PAPER

A Rock, Paper, Scissors
Series

Montgomery Colt

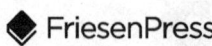 FriesenPress

One Printers Way
Altona, MB R0G 0B0
Canada

www.friesenpress.com

ISBN
978-1-03-919464-9 (Hardcover)
978-1-03-919463-2 (Paperback)
978-1-03-919465-6 (eBook)

1. Fiction, Historical

Distributed to the trade by The Ingram Book Company

To Darla
Thanks for crossing my path

INTRODUCTION

The "hold up", or "sure-thing" or robbing is not tolerated in Dodge City any longer, and the men who practiced the schemes to fleece the unwary have gone to other parts unknown. It will require some months for the removal of the blight on Dodge City's reputation, and the name of "hard town" will soon be in the forgotten past. As the city advances in material prosperity so will its good name come up through the mist of clouds and darkness, shining with greater lustre and brightness, above the dark past.

— *Dodge City Times, Dodge City, Kansas, April 8, 1886*

Paper is the second installment of the *Rock-Paper-Scissors* Series set in the American West in the late nineteenth century. Historical characters such as John Barringer and Fannie May Henderson are ushered into fictional and troublesome events of the time. During the writing of *Paper*, your author discovered that paper — that is, the physical material — in all of its applications, is fundamental in the history of people around the world.

The dominant role of paper was underscored for me during the publication of *Rock*. While patiently waiting for the first copies of the novel, I was advised by my publisher that there would be some delay in printing, due to a worldwide shortage of paper resulting from the COVID-19 pandemic. I had trouble comprehending how our modern "paperless" society could be short on paper. What had happened to all that paper I had been recycling for the last forty years? What had happened to all the newsprint that was no longer required to print newspapers? How could a pandemic have shut down the automation in pulp and paper mills? Was it possible that the hoarding of toilet paper had consumed all of the available wood pulp? All good questions, but to nobody's surprise the industry responded with higher costs for paper and corresponding increases in the price of books (including *Rock*).

Those supply-chain problems awakened my new respect for the pith of paper in history. And, in turn, that awareness led me to give some thought to the changing roles of paper in our lives. On the one hand, we are encouraged to go paperless for environmental reasons. Meanwhile, we switch to paper straws, bags, and packaging — also for environmental reasons. For the sake of efficiency, information technology encourages us to communicate and store important data as a string of zeros and ones. Financial institutions are rapidly converting our money to digital on the pretext that invisible, intangible and insecure assets are more convenient than paper or coins. Yet we are reminded daily that it is our responsibility to keep our digital assets secure.

As a modern-day reader, you can choose old-school paper or digital format, but in 1886 the characters of this story had few choices. Hunters, settlers, ranchers, and townspeople of America relied on paper. In a world without plastic, the demand for new paper products was growing exponentially. Industry responded with automated printing presses, typewriters, paper bags, and cardboard.

Paper was the popular medium for communication: mail, postcards, posters, newspapers, books, magazines, letters, and even carbon copies. Even the most advanced communication technology of the time — telegraph — was presented and recorded on paper.

Paper was the medium for exchanging value. Money, contracts, promissory notes, deeds, titles, and tickets were all printed on paper. Paper documents were typically a combination of handwriting and mechanical printing of ink on paper. In the case of paper money all the printing was done by mechanical equipment on specialized paper.

Paper was a medium for recording images such as technical drawings, artwork, portraits, and maps. Travel was made possible with paper maps and nautical charts. (A paper map appears on the back cover of this book in the tradition of the Dell "Mapback" novels of the 1940s). Paper schedules managed ships, trains, and stagecoaches. By 1888, film technology was available to the masses allowing photographic images on paper (called prints). Prior to that time, plate photography was expensive and difficult to obtain.

Paper is real. Let's keep it around (See Colt's Rant at www.coltfiction.com).

As a genre, most Western novels and movies fall into the broad category of historical fiction. Your author contends that history is best retold as fiction. A fictional story is more interesting to read, easier to remember and more likely to be retold. Even though people and events are unknown to you and me, we are intrigued by the possibilities: that George Washington slept here; that the CIA knows who killed JFK; or that Jesus turned water into wine. And for the last two thousand years of recent history (or five thousand years, if you consider papyrus), the preferred way to distribute these stories was to put them on paper .

While the tale told here is a fictional one, *Paper* is based on actual newspaper reports of the late 1800s. Every chapter begins with a quotation or excerpt from a historical publication (with the exception of quotations from the fictional *Dodge City Fable*). The majority of these articles were obtained from The Library of Congress - Chronicling America series sponsored by the Library of Congress and the National Endowment for the Humanities. Your author is grateful for this directory and the institutions that have contributed to the content.

By today's standards, the language quoted from historical publications may be deemed insensitive. Violent or sexual events are fictional but based on actual events that would be abhorred in 21st century society. There is no disrespect intended where the historical vernacular is quoted.

The preceding quotation from the *Dodge City Times* offers opinion and gilds bias without laying down a single fact. In the 1880s, reporters typically embellished events involving Dodge City and its legendary characters. In hindsight, some newspapers may not have been worth the paper they were printed on. As much as possible, the major events revealed in *Paper* are based on trustworthy historical accounts. The question remains, whether the original readers of such reports were able to separate fact from fiction any better or worse than consumers of today's news sources. On the other hand, the similarity between historical and current events brings to mind a society that remains frozen in a version of the Old West.

Admittedly, there is no confirmation that events happened as told in this story, but they could have. Especially in Dodge City.

THE LAND TITLE

1

Henryville, Lower Canada, British North America, 1861

The West presents superior advantages to such, and with the same industry here which they have exercised in the East, they can, in comparatively but a short space of time, place themselves in the most independent circumstances. Kansas is the place for such men. Here an opportunity is presented for obtaining a home and a valuable farm for a sum insignificant in comparison to the value of the property. This domain embraces as fine farming lands as can be found anywhere in the wide West, and with industry as large fortunes can be upturned from its fertile soil as were ever dug from the golden soil of California.

—*The Kansas News*, **Emporia, Kansas, February 6, 1858**

Thomas Masterson lay awake. His tossing and turning disturbed his wife, Catherine, on this hot August night.

"What's the bother, Thomas?" asked Catherine in her Irish lilt. She had immigrated to British North America at the age of eighteen and met Thomas, the son of Irish parents who had settled in the farmlands south of Montreal. To the French-speaking majority, they were known as *Les Habitants*.

"It's fecking hot. Can't sleep," groaned Thomas. They both knew that the temperature was not his problem. They were both physically exhausted from a long day's work. Yet Thomas had a troubled mind.

"You can gather the clan in maidin," Catherine replied before returning to sleep.

Thomas was unsure how to explain his dilemma to his family. Until now they had been led to believe that they would live out their lives in Henryville, a row of homes along the South River within the watershed of the Richelieu. Like their neighbors, they farmed a long and thin stretch of land measuring three arpents by thirty arpents (seventy-six acres). According to the French seigneurial system adopted in Lower Canada, ownership of the land was granted to a seigneur (nobleman) who employed a local agent to manage the land. Henryville was named for Edme Henry, the land agent for Napier Christie Burton (Lieutenant-Governor of Upper Canada).

Working-class tenants, known as *les censitaire* or *les habitants*, paid *cens* (rent) to the seigneur. Ireland and Great Britain had operated under a similar system since medieval times. Irish immigrants understood this system of feudalism. Little wonder, then, that they had been attracted to the New World and its promises of ownership over vast tracts of fertile land. They arrived only to find, however, that they would be relegated to subsistence livelihood on some nobleman's property. French and British owners maintained the seigneurial system well into the twentieth century.

Several factors converged to weaken the agricultural economy in Lower Canada. Cities along the St. Lawrence shipped in cheaper food products from areas around the Great Lakes. American cattle, sheep, pork and cheese glutted the markets around Montreal. Wheat production in Lower Canada was ravaged by wheat midge (a mosquito-like insect whose larvae feed on the immature wheat kernel). Markets for barley and oats were limited to local consumers. By the mid-1800s, men started to leave the land to work in fur-trading and lumber.

Thomas Masterson remained on the land to be near his growing family. He was optimistic that his talents as a farmer were the best avenue to success. But like immigrants before him, he recognized that success may be elsewhere. After inspecting forty acres of insect-damaged wheat, Thomas realized that he would be unable to pay the rent to his seigneur for the next year. So, in 1861 Thomas Masterson announced to his family that they would leave Lower Canada to seek fortune in America—the America experiencing the beginnings of a Civil War.

Breakfast in the Masterson home was typically finished by 6:00 am so that the older children could complete chores before heading to school. Three boys—Edward, Bartholemew, and James—were of school age. Three younger children—Nellie, Thomas Jr., and George—would remain at home to entertain their mother in the cooking and cleaning tasks of the day.

On this particular morning, Edward, who at nine years was the oldest child, pushed back from the table and declared, "You boys quit pokin' around! Bat, put that book away! It's your turn to milk the cow."

Bat closed the book and shoveled the rest of his porridge into his gaping mouth.

Thomas tapped his spoon on the side of his coffee cup and immediately everyone at the table focused their silent attention on the patron. Edward slid back onto his chair.

"Your mother and I have come to a bitter decision," announced Thomas. "You probably won't like it. Don't waste breath airing your grievances. No chores today. We are leaving Henryville tomorrow."

"But why?" asked two or three children at once.

"Don't you have a contract with the seigneur?" asked Bat. "He must provide for us. His mark is on it."

"That's true, Bat," answered his father. "That is why we came to this place. The men that own the land need us to work it. The land has not given us yield. And our seigneur has run out of patience."

"We need to find a place more suitable for raising a family and growing crops," added his mother.

"What's wrong with the crops?" asked six-year-old James. "They look ready to harvest."

"There's no kernels in most of the wheat. There is not even enough to provide seed for next year," lamented his father.

"Well, we can sell the livestock," declared Edward. "What about the cows?"

"I have sold the cows and chickens down the road, to O'Neill."

"What about the horses?" asked four-year-old Nellie. "You can't sell Patches."

"You are right, lass," replied her father. "Patches is coming with us. We need horses to travel."

"Which way will we go?" asked Edward. "Across the Richelieu to New York or south to Vermont?"

"Some of the other Habitants are also leaving. They plan to travel south to the bend in Riviere du Sud and then west to cross the Richelieu at the narrows surrounding Ile Ash. Those who have been there say that the marsh and sandbars will support livestock crossing."

"I guess that is the good thing about a dry year," responded Edward. "Rivers aren't deep."

"Once across the Richelieu, we travel by wagon to Champlain. There are three families and each family has one wagon. A fourth wagon will have tools and supplies for the group. Lord being our helper, we can get to Champlain before sundown."

"Will anyone be trying to stop us?" asked Bat.

"Not unless the beans have been spilled to the seigneur. They would send soldiers to make us stay past harvest."

"Or put us in the stockade. D'ya think they'd put us all in the stockade?" asked James.

"No. It won't come to that. We will be across the border in less than a day and safe from the Christie family."

Tears welled in Catherine Masterson's eyes. Her children would not see them when she bowed her head. "Let's pray, children. The Lord is my shepherd; I shall not want. He maketh me to lie down in green pastures: he leadeth me beside the still waters. He restoreth ..."

The children joined the prayer in unison, except for one-year-old George, who banged his spoon on the table, oblivious to the shocking announcement. Most of the family was sobbing at the end of the prayer. But not Bartholemew William Barclay Masterson. He sat up straight and looked his father in the eye.

"What can we bring with us?"

2

Lower Canada, British North America, 1861

It is books that teach us to refine our pleasures when young, and which, having so taught us, enable us to recall them with satisfaction when old.

—Leigh Hunt (1784-1859)

Bat spent his last night on the Henryville farm with his collection of books. He knew his father would object to bringing the dozens of books on the wagon, but he assumed maps would be important to their travel.

Bat picked out eight of his favorite books. He cut a map of northeastern states along the folds and glued the sections to the back cover of each book. Then he repeated the process with a map of western states and glued these to the front covers. When Bat loaded the map-books onto the wagon, his father just shook his head.

"So how do you know which book takes us where we want to go?" asked his father.

Bat picked up his most-valued book, *A Tale of Two Cities*, by Charles Dickens. The map fragment on the front cover included most of New York state. The back cover was most of Kansas and Missouri.

Bat stared his father in the eyes and said, "*It was the best of times, it was the worst of times.*"

Bat's father laughed out loud. "You always were a little Dickens, eh?"

The wagon trail to the south was hot and uncomfortable crossing the narrow strips of plowed fields. But the clouds provided some relief to the families riding the pine benches of their open wagons. At the Riviere du Sud the families disembarked to give the horses a lighter load to ford the river. The narrow trickle of water meant that the hooves of the lead horses could gain purchase on the far bank as the wagon wheels entered the near bank. The crossing went smoothly until the wheels of the supply wagon, loaded with two tons of tools and food, sank up to the axles. The wagon jolted to a stop and the driver jumped to the ground. While he pulled the harness of the lead horses, two of the four veered to the left and the hub of one sunken wheel snapped from the torque. When the horses evened up, they dragged the wagon up the bank on three wheels.

"Goddamnit, Paddy. You've broken the wheel."

"Well, you can drive this fecking wagon if yer so damn smart."

"Settle down, lads. We've got the tools. Give us a couple hours."

"The rest of you can help by unloading this wagon. You urchins go play in the river."

Three fathers and two older lads worked on the wagon, while the mothers organized the unloading. True to predictions, the wheel was right again in less than two hours and the convoy continued.

The wagons were traveling along the east shore of the Richelieu River. At noon, they approached a position where sandbars formed an island covered with small groves of maple trees and underbrush. The island split the river into equal necks, each narrower and shallower than the river downstream. The men agreed that the wagons should cross at the island. The women convinced them to stop for lunch before attempting the crossing.

One man and his son rode horses down the riverbank to find the best place to enter and exit the island. Secretly, Edward and Bat Masterson followed them, as curious boys were prone to do. They saw the two riders navigate across the nearest fork in the river. When the riders reached the shore of the island, shots were fired from the trees. Both horses went down, wounded. The father was pinned under his horse, but the son was able to shoulder his rifle and return fire.

When the shooting started, Bat and Edward were watching from a patch of brush along the bank, north of the island. From the puffs of gun smoke, Bat estimated the number of shooters.

"I'd say six or more," said Bat.

"Must be soldiers from Fort Lennox," said Edward. "Taking orders from Christie, I reckon."

"Maybe. But could be American soldiers from Fort Montgomery," speculated Bat.

"They wouldn't be shooting outside the U.S.A. Even if they don't want us traveling there, they'd wait till we cross."

"That's true," agreed Bat. "Either way, they must have a boat."

"I bet yer right. And it's got to be on the other side of the island."

"Let's swim across and sneak up the far side," said Bat with a big grin. "Then we can untie the boat and leave those redcoats stuck on the island."

"What if they see us?" asked Edward.

"They won't. More chance that Pa will tan our hides if he sees us. Besides, old Paddy and his kid will draw their fire for a while yet."

"OK. Let's go," agreed Edward. "But we better strip down for a swim."

The boys unclasped their belts and buttons before hiding the clothes beside a rock. Then, half-naked, they ran down the bank and dove into the river, unseen by any adults.

As they approached the north edge of the island, the sand came up to meet their feet. There was more gunfire now from the opposite side of the island. They waded into the bulrushes until they came to a pair of rowboats tied to willows at the water's edge.

"There's got to be more than a dozen redcoats," said Bat. "I count twelve wet oars."

"They left some firearms in the boat. Let's get them floating, quick," whispered Edward.

The boys crawled up the sandy shore to untie the boats. Then they towed both into the moving water. Edward was attempting to crawl into one when a shot rang out and a piece of the gunwale shattered near his hand. He ducked into the water and swam under the boat to the opposite side, where Bat had already taken cover.

"Kick your feet and hang on with one hand," said Bat. "They can't hit us on this side of the boat."

"It won't give much cover if they keep puttin' holes in it," mumbled Edward.

"The die has been cast. We are crossing the Rubicon!"

"What's that?" sputtered Edward, struggling to keep afloat.

"We either escape with our lives or go down with the ship."

The boys moved one boat slowly but steadily downstream. The other boat followed them at the water's pace. Soldiers on the shore were yelling at the boat snatchers and at each other. When the boys were a hundred yards north of the island, the shooting stopped.

"What about our clothes?" asked Edward. "Should we go back tonight and retrieve them?"

"Not on your life," replied Bat, as he spat out river water. "Bet there will be some extra clothes before this day is done."

Back on the east side of the river, the farmers huddled behind a knoll.

"Is Paddy still kickin'?" asked Thomas Masterson.

"Nah," answered a man with a small scope aimed at the island. "And the boy is bleeding from his head and not moving."

"What ya think, Thomas?" asked a tall fellow.

"I'm low on bullets," replied Thomas. "Maybe five shots left."

"I'm right out of Winchester shells. Not sure my side-arms are going to be much help against an army," groaned the tall man.

"That goddamn Lord Christie. Gettin' the army to do his dirty work. What chance have we tenants got?" asked the man with the scope.

"Give me that scope," ordered Thomas. "It looks like some of them soldier boys slithering downstream." Thomas peered at the boats with the scope for several seconds. "I don't see anyone. You fellas have a look." Then he passed the scope back to its owner, who put it to his eye immediately.

"I'll be jiggered. Those boats are getting away without any crew. It's like they weren't moored properly."

"Might be some shells in those boats. Let's intercept them downstream," said Thomas.

"I'll stay here and watch the island. If soldiers start swimming our direction, I'll fire three shots at them and then retreat to the wagons."

"Aye. Keep a sharp eye through that spyglass."

The men ran back to the wagons and discussed several plans to intercept the boats. The women and children were frantic. They had arranged the wagons in a square and piled some crates and trunks strategically.

"Where's my son? And Paddy?" screamed one woman. One of the men went to her and held her while he explained that her men had both fallen.

"Where's Edward and Bat?" cried Catherine Masterson, searching the expression on her husband's face.

"We left them here with you," shrugged Thomas. "They weren't with us."

"They followed behind you," yelled Catherine. "Do you think they are hiding out there?"

"I'll go look on the riverbank. You follow the others and ford the river downstream," ordered Thomas.

"I'm not leaving my boys behind."

"No, Cate. I'm not either. But you get the wagon to the other side, and I'll catch up. Hurry now." Thomas turned to walk back towards the island.

One of the men was shouting instructions. "We'll go north two miles and cross the river out of sight of the island. Let's get the wagons moving."

Thomas watched the boats coming towards the group. In fact, one of the boats had turned and was aiming at the shore. He watched in disbelief. Two heads were bobbing in the shadow of the boat.

Bat and Edward were anxious to get to shore. They turned the boat east by paddling with their left arms. They tried to call for help, but their lungs were spent. Their legs were tired, and their arms were having trouble keeping a grip on the boat.

"Bat, I can't hold on," sighed Edward. The broken gunwale was cutting his hand. There was blood running down his arm and dripping from his elbow into the water.

"Just a few more paddles," said Bat. "We can make shore."

"I can't. You go," said Edward as he let go of the gunwale.

"You can. We can."

There was no answer. When Bat looked back, there was blood in the water where his brother had been. He yelled out —"Edward!"— then summoned his remaining energy to push his own head below the surface. Bat swung his arms frantically, trying to stay submerged. Among the blood swirls he saw his brother looking back at him, panic in his eyes. Edward was flailing, yet his body did not move upwards.

Bat's mind was racing. *Why can't you swim, Edward? Just swim up two feet and then breathe. If only you could hear me.*

Edward grabbed Bat around the neck and tried to climb to safety. The shadow of the boat moved away, and the refracted sunlight illuminated their skinny bodies tangled together only a couple of feet below the surface.

Why are you trying to drown me, Edward? You just need to swim up. Don't drown me before I save you? Did you see where that boat went? We need to grab the boat.

Bat felt his feet hit bottom. He hugged Edward's bony body and pushed up with spent leg muscles. His lungs wanted to burst. Pain filled his chest. He could not feel his arms and legs. He wondered if this was how it felt to drown.

Please stop holding me down. Edward, will you save me if I get you out of this? Get us out of this. We don't have all day.

Suddenly, Bat noticed pain spreading throughout his body.

I will die so you can live. Edward. You must live.

Without warning, Bat was propelled into the air. Edward was there, coughing into Bat's eyes. Bat gasped for air and his nostrils burned as he expelled the cold water through mouth and nose. Bat felt a far-reaching soreness. His hair felt like it was being pulled out by the roots.

Bat looked up at his father standing in the river, clutching both boys by the hair. His eyes welled up when he saw tears running down his father's face. When he stopped crying and spitting, Bat noticed the rest of the Masterson family gathered on the riverbank. He waited for his father to release his hair. And then he was able to touch the sandy bottom and stumble out of the water. Edward was safe in his father's arms.

Regaining his presence of mind, Bat exclaimed, "Pa, we was up the creek without a paddle till you came along!"

"You can explain yourselves after we get across the river," said Thomas. "Now get on that wagon. And don't piddle."

The boats had been pulled ashore by men who were now gathering the cargo of rifles and munitions.

3

There is a story of an old hunter, who came into Chicago one day, and, after wandering about for a while, looking at the public buildings and other improvements, got into a chat with one of the inhabitants, in the course of which he mentioned to him that he had once had a chance to buy all the ground that the city was built upon for a pair of old boots. "And why didn't you buy it?" "Well, I hadn't the boots just then," was the old man's calm reply.

— *White Cloud Kansas Chief*, White Cloud, Kansas, August 12, 1869

The Masterson family from Lower Canada entered the U.S.A. at the town of Champlain, New York. Many of the families living in Champlain had been there before the international border was moved north of the town. Thomas Masterson had cousins farming in the area, who he hoped would lend a helping hand to his family.

The Mastersons of Champlain County were successful merchants of grain and poultry products. Since the outbreak of the Civil War, many of the able-bodied men from the area had joined the Union Army. Skilled laborers from the community were in short supply. The unskilled

Negro workers were anxious to fight for the freedom of their southern brothers, so there was a shortage of men to work in the fields or haul commodities.

Thomas and Catherine were welcomed with open arms since they could perform a day's work with little supervision. Three of the Masterson children were school age, but after school they worked in the granaries and stock pens. Three younger children were well-behaved and would play with any of the local children regardless of their age or skin color. Still and all, life in Champlain was no more fulfilling than it had been in Henryville.

Catherine became pregnant with a seventh child. The family was happy to be near the town of five thousand people during the first year of the baby's life. But Thomas worried that life would change if the war ended soon and the men returned to Champlain. He was too proud to be a burden to those men who had fought for their beliefs. As soon as baby Emma was old enough to travel, the family set out for Chicago.

In Chicago, the employment situation continued to improve as the war dragged on. Union soldiers were killed or wounded, so more were conscripted from the north. Winters were hard for the large family, but Thomas was a canny negotiator. He took on janitorial work in institutions and row houses each winter, allowing his family to huddle in a small apartment or loft for the coldest months of the year.

Bat spent his days in school or the library. He taught other children how to read and write. In the summer months he became especially useful handling horses or livestock. At ten years old, Bat had earned enough money to buy a derby hat, which he wore everywhere. His peers made fun of him, but the distinctive felt hat added to the boy's image of sophistication and maturity.

When the Civil War ended, men returned to the Chicago area. Emancipated slaves were an economical workforce. Less employment was available to transient families such as the Mastersons. Twelve-year-old Bat and his brother Edward, who was a year senior, took on a larger role in supporting the family.

Bat's language skills were superior to most of his elders. He sought out clerical positions in law offices and publishing houses of Chicago. Under the black derby, the boy was frequently mistaken for a man of experience and professional skills. He landed a position as an assistant to the county judge. Edward was not as successful gaining employment, but Bat used him like a silent partner, performing research and errands. The courthouse had no idea that a pair of teenage boys were researching precedents and drafting arguments for the county. The pair brought home a steady salary, while their father and younger siblings picked up unskilled labor jobs in stables and row houses. The Masterson family was able to put away a few dollars each month. After three years, Thomas could see a light at the end of the tunnel: he began planning for the day they could move west.

By 1870, Bat Masterson had demonstrated his proficiency with written documents. His peers at the courthouse suggested he should send articles to newspapers in the Chicago area. Some editors accepted his articles to be published under the names of older staff reporters. By this time, four of his siblings were bringing him stories. Bat was an expert when it came to embellishing the facts and creating stimulating prose. As a ghost writer he was in his glory. He started to dress like a Chicago businessman to gain entrance to clubs and meetings where nobility would gather and reporters weren't welcome. His outfit started with leather boots, black dress trousers, white high-collar shirt, black double-breasted vest, and black thigh-length coat. Accessories included a silk puff tie and a pocket watch. He valued the comfort and appearance of his tall bowler hat. It was stable in the wind or while riding a horse. But he was also attracted by the cowboys' Stetsons, with sloped peaks at front and back to provide protection from sun and rain.

Bat's sister Nellie had made some hats for the family. When he showed her the modifications that he wanted to make to his bowler hat, Nellie took up the challenge. In a few days, Nellie presented her brother with three separate "Bat Masterson" hats. Each design looked like a bowler, except that Nellie added width to the rim so that it sloped both forward and backward. One of the hats was brown felt and had the valley on the peak. The other two hats were black felt. Bat was pleased with the hats and paid Nellie ten silver dollars.

A local editor caught wind of a pair of buffalo hunters accompanying a wagon train loaded with hundreds of buffalo hides. All of the Chicago reporters were busy covering stories about murders and house fires. The editor saw Bat loitering near the newspaper building and called him into his office.

"Masterson, get in here. There's a story happening."

"I am without surprise that your staff of reporters is fully involved in piddling stories of momentary interest. This writer is available to chase a story of great import."

"Yeah, whatever," groaned the editor. "What do you know about buffalo hunters, Masterson?"

"From my previous research, I know that they have been charged with exterminating the buffalo herds, thereby eradicating the primary source of food and shelter utilized by the tribes of plains Indians. Some say these men are handsomely rewarded by the tanneries and the United States Army. Others say that despite the support of the government in Washington, the buffalo hunters receive meager rewards for the hardship and dangers they face daily."

"Well put, Masterson. But I don't believe it. Hunting with the Winchester rifle can hardly be considered hardship. So get the undeniable facts for the next edition. Apparently, there are some buffalo hunters down at the docks as we speak. Get down there, Masterson, and find out the real story."

"You have chosen the right man for this job, and I am grateful for this consideration. I will not disappoint you on this occasion."

"Save those fancy words for your story. Now take your pencil and pad and get out of here."

Bat was excited to meet some genuine buffalo hunters. He had read about the exploits of Buffalo Bill Cody and Wild Bill Hickok. He rounded up three of his brothers and they convinced a passing carriage to take them to the harbor front. When they got there, they saw a group of teamsters unloading heavy brown furs from the wagons and carrying them onto the deck of a lake freighter.

The wind blowing off the lake was fierce. The brothers wore Irish wool flat hats which flipped off on the breeze, yet Bat's special hat stayed where it belonged. They could not tell if the white flakes in the air were snowflakes or ashes from the fires. Bat saw men looking out the windows of a small building adjacent to the docks. Two of them were wearing Western hats. He walked towards the building with his brothers in tow. Bat knocked on the door to the building before stepping inside.

"Who's this dapper Dan?" asked one hunter.

"Get lost, young fella!" said a man in a gray Stetson. "We're doing business here."

Bat looked at the packs of paper bills on the table. A man with glasses and a visor hat was checking off numbers in a ledger. He did not look up.

"Indeed," agreed Bat. "Gentlemen. I have no intention of interrupting your enterprise prior to its natural completion. However, I come with the honor and pleasure of seeking the true adventures of such men who engage in the pursuance and extirpation of the terrible buffalo in the face of danger."

"Well, get lost anyway," said the man in the gray hat.

"Wait one minute," said another man as he grabbed Gray Hat's shoulder. "I think a reporter is in our midst." This man wore his hat tilted to one side and the brim folded up on the high side. He had a narrow face, goatee, and handlebar mustache. His hair hung down the back of his neck below his shoulders.

Bat had seen pictures in the newspapers of Buffalo Bill Cody. He took a chance and extended his hand. "Would I have the honor of meeting William Frederick Cody?"

The men shook hands. "And who do I have the pleasure…?" Buffalo Bill appeared to be flattered to be recognized in this big city.

"I am indeed a reporter. Masterson from the *Chicago Tribune*. Bat Masterson. Do you have time to regale me with your exploits in the frontier?"

"Certainly. Let's step outside. We can talk in the shelter of the livery stable and leave these men to count these bills. They used to pay us in gold coins, but now everything is paper money."

Buffalo Bill and Bat walked over to the livery stable and got comfortable on some tack boxes. The brothers followed along and stood behind Bat, making notes and whispering to one another.

"These three shavers have accompanied me in my journey and do not wish to cause any interruption or discomfort. Please ignore their presence."

"They have your looks but not your sense of fashion," chuckled Buffalo Bill.

"They are my brothers. Edward, who is the eldest of my siblings. James, who is two years younger than myself.

And young Thomas, who will soon be entering his fourteenth year."

"Splendid. Tell me, lad, have you always lived in Chicago?"

"No. We moved here from Lower Canada. Near the St. Lawrence River."

"I find the world is smaller as you move west. I myself was baptized in Toronto township in Upper Canada. But my parents settled in Kansas. I have lived wherever I could find employment. I fought for the north in the war. After the war I worked as a scout for the army. But most of that work has been in Kansas or the bordering territories."

"So how did you get the nickname Buffalo Bill?"

"I have a contract to feed buffalo meat to the railway construction crews. And the hides are my profit for that work."

"How many hides does it take to make a profit?"

"That's a question I don't have an answer for. A good hunter can make an excellent living. I have personally killed over four thousand buffalo in less than two years."

"Are there four thousand hides being shipped today?" asked Bat.

"These hides are only some from the last few weeks. Some belong to the feller you met in the office."

"Do you always have a wagon train to carry the hides on your hunting excursions?"

"That depends on the hunt. On occasion, the army provides a contingent of soldiers, including wagons, horses, and chuck."

"Why is the army assisting you?"

"In anticipation of any opposition. The survival of the western tribes is dependent on the survival of the buffalo. They rely on the buffalo for meat and hides."

"As in food and shelter?" asked Bat.

"Indeed. Since the Civil War, General Sherman and Major General Sheridan are charged with enforcement of the treaties and reservations. They believe the path to controlling the Indians is through the eradication of buffalo. Manifest Destiny, they call it."

"And what is a typical hunt when the army is not involved?" asked Bat as he scribbled in his journal.

"Those generals think that every sportsman from England and America should be invited to a grand hunting adventure. So there is a great demand for buffalo guides in Kansas, Wyoming, Montana and the Dakota Territories. I have payin' customers from the east who hire me as a guide on a buffalo hunt. Then they absorb the costs of wagons and feed, as necessary."

"Does it pay to take out one hunter to bag one animal?"

"It's never just one animal. The tanneries in Kansas pay up to three dollars and fifty cents for a buffalo hide. Bullets cost two bits each. So when a man is riding alongside a herd of two hundred buffalo, he never stops at killing one. Take the gentleman that's with me."

"Who is he?"

"A dentist out of Minnesota. Name of Palmer. Bit of an asshole. You know the type. Thinks he's entitled to shoot anything anytime. Hired me for a buffalo hunt in Wyoming. Said he wanted to set the record for most kills in an eight-hour day."

"And did he set the record?"

"It was an impressive day. I shot sixty-eight. Palmer killed forty-two buffalo and one mountain lion. So, sixty-eight stands as the record. Last year, I hunted with a feller who got forty-eight in a day. That's probably the next best."

"So would you say it was a profitable day?"

"Certainly. Even when the market drops. Normally the hides get tanned before they are shipped east. But in the winter they can be shipped in a frozen state to tanneries in the east. Palmer and I bagged four hundred animals last month and by bringing them here we get ten dollars per hide."

"Why didn't you bring them by rail?"

"Rails stop in Kansas. So we loaded wagons in Wyoming and took the shortest route to Chicago. Followed the Platte Rivers to the Missouri and crossed through Iowa.

"I heard you have a name for your gun, Mr. Cody."

"Yes, sir. Lucrezia Borgia. She is a character in a Victor Hugo book. Highly recommend you read it."

"Thanks, I have. But, tell me, what kind of rifle is best for hunting buffalo?"

"Lucrezia is a Springfield Model 1866. Some people use a Henry repeating rifle."

"Where do you call home, Mr. Cody?"

"Most of my associates settled in Ellsworth County. There are stockyards where the Chisholm Trail meets the Kansas Pacific. I stay there often to meet other buffalo hunters. Cowboys coming up the Chisholm Trail cause trouble all through the fall and winter. So I have an interest in developing some properties up the line in a place called Rome."

"The Chicago readers will be very interested in these tales of the buffalo hunt. Thank you for your candor."

"Can you put your pencil down now?" asked Cody.

"OK. Off the record. Can I ask if there are still buffalo to hunt?"

"Off the record. The task has barely started. There are millions of buffalo still roaming the prairies. You boys should come on out. Hunt buffalo. Do some farming. Land is cheap in Kansas. Take a look down in Sedgwick County. The railway hasn't got there yet but when it does land values will climb."

"Hunting buffalo sounds like an exciting life. I hope we make your acquaintance again."

"Look me up when you get to Kansas. I keep the army informed of my travels, so check at the forts."

4

Chicago, Illinois, 1870

A parry of young men were telling what they would do if they were shipwrecked far out at sea, and left buffeting with the waves without a plank to sustain them. Each one gave his opinion excepting Paddy Murphy, who, after being asked, replied: "Bad cess to ye for a cowardly set of spalpeens; ye'd all be after savin' yourselves, an' not thrying to save anuther. Why it's Paddy Murphy that would swim to shore an' save himself an' thin come back and save anuther."

—*The Workingman's Advocate,* Chicago, Illinois, September 24, 1870

George Hoover of Caistorville, Ontario, had requested and received a manual from the U.S. immigration office in New York. *The Handbook to Kansas Territory,* published in 1859, provided detailed information for anyone who was interested in moving west. After years of watching his father slaving as a sharecropper for the British nobility, Hoover was determined to leave his home in Caistorville, in the newly confederated Canada. By the summer of 1870, Hoover had accumulated traveling money from piecework and scrimping. He planned to travel across the

Great Lakes to Chicago and take trains as far west as the lines were built.

Hoover's large frame and muscular build were welcomed by the captain of the first ship that he approached. The *Edmond Fitzgerald* was the namesake of a shipbuilder in Port Huron, Michigan. The ship had been christened that year and in the first months of operation had successfully hauled iron ore, lumber and grain across the Great Lakes between Ontario and U.S. ports. Hoover proved his worth during the loading of the two-masted schooner on his first morning in Port Colborne, Ontario. The crew loaded 26,000 tons of grain in one-hundred-pound bags. A few days later, Hoover was traveling alongside those sacks of grain destined for flour mills in Chicago. He was eager to get to Chicago, even though it meant unloading the same sacks of grain. Hoover ate well and slept soundly for the two weeks in transit.

Chicago was connected to the Mississippi River via the man-made Illinois River Canal system. The river traffic carried grain, sugar, coal, salt, lumber, and finished goods to and from the Western frontier. Railways carried iron, cotton, tobacco, and finished goods from the West to the ports on the Great Lakes. Those shipments were destined for the eastern states or Europe. Regardless of the type of cargo, there were transfers between modes of transport. At those inter-modal hubs, teamsters handled freight with horses and wagons, heavy work critical to the growing economy of the U.S.A.

Chicago had a population over 300,000 when twenty-two-year-old George Hoover landed in 1870. When he disembarked from the *Edmond Fitzgerald*, Hoover was paid twenty dollars—thirty for his work, less ten for travel and lodging. He had never received that much cash in his young life so felt like a king as he walked through the waterfront streets. He found a hotel that offered low monthly rent for a room with a bed and a chair. There was lots of work for strong men along the waterfront, so Hoover picked up employment manhandling bags of grain between ships and wagons. As soon as he could afford a team and wagon, he worked as a teamster, transferring goods from freighter ships to trains and vice versa. He was surprised at the number of buffalo hides being shipped from tanneries in Kansas to ships destined for Britain.

In the dark of night, on October 8, 1871, Hoover was transferring sixty buffalo hides to the harbor front. As he crested a hill, he could see flames and smoke to the south. He knew the fire crews had been busy on the previous night, so he turned the wagon towards the fire in case he could be of assistance. In less than five minutes the fire had spread north and east of the canal. People were running in every direction. A crowd of seamstresses and millinery workers emptied onto the street. As they came towards his wagon, the women were screaming and tripping over their long dresses. His startled horses bucked and one snarled the harness around its front leg. Hoover tried to hold the animals, but they too joined the panic. The tangled horse fell forward and the other horse jumped over it, causing the wagon to spin sideways. Spokes on the wheels broke and the hub dug into the road, causing the wagon to flip on its side. Hoover was thrown towards a throng of women running up the road towards him. He landed at their feet and knocked two of them to the ground. One of the young women was knocked unconscious. The other stood up quickly and kicked him in the groin before retreating from the smoke and flames.

Hoover lay groaning on the street beside the unconscious girl. She blinked when he swept her hair aside.

"Are you OK, Miss?"

"Ow. My leg is not."

Hoover pinched one of her ankles. "Can you feel that, Miss? I hope nothing is broken."

"No," she groaned and propped herself up on her elbows to look.

"You can't feel that? That's not good," Hoover speculated.

"No, I mean I don't think they are broken. The left one really hurts."

"I'm sorry about knocking you down."

"Probably a sprain," she sighed.

"I can help you stand if you want," said Hoover.

"If you are able. You also took quite a tumble."

Hoover put an arm under the girl's shoulders and lifted her gently. "Can you put weight on it?"

The girl tried to take a step but retracted her foot instantly.

Hoover noticed her grimace as tears formed in her eyes. He picked her up in both arms.

"Sorry if I seem bold, Miss, but there is fire coming and I reckon you can't outrun it."

"I think I can ride a horse," cried the girl.

Hoover looked back at his overturned wagon. One horse was still attached and was standing patiently. He carried the girl and set her on the mound of buffalo hides, now piled on the street.

"My name is Nellie. I am much obliged, Mister…?"

"Hoover. George Hoover. I'll get this horse unhitched and then you can ride it. But I'll stay with you till we get to safety."

The flames were leaping above the nearby buildings and illuminating the street with an orange glow. Hoover felt the heat on his back as he removed the harness from the horse and attached reins to the halter. He threw a buffalo hide over the horse's back before lifting Nellie onto the horse. Then he led them towards the harbor, where he hoped to find safety.

The cause of the fire that night was never determined. Some say it broke out in a barn when a lamp was kicked over. Others say it was sparks from the house fires that had occurred the previous day which had also exhausted the water available for firefighting. Regardless of the source of ignition, within thirty-six hours, fire had spread to more than eighteen thousand buildings, resulting in losses estimated at approximately two hundred million dollars. Over three hundred residents died in the Great Conflagration. The city lost one-third of the property value, including the commercial district and municipal buildings. The pumping station for Chicago waterworks was destroyed. Gas lines were damaged and disconnected in most of the city.

When Nellie Masterson and George Hoover reached the harbor, they encountered crowds of people. Some were passing buckets of water from the lake. Some were looting nearby warehouses. Some were comforting the injured and frightened. And most were holding each other close.

Hoover tied his horse to a rail and helped Nellie dismount. She was barely conscious. He wrapped her in the buffalo hide and carried her down to the docks, where he found a dinghy tied to the pier. He stepped into the boat and then lifted Nellie down from the dock. Hoover calmly paddled into the lake, away from the commotion. The breeze was colder than either anticipated, so Nellie shared the buffalo hide with her new-found friend.

During the fire, the Masterson family had sheltered in place with six of the seven children. Nellie was unaccounted for, and the building where she had been working was completely destroyed. In the light of day, her father walked through the rubble and ashes, looking for Nellie. Ed and Bat managed to escape the arms of their mother for a few hours to search the streets, but to no avail. Nellie did not come home that day or the following night.

Two days after the fire, Nellie limped up the stairs to the room where her mother was preparing supper. She set a book on the table with the words "Handbook to Kansas Territory" printed on it.

"A man gave me this book," said Nellie. "For Pa."

Her mother embraced her and started to cry.

"I'm alright, mother. Don't cry."

The boys shouted, "Nellie's back. She didn't burn."

Catherine understood that her daughter would tell her more when the time was right. "Boys, go find your father and tell him to stop looking for Nellie. And be back here before dark."

The Great Conflagration left George Hoover desperate. The building where he boarded had been destroyed, along with his spartan possessions. He recovered twenty-six dollars in silver coins from the ashes of his room. Wagons and teams were in high demand during the period of recovery and rebuilding. Hoover sold his horse and stuffed the cash in his pocket.

Residents of Chicago struggled to find food and shelter, so the city council offered free train tickets out of the city. Hoover took advantage of a free railroad ticket on the Kansas Pacific Railroad. The ticket would take him to the furthest point that a west-bound train could travel in that year. Since there was no water in the Chicago waterworks, Hoover had not washed his body nor his clothes for some time. He smelled of stale beer, sweat, and smoke. Where he sat, he left a black stain on the bench, yet he felt no shame among the other refugees from Chicago.

Passengers gradually disembarked at stops in Illinois. After two nights the train crossed the Mississippi River. Passengers detrained at several stops in Missouri. Hoover was determined to reach the frontier. On the fourth day, there were only five passengers remaining in his same car, which had seated twenty. The conductor came through the car, bellowing the words that Hoover was waiting for.

"End of the line. Ellsworth, Kansas. All passengers must detrain. Ellsworth."

When the train came to a stop, Hoover climbed down to the platform, rubbing his stiff legs. For the coming fall and winter, Ellsworth, Kansas, would be home.

In 1871, Ellsworth was home to over two thousand residents and almost as many cowhands bringing Texas cattle to the rail head. Cowboys, prostitutes, and saloons contributed to the reputation of Ellsworth as the wickedest town in Kansas. Wild Bill Hickok and Wyatt Earp served the area as lawmen for brief periods. Gunfighters and killers were both feared and revered by the residents of Ellsworth.

This was where an enterprising twenty-four-year-old Canadian would soon learn hard lessons in survival and commerce.

5

Fort Dodge, Kansas, 1872

Abilene was the first northern market established for the sale and shipment of Texas cattle, and the reputation it then gained was the solid foundation upon which rests its present size and prosperity.

The average reader can well imagine the tumultuous and exciting scenes attendant upon the receipt and shipment of thousands and thousands of wild, untamed steers. Add to this the pandemonium created by the carousing, drunken ruffians, who are always to be found where the law is but loosely enforced; gambling saloons, rum holes, houses of prostitution and dance houses upon every hand; rows and shooting matches of daily occurrence; cowboys, desperadoes, adventurers and lewd women, and you have a pretty fair description of what Abilene was in cattle days.

—*Abilene Reflector*, Abilene, Kansas, April 21, 1887

George Hoover stood on the porch in front of Sutler's store inside Fort Dodge. For two long days, he had traveled across open prairie to investigate the price of land and business prospects. To quench his dry throat, Hoover came to this mercantile store to purchase a bottle of whiskey.

"Sorry, mister. Can't sell you any whiskey."

"How about beer then?" asked Hoover.

"Again, I have to apologize. Can't sell you no beer."

"I see a keg on the shelf. Is my money no good here?" Hoover was getting more annoyed than thirsty.

"I'm sorry to be the bearer of this news, but Colonel Richard Dodge, commandant of the Fort, has restricted alcohol sales. Only officers of the United States Army can purchase alcoholic beverages within a five-mile radius of Fort Dodge. And you do not appear to be an officer of the army."

"What else have you got to drink?"

"There is a pot of coffee on the stove. No charge for coffee or water."

Hoover stomped over to a table where a pitcher of water was sitting. He poured a tall glass and swallowed it. It was tepid, but he went ahead and poured another while he asked the storekeeper more questions.

"You the owner? Sutler?"

"Yeah, mister. Set up shop here five years back."

"You think you can stay in business without selling liquor?"

"I am hoping the railway coming to town will bring in some more customers."

"How do you figger railway's coming?"

"They gave us a map to put on the wall. It's got dates and schedules for the whole shebang."

Hoover went and had a look at the map. It showed the Atchison, Topeka and Santa Fe Railway (AT&SF) line routed from Kansas City along the Santa Fe Trail through towns and watering holes in southern Kansas. On the map, handwritten beside Fort Dodge were the words "October, 1872."

Hoover was living in Ellsworth, Kansas, at the time. His travel to Fort Dodge was instigated by a newspaper article predicting that the line would intercept the Western Cattle Trail near Fort Dodge, providing a new location for stockyards. Cattle could be loaded on AT&SF trains at Fort Dodge instead of traveling several days north to the existing rail yards at Ellsworth. This map on the wall of Sutler's store confirmed the railway's plans to build there sooner rather than later.

To Hoover, this signaled an opportunity. The area around Fort Dodge would need to be developed to support the influx of railway workers and trail hands. And those same workers and hands would be looking for liquor. Liquor not available in Fort Dodge. The closest towns with liquor sales, entertainment and rail service were Great Bend and Newton, but they were located a ten-hour ride and a fifteen-hour ride away, respectively. Hoover believed that a community could be developed outside the Fort Dodge prohibition zone. He was determined to establish a site for such a community.

Hoover recruited a partner, Jack McConnell, to assist in the endeavor. They stopped at the gate to the fort and talked with two soldiers.

"Tell your cohorts that we are selling whiskey five miles west of here, just north of the river."

"Got any beer?" asked one guard.

"No, just whiskey today," answered Hoover, as he flipped the reins to get the horses plodding west.

"We should have brought beer," said McConnell. "I like whiskey, but it is a warm day."

"Beer takes up too much space. A barrel of whiskey has five times as much value. Whoa, horses. Whoa."

"What are you doing?"

"We have to measure off five miles," replied Hoover. "I measured around a wagon wheel and did some ciphering. That front wheel needs to turn twenty-six hundred revolutions to travel five miles in a straight line. So, to be safe we'll count off twenty-eight hundred and then set up a site to sell our wares."

"How we going to count that high?" asked McConnell between swigs on a whiskey bottle.

"I'll tie my handkerchief to the wheel and count every time it goes past. It will also leave a mark in the dirt if we need to recount."

"Hell, I ain't never counted past a hundred before," mumbled McConnell.

6

The young man should emigrate to Kansas. A couple of years of toil will secure to the energetic and economical young man a competence. The hard-working farmer, who finds it difficult to keep out of debt, should come to Kansas. Health and independence he will be sure to find. The city mechanic should come to Kansas. There is great demand for all kinds of mechanics. Wages are good, and will continue so. The young woman should come to Kansas. The demand for school teachers and for household help is great, and the increase of population will bring with it an increased demand.

—*Handbook to Kansas Territory*, James Redpath and Richard Hinton (New York: J.H. Colton, 1859)

The Masterson family — seven children and both parents — acquired an eighty-acre homestead in Sedgewick County, Kansas. In the first year, they broke the land; seeded the crops; constructed a house and outbuildings; and purchased some livestock. Now the family waited for nature to bring on a bountiful harvest so that they could pay for supplies and feed the family.

Four of the seven children were now over the age of fourteen and were considering life off the farm. On

September 16, 1872, the Masterson family was celebrating the end of harvest and the seventeenth birthday of James Masterson.

Bat offered a toast to his younger brother. "May you live as long as you want and never want as long as you live." Glasses were lifted and clinked. The younger children drank sarsaparilla, while the adults celebrated with a rare bottle of Irish whiskey.

"Thank the Lord for rewarding our efforts in this land of opportunity," responded his father.

"And we are blessed with even more opportunities," said Bat. "I have been invited to join the buffalo hunt."

"Who says?" asked his mother.

"Buffalo Bill Cody put in a good word. The army is hiring civilian scouts to hunt buffalo and put down any Indian troubles."

Edward and Jim stood up from the table. "We're going too if they will have us."

"You boys sit down right now! What has got into you, Bartholemew? This family stays together through thick and thin. And your father needs your help on the farm."

"We can't spend our whole life helping on the farm," replied Bat. "We need to make some money and meet some girls."

"Oh, so that's it. You need to meet girls. And what dance hall would that be in?" asked Catherine.

"No, Ma!" shouted Edward. "We want to have our own lives and our own families. You still have Nellie and the young'ns. Heck, even baby Emma is already ten years old."

"Pa, put a stop to this!" ordered Catherine, her head in her hands. "Keep this family together."

The three boys stood facing their father, fully expecting continued parental objections. To their discomfort, Thomas stood silent, turning his stare to each of them in turn. He was proud of these boys cum men. Edward, the oldest, stood tall and slim with his light-brown hair and mustache. He reminded Thomas of the man he saw in the mirror twenty years earlier.

James was now seventeen. His dark hair and handlebar mustache added years to his baby face. Thomas marveled at how much James had changed in the last year.

Bat would be nineteen in November. His face was thin like Ed's but was distinctive due to his dark eyes, heavy eyebrows and thick black mustache. Bat always dressed like he was going to church or a meeting at the bank. His three-piece suit was buttoned closed over a white shirt and bow tie. He accented his image with a pocket watch and the bowler-esque hat. On this day, the only clothing he had in common with his brothers were the leather chaps which looked out of place on his rakish figure. Bat was confident in his appearance, and this confidence would influence the people he encountered throughout his life. It was also not lost on his father.

"The boys are right, Ma. It's time they made their own way," conceded Thomas, facing the woman who had raised these fine men.

"What? Are you…? I don't know," stammered Catherine.

Then Nellie jumped up from her chair. "And me, too. I'm fifteen now, and in the spring I'm going to New York."

She looked resplendent in a simple dress she had fashioned herself.

"What are you going to do in New York?" asked Thomas, assuming he already knew the answer. Nellie had proven her ability to make clothing for each member of the family.

"I am going to be a milliner, like in Chicago. Even if I have to work as a cleaning lady off the start."

Thomas Masterson looked around the room and realized that he was no longer in charge. Half of his children were determined to make their own way in the world. When he shrugged and looked to his wife, Catherine, she nodded her approval.

"Pa, will you drive us to the station in Wichita?" asked James.

"No, I don't think you need to take the train. Boys, take your three horses. Nellie can double up with one of you on the way to the station. I can't spare my rifle. Ed, you have your pistol, and the others will have to buy guns."

Edward, Bartholemew, and James saddled the horses that their father had given them. The horses were old and the tack was worn, but they would get them down the road. The boys each had a saddlebag, but Nellie also made them carry two hat boxes and two large carpet bags. The trip to Wichita station took four hours with stops for water and grazing. Nellie had enough money to purchase a ticket for the two-week ride to New York City.

The Masterson boys galloped their horses to the army recruiting office before it closed. There they received

Winchester rifles and civilian contracts to hunt buffalo in Kansas, Texas, and Indian Territory. Their next stop was Dodge City.

7

Dodge City, Kansas, 1873

Buffalo usually go in herds varying in number from a few stragglers to thousands in the same herd. Occasionally fifty thousand are seen together, yet the most frequent size of the herd is from three hundred to a thousand. They roam over the plains and travel northward in spring and summer and southward in autumn and winter.

For a number of years past buffalo hunting has been a trade which has proven very profitable to those engaged in it, but now it is not profitable as the buffalo are too scarce—that is they go in too small herds to be easily hunted. Hence the hunting as heretofore for the hides alone has about ceased. The cost of preserving the meat at this season of the year is much more than during the cold weather, hence this branch of the business has played no important part in the slaughter of these immense herds. It is estimated that the meat which has gone to waste on the plains during any winter of the past five years would have furnished an abundance of meat for the poor of the entire nation who depend upon charity for food.

—*Dodge City Times*, Dodge City, Kansas, September 14, 1878

The temperance zone imposed at Fort Dodge, inspired George Hoover to build a beer and liquor store at the preeminent site for Dodge City. By good fortune, more than by planning, Hoover's site was perfectly located for those with a sense of adventure and ambition. A bridge had been constructed over the Arkansas River, attracting travelers and trade. Dodge was located on the Atchison, Topeka, and Santa Fe railway, as well as adjacent to the Santa Fe trail. Its proximity to Fort Dodge provided protection from any warring Indian tribes.

In its early years Dodge City served as the best location for tanning and shipping buffalo hides. The hides of one and a half million buffalo were shipped from Dodge to customers in the eastern states. Some meat was shipped, but most was left to rot in the heat of the prairie summers. Buffalo bones were collected and sold for several dollars per ton. Men involved in hunting and skinning carcasses became known as "stinkers" due to the odor from decaying carcasses.

The Medicine Lodge Treaty of 1867 stipulated that the Kiowa, Comanche, and Plains Apache would surrender thirty-eight million acres in exchange for three million acres in the southwest corner of Indian Territory. This treaty preserved traditional native hunting grounds south of the Arkansas River and north of the Canadian River. Nevertheless, cattlemen in Texas opposed buffalo ranging freely where they intended to graze beef cattle. The support of the powerful cattle barons, allowed Dodge City buffalo hunters to move into the preservation area.

By the time the buffalo herds thinned, two major cattle trails led the way to Dodge City stockyards. In the next decade, over five million Texas longhorns were loaded onto rail cars in Dodge City for shipment east to the large population centers. Trail hands were paid out at the end of the drive, and Dodge City was a good place to spend money on alcohol, gambling, sex, and any wild entertainment that could be dreamed of.

Everything had a price and for most things the price was two bits. The booming economy created demand for all types of goods, which were brought in by train. Dodge City became the distribution point for three army forts and many settlements to the south. Trading posts in Indian Territory and the Texas panhandle were a two- or three-days' ride.

Bat Masterson and his brothers thrived on life in the frontier. Working out of Dodge City, they found no end to the opportunities available to them. In the peak years, a crack shot like Bat could make a hundred dollars a day by killing thirty to forty buffalo. The U.S. Army supported the buffalo hunters by offering protection and supplies at forts established in Kansas and Texas — all part of a government strategy to eliminate the buffalo in order to deprive the Plains Indian tribes of an important source of food and shelter. Buffalo hunters earned an extraordinary amount of money, but they could also earn additional money by guiding game hunters or clearing the range for cattlemen.

By the time Bat Masterson reached the age of twenty, the money meant less to him than the adventure. His travels in pursuit of buffalo landed him in Adobe Walls, along the Canadian River in the north of Texas. The Adobe Walls trading post had been destroyed ten years earlier during a battle between Kit Carson and the Plains Indians, but the location attracted some traders to rebuild the site. Bat worked on the crew that constructed a buffalo hide trading post, new store, blacksmith shop, and the obligatory saloon.

At dawn on June 27, 1874, a party of seven hundred Comanche, Cheyenne, and Kiowa warriors, led by Quanah Parker, attacked the post. One woman and fewer than thirty men defended the camp from windows and doorways. Bat Masterson and eight others were pinned in the saloon throughout the first day. The warriors pounded on the saloon door with rifle butts, but the occupiers were able to repel them with pistols and close-quarters weapons. By afternoon, the attackers had the buildings under steady fire from stationary positions. At the end of the day, the raiders moved out of rifle range but kept the camp surrounded. Three men within the trading post were killed, and their bodies were buried that night. The bodies of fifteen dead attackers lay on the ground. On the second day, a few hunters rode into camp to reinforce their besieged peers. Subsequent incursions by the Indians were met with increasing firepower over the next five days. Quanah Parker suffered a wound, and more than two dozen of his party had been killed. The standoff lasted weeks, until a cavalry troop evacuated the buffalo hunters later that summer. The hunters, including Bat Masterson, and other survivors abandoned the camp, leaving it for the attackers to burn to the ground.

The buffalo hunters who survived overwhelming odds in defense of Adobe Walls were celebrated by newspapers across the country.

8

Cantonment Sweetwater, Texas, 1876

Now all the people that came out were circumcised: but all the people [that were] born in the wilderness by the way as they came forth out of Egypt, [them] they had not circumcised.

—Joshua 5:5 [King James Version]

Undaunted by his near-death experience at Adobe Walls, Bat Masterson continued to hunt buffalo in the Texas panhandle and Indian Territory. Since the buffalo herd was thinning, he garnered work as a teamster, transporting supplies into the same areas. The army had established a supply depot at Fort Elliott. The depot was named Cantonment Sweetwater, based on its proximity to Sweetwater Creek.

Bat Masterson had seen the growth of another place next to an army fort in the middle of nowhere. He speculated that this location might have the same success as Dodge City, so he surveyed a forty-acre town site at the cantonment. The businessmen encouraged Bat's plan for their growing community, and he became a celebrated character in Sweetwater. But popularity also breeds jealousy and contempt. Bat never suspected his renown would lead to a deadly confrontation — a confrontation that would follow him for the rest of his life.

On a fateful day in January, Bat was driving a wagon load of whiskey barrels and beer kegs from Dodge City to the saloons in Sweetwater. Business was booming, due largely to the estimated four hundred buffalo hunters spending that winter in town. Bat had no problem arranging a back-haul for his team and wagon. His plan was to return to Dodge the following day with a load of buffalo hides. His freight service thrived in both directions and earned Bat a great deal of respect among the pillars of the community.

As a young man, barely twenty-two years old, Bat was healthy and physically fit. Toting barrels and buffalo hides was arduous and taxing. He knew that it would not be a lifelong career, but for now he was enjoying the travel and adventure. Although he had grown accustomed to the odor, Bat did not enjoy the smell of rotting buffalo flesh. This night, the stench followed him up the steps of the Lady Gay Saloon.

"As I live and breathe," said a buffalo hunter sitting on a stool outside the saloon. "Bat Masterson is in town tonight. Can I roll you a smoke?" asked Billy Thompson.

"Sure, Billy. What are you doing out here?"

"Mollie decided to close the dance hall tonight and spend some time with the rubes in the Lady Gay."

"Sales and marketing are the key to any enterprise. And Mollie is a costermonger if I ever met one."

"That's what she said," agreed Billy. "I am just her bodyguard tonight. Had some trouble in the dance hall last night."

"Anything of which I should be aware?" asked Bat.

"You ever heard of Sergeant King?" Billy waited for Bat to nod. "Well, he's stationed at the fort and spends his evenings in town. Mostly playing cards but last night he was in the dance hall."

"Fancies himself as a dancer, does he?"

"I shudda noticed him sneak upstairs. But I was distracted by a piece of calico twirling around the floor. Seems he tried to have his way with one of the Jolly twins."

"I was under the impression those girls were just handmaidens to the girls on the line. Pretty young, if I am not mistaken."

"They're older than they look. Mollie knows the risks even for the girls that aren't on the line." Billy spat his tobacco into a nearby spittoon.

"So Mollie closed up shop to keep King out?" asked Bat. "Seems unlike her."

"She closed because all the girls are afraid of King. Big hullabaloo this morning, so Mollie asked old Norton to close his hall for a night."

Bat pulled up a stool beside Billy and lit his cigarette. He looked across the street in silence while he drew several drags on the smoke.

"King is bad news," continued Billy. "Heard he's been in and out of the army several times. Every kind of crime from shooting a dog to killing some card players in Abilene. Some say he changed his name to Melvin King after a court martial," Billy added.

"Who was he before?" asked Bat as he flicked ashes off the end of his cigarette.

"Sergeant Anthony Cook. But from the posters I've seen they both look like the same horse's ass."

"So he needs a new face more than a new name," chuckled Bat. "My understanding is King has never risen above Corporal due to his unbecoming behavior."

"Well, he insists on being called Sergeant King around here. And since he showed up, he figgers he is the law in Sweetwater. The army doesn't see a need for a marshal in town."

"I have never actually been in his presence. What's he look like?" asked Bat.

"Yer in luck, Bat. Come here," Billy said, as he stood to look over the saloon doors. "That's him playin' faro. In uniform tonight. Brown hair. Short feller but wiry."

"Looks like Mollie is watching him close," said Bat. "It's a good chance for me to make his acquaintance. Keep your head up, Billy. This promises to get interesting."

Bat walked up to the bar to stand next to Mollie Brennan. Mollie was the longest-serving harlot in this new cantonment of Sweetwater. Prior to that, she had been a popular dance-hall girl in Ellsworth, Kansas. Mollie knew most of the regular trail hands and buffalo hunters from the days when Ellsworth was all the rage. Like Bat and the businessmen, Mollie saw potential in a town beside an army fort. She convinced a number of other girls, including seven sisters with the surname Jolly, to join her in Sweetwater.

Tonight, Mollie was focused on the table where King was sitting and didn't notice Bat step up beside her.

"Which way does he gather?" asked Bat in a whisper.

Mollie flinched at hearing the familiar voice next to her. "Bat Masterson, what are you insinuating?" laughed Mollie.

"You know what I mean. Which side is it on?"

"Just like you, he gathers left. But unlike you he is left-handed."

"Well, not everyone is perfect, as you know."

"As I know and appreciate. What brings you to the Lady Gay tonight?"

"Trouble brings me here. Trouble, as you will appreciate. What else do you know about Sergeant King?"

"I know things. I know he was born in Lower Canada, probably not far from the Masterson estate."

"Interesting. What else?"

"I know he is circumcised like you."

"Maybe we were delivered by the same Jewish doctor. But I prefer you keep that information under your hat, so to speak."

Mollie laughed. "That's stock-in-trade among us girls. Some peckers are just more inviting. Mm-mm."

"Sakes alive!" exclaimed Bat. "Mollie, how much have you had to drink?"

"No one's counting, tonight."

"I heard a maiden had some trouble."

"Actually, two of them. They're identical twins. Sergeant King seems to have a fetish. He groped them both last night and made it clear he would be having his way with them soon. Scared the shit out of those poor girls. They are still god-fearing and chaste ladies. And that's just the way they will stay."

"Who is King playing cards with tonight?"

"A couple of fledgling buffalo hunters. They are holding their own. The dealer's new. I'm helping him out by watching for King to cheat."

When Bat sat down at the faro table, facing Sergeant King, his presence was acknowledged immediately.

"Do you fellers smell something?" asked King. "Smells like something died."

Bat Masterson looked around the table. "Gentlemen, would you be kind enough to tell me, was this chair taken?"

"Hard to say," said King.

"Well, the chair was either occupied or available," said Bat. "So, tell me your impression, mister. King, is it?"

"Sergeant King will be fine."

Mollie came over to the table.

"Well, good fortune shines a light on all of us tonight," exclaimed Bat. "The immortal Miss Brennan deigns to entertain us."

"Why are you not dancing over at Norton's Hall?" asked King.

"Norton closed the hall tonight," replied Mollie. "Trouble with a patron last night." She glared at King.

"To whom do you refer?" asked Bat, pretending to look around the bar.

Mollie scowled at Bat and turned towards King. "Sergeant King. Have you met the notorious and insufferable Bat Masterson?"

King frowned and shook his head.

Mollie continued, "Well, you are in his company. And tonight he does smell like a dead dog."

"That seems to be the popular opinion around this table," said Bat.

King stood up. He was even shorter than Bat had suspected, no taller than five and a half feet. The buttons of his army coat were unfastened. Bat noticed two gun-belts. One holster on each side with the pistol grips facing forward, indicating that King liked to reach across his body to grip one gun at a time. If Mollie was correct, King would draw with his left hand, using the gun on the right hip. Bat kept his hands on the table, waiting for King's next move.

"Take a bath, buffalo hunter," said King. He turned and left the saloon. Two soldiers at the next table got up from their chairs and tipped their hats to Mollie as they followed King out.

Bat chuckled, then shook hands with the youngsters sitting at the table and introduced himself.

"We know who you are, mister," one of them said.

"You should have put a hole in that Sergeant King," said the other.

"I guess he left too soon. I'm inclined to do some drinking and gambling before the shooting starts."

The youngsters gaped at Bat and then looked to Mollie.

"He's pulling yer legs, boys," laughed Mollie. "He's a lover, not a killer. Reckon there won't be any shooting tonight. Now let me buy you boys a whiskey."

"Make 'em doubles, on me," said Bat.

Just after midnight, Billy Thompson came into the saloon and whispered something in Mollie's ear. She nodded and then leaned down beside Bat to get his attention.

"Let's go across the street. Someone's upstairs. Might be nothing."

"Or is it a ruse to draw me the bath I need so desperately?" asked Bat.

"I'm serious, Bat," replied Mollie. "There is a candle lighting the window where the Jolly twins are sleeping. And that is not normal!"

Norton's Dance Hall was dark except for a window on the second floor. Quietly, Billy unlocked the front door and held it ajar for the others to enter. He stood silently at the bottom of the stairs while Bat and Mollie started up. Bat looked at Mollie when he heard a bed creaking and someone grunting. Before she responded, they heard a man's voice, "Stay there, sister. Wait your turn."

"That's King," said Mollie, as she bolted up the stairs.

"Wait, Mollie," Bat warned, but she was already ten steps down the hall. As he followed her into the dark corridor, Bat drew his sidearm.

Before Billy started up the stairs after the pair, he noticed two soldiers coming across the street towards the open door. He ran to the door, slammed it shut, and turned the deadbolt. In the same instant, a shot rang out from above. As Billy ran for the stairs, he heard two more shots in rapid succession.

"I'm here, Mollie! Run to me," shouted Billy, climbing the stairs two steps at a time.

9

Cantonment Sweetwater, Texas, 1876

Garner, the young man who attempted to commit a rape on a ten-year old girl near Cat Springs, Austin county, last week, had an examination at Bellville on Tuesday. The girl identified Garner while standing with a dozen other men in the court room, and also identified his horse while it was hitched at a rack with numerous other animals. He was committed to jail at Bellville. The girl's straightforward evidence leaves no doubt as to his guilt.

—*Brenham Weekly Banner,* Brenham, Texas, December 6, 1878

On any given night, men were milling around the streets of Cantonment Sweetwater into the early hours of the morning. This night there were soldiers among the men in the street. They looked up after hearing a gunshot from the second story of Norton's Dance Hall. Two muzzle flashes in the candlelit window coincided with the second and third gunshots. They ran to the door, but it was locked from the inside. One man shook the door and pounded on the frame, while the other jumped into the street to watch for more gunfire.

Patrons of the Lady Gay Saloon poured into the street, asking questions and shouting theories. The soldiers tried to explain what they had seen. There were several buffalo hunters in the crowd and more running down the street. The buffalo hunters quickly took control of the situation and pushed the two soldiers away from the dance hall. With guns drawn, they formed a perimeter across the front and down the narrow side alleys.

Buffalo hunters were experienced at working with a team of men or horses. They did not need a commanding officer to make decisions for them. Situations like this night were commonplace in their travels. And in this part of the world they were the majority and could enforce the law as they saw fit. The buffalo hunters did not know what had started the hullabaloo, but they were in control of the situation at Norton's Dance Hall.

As the crowd waited, minutes seemed like hours. Finally, Billy Thompson came out of the dance hall. He talked to the group of buffalo hunters that had gathered there.

"Send two soldiers for the army doctor. Get some of your crew to guard the back doors and don't let anyone in," ordered Billy.

"They are already in place," answered one of the hunters near him.

"I need two of you to come with me." Two hunters entered and, after he locked the door, followed Billy upstairs.

Two soldiers mounted up and rode hard to get the doctor. In twenty minutes, the captain of the fort, eight officers, and the army medic arrived at the dance hall. The doctor climbed down from a horse with a large black medical bag and waited at the entrance. Everyone was watching Billy open the door for the doctor. No one in the crowd saw two figures exit at the rear of the building. They were whisked into the darkness of the alley by two larger shadows.

Dr. Finley arrived to find the hallway and bedroom well-lit by lanterns and candles. Sergeant King was lying face-down in the doorway of the bedroom. Blood was soaking into a rug underneath his upper body. He did not appear to be breathing. King was dressed in the same uniform he had been wearing in the saloon.

Bat propped himself up on his elbows and said, "Thank God for the army and their doctors." He was lying on a four-poster bed, wearing only underclothes and covered by a blood-soaked sheet.

Mollie Brennan lay motionless in a pool of blood at the foot of the bed. Her arms were folded over the blood-stained bodice of her dress. There was a tin washtub next to Mollie's body. The six inches of water in the tub was pink. A sponge and white bubbles floated on the surface. A tufted velvet armchair was positioned near the tub. Bat's clothes and chaps were neatly folded over the back of the chair and his boots were standing in front of it.

The doctor quickly scanned the room. He stepped over King's body and bent down beside Mollie's head. He placed two fingers on her neck, waiting for a pulse. Having no success, he moved back to King. When he checked for a pulse, his eyebrows rose.

"This man is still alive. Help me roll him on his side."

"Shit, I was sure he was a goner," said one of the buffalo hunters who kneeled down to help the doctor.

"Appears the bullet went in just under his right arm but never came out. I'll put on this bandage and then he needs to go the infirmary at the fort." Three minutes later, some buffalo hunters were hoisting the rug by the corners and carrying out the bandaged Sergeant King. The doctor was examining Bat even as the others left the room.

"What happened here, Bat? Can I call you Bat?" asked the doctor as he lifted the blanket covering both of Bat's legs. "Did you get shot twice? These holes don't line up." Although the wounds were covered in blood, it was clear that there were two bullet holes, one in his lower abdomen and one in his hip.

"Just one lucky shot. Must have ricocheted off a bone," groaned Bat. He was fighting to stay conscious.

"I am going to treat you here," said Finley. Just then, two buffalo hunters came back to the room. "Someone bring me a bottle of whiskey. And some boiling water if you can. He will need a bullet to bite on."

Bat was lapping a trickle of whiskey poured by one of the hunters until the other placed a bullet in his mouth. Then the doctor took a cloth handkerchief and a debarked willow branch from his bag. He wrapped the cloth around the thin stick and then poured the rest of the whiskey over it. Then he dipped the device into the pail of hot water.

"OK, Bat. Now is the time to bite down. This is going to hurt," said Finley as he wiggled the cloth into the wound. Bat screamed and then passed out. One of the hunters gagged and turned away.

The other hunter spoke up. "What are ya doing, doc?"

"Your friend will not die from this wound unless it gets infected. And I need to disinfect the wound along the path of the bullet."

"With whiskey?"

"Whiskey will do it. Ninety percent of most medicine is whiskey," laughed Finley. "You boys are probably real healthy, aren't you?"

"I reckon. Whiskey does the trick."

"Go ahead and take Miss Mollie downstairs. The undertaker will collect her in the morning."

Bat awoke in pain. Then he remembered that he had been shot. But where was he now? The pillow smelled of Mollie's perfume. But where was Mollie? Why was the room spinning? There was a candle burning on a nightstand. Across the room, he could see Billy Thompson sitting in an armchair, asleep.

"Billy," said Bat in a hoarse voice. He tried again but the sound was even weaker. There was a small glass of whiskey on the nightstand. He drank it and tried to remember. Then he fell back asleep.

At sunrise, Billy shook Bat on the shoulder.

"Wake up, Bat. How did you sleep?"

"Stop!" groaned Bat. "Land sakes, where am I?"

"You are in Mollie's room, at the dance hall."

"Yeah. I thought it looked familiar. Where is Mollie?"

"Bat, you probably don't remember much."

"Remember much of what?" asked Bat.

"Mollie's dead," replied Billy, hanging his head.

"Miss Mollie's dead!" exclaimed Bat. "I thought that was just a nightmare. Did one of the girls shoot her, too?" Bat grimaced and started to rub the bandages on his abdomen.

"Listen, Bat. You need to get the story straight. There weren't no girls here."

"What ya mean? I thought King had a couple of twins across the hall."

"No, Bat. That's not the story. Here's what you say. The dance hall was closed. You were up here having a bath. Mollie was bringing hot water for you when Sergeant King stormed into the room holding his revolver. He cussed out Mollie for allowing you to corrupt her. He threatened to kill you both. When you jumped out of the tub to get to your gun, King shot you through your gullet and damaged your hip. You fell to the floor and Mollie tried to disarm King and got herself shot. You were able to reach your gun-belt hanging on the bedpost, draw your pistol and fire from a laying-down position. King hit the floor, with a wound in his right side. That is how we found the three of you when we rushed up to Mollie's room."

"Plausible," said Bat. "You're suggesting that King would tell a different story had he lived?"

"Oh, he's alive. He's in the infirmary at Fort Elliott. Far as we know, he can't talk. And if he could, he won't be telling what he was really doing up here."

"What about those twins? And the blood across the hall?" asked Bat.

"The boys got the witnesses out of town already. Most of the blood was on the rug and we just dragged it over to this room with King on it."

"It appears that the legend will be more plausible than the truth," said Bat.

"Only you and King know what really happened. And King won't be telling it. My boys helped move some bodies around, but they never saw what happened. As far as anyone knows, yer a goddamn hero. The legendary Bat Masterson guns down a crazed gunman before he can kill again."

"If someone has to be the hero, I'll take a shot at it," surmised Bat.

"Doc Finley figgers you'll be needin' a walking stick for a long-time. Some of the boys cobbled this for you to use fer now." Billy held out a wooden cane made from a metal handle attached to a wagon wheel spoke.

"I am inclined to have a selection of custom sticks fashioned. A hero needs a scepter one day and a shillelagh on the next," chuckled Bat as he looked at the roughhewn cane.

"There is something else," added Billy. "Mollie whispered something before she went, but darned if it makes sense to me."

"What did she say?" asked Bat.

"She said 'Twins have the list'. Does that mean anything to you?" inquired Billy.

"Good to know. But don't repeat that."

"I might have mentioned it to Doc Finley," admitted Billy.

"Shit. That could be trouble for those girls. Make sure they are protected till I make a plan."

The two buffalo hunters sat in silence, thinking about the night's events. Eventually, they came around to sharing memories of some nights with Mollie. Other buffalo hunters had driven Bat's team and wagon to Dodge during the night. The cargo was listed as buffalo hides. However, there was more precious cargo under wraps.

Corporal Melvin King died the next morning, January 25, 1876. As company commander, Captain Gunther was required to investigate the death of his corporal. He waited a few days for the emotions to settle before scheduling a short hearing at the fort. Due to his injuries, Bat was unable to attend but sent Billy Thompson to represent him. Testimony was provided by army personnel that were across the street in the Lady Gay prior to the shooting. Those men witnessed a heated discussion between Bat and Sergeant King. They could not say how much either man had to drink but admitted King had been belligerent for some time before Bat entered the saloon.

Billy Thompson agreed with the army witnesses and relayed the conversation between King and Bat about the need for a bath. He presented the story of Bat's incredible poise and courage. Even though Bat was caught in the delicate position of bathing at the time, he tried to protect Mollie Brennan.

Newspapers of the day stated that Corporal King, stationed at the Cantonment on the Sweetwater in Texas, died as a result of gunshot wounds sustained in a quarrel at a public house on the previous evening.

Several weeks later, the army dispatched a letter to Susan B. Cook, next of kin to Anthony Cook aka Sergeant King. The letter described King as a *"favorite throughout the regiment with officers and enlisted men"* whose untimely end resulted from a mortal wound sustained in an affray at Cantonment Sweetwater, Texas.

In the spring of 1876, Billy Thompson and Bat Masterson returned to Dodge City. Bat was using a cane to walk. He was able to ride a horse by storing the cane in a rifle scabbard.

10

Dodge City, Kansas, 1876

**Men willing to work at any manual labor may safely emi-
grate to the Territory, and find little difficulty in procuring
steady work and remunerative wages. Physicians, clergymen,
lawyers, real estate brokers, gamblers, politicians and the like
had better stay at home, for the territory is already bounti-
fully supplied with them.**

—*Handbook to Kansas Territory*, **James Redpath and
Richard Hinton (New York: J.H. Colton, 1859)**

Like most boom towns, Dodge City grew as a result of its
location and a single industry. From the arrival of the railroad in 1872, Dodge City was the home base for most of
the two thousand buffalo hunters roaming western Kansas.
These men were protected by the federal government and
supported by the U.S. Army. Some of these hunters were
trained marksmen. Some had survived the Civil War, the
Indian Wars and the Mexican-American War. Some had
worked in law enforcement. But there were two things
they all had in common: money and power.

By 1876, though, the buffalo herds had been virtually
eliminated from Kansas and Texas. Buffalo hunters had
to adapt to a new way of life in the West. In order to keep

Dodge City vibrant, the buffalo hunters worked with the business community to bring in cattle drives and cowboys. Texas longhorns were the new buffalo, and the cowboys were the new hunters. But the buffalo hunters realized that there was little money and no power in working on the cattle trails. The real money and power were gained by servicing the influx of cowboys and railway workers. And those people were looking for entertainment.

The hunters formed partnerships in all types of businesses, but especially those that catered to the entertainment preferences of cowboys. These involved, of course, gaming, alcohol, sex, and guns, the same things that had entertained the buffalo hunters in times previous.

So the buffalo hunters built bars, saloons, and bordellos. As businessmen, they needed law and order. But because the political organization of these young communities often lagged behind the demographics, the buffalo hunters themselves organized to create laws and elect the officials to enforce them.

In 1872, George Hoover founded Dodge City in Ford County by opening a liquor store, but the town was not incorporated until 1875. Hoover was officially elected mayor in 1876 but had been the defacto mayor prior to that date. Hoover had never been a buffalo hunter, but he understood their desire for money and power.

In its early days, Dodge City had no elected lawmen, but relied on the Ford County Sheriff, Charlie Bassett, as the primary peace officer. Bassett was able to reduce the amount of vigilante justice but faced fierce opposition from the powerful gang of buffalo hunters that promoted prostitution, gambling, and public drinking establishments. That group became commonly known as the Dodge City Gang. It included Bat Masterson.

The Gang had a loose structure in its early days, and various sub-factions developed. Bat Masterson led by example, and his supporters included legends such as Wyatt Earp, Doc Holliday, Luke Short, Frank McLain, Neil Brown, W.H. Harris, and William Tilghman.

After the Sweetwater shootout, lore of Bat's ability with a gun garnered respect from both lawmen and gunfighters. Bat realized his hunting days were done, due to the combination of waning buffalo numbers and his reliance on a walking stick. He cultivated this reputation and natural leadership ability to become a respected entrepreneur on both sides of the law. In 1877, Bat succeeded Charlie Bassett as Sheriff of Ford County with a commitment to oversee the on-going vice activity in Dodge City. And former Sheriff Charlie Bassett was welcomed into the Gang under the authority of Bat Masterson.

11

However, as long as the drive can be maintained through to Kansas, it will find its outlet at Dodge City. This is established from the fact that the route to this point has natural advantages over other routes. We lie in a bend of the river which brings this point nearer to the range and outside of the heavy settlements. We are at the terminal courses of the numerous creeks and streams that find their source south, east and north of us. This point on the river is the only one within the western limits of Kansas that affords an easy ingress to the railroad. The route from the Pan Handle to Dodge City is good at all seasons of the year. There is a good trail, plenty of water and abundance of grass at all times. No other point along the river west within Kansas possesses these natural advantages.

—*Dodge City Times*, Dodge City, Kansas, September 14, 1878

Bat called an early morning meeting at the Long Branch Saloon. He invited Wyatt Earp, Doc Holliday, and Charlie Bassett. The barkeeper was instructed to make sure that they were not disturbed and that there was always a full bottle of bourbon on the table.

"Gentlemen," Bat said, raising the first glass of whiskey. "To the Dodge City Gang and our successful enterprise."

The other men raised their glasses and mumbled approvals: "Hear! Hear!" "To our success." "For the good of the Gang."

"As you are aware, the demise of the buffalo herd has seen the departure of many men and their affluence. Where we once had thousands of buffalo hides piled, we have dog excrement and tumbleweeds. Bankers that formerly were challenged to count the money in their vaults are now closing their doors. You only have to visit Cantonment Sweetwater to see what could happen here in Dodge. Sweetwater sustains nary a harlot today. And there is no truer indicator of economic decline than the departure of experienced whores." Bat paused to take a swallow from his glass, while the others nodded their agreement.

"It will, dare I say, it *is* disheartening and lugubrious to consider the demise of our fine city before celebrating the sixth anniversary of its founding by George Hoover. Last year our city had twenty saloons, five hotels, six brothels, four dance halls, four banks, three mercantiles and two tanneries. Now with a steady population we have only twelve saloons and three hotels and no tanneries. The money to build and operate these establishments did not come from a thousand residents. It came from buffalo hides. Without the buffalo trade, some would question the necessity of this town on the Ar-Kansas River."

"Good sir," said Earp. "Would you not suspect that the cattle trails will bring life to our town?"

"Can we count on that?" asked Doc Holliday. "Cowboys only get paid a dollar a day."

"But they receive the whole wad as soon as the beeves are in the yard. Which will be right here in Dodge," declared Earp.

"I believe Wyatt is largely correct," answered Bat. "As long as the trail ends here, the cowboys will have money to spend. However, the cattle trade depends on many factors which we do not control. In the same way that we did not control the buffalo herds, we do not control the ranchers and the railways."

"Please explain what you mean by that," said Holliday. He coughed into his handkerchief.

"My meaning is that ranchers choose the most convenient destination for the cattle drives based on two considerations. Firstly, the location of the closest rail yard. And secondly, the price they will receive." Bat paused to finish his glass of whiskey. "Today the cattle trails terminate at stockyards in Dodge, Newton, and Ellsworth. However, I would like to propose that there are methods at our disposal to divert those trails to our yards in Dodge, exclusively!"

Bat pulled some papers from his breast pocket and unfolded one sheet. Handwritten at the top were the words, "**All Roads Lead to Dodge**." He passed the page to Charlie Bassett. Below the heading were eight words written in pairs.

Cattle trails. Rustlers.
Liquor. Reformers.
Money. Property.
Women. Newspapers.

"What's this mean, Bat?" asked Bassett. He passed the paper to Doc before Bat answered.

"Dodge has always been reputed for four profitable interests. Those interests are the first word on each line. The second word on each line is the method we will use to promote those interests."

"I can't say I am reading this correctly," moaned Doc. "Liquor and Reformers don't mix."

"You have to grind 'em up real fine and then strain out the bones," chuckled Earp.

"Go heavy on the whiskey when yer mixin' that drink," added Bassett, grinning.

Doc coughed while the others laughed at the idea.

Bat handed a handkerchief to the sickly man before continuing. "The best way to perpetuate cheap and plentiful liquor in Dodge City is to assist Reform in other towns. Reformers seem to be moving in from the east. Hopefully, they will have great success in Newton and Wichita."

"I see what you mean," replied Doc. "We can convince some folks that Prohibition is coming. The reformers will celebrate, and the drinkers will move this way."

"Doc, I want you to talk with Mayor Hoover about temporarily reducing his wholesale deliveries east of Dodge. Start with Wichita," ordered Bat.

"Your Canadian friend might take issue with cutting off the liquor supplies to other towns. He makes a lot of silver with that wholesale business," Wyatt Earp said.

"Good point," replied Doc. "I will convince Hoover to start rectifying the liquor sold outside Dodge. Then as the market dries up, he can demand a premium for the product sold here and we'll help drive the customers his way. I am confident he will see the benefit of this plan."

"Exactly." Bat nodded and tapped his cane on the floor. "Charlie, can you arrange cattle rustlers to divert the cattle away from the Chisholm and Shawnee Trails?"

Bassett scratched his chin and broke into a big grin. "Should be easy to get the tribes to rustle a few head on those trails. In fact, there's good money in cattle rustling for ourselves."

"Just be discreet, my friend. We don't need the ranchers and trail hands up in arms next spring."

"Hey, when I talk with Hoover, I'll suggest he cut off whiskey supplies to the trading posts on the Chisholm trail," Doc volunteered. "But keep the Western Trail well supplied."

"Now you are thinking!" exclaimed Bat. "Let's make sure the teamsters all know to give preference to the posts along the Western Trail."

"I am assuming you want me to handle the property category," Earp remarked. "Just clarify what yer including in property."

"In the short term I mean liquid assets. We need some cash for operating costs. If necessary steal some chattels that we can sell to settlers. Saddles, tools, wagons. But be sure these crimes don't lead back to Dodge. Never in Dodge."

"Might be easier to rob a few banks, trains, and stagecoaches, just to get started," said Earp.

"Focus on trains and stages west of here," said Bat. "We want them to feel secure servicing Dodge from the east."

"Indeed, and we should consider which banks we use for the deposits," Earp suggested.

"Let's analyze that later," answered Bat. "After a couple of years, the deposits will allow us to do some land deals. We can buy up undeveloped properties in communities where we can influence the growth."

"So who's taking care of the last item?" asked Bassett. "The womenfolk?"

"Good golly. I miss Mollie," whispered Bat. "If only she was here, God rest her soul."

The other three men went quiet and held their hats over their hearts. After they muttered tributes to Mollie, Bat interrupted, "I'll take care of the recruiting side. We will need a flock of fine women and a pair of experienced matrons. Someone who the youngsters will trust and respect."

"How will you recruit these gals?" asked Earp as he winked at Bat. "Your handsome face?"

Then Earp nudged Bassett with his elbow. The gangsters started to chuckle.

"Say no more. Say no more," laughed Bassett.

Bat contrived a deep "Har-har" before returning to his role in the plan.

"Fred Harvey is recruiting his Harvey Girls through newspaper advertising. Newspaper advertising is being used to solicit mail-order brides. We are going to be in the newspapers."

Three men laughed spontaneously. Holliday spewed whiskey out his nose and endured another fit of coughing.

Bat tapped his cane on the floor. When the others regained their composure, he said, "Alea iacta est."

"Why don't you speak plainly, Bat?" asked Bassett.

"What's that you say?" Earp asked.

"That's Latin for *the die is cast*," mumbled Doc between coughs.

"How do you know Latin?" asked Bassett.

"The benefits of dental college," said Doc.

Bat continued to sermonize while he flattened a hand-drawn map on the table. The drawing showed cattle trails, river crossings, and rail lines.

"Forty-nine years before Christ, Julius Caesar cast the die by crossing the Rubicon River. In our plan, we have cast a die today that will bring all roads to Dodge across the Red River, the Canadian, the Arkansas, and the Cimarron. Memorize this map. Use the words, *'the die is cast'* when you want to review your progress with other members of our gang. Otherwise we will meet back here in one month."

"When we leave this table today, we have crossed the Rubicon," Earp said, raising his glass to the others.

"I'll keep my rope handy and my powder dry," replied Bassett. He placed his empty glass on the table with the bottom up.

"Bat has cast the die," declared Doc Holliday, struggling to get up from the table.

For the months that followed, the Dodge City Gang honored the plan as Bat Masterson had laid it out. The leadership of the Gang developed missions for buffalo hunters and rewarded them by preserving the lifestyle in

Dodge City. Bat was elected Sheriff in Ford County and Wyatt was appointed assistant Marshal for Dodge City. Both lawmen exploited political connections at the state and federal levels.

The gang's membership grew to include businessmen of Dodge who could profit from liquor, gambling, and prostitution. Eventually, distinguished members of the community provided anonymous support for the Gang's efforts to maintain and grow their city. More than half of the Board of Trade were supporters of the Gang in some fashion.

Bat also kept close contact with a string of reporters in other towns to publish articles that deflected suspicion away from the Gang. He was intrigued by the newspaper business and recognized the impact of words on any form of paper. Fake telegrams or letters could be supplied as evidence for ambitious reporters to publish questionable news.

Members of the Gang came and went from Dodge with impunity. When and where their skills were required, buffalo hunters moved to neighboring counties or states. Bat, Earp, Bassett and Holliday organized gangs in Texas, Arizona, New Mexico, Colorado, and Montana. When time permitted they met in person. Otherwise they relied on Western Union telegrams or Wells Fargo express mail.

Despite Masterson's firm grip, and the dedication of gang members, the cash returns from these exploits were far less than Dodge was built on. The town that once had twenty saloons, now had only three. A prohibitionist sentiment was sweeping the country and Kansas, with a history of violence and debauchery, was an easy target. More and more, elected officials sought to reform the way the people of Kansas lived.

12

Dodge City, 1878

Close his eyes, his work is done!
What to him is friend or foeman;
Rise of morn or set of sun,
Hands of man or kiss of woman?
Lay him low, lay him low,
In the clover or the snow—
What cares he, he cannot know.
As man may he fought his fight—
Proved his truth by his endeavor;
Let him sleep in solemn night—
Sleep forever and forever.
Lay him low, lay him low,
In the clover or the snow —
What cares he, he cannot know.

After the services, the large crowd that had assembled to show respect to the departed, formed in procession, the fire company, in uniform, marching in front. This was the largest procession ever witnessed in Dodge City, and the most solemn.

—*Dodge City Times*, Dodge City, Kansas, April 13, 1878

Crime within Dodge City was discouraged by the law and the Gang. There was no justification for stealing money from a trail hand who was likely to spend that money in a saloon or brothel. Still and all, fights and shoot-outs were commonplace. Disagreements could escalate quickly over women or cards, especially under the influence of alcohol. So, the lawmen of Dodge City kept a close eye on people in the gambling and drinking establishments. As the elected marshal of Dodge City, Ed Masterson deputized his brother, James, and Wyatt Earp. At the same time, Bat Masterson was the sheriff for Ford County, including the county seat in Dodge City.

On an April evening, Marshal Ed Masterson was in the Lady Gay Saloon (named after the infamous saloon in Sweetwater), when he noticed a cowpoke waving his six-shooter around in a drunken stupor. When Ed asked him to check his gun with the bartender, another trail rider spoke up.

"Hey, Marshal. Don't be preachin' no gun laws 'round here! This is Dodge City, and a man has a right to protect his-self."

"Fellers, ain't no law against guns," said Marshal Ed. "But there is a law about being disorderly and pissin' off the men around ya. So I'll ask you politely: please leave your sidearms with the barkeep and have a drink on my tab."

"Well, alright. Set 'em up, barkeep."

Marshal Ed had hardly left the saloon before the same two cowpokes came stumbling into the street. Both men were still armed, and one was waggling his barrel towards Marshal Ed.

"Holster yer gun, fella, or come down to the hoosegow with me."

"Ain't and won't."

Marshal Ed grabbed the man's arm and tried to wrest the gun away. The second cowboy drew his gun and pushed it into Marshal Ed's side.

"Let him go, Marshal!"

"Let's settle down, fellers. No need for any shootin'." As he released the arm of the first cowboy, a gun went off. Marshal Ed fell to the ground with a bullet in his stomach. Smoke rose from the hole where his coat was burnt by the muzzle flash.

In an office across the street, County Sheriff Bat Masterson heard his brother shouting. As Bat rose to look out the door, he heard the single shot. Grabbing his cane, he hobbled out to the street.

Two cowboys were running away along the middle of the street. When he saw his brother in the dirt, Bat aimed and fired at the two men trying to escape. By the time he had emptied his pistol, both of the fleeing men were writhing on the ground.

A witness came out of the Lady Gay. "Those fellers were lookin' for trouble with the marshal. We all seen 'em."

"Get the doctor! And pronto!" ordered Bat. When he kneeled down beside Ed, he could see his brother was bleeding profusely from his abdomen. Bat remembered words that rang in his head when the boys were in a river. *Edward, I will die so you can live. You must live.*

Bat said, "You're going to be OK, brother. They've gone for the doctor."

"Yeah. Probably just a flesh wound."

"Sure. Does it hurt much?"

"Like that time Nellie made them jalapeno pancakes."

"Ooo. That's real hurtin'. But she's gonna hurt you worse when I tell her you said that." Bat forced a smile as he looked his elder brother in the eye. Except for a mustache, he was looking at the same thin Irish face he remembered from the farm in Henryville.

"It's getting dark already. Feelin' mighty tired." Those were last words of twenty-five-year-old Marshal Ed Masterson.

The bystander returned carrying a medical bag and the doctor trotted behind.

"Looks bad, sawbones," said Bat. "He stopped breathing."

The doctor checked for a pulse and shook his head. He looked down the street where Deputy Earp was now standing over the wounded cowpokes. "I'll go check the offenders."

"Just a minute," said Bat. "For the record, Ed shot them both. Dead or alive, he got six shots off and dropped them both."

The bystander started to object, "But, I thought..."

"Wrong, Marshal Ed shot them," Bat said looking the man in the eye. "I didn't get here in time."

The doctor joined Earp at the two cowpokes. The one who shot Ed had crawled a couple of paces but was now deceased. There were two holes in the other cowboy, but he was alive.

"Well, feller. You might just see another sunrise," said the doctor, as he opened up the cowboy's vest to examine the wounds.

"Can you fix me up? Who was it shot me?"

"Er, I believe Marshal Ed Masterson shot you. And now he's dead. If you survive a couple of days, you can tell the judge your story."

"Well, I never shot anyone. Wagner did the shootin'. Tell 'em, Wagner!"

"Yer friend is not talkin'. Probably for the best, since he would be facing the noose."

The surviving cowboy rode out of Dodge a few days later in the knowledge that he had aggravated the law in Dodge City and the Gang would want revenge. The cowboy knew his future was uncertain at best.

The next day, Edward Masterson was buried in a pine box at Fort Dodge, Kansas. By acclamation, the city council promoted James Masterson to city marshal for the remainder of the term. The Gang members wanted to pay a lasting tribute to Ed with a funeral and burial in Dodge City. For a year they argued that the Dodge City marshal should be exhumed from his grave in Fort Dodge and buried at the Prairie Grove cemetery in Dodge City. Eventually, they prevailed. The Dodge City Fire Department arranged the transfer of Ed's casket, and a funeral ceremony was held on April 15, 1879. The Gang was in attendance in full force, and Bat took the opportunity to meet with his lieutenants. Neither Edward nor James had been active in the Dodge City Gang, yet Bat relied on their cooperation in local matters.

Bat cornered James after the burial, out of earshot of the other mourners.

"How are you standing up through this, young brother?"

"I'll be OK. Still want to put a hole in that Walker feller who consorted with Ed's killer."

"A natural inclination to avenge a brother's killing, especially since Ed was like a father to both of us," said Bat. "But you are the law in this town now. And you need to stay clean. Ed would want it that way. Maintain your integrity for the sake of the Masterson name."

"But what about you? Won't you be takin' his place in the family?" asked James.

"No. I'm overly involved in the Gang. It will be best for everyone if we steer clear of each other for awhile."

"OK. I reckon yer right," James agreed. "But Ed had some unfinished business."

"Are you referring to the Jolly twins?"

"Yeah. They were good company to Ed but since he has been gone they are paintin' the town red. I've had to lock them up more than a few times. In fact they are in the brig today so they didn't cause a ruckus with all these folks at the funeral."

"Did Ed know them in the Biblical sense?"

"S'pect so. He kept it private mostly. You could tell, though, by the way they doted on him."

"How old are they? Twenty?"

"Maybe a year or two more. Truth is, I can't coddle them any more. I have enough trouble with all the other pieces of calico in town."

"I'll take them on for a spell. They owe me." said Bat. "And it's been a while since I had a cook or a concubine."

"So, you take both. Two fine young ladies, despite what they bin through."

"A year from now, they'll be married off to some rancher or cowboy. I'll even put up their dowry."

"You take care of that, Bat. As you say. I should steer clear of agitation when I can."

The brothers shook hands before James walked down the hill towards town. Bat continued to receive condolences from the single line of men approaching him. He leaned his left arm on his cane as he glad-handed the members of the Gang.

The Lady Gay Saloon was closed that night, except for invited guests of the Gang. Bat stomped his walking stick on the floor to propose a toast. "The Masterson family thanks you for attending the funeral of our brother and friend, Edward John Masterson. The people of Dodge City are better for his bravery and compassion. As our eldest brother, Ed taught James and I about loyalty and chivalry. I think that some of you outside the family would agree. Wyatt, Doc, Charlie, and all of you — join me in a glass of whiskey. To Ed."

Depressed after losing his older brother, Bat was seldom seen outside the Ford County office. His associates in the Gang decided to join Bat one evening for supper. Charlie Bassett brought a pot of beef stew and enough biscuits for them all. Wyatt Earp sat in a wooden chair. Doc Holliday stood by the door, coughing and spitting into the street.

Bat was sitting at his desk, staring at some wanted posters, when Earp exclaimed, "The die is cast!"

Bat was the first to respond. "I know why you have chosen to bless me with your company," Bat replied. "And I appreciate the effort."

"Since we lost Ed, it seems like we're floggin' a dead horse," said Wyatt.

"It's time to do something different," added Bassett. "Dodge is like a cold stone."

"Can't get blood out of a stone," said Earp.

"So, it's not just me that senses the loss," added Bat. "Ed was a big part of our success."

"Shor'nuff," replied Earp. "We've got gambling halls and saloons that used to rake profits under the table. And that's what kept them goin'."

"Wyatt's right, Bat," concurred Bassett. "We need to stir up some more money in town."

"Money comes from other towns. It comes from ambition. It comes from the frontier. But it can't come from Dodge residents!" Bat shouted.

"Fine and dandy, Bat. But how do we get it here?"

"We need to cast a net. And that means we need to spread out."

"Not sure what yer meanin', Bat," Bassett said.

"You will. I'll build a plan, but we will have to get out of Dodge. In fact, we will have to get out of Kansas."

By the end of the day, the members of the Gang had received their orders from Bat. They rode out of Dodge in all directions.

As sheriff of Ford County, Bat achieved a myriad of success during his two-year term. He was credited with apprehending the Rourke-Rudabough gang for a series of train robberies. He captured the murderer of popular stage star Dora Hand. From horse thieves to trespassers, there were plenty of half-witted criminals to whom Bat extended the long arm of the law. And from each jailed miscreant, Bat solicited a colorful story for the courts and the local newspapers.

Nevertheless, Sheriff Masterson had detractors within the county, especially those within the Dodge City Reform movement. Residents were growing tired of the reputation Dodge was gaining in the newspapers of New York and Philadelphia. When it was time for re-election, the reformers supported another candidate, ending the political career of Bat Masterson. As always, Bat took away several valuable lessons from the experience.

The Reform movement actually improved the profits to saloon-keepers. Alcohol prices were doubled, with the excuse that reformers were making it difficult to obtain a reliable supply. If demand was impacted by price, the saloons would "rectify" the product by diluting it with water, oil, or local moonshine. Prostitutes raised their rates in Dodge City, based on the persecution they faced by Reformers and the dwindling number of women in the profession. Like Colonel Richard Dodge, who seven years previous had banned alcohol on his army base, the Reformers indirectly contributed to the profits from the enterprises they so vehemently opposed.

Cowboys continued to flock to Dodge with their cattle drives. They filled the saloons. They drank the whiskey, whether pure or rectified. They womanized. They gambled. The local lawmen looked the other way. In fact, many lawmen invested in saloons. Bat's brother James bought a partnership in the Lady Gay Saloon during his term as city marshal.

The primary lesson that Bat received from political life was the thrill of victory and the agony of defeat. If he had set his sights on continuing as Ford County Sheriff, he would have used the influence of the Gang to achieve the win. But Bat was young and eager to learn what lay beyond the horizon of Ford County. His leadership role in the Gang was enough authority and responsibility to feed his ego for now.

Bat uncovered the power of the newspaper. This revelation unlocked a world of opportunities that would become significant in his future. He recognized that readers seldom questioned the validity of the stories in this media. Bat watched news stories spread far and wide—whether they were true or false—especially with the introduction of the news wire services. He subscribed to newspapers and immersed himself in stories from around the world. He clipped and collected articles related to his personal interests, such as crime, Kansas, gambling, mining, and railways. These were the topics of the day that would open doors for this bright young man.

Bat learned enough lessons to plan for a long and fruitful life beyond the age of his dead brother.

13

Soon after the order reducing the issue of beef from 125,000 to 83,000 pounds per week, the Indians, pursuant to a request from the Agent met at his office for consultation... They said that their crops had failed, which rendered them entirely dependent upon the Government for subsistence. They had behaved well and deserved no punishment. They had barely enough before and did not see how they could possibly subsist on two-thirds of the amount. They must have beef; no other food will answer, and even if it would there is very little now in store. They thought the outlook very gloomy, but showed no signs of hostility. They asked Agent Miles and Major Randall to do all they could to restore the regular issue. Last Wednesday Major Randall received an order from the War Department to supply the deficiency. This is good news, not only to the Indians but to all who live in this country. No man, no matter what his color, will starve if he can help it by any means, however high-handed or disreputable. Had there been no remedy for the reduction, the Indians would probably have gone to killing cattle wherever they could find them.

—*Cheyenne Transporter*, Darlington, Indian Territory, April 10, 1882.

The diversion of cattle trails into Dodge was a very effective achievement by the Gang. Originally, the trails running north from Texas had been created by nomadic Native Americans. During the Civil War, both armies relied on Native guides to navigate the trails. Following the war, forts at strategic locations were converted to assist travelers. Trading posts were built to serve the trails. The United States government encouraged settlers to move west into Indian Territory, a policy which pushed the larger Native tribes to the west. The settlers soon fenced their property to prevent grazing by cattle drives. As a result, the Shawnee Trail was no longer suitable for grazing or moving cattle. Texas cattle drives were diverted along either the Chisholm Trail or the Western Trail.

The Chisholm Trail terminated at Ellsworth on the Kansas Pacific Railway. Later the AT&SF line intercepted the Chisholm Trail at Newton, creating a closer stockyard. Settlers were gradually moving their fences towards the Chisholm Trail, but the Dodge City Gang did not have patience to wait for external forces. Gang members organized rustlers to stampede cattle off the Chisholm Trail at the border with Kansas. Meanwhile, the Gang trained guides that could divert a cattle drive to follow the Dry Route (aka Cimarron Cutoff) into Dodge City. As a result, over 100,000 head of cattle traveled to Dodge City each year from either the Western Trail or the Cimarron Cutoff. The majority of these were shipped by the AT&SF railway to the east.

Each cattle drive brought its share of cowboys and commerce to Dodge. Between five hundred and six hundred cowboys would arrive in Dodge before the end of summer. Typically, each drover would receive one hundred dollars as soon as the cattle were corralled. Then he had enough money to purchase food, lodging, whiskey and female companionship for a month.

Charlie Bassett was supervising the Gang efforts on the cattle drives coming north on the Chisholm Trail. By creating disturbances in Indian Territory, this bunch was able to divert drives from the Chisholm Trail westward, following the Cimarron and Canadian Rivers to arrive in Dodge City. This activity maximized the number of cattle sold through Dodge.

Bassett borrowed his plan from the fate of an Irish-Canadian immigrant, Pat Hennessy. Legend rumored that a mule train of four men and three wagons was hauling coffee and sugar from Wichita to points south. Hennessy and his crew were warned of unrest among the Cheyenne Indians on the Chisholm Trail. On Independence Day, the warnings proved true when their wagon train was attacked ten miles north of the ford on the Cimarron River. All four men were found killed and mutilated. A trading post was created near the site where the men were buried. Although named after Hennessy, the official name of the post was misspelled as Hennessey.

Rumors that the attackers were white men dressed as Indians played into Bassett's plan. By 1880 the stories had been overblown and exaggerated in the retelling. And each attack on a cattle drive at that location added to the fear among drovers. Word spread that a cattle drive could follow the Cimarron River to avoid the potential

Cheyenne raiders at Hennessey. So Bassett recruited gangsters and local Cheyenne to attack cattle drives after they crossed the Cimarron. In the night, they would steal a few head and shoot a couple of horses. Then, the next morning, a group of riders in warrior costumes would assemble in plain view, across a ridge on the trail ahead.

Sometimes tempers got inflamed and the cattlemen suffered fatal wounds. But eventually, the drive would turn west towards Dodge City. Then a small party from the gang would follow until the herd was safely out of Indian Territory.

In July 1880, Bassett watched a cattle drive of two thousand longhorns as it approached the site where Pat Hennessy had met his maker. Bassett stood in a grove of trees with a spyglass, panning the herd.

"What d'ya think, Charlie?" asked one of the gangsters.

"Typical formation of two wagons in front. Looks like ten or twelve drovers with the cattle," said Bassett. "They must have been on the far side of the river last night and broke camp early. They'll be in the flats in a few minutes. Reckon we lose the advantage if they get up over the ridge by dark."

"Shor. Once they get up there, it's a bear to survey the whole outfit. Boss, we were here last year. Some of these trail bosses might have a long memory."

"Yep. Could darn well be a trap."

"Maybe trouble, boss."

"Tell ya what. I will mosey on down there for a chinwag," chuckled Bassett.

"By yer self?"

"Yeah, but as soon as I get within a hundred yards of the chuckwagon, you take the rest of the gang up on the ridge where they can get a good look at ya. I'll see if they care to dicker."

"What if they get ornery?"

"If you hear gunfire, come hell bent for leather. Otherwise, I will ride back here with their answer."

"The men are ready. I'm lookin' for a little taste of whatever is in that chuckwagon."

As the last of the cattle reached the clearing, Bassett rode by himself towards the chuckwagon. By the time he reached it, two of the point riders had trotted up the line. Bassett looked over his shoulder to see that his gangsters had followed instructions. The line of twenty riders on the ridge looked imposing.

"Howdy, fellers," said Bassett. "I'm looking for the trail boss."

"That'd be me, mister," answered a middle-aged cowboy facing the intruder.

"My name is Charlie Bassett from Dodge City. I am here to ask your cooperation."

"What d'ya mean by cooperation?"

"My friends and I are hoping you will take the Cimarron-Cutoff from here on. Just for everyone's safety."

"You know that adds a week to our drive. And that means another seven dollars wages for each man."

"Well, I never took that into consideration. How careless. Let me ask you this, how much is owed to these men if they were done today?"

The trail-boss frowned. "Don't figger to understand yer question, Mister Bassett."

"Well, I am just spitballin' now, but the way I see it is you got fifteen men who have been riding for seventy-five days. For easy figures, that's twelve hundred dollars if you turn out those doggies right here." Bassett waited for some inkling that the drover understood him before carrying on. "Or on the other hand, you can turn west right now and pay those men the hundred and seven dollars they each deserve when they get to Dodge."

"Are you suggesting we abandon the herd right here for twelve hundred dollars?"

"Yes, I am. And just so there are no hard feelings, each fella can keep the horse he's riding."

"I can't do that, mister. I'd be fired for turning over the herd to rustlers. I think we'll take our chances on the trail ahead."

"Well, there ain't no rustlers involved. The cattle would be sold in Dodge same as if you finished yer job. But like I said, I was just spitballin'. Ya know, hypothetical like."

"Kindly tell your men on the ridge that we are going to ride on north, following this trail all the way to Newton, Kansas."

"Oh, I will. In fact, they were hoping you would say that."

"Why's that?"

"'Cause they are going to ride up to Hennessey tonight. And they are going to tell everyone there that the drovers coming along behind them were offered full pay and a horse just to transfer the responsibility to my friends and me. And then when your crew gets there, you can explain to them that in two days they will have to fight their way out of Indian Territory before they get paid a single penny."

By the next morning, each of the drovers had received seventy-five dollars from the Gang. Every drover headed south on a horse they had chosen from the remuda. The chuckwagon and former trail boss turned west under the direction of Charlie Bassett. Charlie's gang drove the herd. They were not experienced cowboys, but there were twenty of them. And when the Gang sold the cattle in Dodge, the payment was made to Charlie Bassett, who paid out the gangsters as well as any brand inspectors who looked the other way as cattle were shipped.

That made for a wild night in Dodge City. And more wild nights followed. Bassett's crew brought in two or three herds each summer. By the time the herd owners were informed of the theft, thousands of dollars had been safely deposited in the Dodge City Peace Bank.

14

**SHILOGH'S COUGH AND CONSUMPTION CURE is
sold by us on a guarantee. It cures Consumption. For sale at
McMurray's Drug Store.**

—*The Delta Independent,* **Delta, Colorado, December
7, 1886**

The street was quiet in the morning. A scrawny man in
a long black Victorian coat limped up the steps of the
Columbian Hotel. At the top stair, he bent over in a coughing fit. After almost two minutes of coughing, the man
spat blood and phlegm into a spittoon by the entrance. He
stopped inside the saloon doors while his eyes adjusted to
the dark interior.

A man polishing glasses behind the bar looked up in
anticipation of a new customer. Three figures leaned on
the long wooden bar, oblivious to their reflections adorn-
ing the mirrored wall. A hanging candelabra reflected
light off the ceiling of embossed metal tiles, which once
were white but now reflected a tobacco-smoke amber.
Candles illuminated each of four tables at the far end of
the tavern.

The scrawny man moved slowly into the dimly lit cavern of tables and chairs, looking for some familiar faces. He passed within earshot of the men at the bar, whom he judged, by their conversation, to be coal miners enjoying some time in a room not as dark as the shafts where they toiled. The miners hunched over their drinks, not far from bending over a seam of ore.

Two mustached patrons sat at the table furthest from the entrance. Both men sat at angles that provided a view of the long saloon. The scrawny man looked at the bartender as he limped past and mumbled his drink preference. The bartender nodded and mumbled something to the miners at the bar. Their discussion halted while they glanced over their shoulders at the man in his affliction.

The men sitting at the table watched him approach. As he walked towards the pair, they offered no greeting. They both kept their hands hidden below the table and offered no assistance.

The gaunt figure stopped to lean on a chair at their table before speaking, "I'd be much obliged if one of you gents could offer me your chair. I don't want my back to the door."

"We know you want the calico seat. In case any ladies descend the stairs," laughed the man with a walking stick propped on the side of his chair.

"You overestimate my stamina, Bat," said the coughing man.

"What's the matter, Doc?" asked the other, as he withdrew a pistol from under the table and placed it in plain sight. "Is the State of Colorado after you?"

"That's only one of many," sputtered Doc Holliday. "Suddenly, I have a new appreciation for Colorado Governor Pitkin." He coughed before asking, "Which one of you am I obliged to?"

"Call it Divine Intervention," answered Bat Masterson.

"Trinidad Marshal Masterson is too modest," said Wyatt Earp. "He laid the bunco charges here in Colorado. I always suspected you were a better fraudster than a gunslinger."

"State of Arizona will be consternated," Doc Holliday said. "I would like to see the judge's face when you inform them that I can't be extradited to face any trumped-up murder charges in Tombstone." Again, Doc coughed at length.

"Gentlemen," said Bat when the coughing subsided. "I must give credit to some advice I received from an Italian family who have settled here in Trinidad. As fate would have it, those families think along many of the same lines as our Dodge City Gang. It was during a conversation with one of these Italians that the idea of bunco charges in Colorado came up. And as long as you stay in Colorado, you cannot be extradited until those charges are resolved."

"How did you get the Governor to agree, especially on short notice?" asked Earp.

"I called on a friend. You may have read some of his reporting in the *Denver Tribune*. A good journalist knows how to get the Governor's attention in the eleventh hour."

"I guess it's who you know," mumbled Doc.

"That's true if they are newspaper people," agreed Bat. "The real power in the West is shifting from men with firearms to men with ink and paper." Then Bat Masterson lifted his cane and tapped the silver star on his vest. "Gentlemen, I remain your humble friend and confidante, regardless of the powers behest upon me by the good people of Trinidad, Colorado. It behooves me to celebrate in the knowledge that I was able to ensure that Doc Holliday, this agent of devilment and disaster, will face justice at the hand of the residents of Colorado and their appointed officials of which I am but one, lowly servant."

"I think Bat is trying to say that he was glad to help," chuckled Wyatt Earp.

Doc Holliday coughed several times before reaching into his coat pocket and pulling out some silver dollars. "I guess you both earned a whiskey. See if you can get the bartender's attention. I have to sit down," groaned Holliday, as he waved his hand for Earp to move to another chair. Doc slowly lowered his frail body onto that chair while Masterson and Earp watched with trepidation.

"I hate to see you sit in that chair, Doc," said Earp.

"Well, I am hoping to get some of my strength back now that I am out of the calaboose," coughed Holliday.

"You misunderstand, my friend," replied Earp. "That's the chair Frank Loving died in. Hand to God." The men broke into laughter infused with Holliday's coughing fits.

Baited by the silver coins on the table, the bartender suddenly appeared with three glasses of whiskey.

Bat Masterson entertained himself in Colorado for several years as part-time lawman, faro dealer, gambler, and ladies' man. He continued to dress to the nines and was easily recognizable by his hat and cane. The Gang continued to rely on Bat's remote leadership via telegrams or word of mouth. But in the spring of 1883, the Gang recalled him to Dodge City.

The Gang's influence in Dodge City had diminished since the last civic election in 1881, when so-called Reformer candidates became mayor and marshal. In practice, those officials were only interested in lining their own pockets as majority owners of several saloons. By the time of civic elections in April 1883, the graft and violence in Dodge City had aggravated the rail line and its workers. AT&SF and the *Dodge City Times* used both legal and illegal tactics to throw the election to the anti-Gang movement.

Ordinances were passed on April 26, 1883, that levied fines up to a hundred dollars on prostitutes, brothel keepers, vagrants, or any citizens involved in activity deemed unlawful. Gang member Luke Short was half-owner of the Long Branch Saloon and had been paying the city officials for protection. However, only two days after the new ordinances, lawmen arrested three of the Long Branch dance hall girls. No arrests were made at any other saloons, so Luke Short sought to rectify the situation by attacking the jailhouse that night. The jailbreak was thwarted by city officials. Despite an exchange of gunfire, no party was injured. The next day, Luke Short was arrested on assault charges. He was able to pay a bond of two thousand dollars to regain his freedom.

Two days later, the city officials exercised the vagrancy law and again arrested Luke Short, as well as five gamblers, for being undesirables. The six were denied legal counsel and escorted to the train station by armed guards. After receiving a wire from Bat, Short took a train to the state capital, Topeka. There, he planned to take his plight to Governor Glick, a known opponent of the reform movement.

The *Kansas City Evening Star* reported that in Dodge City a vigilante committee, formed by "the proprietor of one of the hardest dance halls that ever existed in the west," had taken the law into their own hands. The vigilantes were running other residents and business owners out of town without due process. Any reporters or legal representatives arriving by train were threatened at gunpoint to stay on the train. The article ended with a blunt statement: "That there will be trouble of a very serious character there, is anticipated."

Governor Glick was quick to intervene. His first telegram to the de facto Dodge City sheriff asked for a description of the situation and, upon receiving the answer, a second telegram berated the sheriff and mayor for bringing disgrace upon Dodge City and the State of Kansas. However, there was no threat of legal action or indictment of either side. Luke Short was still banned from his home and place of business in Dodge City.

After the situation had dragged on for two weeks, Bat Masterson assembled his lieutenants: Luke Short, Wyatt Earp, Doc Holliday, Shotgun Collins, Rowdy Joe Lowe, and Charlie Bassett. The group gathered in a Methodist Church in Kansas City on Monday, May 14, 1883.

"Gentlemen. This is an extraordinary occasion. You represent the spirit of Dodge City, with your experience, your skills, and your passion. We have reaped the profits of our fellowship over the last five years, but today we are faced with an enemy that believes those profits belong to them."

"We are the founders!" shouted one man, followed by exclamations from others.

"Well said."

"Damn them all to hell!"

"Hang the sons of bitches!"

"You are all entitled to your emotions," responded Bat. "But air your grievances here today. We consider the Gang's destiny will be to control alcohol and entertainment in Dodge."

"How do you reckon we go about that?" inquired Earp.

"We kill some bastards!" shouted a frustrated Luke Short.

"Patience, gents. Patience," responded Bat. "Before we resort to violence, remember that while we are aging, the world around us is changing. It is impossible to stop either of those. And when you can't stop it, you must learn to work within. The Gang must adapt."

"How must we adapt?" asked Earp.

"In order to mold our future, we must mold public opinion. I have been in contact with journalists across the country. They are telling our story. Their readers are calling upon us to respond. They are soliciting funding to support our righteous cause. And, as usual, the politicians in Washington and Topeka are following their perception of public opinion. The current vigilantes in Dodge will piss their trousers when they read about the return of the Dodge City Gang."

The next day the *Kansas City Evening Star* published the names and credentials of all who sought to descend on Dodge City. The newspaper said it had "no hesitancy in predicting that there is going to be trouble of a bloody nature if resistance is offered to Short's return." The *Star* had predicted what later became known as the Dodge City War.

Members of the Gang assembled in Caldwell and Cimarron in the last days of May, a month after Luke Short had been expelled from town. The Dodge officials requested the governor send in troops in response to the influx of gunfighters that was expected. Instead, the governor offered a lone negotiator.

Sentiment among the vigilantes and Reformers was wavering even before the Gang members arrived in Dodge. Wyatt Earp arrived with four other gang members on May 31. He successfully negotiated the return of Luke Short to run the Long Branch Saloon unmolested. Bat and other heavily armed men accompanied Luke Short into Dodge on June 4, 1883. Each day following, additional Gang members arrived by train and stationed themselves in the Long Branch. By the time the governor's negotiator arrived, there were more than forty men in league with Luke Short.

Negotiations resulted in concessions by both sides. Gambling would be permitted in areas screened off from the bar and dance hall. Short committed to removing crooked gamblers from the saloon. Women working in the dance halls were to be more discreet. The Dodge City War ended without a shot being fired. Bat credited the newspaper reports for establishing their side of the conflict in a manner that left the Reformers with little to no support.

For nearly five years, the Dodge City Gang had followed the plan as Bat Masterson had laid it out. Through the efforts of buffalo hunters and many gang members, they had successfully diverted cattle drives towards Dodge City by creating deterrents on the alternate trails and by smoothing the paths to Dodge. Monies were gained from heists, bootlegging, and illegal gambling. Despite their efforts, the Gang was unable to return Dodge City to its former glory. As Bat predicted, the world was changing.

The members of the Gang took on wives and families. Only a few continued to seek fame, fortune, and adventure. Before the Gang disbanded, Bat arranged for a local photographer to stage a group picture of his lieutenants. The photographer set up in an empty room at the Long Branch Saloon and captured the legendary photo of the notorious Dodge City Peace Commission.

The die had been cast. Bat Masterson realized the Gang no longer required his leadership. All the same, Bat maintained his thirst for adventure.

DODGE CITY PEACE COMMISSION

Back Row - W.H. Harris, Luke Short, Bat Masterson, W.F. Petillon
Front Row - Charlie Bassett, Wyatt Earp, Frank McLain, Neal Brown
Photo courtesy of Kansas Historical Society

THE LEGAL TENDER

15

Dallas, Texas, In the year of our Lord, 1882

Judge in yourselves: is it comely that a woman pray unto God uncovered? Doth not even nature itself teach you, that, if a man have long hair, it is a shame unto him? But if a woman have long hair, it is a glory to her: for [her] hair is given her for a covering.

—1 Corinthians 11:13-15 (King James Version)

On this night, Una looked forward to the following day of worship services. Her mother encouraged her to gussy-up before church. She brushed the long auburn strands of hair cascading over her shoulders and ending just below her navel. Her hair had been her source of pride since the age of five. The mirror mounted above her four-drawer dresser, reflected the girl's youth and beauty. She whispered the words she had heard her mother say to her, "You are Una. You are strong. You are beautiful."

Now that she was fourteen years old, Una Clark was struggling to understand her role as a female in the assembly. Changes to her body were troublesome on occasion, but her newfound shapeliness garnered the attention of her brethren. When men paid attention to her, Una was bedeviled by feelings ranging from guilt to yearning. She responded to their endorsements with a demure smile and downward glance. And as they parted, Una would speculate whether those men had more to offer beyond physical appearance.

As Una put down her brush, she thought she detected a movement in the mirror. She turned to see sawdust falling from a knothole in the fir-plank walls. She quickly grabbed her brass candle holder and crouched to see if there was a mouse or snake in the wall. The knothole was waist-high and about the size of her index finger. Una knelt in front and held the candle close to the hole. There was no sign of any animal pest, only blackness on the other side. However, sawdust in the base of the hole and on the floor below suggested that this hole had been drilled or filed. She also knew that her brothers' bedroom was on the other side of that wall. Had they bored this hole to torment her with some vermin? Did they plan to listen or speak to her through this hole? Or were they planning to watch her undress in the morning or at night? Perhaps the movement she had seen was an eye blinking on the other side of the wall.

Una was baffled. Her brothers were ten and eleven years old. At that age, did they really want to see their sister naked? They had probably caught glances of her bathing in a washtub on many occasions. Why go to this effort? Una blew out the candle and quickly finished her nighttime routine before she crawled under the covers. But sleep did not come immediately—not until Una had decided how she would respond to the peephole.

The Assembly of Dallas Paramount Brethren met every Sunday at a place of worship constructed in an abandoned stable. The building had been donated by a now-deceased elder who had raised quarter-horses. The brothers of the assembly commonly referred to the Gospel Hall as the "stable," taking advantage of the allusion to the birth of Christ. Most of the partitions between stalls had been removed, except for a cloakroom and storage stall. Benches lined both sides of the ground floor, and chairs were available in the loft.

There were no officially ordained preachers in this assembly, but devoted believers, exclusively male elders, took turns preparing and delivering the word of God. The moral code was strict in the Dallas Paramount Brethren Assembly. Members of the assembly were to have little or no contact with non-brethren. Brethren could not attend schools, weddings, hotels, restaurants, or halls where non-brethren may be present. Any residence or place of business owned by a brother must not be in physical contact with any building occupied by non-brethren. Only men were allowed to conduct business with outsiders. Since most of the members were farmers, these restrictions were easy to practice.

The Dallas Paramount Brethren were expected to marry early and to marry another believer in the Brethren gospel. Travel to visit Brethren relatives required permission from the local assembly. This permission would be granted in writing in order to introduce a visitor to another Brethren assembly.

The assembly permitted alcoholic beverages to be consumed in moderation within a private residence.

Smoking and gambling were strictly forbidden. Pets were not allowed in the home, although animal husbandry was permitted as part of farming or ranching. Reading materials were limited to the Bible and the teachings of Brethren elders. Magazines and newspapers were banned.

There were punishments to enforce the church's conventions, and people who broke these rules were regularly shut up (shunned). At the discretion of church elders, *shut up* members were permitted to rejoin the assembly only after they openly admitted their sin or transgression.

Women and girls of the assembly were expected to dress in formal garments yet maintain a conservative appearance. An ankle-length cotton twill skirt and Wichita blouse in white or pink were common attire. Only the brazen women would flaunt ruffled blouses or bustles under printed skirts. Feminine footwear included Victorian ankle boots or Ladies' Spats in white or black. All the females were expected to leave their hair uncut and partially covered by a headscarf or muslin bonnet. Women were not permitted to wear lipstick or makeup.

Although the dress code for men was not as strict during the peak farming seasons, they tended to dress formally on the day of rest until changing for evening chores. Men were expected to be clean-shaven, with conservative haircuts. Most wore tweed or canvas coats over a canvas double-breasted vest and white club collar shirt. Black canvas trousers, black suspenders, and pocket watch completed the costume. Ties were not permitted at worship services but were tolerated in places of business. Young men would be dressed similarly, with allowance for some blue or brown tones. Every male wore black leather boots. Black Stetson hats were the most common outdoor headgear for brothers of the assembly.

On Sunday, the women and children of the Clark family, including Una, her mother, and two brothers, traveled in a wagon pulled by two horses, through the streets of Dallas on their way north to the Gospel Hall. Their route took them past several hotels and saloons. As believers, they had never darkened the doorway of any such establishments. Those enterprises catered to the cowboys who were passing through or waiting for their next cattle drive.

The Clarks' wagon passed several cowboys who, without current employment, were loitering along the street this Sunday morning. Two such loafers were leaning on a hitching rail, passing a whiskey bottle between them. Both cowboys noticed Una and her mother sitting on the bench at the front of the wagon.

"Well, I'm havin' a dream, gulp," a short stalky cowboy belched. "Take a gander at them fine specimens comin' our way."

"Reckon them's the real McCoy. Genuine and mighty fine. Hey, Stubby, let's jaw with them," slurred the other cowboy. Grinning through buck teeth—stained and rotting—he stumbled onto the street in front of the horse and wagon.

"Whoa, Leviticus. Whoa, Malachi," shouted Mother Clark as she pulled back on the reins. She glared at Bucktooth, but despite her anger, she did not speak.

"Well, that's right friendly, ma'am, haltin' your wagon to parlay with a couple of cowpokes."

The Clark boys stood up in the box and looked over the ladies' shoulders. "Who's that, Ma?" asked one of the boys.

"That's not someone we can talk to, boys," Mother Clark whispered. The boys understood from the whisper that the rules of their religion were involved, and they sat back down quietly.

Stubby staggered toward Una's side of the wagon and mumbled, "Well, tie me up to this heifer for a night."

Una could smell his rancid breath, even though the man's face was several feet away. She held her tongue because she was more afraid of her mother's religious teachings than she was of these drunkards. When Stubby grabbed her arm, Una spit on him and screamed, "Giddy-up, Ma!"

Mother Clark loosed the reins, but the horses were being held by Bucktooth. Then Stubby grabbed the bottom of Una's dress and tried to pull her down from the wagon. The youngsters took the lead from their older sister and spat at the attacker. Una kicked the side of his head with her Victorian boot. He grabbed her ankle and pulled hard enough that she fell to the street.

When Stubby put his knee on her abdomen, Una swung her fists and started screaming.

"Don't scream. I just want to get a good look at you," Stubby growled, as he pushed her head from side to side. Mother Clark leaned across the wagon bench and struck the attacker vigorously with her horse whip—but to no avail. Una continued to kick with bare legs, now exposed from under her Sunday dress.

The smell of the man's sweaty hand on Una's face, his whiskey-breath, and his unbathed body mingled with the stench of horse manure and urine on the street. She felt helpless as Stubby pinned her right arm across her neck. Bile rose to her mouth, fettering her efforts to scream. Una closed her eyes and prayed silently that her brothers would not interfere. She prayed that god would protect her family from this violence. She prayed for the swift return of her father from his travels.

"Hold on there, feller," boomed a voice from behind the wagon.

Una opened her eyes to see a pair of gray cowboy boots walking towards her. She squirmed to get free, but the weight on her midsection made her efforts futile. And now there was a single gray boot in front of her face, like she was being straddled by yet another man. She prayed it was not the bucktooth cowboy. She prayed to her Savior that the gray boot was a protector, to deliver her salvation. Una mumbled the words from Psalm 25, "Unto thee, O Lord, do I lift up my soul. O my God, I trust in thee: let me not be ashamed, let not mine enemies triumph over me. Yea, let none that wait on thee be ashamed..."

Someone kicked dust in Una's face. She heard feet running. Men were grunting and shouting words she did not understand. After a short fracas, Stubby's body was off her. When she turned to see where the next attack was coming from, a tall man wearing gray boots was silhouetted against the bright morning sun. He had a muscular build and was gripping both Bucktooth and Stubby by the collars of their shirts. Una sat up and pulled her knees up to her chest while rearranging the proper whereabouts of her dress.

"These two won't bother you ladies anymore," stated the tall man who had appeared from nowhere. The man who had answered Una's prayer. Her protector.

Una watched their rescuer push the cowboys back to the hitching rail before releasing his grip. Bucktooth relaxed against the rail and tipped his hat towards Una and her mother. But Stubby's adrenaline was still flowing. He pulled a knife from his belt and stepped towards the street.

Una did not see the actual point of impact. She only saw a gray boot return to the ground. At the same time she heard the metal blade striking the road. Stubby had blood leaking from his nose and mouth. Bucktooth watched wide-eyed as his associate rebounded off the rail and fell, face forward, into the street. Stubby lay motionless except for occasionally coughing up blood.

"Had enough?" asked the tall man, looking at each of the cowboys. Bucktooth nodded as he tended to his fallen partner.

The man with the gray boots walked slowly towards Una and extended his hand to help her up. As she stood up, her eyes were welling with tears. The man held her close for an instant and then whispered, "Name's Cotton. What's yers?"

Una climbed up onto the bench of the wagon and dusted off her dress as much as possible. Then she looked Cotton in the eye and said, "Una Clark. I am beholding to you, Mr. Cotton."

Mother Clark gasped and flicked the reins to get the horses moving. Una turned her head to gaze at Cotton as they pulled away. He politely raised his hat and exposed his curly blond hair. In the sunlight it looked almost white. Una wondered if that was why they called him Cotton. Her brothers waved to Cotton, the man who had saved their sister. A protector.

Members of the Dallas Paramount Brethren Assembly noticed the Clark family sitting in the loft, while more than enough seats were available in their usual sitting place on the main floor of the Gospel Hall. Mrs. Clark looked angry, and Una looked disheveled. Their appearance and behavior were cause for speculation, and Una expected that the elders would seek some explanation after the service.

The typical service was two hours, followed by lunch with the other members. Una spent most of the service checking her appearance and rubbing dirt off the pleats of her clothing. She stayed in the loft after the service, waiting for others to leave the hall. Her mother and brothers left her alone in the loft while they visited over the lunch served in the yard. Una suspected that she was going to be shut up by the assembly, and possibly by her own family. They would contend that *she had spoken to a non-brethren. She had been touched* and had touched a man who was non-brethren. She was a woman who had been seen and heard. She waited.

The assembly finished lunch after another hour. The elders met with Mrs. Clark for ten minutes, before sending her home with her sons. Then most of the elders left on foot or horseback. Two elder men waited in the Gospel

Hall. They each said a prayer and then called for Una to come to them.

One of the elders motioned for her to sit. Una had seen him in assembly regularly. She did not know the other man. He took a stool and sat directly in front of her—so close that their knees were touching. Una looked down, but the elder reached out and lifted her chin. As he held her face, he looked into her eyes. She said nothing and did not move away. Una bit her lip to hold back tears. Then the elder grabbed both her shoulders and pulled her body towards his. He wrapped his arms around her torso and held her tight. Una waited, but his grip only grew tighter. Now she felt that she could not breathe. She felt like her body was being violated for a second time that day. She pushed the elder away, at which point both men sighed.

The elders took turns speaking to her. The first one said, "Una Clark, you are to be shut up for the rest of this year, if you do not repent."

Following a pause of only a few seconds, the second elder said, "Una Clark, you did not repent, so you are to be shut up until the end of 1882."

"Una Clark, you will be shut up indefinitely if you do not repent or if you sin in the future."

"Una Clark, you must leave this hall immediately."

Both men rose and waited for Una to leave.

Una wiped her eyes and looked back and forth between the elders before speaking. "What shall I repent for? What do you think happened today?"

There was no reply from the elders.

"My father is coming home. He will find out what happened here today, and *he* will decide whether I am shut up. You know who my father is. He is Pinkerton Agent H.A. Clark. And he is an elder in this assembly. You will see who needs to repent when H.A. Clark comes to this assembly."

The elders looked at each other and then, without speaking, each grabbed one of Una's arms and dragged her to the door. Outside, they let Una fall onto the gravel walkway before they locked the door of the Gospel Hall. Una lay still until the elders walked away. Eventually, she stood and brushed the dirt from her clothes for the second time that day.

Una removed her bonnet to shake the dust from her hair. She sobbed as she rubbed a knot in her neck. Her head ached. The emotional distress of the day was taking a toll on her physical well-being. She stopped in the shade of a live oak tree, mumbling to herself.

"Stop crying. You did nothing wrong. You are Una. You are strong. You are beautiful."

"You don't need to convince me, ma'am," said a man's voice from within the grove of trees. Before Una could recover from the surprise, a man stepped out of the shadows, the same man who had saved her from the drunk cowboys.

"I don't know what you mean," Una replied, wiping dried tears from her cheeks.

"I reckon you are strong. Y'all were brave when you spat on that drunkard in the street. That impressed me!"

"I am much obliged to you, Mr. Cotton. Now I need to get to my home."

Cotton walked up to Una, holding a canteen. "Water, ma'am?"

Una held the container in both hands and drank several mouthfuls, instantly realizing she was extremely thirsty. As she returned the canteen, she noticed the cowhand's deep blue eyes shining out of a tanned face. When he smiled, his teeth gleamed from beneath a thin mustache. Cotton had demonstrated his physical strength during the earlier rescue, but now it was Una who was feeling empowered. The cowboy's presence solicited Una's trust and confidence.

"Thank you. I have to ask what you are doing here, mister?" She had her suspicions.

Cotton noticed the narrowing of her eyelids. "I declare, ma'am, that I was struck by your loveliness. And as I said, standin' up to those cowboys took some gumption. So I made an effort to meet up with you after you were done worshippin'. Meant no offense."

"I guess none taken. You might be the only man that has *not* offended me today."

"May I apologize for the rest of mankind by offering a ride home?"

"I would be obliged. Do you have a wagon?"

"Just my horse, ma'am. But we can ride double if you like."

"That would be fine. And my name is Una."

During the half-hour trip, Una learned that Cotton was a lead hand for a rancher in south Texas. He was planning to leave on a three-month cattle drive to Kansas along the Chisholm Trail.

When they rode within sight of the Clark home, Una interjected, "Stop here. I will walk from here."

"Could I call on you next spring when I get back from Kansas?" asked Cotton.

"I would like that. And I will cook a meal for you," declared Una.

Cotton helped her dismount. When he kissed her hand she moaned softly and quickly turned away.

Una walked into the farmyard at the regular time for evening chores. She would have to change her clothes quickly. Her mood had improved dramatically as she looked forward to the love and security of home.

Una noticed her brothers playing with the chickens. She wondered if some zealots of the assembly might interpret that action as playing with a pet. After her punishment and banishment today, she wondered if her brethren had even a lick of common sense. The elders certainly lacked compassion. She imagined elders talking in the corners. "Those boys should be shut up for having pets. Who knows what evil lurks behind that chicken coop?"

Una had to grin at her own daydream, and she smiled as the boys ran towards her. "Una, you're back. Una, come see the chickens! I gave one a bonnet!"

"Hey, Una. Where have you been? Ma wouldn't tell us."

"It's OK, boys," she assured them, unsure of what version of events their mother had told them. "I had to thank that nice man who stood up for us this morning. Go play with the chickens while I go change into my work clothes."

Una went to the house and entered the main room, which functioned as kitchen, dining, and living space. She watched as her mother looked up from peeling potatoes. Una thought she saw a flash of empathy in her mother's gaze before it returned to a half-peeled potato and a knife that remained motionless.

"Ma. Did the elders say anything to you? Tell me," Una pleaded.

Her mother remained silent.

"Did they say that I was to be *shut up*?"

Her mother looked at her and silently mouthed, "I am sorry."

"But why? I was attacked. And I fought to remain chaste. Did I ask for that man on top of me? Then the assembly would have good reason to shun me. And that Mr. Cotton saved me. And he saved you and the boys from an attack in broad daylight. So there was no shame in thanking him." Una paused to catch her breath while her mother bent over the sink and closed her eyes. "Ma, I prayed that someone would save us. God answered my prayer with Mr. Cotton. He was my protector!"

Mother Clark put down the knife and potato and, without looking at Una, walked out of the house.

Una went to her bedroom and looked in the mirror. She saw mud and dirt and torn fabric. She saw straw in her hair and realized that she smelled like a horse. Una wondered why Cotton had been so kind to her.

After removing the grime from her body, Una felt better. She felt righteous. No man could take that from her. Nor give that to her.

For the next few days, life in the Clark household was uncomfortable for everyone. Mother Clark would speak to the boys but not to Una. The boys were warned not to talk to her. They were told not to touch her, nor should they enter her room. But the boys knew how to communicate non-verbally. If Una was watching, they would pantomime their thoughts. If they wanted her to pass the potatoes, they would pretend to lift an invisible bowl and pass it to each other. If they wanted her to help hitch up the wagon, one of them would get on all fours and start to whinny like a horse while the other pretended to attach the harness.

In some situations, the boys would simply talk to each other, referring to Una in the third person. "Brother, do you think our sister will water the horses tonight?"

"Yes, brother, I do. Do you think our sister will feed the pigs tomorrow?"

"Of course, brother. I think I saw her agree to that."

Then Una would reply, "You can pretend I am not here, but you are mistaken if you think I'm doing your chores just because of some daft religious customs." The boys would giggle until they noticed their mother's glare. Then they would leave to do their chores.

When the women were alone, Una would ask, "When is Father coming home? I want him to sort out this poppycock. Father won't leave me in this fix."

16

Mrs. Woodhull having said something as to Beecher's preaching to a dozen of his mistresses, the witness said that he could not believe it; either Tilton or Mrs. Woodhull spoke of the number of Beecher's mistresses as being forty; the name of Mrs. Proctor was mentioned in this connection; Mrs. Woodhull in a tone which might have been heard by Tilton, spoke of Mrs. Tilton as [a] woman with whom Beecher had long been enamored; she said there was some doubt as to whether Beecher or Tilton was the father of one of Mrs. Tilton's children.

— *The Dallas Daily Herald*, **Dallas, Texas, March 12, 1875**

Agent H.A. Clark, detective for Pinkerton Detective Agency, arrived by train in Dallas after a drawn-out trip from New Orleans, where he had captured a notorious thief attempting to flee on an ocean-going vessel. Clark had been away from his family for several weeks and decided to treat them to some fresh seafood. He had obtained fresh lobsters, which were wrapped and packed in an ice-filled crate.

At the Dallas train station, Agent Clark hired a horse-drawn carriage to take his luggage and person to the Clark farm. He was delivered to the house at sunset on a hot August evening.

"Pa is here, Ma!" yelled one of the boys from the yard.

Una came out of her room and exchanged glances with her mother. Mother Clark held up the palm of her hand to signal for Una to stay where she was. Una nodded. She understood that her mother would be first to explain the situation to her father, assuming the boys did not lay bare the drama of the last few days.

"Hey, Pa. What's in the box?" asked one of the boys.

"Did you hear Una got in a fight?" asked the other. "Right in the street, Pa!"

Agent Clark held out his arms to hug the boys simultaneously. Then he opened his arms wide above his shoulders and looked to his women for answers.

"Go get cleaned up before bed," said Mother Clark, as she whisked the boys towards the door of the house. Agent Clark stood, listening quietly as she explained the events from last Sunday which had led to shutting up Una.

"I will have a talk with her," stated Agent Clark.

"No, that is a sin!" warned one of the boys still within earshot.

"The Elders said that she is shut up," confirmed Mother Clark.

"I understand. And I ask you not to report my sin. My inquiry will be as a Pinkerton detective, not as the father of a shunned girl. I need to hear from Una."

Mother Clark nodded. She carried a suitcase for her husband, while he carried the small crate to the kitchen table.

Agent Clark announced, "Leave this crate for Una to unpack in the morning." Then he went to Una's room, where he found her sitting on her bed, her hands folded in her lap and head bowed in prayer. He waited until she looked up at him.

"Una, I expect you to tell me what happened on Sunday to determine why you were shut up by the elders."

"Thank you, Father," whispered Una. Then she related the events of Sunday morning, including the drunkards, the insults hurled, and the assault by the man called Stubby.

"How did you escape his grip?" asked Agent Clark.

"I was hitting him to no avail, so I prayed that the boys would not be harmed by what was happening, and suddenly a man named Mr. Cotton came and lifted him off."

"This man called himself Mr. Cotton? Had you met him before?"

"No, sir. That was the first time I saw him."

"Your mother thought there was an embrace. Like you were familiar with this Mr. Cotton."

"I swear Pa, I never saw him before that moment. He did what he did, and I thanked him for rescuing me."

"What did the elders say?"

"They wanted me to repent. But I don't see what I had to repent. I was a victim, not a sinner!"

"But you are a young woman, and your virtue came into doubt when one man lay on top of you and another man embraced you. The assembly will want you to know your shame and show penitence before you are welcomed back to services."

"So I am to blame for everything a man does to me, whether invited or forced. So our brethren want me to apologize for the actions of those men. And how about you and Ma? What do you want?"

"We want you to abide by the beliefs and wisdom of the elders. That's the only way we can absolve your sins and prevent them from corrupting the people around you. You need to beg forgiveness from the elders and the assembly."

"How, Pa? How can I do that when I am shut up?"

"The elders will show you the way when the time is right. I am sorry, Una, but that is the path you must take," proclaimed Agent Clark, as he turned and left the bedroom.

The next morning, Agent Clark showed the crate of seafood to his family. Then he turned his back to Una and said, "Thank the Lord for this bounty from the sea that Una is going to prepare for us today. Finish your breakfast, and we will leave her to prepare the lobsters while we tend our crops and animals."

Una waited until the others had left the house before unpacking the seafood from the crate of melting ice. Ice was rare in Dallas and Una marveled at the feel of the remaining chunks. The ice cooled her fingers. She rubbed a bite-sized piece across her cheek and down her neck. Melt-water ran through her fingers and wet her skin. Then she popped the remaining piece into her mouth and swished it around with her tongue until there was nothing left except a swallow of water.

The lobsters had been wrapped in newspaper. Una was aware of newspapers but had never been allowed to read one. She noticed that some of the wet pages were still legible. The pages from the *New Orleans Times-Democrat* covered stories over the last decade. She laid the pages out to dry while she finished unpacking the lobsters which she then placed in a pot of water on the wood stove. She hoped she remembered correctly how her mother had cooked shellfish on previous occasions. In any case, Una believed extra boiling would not harm them, which would give her time for reading. Confident that she was alone for the next few hours, Una spread out several newspaper pages, knowing full well that reading these was considered sinful. Nonetheless, she was captivated by the variety of information available in these pages. Compared to her Bible readings, this soggy newspaper was surprising and fascinating.

The newspaper had stories about American presidents and politicians, about crimes and court cases, about developments in towns and cities, about animal husbandry and miracle cures, about weather events and natural disasters, about abolition and prohibition. And there were advertisements of items for sale and of professional people offering to perform chores and miracles. There were drawings and photographs of people and places. Some of the stories contained Latin, French, Spanish, and German words.

Una devoured the words, most of which were alien to her adolescent mind and cloistered upbringing. She was shocked to read about elders in the Plymouth church

accusing each other of sins of the flesh. She was morti-
fied by the number of crimes committed and miscarriages
of justice.

Moreover, the pages of advertising fascinated her. Most
of the advertising was selling medicines and cure-all pills.
Then a column titled **FEMALE HELP WANTED** caught
her eye. One of those advertisements read:

> *Wanted: Young women 14 to 20 years of
> age, of good moral character, attractive
> and intelligent, to waitress in Harvey
> Eating Houses on the Atchison, Topeka
> and Santa Fe Railway in the West.
> Wages, $17.50 per month with room
> and board. Liberal tips customary.
> Experience not necessary. Write in care
> of The Fable, Dodge City, Kansas.*

Una read the advertisement several times. It seemed
incredible to her that a girl of fourteen could earn such
wages, simply by serving meals. She had not heard of
Harvey Eating Houses, but Una was vaguely aware of
Dodge City as a railroad terminal for the cattle drives
leaving from Texas. That she had heard of this town meant
that people from her community had been talking about
Dodge. It must be a place of excitement and opportunity.

Una heard footsteps approaching, so she tore the
section of the page with the advertisement and folded it to
the size of a biscuit before tucking it in her sleeve. Before
she could remove the mushy newspaper spread out on the
table, her father entered the room. She crossed her arms
and leaned on the pages. Una saw her father's face turn

from query to anger. But he spoke not a word. When he raised his hand, Una closed her eyes, anticipating a slap.

Wham! Una's eyes burst open to see her father's clenched fist rising from the table with newspapers crumpled between his fingers. He pulled the remaining pages towards him, crumpling them with both hands into a spherical wad. Then he slid the pot of boiling lobsters to one side so he could open a lid on the stove and pitch the paper ball into the fire.

Una was surprised when her father spoke to her. "Reading the words of liars and heathens? More sins for you to repent? Leave this house until I call you back!" he yelled.

Una did not argue. She was glad to leave. She dashed from the kitchen into the yard, where she immediately collided with her mother. Their eyes met briefly, and they exchanged scowls. Una whirled out of the way and ran towards the livestock pens, disappearing behind the barns.

17

Returns to the National Board of Health show the general health of the country to be good, save that small-pox, scarlet fever and typhoid fever are epidemic in some localities. Scarlet fever is very severe in New England; typhoid fever is prevalent to an unusual extent in the South and West, and especially in the Mississippi Valley.

— *St. Landry Democrat*, Opelousas, Louisiana, December 24, 1881

Una returned to her room at sundown. She was hungry but had no regrets about leaving her parents to clean up after the lobster feast. In her room, she removed the scrap of newspaper from her sleeve and trimmed around the Harvey girls item. Then she folded the small advertisement and slid it behind the cloth lining inside her music box, safe from prying eyes. She lay on her bed imagining what life would be like in a luxurious Harvey hotel.

The Clark boys felt the tension among the other family members. The period of shunning felt like punishment for everyone in the family. In the silence, the boys wondered whether perhaps they, too, carried some blame. The older boy had already learned to avoid culpability by incriminating another sibling in trespasses. He elected to further incriminate his sister.

The boys were typically in bed before Una had extinguished her candle or lamp. This resulted in light from Una's bedroom streaming through the hole they had drilled in the wall, a hole that their parents had not yet discovered. There would be hell to pay for drilling such a hole, regardless of the intended purpose. The boys agreed to blame Una for the hole and called for their father.

"What's going on? You boys are supposed to be sleeping."

"Yes, Father," whispered one of the boys.

"We can't sleep because Una keeps talking to us through that hole."

Clark saw the light where they gestured. He tapped his finger to his lips to keep the boys quiet before removing some sawdust at the edge of the hole. Then he got down on his knees and looked into his daughter's room.

Una saw movement in the hole and sawdust falling. She had been waiting to catch her brothers at the peephole. Silently, she grabbed her bottle of perfume and lowered it along the wall. When the nozzle lined up with the hole, Una squeezed the bulb with all her might. Atomized cheap perfume blasted into the hole and the fragrance filled the air.

"By all that's holy, what have you done to my eye?" yelled her father. When Clark tried to stand, he lost his balance, falling onto the bed between his sons. "Woman," he yelled to his wife. "Get me some water! Your vixen daughter has blinded me."

Una did not understand why her dad was yelling. She had fully expected a reaction from one of her brothers. She swung her door open and looked into the adjoining bedroom. Her father was writhing in pain with one hand covering his right eye, while her brothers stood beside the bed, in shock.

Clark grabbed Una's arm and pulled her towards him. "God will not forgive this. You have disrespected your family and your father."

"I don't understand," cried Una. "Why were you peeping at me while I undressed?"

"Why did you perforate the wall if you were worried about peeping?"

"Yeah, why did you?" chimed in one of the boys.

"Get out of my sight!" commanded Clark. "I don't want to look upon you with even one eye. And you better pray that there is no lasting harm to my vision."

Una climbed the makeshift ladder to her sanctuary inside a rectangular granary. The creaking ladder would warn her if anyone followed her into the bin. The boys had not discovered this hiding place, and her parents only checked the level in the bin when it was near empty. At present, the bin was nearly full, with wheat ten feet deep.

The Clark children knew that granaries were a dangerous place to play, depending on the type of grain. Some grains behaved like fluids, while others were more like sand. More than a few farm families had been devastated by the drowning of a child or even an adult in a bin of rapeseed or flaxseed.

But Una knew that on this hill of wheat she would find safety and comfort. She knew that if she jumped from the ladder into the stockpile, her body would submerge up to her waist in the oblong kernels. Loose clothing, such as dresses or petticoats, would float on the surface of the wheat, creating a sense of bliss where the cold seeds touched her skin.

Una leaned back on the grain like she was floating on a lake. As she wriggled her arms and body, she sank deeper into the kernels, until her clothes puffed full of air. The sensation was indescribable and Una could not imagine any similar feeling. When she closed her eyes, she imagined thousands of tiny fingertips ferrying her across a river. She settled into the wheat, only her face exposed. She vowed in the dim light of the granary that she would no longer be guided by guilt. She prayed that her adult life was about to begin. Life without elders. Life free of guilt.

The next morning, Una was awakened by the sound of the boys shouting over the crowing of a rooster. Someone was clanking pails outside the granary and she noticed a depression where grain was sinking along the bin wall. Outside, someone was drawing wheat out of the bottom of the bin.

Una struggled to free herself from the flowing grain. Her arms were weak and her head ached. There was an unusual pain in her lower abdomen. In a panic to escape the wheat moving below, she managed to roll onto her stomach and paddled with her arms towards the sunbeams entering the opening in the upper wall. The flow stopped and the girl scrambled to the ladder outside the opening.

As Una descended she noticed a rash on the back of her arms. Weary and rushed, she missed the bottom rung of the ladder and fell on her back.

Mother Clark set down the pail she was carrying and kneeled beside Una. Una's cheeks were red and her eyes were cloudy. Mother put her hand on Una's forehead. Then she lifted her arm to see the rash.

"I'll be fine," grumbled Una. "Leave me alone like a good member of the Plymouth church."

"No, I don't care what the church says!" exclaimed Mother Clark. "You are sick! Maybe it's just from being in that dusty granary. But you need to be in bed until you feel better. If you don't feel better tomorrow, I will fetch the doctor."

Doctor Bulliss was still in Una's bedroom two hours after he had arrived. Una was unconscious and her breathing was labored. The rash had spread to her torso. Mother Clark was placing wet towels on Una's forehead and abdomen as instructed by the doctor.

Finally, the doctor put away his stethoscope and asked Mother Clark to fetch Una's father.

Mother Clark went into the yard and called for her husband to come. When they came back inside, the doctor was thoroughly washing his hands and arms in a basin. As he shook off the water, he said, "I believe your daughter has typhoid fever."

"Where would she have gotten that?" asked Mother.

"Typhoid is usually spread by food or water that has come in contact with an infected person. Where do you get your water from?"

"From a well, just behind the buildings. We have been drinking that water for years."

"Then she may have sampled some contaminated food. Something raw."

"We always cook our food," said Mother Clark.

"Except garden fruit or vegetables," said Agent Clark.

"Well, cook everything now. And make sure you wash carefully after touching your daughter."

"How long before the fever breaks?" asked Mother Clark.

"That's hard to say. People with typhoid either die quickly or recover slowly. Lots of times the fever breaks but the patient does not wake up and they starve. In other cases, patients are back to normal in a few weeks."

"Oh, dear God. And we have been so cruel to her of late," cried Mother Clark. She sat down at the table and hid her face in her hands. "What have we done?"

"Will we all get the fever soon, doctor?" asked Agent Clark.

"I don't think so. Only if your well has been contaminated. But then I would have expected other cases in your family. Make sure Una is kept cool during her fever. And if she wakes, make sure she drinks."

"We will," agreed Agent Clark.

"Mr. Clark. May I look at your eye?" asked the doctor. "You seem to have injured it."

After a brief examination, the doctor applied some ointment to the injured eye. He retrieved an eye-patch from his bag and handed it Clark.

"Keep that on until I see you next time," ordered the doctor. "I will come back in three days."

When Doctor Bulliss returned three days later, he was able to determine that Una's temperature had dropped to a safe level, yet she remained comatose. The doctor shook his head as he put his thermometer back in its leather sleeve.

"What is it doctor?" asked Mother Clark.

"Your daughter has suffered an extreme fever. On my last visit her temperature was above 105 degrees and brain damage may occur above 106 degrees. That damage has caused Una to go into a coma. She may wake up anytime or she may never wake up."

Mother Clark leaned into her husband's vest, sobbing uncontrollably. Agent Clark fiddled with his eye patch to wipe away a tear. After the doctor had packed his bag, he asked the Clarks to sit down at the kitchen table to talk about options for Una's care over the next few weeks. He explained that in her present state Una would die from dehydration or starvation in the next few days, but that there were some doctors experimenting with feeding tubes made from eel skin. In fact, President Garfield had been fed beef broth and whiskey for eighty days after being shot last July.

"But the president was awake for those feedings," objected Agent Clark.

"Granted, but the techniques are improving," assured the doctor. "A feeding tube could be inserted into Una's rectum until she regains consciousness. When she can swallow food and drink normally we may find that her brain is undamaged."

The Clark's agreed to the doctor's treatment plan for their daughter. Doctor Bulliss hired a covered wagon and driver to transport Una and a nurse to an infirmary in Waco, Texas. Fortunately, she survived the trip and was placed in a private room. Another doctor arrived from St. Louis later that day to meet with Doctor Bulliss.

After examining the patient and her medical history, the doctor from St. Louis handed a sealed envelope to Bulliss. "Thank you for bringing the patient here. I may not be able to save this patient, but she provides a strong young body to test my theories."

"Should I count this?" asked Bulliss looking inside the envelope.

"The five hundred as agreed is in there. Also there is a letter to the Clark family."

"Thank you," Bulliss said with a wide grin. "I will be sure to deliver the letter to the family on my return to Dallas. What will you do when the girl dies?"

"There will be additional tests to be conducted even after she dies."

"I mean will you keep the Clark family advised?"

"That is taken care of in the envelope you are delivering," assured the doctor from St. Louis. "It includes a death certificate dated for today. The trip was just too hard on this girl."

18

Yesterday, as the engine on the road from this city to the quarry was leaving the yard for the quarry, the main shaft connecting the driving wheels broke, and threw the engine down an embankment, completely demolishing it. Fortunately, there were no cars attached to it at the time, and only a few persons on the engine.

—*The Austin Weekly Statesman*, **Austin, Texas, September 30, 1886**

John Barringer was standing on the wooden sidewalk in front of a telegraph office on a familiar street in a familiar town. The street stretched to the horizon. As he leaned on the post supporting the portico, he tried to put a finger on the name of this city. He recalled that on a recent trip to Austin, he had been impressed by the grandeur of the structures made of granite but saw no stone of any kind on this street. The buildings were made entirely of wood. The facade reminded him of Bluffton or Llano. Yet Barringer could not imagine that the streets in those towns would ever grow to be this long.

As Barringer pondered how he had arrived on this mysterious street, he heard a thundering noise coming from his left. At the south end of the street, he saw a herd of Texas Longhorn cattle stampeding towards him under a cloud of dust. The herd smashed wagons, trampled horses, and sent a scattering of bystanders running for cover. Barringer stood dumbfounded as he watched the herd continue past his vantage point. The sounds were deafening: hooves pounding, cattle bawling, people screaming, and wood snapping. Barringer estimated that more than five hundred cattle had passed his position, yet he was untouched. The stampede continued down the pike, causing havoc among the living and obliterating any encumbrances in its path. A breeze pushed the wall of dust, like an invisible drover riding drag on the herd.

John Barringer now noticed sheets of paper wafting in the air above the street, as if the bovine criers had delivered the daily news. An adolescent woman ran from a doorway, gathering the papers and stuffing them into a shoulder bag. She had russet hair and a milk-white complexion. Her white dress and hat were unsullied by the previous chaos. The angelic young woman snatched a paper as it drifted past her, then walked directly towards Barringer and handed him the page with a smile.

Barringer stretched the corners of the page so that he could read the message this woman was relaying to him. A headline on the scrap of newspaper read:

Schoolteacher to Hang for Murder of Westinghouse Engineer

Bile rose up in Barringer's throat as he stumbled into the street. He grabbed more pages as they twisted in the breeze. Each page was torn from a different source, but they all had the same headline. Some had a picture of the schoolteacher, Fannie May Henderson. Barringer had never seen such a clear likeness of her face on paper. He stuffed one into his pants pocket and stumbled along the street in a daze. When he had gathered his wits somewhat, he looked up the street and could see the herd of cattle returning. Now the five hundred were stampeding back towards him, towards the south. Barringer had no time to retreat, so he leaned forward into the charging herd. The sound was deafening until he opened his eyes. Then the noise was gone. There was no herd.

Barringer lay on a bare plank floor. He wondered how he came to be there. He had expected to be mortally wounded in a dusty street. He checked his arms and legs for injuries. He felt for a paper in his pocket but he had no pockets in the threadbare pair of long johns he had worn to bed. Except for a stiff leg and morning haziness, he seemed alive and kicking. Then Barringer recognized the floor of the schoolhouse that he had built. Of course, it was still standing, here in a meadow outside of Bluffton. There were no other buildings. There were no stampeding cattle. This was the schoolhouse that Fannie May and he had designed and built after the fire of 1883. The empty bed beside him was where they made love in 1886.

But now she was not there.

This was not Barringer's first nightmare. Dreams had visited him frequently since his childhood. He recalled the words of his father. *"You have to live your nightmare until it makes sense."*

Barringer jumped to his feet, indecent and unashamed in his timeworn underwear. He flung open the door to the classroom to see Fannie May packing clothes into a steamer trunk near the entrance of the schoolhouse.

"We have to get you out of here! You're the school-teacher!" shouted Barringer.

In the privacy of the closed schoolhouse, in the heat of this August morning, Fannie May was dressed only in her night shift. The sun was creeping over the eastern hills and shining directly into the schoolhouse windows. Barringer's gaze descended along her dark brown hair to her waist, where the sun shone through the thin fabric, silhouetting her shape. As she bent over the trunk—which appeared to be filled with under-drawers, petticoats, Millie skirts, and Weddington blouses, and more clothes than a schoolteacher could wear in a year— the shift rode high to expose the soft white skin of her calves.

"What you are getting at, John B?" asked Fannie May, as she stood erect and gazed at her beloved.

"Just living my nightmare."

"Your nightmare? I am the one who has been dismissed by the self-righteous trustees of the Bluffton-Burnet school division. To them, I am just another fallen woman."

"Of course, but I reckon it's best if we hurry out of here," stammered Barringer, as he raised his gaze to meet her ice-blue eyes.

Fannie May took this opportunity to arch her back to relieve the strain of bending over the trunk. As she did, she smiled at the strapping man across the room. Not a tall man, but a man whose hairy upper body was muscled and firm.

Both arms were brawny from physical exercise, but the right arm was obviously thicker and more powerful as a result of the carpenter's trade. His hair was thick and black, including a full mustache which concealed his mouth unless he was expressing his erratic sense of humor.

Fannie May glanced towards his undergarment. "John B! What are you thinking? Show some modesty!"

Barringer looked down at his hairy self and tucked his manhood back from where it had escaped. The corners of his mustache curled up when he answered. "Oops. No time for biology class."

Fannie May blushed and attempted not to laugh. "As you say, we need to pack out of here before my replacement turns up."

"Do you reckon the Bluffton school board will latch onto a new teacher real quick? You just got the telegram yesterday."

"I expect the board had started looking for my replacement before the telegram was composed. I'm sad to leave the Bluffton children and their families. It's not fair to punish those eager minds because of my misspent youth," she sighed. "And it seems the past will haunt me wherever I go. I am so sorry, John B."

"Don't fret. There's lots of time for learnin' the folks in Arizona when we get there."

"I am grateful for your support, John B. So, what is bothering you this morning? You seemed aggravated when you awoke."

"Bad dream. Because I am worried that folks here are still riled up for what happened to Mr. Wills and that murdered rail boss."

"John B. We both know that you didn't kill the railroad boss. You were found innocent by trial. As for Wills, he died of natural causes, also known as liver poisoning."

"I reckon someone will find that freight car with the dead Westinghouse man inside," said John B.

"There is no proof that we knew anything about how he got in there or what the railway did with the car."

"That's been eatin' at me. We do know that the man was trapped in a box in a rail-car that was parked on a siding. And people might think we had motive to kill him."

"Don't be feeling guilty for any of those events," ordered Fannie May. "And we don't know who put that Westinghouse man in a crate on a train. Whatever knowledge I had does not make me legally responsible for the outcome. The sheriff will see it that way."

"I hope yer right. But some locals might see things different." Barringer paused, while Fannie May continued sorting and packing. "I figger I'll walk up to Bluffton and see about catching the stage to Llano. I've got to get my horse and the money from the bank before we head west."

"I suggest you acquire some clothes en route. Drawers should be first on your list. If only for the protection of the righteous and moral women of Texas Hill Country."

"You mean the way I'm dressed is a might too *hole-y*?" chuckled Barringer.

Fannie May shook her head and returned to packing. She assured John B that she would be done packing by midday.

19

Llano County, Texas, 1886

On the night of the 8th a horse, the property of Dr. Dubose, was stolen from a livery stable at this place. The night following the town of Bluffton, in this county, was destroyed by fire; only one business house, a drug store, escaped. The burning was evidently the work of an incendiary.... Considerable excitement exists here and it is sincerely hoped that more vigorous measures will be instituted by the authorities to arrest the perpetrators of these and all other crimes and to execute upon them that vengeance of the law they so richly deserve.

—*Austin Weekly Statesman*, Austin, Texas, November 22, 1883

In 1883, fire had destroyed the town of Bluffton, leaving only one place of business and the Masonic Hall. In the three years that followed, the townspeople employed local carpenters, including John Barringer—known as John B to his friends—to rebuild the homes and commercial buildings near the original town-site. In order to attract an accredited teacher, the Bluffton-Burnet School Board had commissioned Barringer to build a modern country school for the children from towns and farms in the area. Barringer tackled the project with keen interest and was able to involve the new schoolteacher, Fannie May Henderson, in the design and construction. Together, in the spring of 1886, they completed construction of the classroom, teacher's quarters, privy, and barn.

One of the churches destroyed in the Bluffton fire had salvaged a large bell from the debris. Since the church bell had not been in use for some time, the church elders had donated it to the schoolhouse project. Inspired by the extraordinary donation, Barringer had constructed a belfry above the entrance of the school to accommodate the seventeen-inch cast-bronze bell. Barringer had been fascinated by the artisan-ship of the bell. Removing the soot and rust had taken several hours of brushing and polishing, but eventually the glory of the bell and its appurtenances was revealed. The manufacturer had cast some letters onto the surface of the bell: **Clinton H. Meneely Bell Company, Troy, NY, A.D. 1870.**

A yoke mounted on metal stands was supplied with the bell, and a cast-bronze wheel twenty-four inches in diameter had been attached to the yoke. That wheel operated like a pulley, with a long rope looped through the groove on the rim. The bell-ringer could pull the rope hanging from either side of the wheel to cause the bell to swing in either direction or to stop the motion.

As a carpenter, Barringer had experience using block-and-tackle pulleys to lift large items into place. With the assistance of his draught horse, Clyde, the bell was lifted into place almost twenty feet above the ground. A rope of the correct thickness to fit snugly in the groove on the wheel could be pulled to swing the bell. Based on trial and error, Barringer had determined that he could pull down on either side of the rope for more than two feet before it lost purchase on the wheel rim.

Barringer and Fannie May rang the bell proudly for the opening of the school in the spring of 1886. It was heard for miles around. And students from miles around attended the school during that first spring.

During the several months required to build the school, Fannie May and John B had learned about each other's hopes and dreams. Barringer took pride in his workmanship, the importance of which was second only to the relationship he had developed with the schoolteacher. Fannie May was excited by the opportunity to build a new life in the progressive community of Bluffton. A series of events over the summer of '86 changed the lives of the carpenter and schoolteacher.

Barringer was falsely accused of the murder of a railway construction foreman. He was apprehended by a Pinkerton Agent named H.A. Clark and incarcerated in the Llano jailhouse. While awaiting trial, Barringer relied on his savvy fiancée, Fannie May, to protect his only asset—a rocky mound which contained a mineral sought by both Thomas Edison and George Westinghouse. Fannie May determined that she and Barringer were contending with three adversaries, each with a different primary motivation: one was motivated by fear, the second by greed, and the third by love. By implementing a game of Rock-Paper-Scissors, Fannie May successfully exploited those motivations to turn these three enemies against each other.

Barringer was acquitted of the murder charges, but during the trial, Fannie May was identified as a former dance-hall girl from Paris, Texas. Amid the ensuing furor, the couple escaped the town of Llano on the newly christened railway.

They were holed up in the schoolhouse, which was closed for the summer, when they received word that Fannie May had been terminated. The news was disappointing but not surprising. They had already formulated a plan for a new life: they hoped to benefit from an extravagant uncle, Daniel Moreau Barringer, who was mining near Winslow, Arizona.

Neither had ever undertaken a journey of that magnitude before.

Sheriff Russell was relaxing on the porch in front of the Llano County jailhouse. He spent most mornings enjoying the sunrise from this stoop. The slats of the bench supporting his hefty figure creaked their surrender as he rocked forward to empty the briar bowl of his pipe onto the ground. After repeatedly reaming the dottle out of the pipe, he reached into his vest pocket and retrieved a new quota of Virginia tobacco. As he tamped the bowl, a horse and rider rounded the corner and approached his position.

"Are you the county sheriff?" asked the man on the horse.

"Either that or I stole this badge," laughed the sheriff. "How can I help you, friend?"

"I'm lookin' for my son. Rumor has it that he was in your custody not that long ago."

"Then you'd be Old Jack Barringer?" inquired Russell, noticing the family resemblance. He stood to meet the man dismounting from his horse. "I am glad to say that John B is no longer a guest in the hoosegow."

"I'm ashamed to say that I haven't been in contact with my son for a few years. But when his ma heard he had been arrested, she sent me to find out what happened with him."

"Well, he was in a tangle for most of the summer. Fortunately, the judge saw it different and John B was released a couple of weeks ago. Left town in a hurry, though. Lots of folks still think he murdered a railroad boss. I am told he and his lady friend took a train out of here. Left his horse behind. And I still have his guns and saddlebag here. As far as I know, he and the schoolmarm are back Bluffton way."

"I guess I came this far for nothing. I heard he had something to do with a mine back there. I'd be much obliged if you point me in the right direction."

"There is probably more trouble comin' his way. Trouble that he don't deserve. I'll ride there with you. We can return his horse and possessions when we find him. I owe your boy, Mr. Barringer. John B has done more carpentry around here than anyone else. Built this here jailhouse a few years back. Broke my heart to lock him up in it."

"I'd be obliged to ya," replied Old Jack.

"Why don't you grab a bite over at the Dabb's Hotel while I liberate that big horse of John B's."

Within the hour, Sheriff Russell had paid the livery to release the black Clydesdale, loaded all of young Barringer's possessions in a pack, and relit his pipe. Both men and three horses set on their way to the mine known as Barringer Hill, where they expected to find John Barringer or some clue to his whereabouts.

John B grabbed the red checked shirt he had been wearing for four days and a pair of dark canvas trousers, also due for a washboard. After he connected the Y of his suspenders to the back of the trousers he pulled on his black leather boots.

Fannie May had prepared a plate of biscuits and cheese. As he ate his morning repast, John B wondered how Fannie May expected to transport the large trunk and several smaller boxes to Winslow. By his estimate, the trip was over a thousand miles. On a good horse, in good weather, that would take two months. A wagon with a pair of draught horses would take even longer, depending on the condition of the trails. As a carpenter, Barringer owned a good wagon, and his Clydesdale horse could lead a team. But Barringer predicted that using a wagon would eventually result in unexpected delay. A wheel could fall off. The wagon could get trapped in rocks or mud. The most likely fate would be that the wagon floated away as they crossed any number of streams and rivers between Bluffton and Winslow. That would spell the end of the trunk full of fine clothes, as well as items they would need for survival. Regardless of their mode of transportation, John B knew that he had to retrieve his horse and acquire another for Fannie May to ride. Fortunately, he had more than enough money in the First National Bank in Llano. He had deposited five thousand dollars from the sale of his mine at Barringer Hill. That amount was untouched and would finance the next few years of married life.

Upon his release from Llano jailhouse, Barringer and Fannie May had eluded an angry mob, unable to fetch his horse from the livery. He also planned to retrieve his harness, saddlebag, Navy Colt pistol, and Winchester rifle. As he thought about his pistol, he wondered if it was time to look for a new gun. He had never fired a gun at another human, but anticipated that his travel plans may involve gun-play. His father had once told him, "The road to peace is through prayer. So ask God to keep your powder dry and your aim true."

By late afternoon, Fannie May had filled her steamer trunk and one suitcase with her clothes. She also packed nine boxes with books, newspapers, and paper supplies. Barringer was mapping out their trip in his mind when he heard voices outside. The distant words could not be deciphered, but the tone indicated a multitude in bad temper. John B and Fannie May looked out the windows in time to see an angry mob emerge from the edge of the forest carrying signs and tools, including a few rifles.

Fannie May ran to her closet and removed a double-barreled shotgun. She opened the chambers and was feeling through a drawer for ammunition when Barringer came up beside her.

"There's at least a half-dozen guns out there. Let's not start a battle that we can't win," whispered Barringer. "Least not until we find out what they want. If it is the same bunch that chased us out of Llano, they probably just want to get me back in a courtroom for murder of that rail boss."

"I guess you're right," conceded Fannie May, as she tucked the shotgun under her bed-covers. They joined hands as they walked to the front step of the school and watched the approaching crowd.

Fannie May recognized some parents of schoolchildren carrying signs that read:

Liars can't save Killers

Miss Fannie go back to your Brothel

Trial was Fixed

Barringer identified Dora-lee, a harlot from the Dabb's Hotel in Llano, followed by several of her patrons. He recognized some saddle tramps that frequented the saloons in Bluffton. The Llano undertaker's wagon was at the back of the group.

Barringer held up his arms and shouted over the cacophony of angry voices. "We know you have reasons to be mad. Fannie May and I are packing our bags today and leaving the county."

"That's what you think, Barringer," yelled a cowpoke, who stepped forward. "Not until these people get their pound of flesh."

"Yeah, you yellow-belly. Yer not goin' nowhere," shouted Dora-lee.

Two irate cowpokes pulled out sidearms and jumped up to the top steps beside Barringer and Fannie May. They shoved the couple back into a corner of the classroom. Another young drover with an egg-sized tumor on one cheek stumbled up the steps, where he grabbed one side of the bell rope. The bell chimed loudly. The ruffian finally gained control of the ropes after the fifth chime.

"No need for the ruckus, Chewy," ordered one of the older saddle tramps. He called the hooligan by a nickname owing to the stream of brown spittle running from the corner of the punk's mouth.

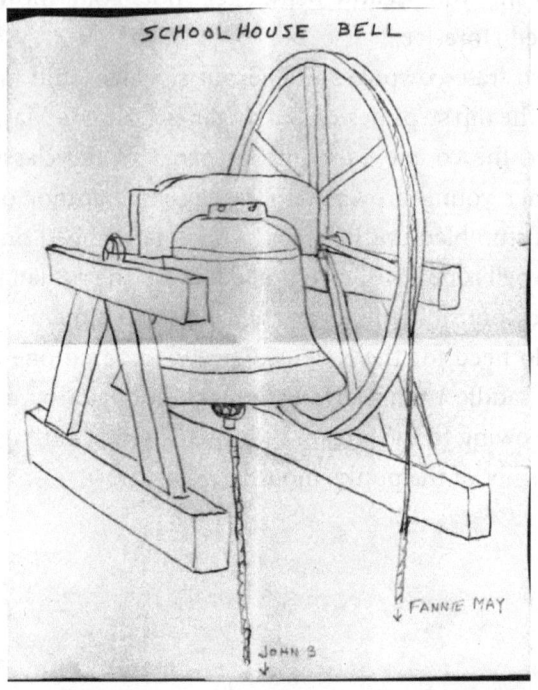

SCHOOL HOUSE BELL

FANNIE MAY

JOHN 3

"There's a couple of good ropes here if we cut it at the bottom," slurred Chewy, before he spat on the floor. "I can fashion up a necktie for each of them."

"Do it, kid!" yelled someone in the crowd. "That's what they deserve."

Fannie May could not believe her ears. The mob outside the school intended to execute them. She started kicking the man holding a gun on her and screamed, "You can't hang us without a trial!"

Barringer stepped forward. "You might think I murdered that rail boss, but you have no call to lynch the schoolteacher."

"Well, she's a liar and a whore. In my books that's a hangin' offense. B'sides, carpenter, won't she want to be with you?"

One of the men from the mob, a large muscular man, lowered his sign and came into the school. "No need to hang these folks. They said they were leavin' the county, and that's good enough for me and most others."

"You git yourself out in the yard and watch this hangin'!" ordered a cowpoke, as he pushed the big man down the steps. "And if you can't bear to watch, then cover your eyes."

Chewy held up the looped knots he had fashioned. "Yessir, we're gonna hang us a whore and a murderer," he snickered savagely. "Take a gander at them nooses."

The older cowpokes dragged two desks into the vestibule, where the ropes hung. They forced Fannie May and John B to each stand on a desk before tightening a noose around each of their necks. Even in the shade of the porch, the gathering outside had a clear view of the doomed couple. Some parents were praying. Some women covered their children's eyes. Other women in the crowd started pleading for mercy. But not Dora-lee.

Dora-lee was grinning. She believed that this couple had murdered a man and conspired to pin the blame on Andrew Wills, her long-time customer and friend. In her mind, Wills had died from the anguish of the trial and these two should pay. In truth, Wills had been a good friend to Barringer before and after the murder charges. Barringer had been shocked when he heard that Wills had died in the Llano jailhouse.

John B grabbed Fannie May by the hand and waited for her to focus on his face. He spoke softly, "I'm not sure how this is going to play out." As he looked up towards the bell wheel, he added, "But when they pull the desk out from under you, try hard to wrap your legs around my neck."

"Even if I can, that will put all my weight on you. You'll die."

"Please trust me, Fannie May," pleaded Barringer. "It's our only chance. I love you."

"I know you love me. But they'll probably shoot us if the rope doesn't work."

"What's all this whisperin'?" growled Chewy, as he tried to shush them with a finger held to lips the color of dung. With a nod from Chewy, the other cowpokes pulled both desks away quickly.

All those that witnessed the moment gasped in surprise. As expected, Barringer's body dropped. But it lowered slowly, noticeably slower than expected by men who had witnessed previous lynchings. Fannie May felt the noose tighten and yank her upwards. The bell wheel was acting as a pulley between the two ends of the rope. And the inertia of the bell dampened the speed of the reaction until it stopped with a single, low-pitched clang.

Unable to breathe, and on the verge of panic, Fannie May recalled John B's last words. The instruction made no sense to her, but she trusted that he had a plan. Fannie May raised one leg onto John B's shoulder, then the other, and was able to squirm her bare legs into a sitting position. The rope around her neck went slack, and she was able to breathe. She heard John B gulping for air underneath the folds of her gown. Modesty aside, Fannie May hiked up the shift to see his wide eyes staring up at her. He could not speak. The noose was tight around his throat and his mouth was pressed tight against her body, his thick black mustache pressing into her thighs.

As Fannie May looked at John B, the pupils of his eyes rolled back into his head. When she glanced past him, she could see his feet swinging several inches off the floor. She screamed, "John B! Don't go yet, John B!"

Fannie May looked at the cowpokes with fury in her eyes. Chewy was flicking his tongue in and out between brown and yellow teeth, while he stared at her exposed legs.

"Like what you see?" Fannie May asked. "You can have me if you cut us down. Take me."

Some women in the mob turned their gaze away. Dora-lee screeched, "Chewy, I can give you that anytime. Don't let them down."

Fannie May's mind was still clear and her breathing was unrestricted. She suspected that John B would be dead within minutes unless she could get his feet to the floor. She pulled down on the rope that suspended him but it did not move. The rope was jammed on the pulley. Her efforts seemed futile, as valuable seconds ticked away. She pulled herself up to stand on his shoulders, creating more slack on her end of the rope. But now, her entire body weight added to his own served to tighten the noose on her lover. Her effort to budge the rope risked shortening John B's life. Even though she was temporarily safe, John B was no longer breathing.

20

Barringer Hill, Llano County, Texas, 1886

Friday morning, October 1, a mob gained entrance to the jail, seized Wallace, dragged him from the cell and strung him up. He was cut down, after being allowed to hang for a short time, in order that a confession might be forced from him. He refused to own up to the crime, and before the crowd could hang him again, the sheriff gained possession of him and carried him back to the cell. The crowd was prevailed upon to disperse and it was supposed that the law would be allowed to take its course.

Last night, however, a second and successful attempt was made to mete out justice to the murderer.

—*Austin Weekly Statesman*, Austin, Texas, October 7, 1886

Sheriff Russell followed a hand-drawn map to the location of Barringer Hill. After tying the horses to some live oak trees, the men walked across the site, which was in disarray. Barringer's wagon was tipped on one side with the harness still attached. A wooden box of carpenter's tools had broken open at the base of a tree. A broom, fork, coffee pot and frying pan were strewn beside the wagon.

The hill was still an imposing formation, despite having had many of the rare-earth minerals removed from it.

Standing forty feet high at its peak, and eighty feet on its longest axis, the gravel-covered hill had an opening at one end where material had been removed. The two men discovered tattered clothing, broken shovels, and ten-dollar bills scattered among the debris surrounding the hill.

"Looks like there has been an explosion here," commented Sheriff Russell.

"Agreed," said Old Jack. "And these timber rails run right down to the river for no rhyme or reason that I can see."

"Do you think we can harness up Clyde to his wagon and drive up to the schoolhouse? I bet we will find John B or his lady friend there."

The two men tipped the wagon onto its four wheels and harnessed Clyde to it. The sheriff rode lead on his horse while Old Jack drove the wagon with his own horse tethered in back. The trip took the better part of an hour, along a trail that meandered west then northeast. When the trail turned, they heard the school bell toll five times in succession.

"Well, someone's at the school," remarked Old Jack.

Just before they emerged into the clearing surrounding the school they heard one very loud chime of the bell. Once in the clearing, the two men could hear the noisy throng gathered at the door of the school. Sheriff Russell stopped his horse. With a small spyglass he removed from his vest he was able to get a clear view of the commotion. He could see the figure of a man swinging from a rope, with a woman standing on his shoulders. For all appearances, they could have been playing a game. But he heard a woman scream "John B," followed by other words in a desperate tone.

"Goddamn! That's a lynching!" yelled Russell, as he kicked his horse in the ribs and galloped towards the school.

Old Jack assumed the lynching might be over by the time the big Clydesdale could get to the school. "Whoa, big fella. Whoa." As the wagon came to a halt, Jack Barringer grabbed his son's Winchester rifle from the back of the wagon. Quickly but calmly, he leaned the rifle stock on the edge of the wagon and took aim at one of the ropes. He fired once and jumped back on the wagon when he heard the plaintive response from the bell.

Fannie May was screaming and crying as she tugged on the rope that was choking John B. She managed to climb off of his shoulders, her weight supported by both hands gripping the rope above him. By now, her bleeding hands were making it difficult to concentrate. Yet, she continued to tug and swing the rope in an effort to release it from the wheel of the bell — but it would not let go.

Then, without warning, without moving, the bell rang. The single peal was loud enough that Fannie May did not hear the report of a distant rifle.

The toll created vibration in the bell, which traveled through the yoke and out to the wheel. That vibration broke the rope free to slide in its groove. Fannie May's hands were yanked from their grip on the descending rope. Barringer's limp frame dropped until his feet touched the floor. His knees buckled and his body crumpled onto the floor. Fannie May felt a wave of relief, but it was short-lived. Without warning the rope around her throat tightened and she was lifted by the neck up into the belfry. Pain shot through her spine. The skin on her neck burned from the rope. She could hardly see through the sweat and tears that filled her eyes. Could it be that the toll which had released John B was the death knell for Fannie May?

In the shadows of the belfry, with waning consciousness, Fannie May caught a glimpse of some ladder treads that Barringer had installed when he was raising the bell. In a blind panic, she waved both arms until she gripped one of the boards. Then, with only the strength in her arms, she climbed each board until at last her weight was off the rope and the noose drooped at her back. She dangled there, supported by the tendons in her arms, exhausted, without any clear options.

Most of the men and women watching from outside were baffled by the sequence of events they had just witnessed in the space of less than a minute. Chewy stared up at the schoolteacher now suspended high above. His own intoxication and stupor caused him to lose his balance and fall backwards onto Barringer. When Barringer emitted a groan, several bystanders ran into the school and pushed the cowpokes away while others eased the strain in the noose. Some ladies fetched pitchers of water to pour on the victim and to quench his thirst.

A horse and rider thundered into the crowd. Sheriff Russell did not wait for his horse to come to a stop before dismounting. The agility of the burly lawman was astonishing to the onlookers as he deftly maneuvered his way into the school. He saw Barringer being attended to, then looked around for Fannie May. Several bystanders were looking up into the shadows of the belfry. Sheriff Russell followed their gaze and saw the schoolteacher precariously clinging to slats on the wall. He quickly went to her chambers and retrieved a stiff wool blanket, then drafted four large bystanders to each hold a corner of the blanket at shoulder height directly below Fannie May.

"Hang on for a minute, Miss Fannie. Can you get the noose off?" asked the sheriff as he looked up.

"No, I need both hands to keep me from falling. Can't hold much longer," she croaked.

"Hold on just a bit. When I cut the rope down here, you should be able to fall onto the blanket these fellers are holding."

Fannie May grunted. The men holding the blanket nodded when the sheriff looked at them. One of the cowpokes took a knife off his belt and presented it to the sheriff, handle first. Then the sheriff bent over the ladies tending to Barringer. They had loosened the noose around his neck, but it was still firmly attached to him and was under some tension from above. The Sheriff gripped the rope with one hand and hacked at it with the other. In a moment, he had sliced all of the braided strands.

"OK, Fannie May. Let yourself fall," yelled the sheriff.

Fannie May relaxed her grip and dropped about eight feet to the waiting blanket. She was aware that her backside was exposed as her shift ballooned from the air rushing past her. But before she could make amends, her legs crumpled into the cot. Without delay, the trailing end of the rope struck one of the men holding a corner of the blanket. He groaned but kept his grip as they lowered the teacher gently to the floor. Immediately, one man covered her with a fold of the blanket. The Sheriff bent down to loosen the noose and pull it gently over her tangled brown hair.

"Is John B alive?" she gasped.

"Yes, ma'am," said several of the men bending over her.

"How did the rope finally give way?" gasped Fannie May.

"Someone shot the bell. That loosened the rope," replied the sheriff.

"I hit the bell," declared Old Jack, who had just arrived at the steps of the schoolhouse. "Was trying to shoot the rope, but I hit the bell."

Clyde pulled the wagon carrying Fannie May, John B, and Old Jack from the schoolhouse to Bluffton. Sheriff Russell rode his own horse alongside. The third horse trailed behind the wagon. The rough trail rambled through coulees and across streams. Lying in the back of the wagon, Barringer was quiet except for an occasional cough to clear his throat. Fannie May crouched next to him, occasionally rinsing her torn hands with water from a canteen.

When they stopped to water the horses at a trough in Bluffton, the sheriff leaned over the side of the wagon to look at both of the victims. Fannie May was scratched and bruised around her neck and arms. John B had a bloody wound running from ear to ear around his lower jaw. The upward curve of his injury gave the impression of a villainous smirk. Unfortunately, the sheriff had seen similar scars on lifeless victims of past lynchings where the knots were not cinched properly. John B's survival may have been attributable in some measure to the greenhorn who fashioned the noose.

"Before I leave you in the care of your family, I need to talk to you, John B. Can you hear me?" asked the sheriff. Barringer groaned and nodded.

"I got a cable from the Pinkerton man," continued the sheriff. "You remember, Agent Clark was at your trial. He says that two employees from Westinghouse have gone missing. Hanks and Chico. I wonder if you know what happened to them?"

John B shook his head and looked towards Fannie May. The Sheriff turned to Fannie May and raised his eyebrows without repeating the question.

Fannie May shrugged and asked, "Did they leave together?"

"Nobody seems to know. But I thought you might have heard from them," speculated the sheriff. "I will telegram the Pinkerton man that we have not seen them since the mine at Barringer Hill closed." Then he pulled out his pipe and started the whole process of cleaning and lighting it.

When his horse had finished drinking, Sheriff Russell mounted and rode up to the back of the wagon. "I suggest you both wait until you are hale and hearty before going to see the doctor. No use getting snared by the sawbones if you can recover on the farm."

21

Barringer Homestead, Llano County, Texas, 1886

Crops in Burnet and Llano counties are very promising. The corn fields are clear of weeds and grass and cotton chopping is now under full headway. Farmers say that it has been the best spring season they have ever seen—just enough rain and not too much.

The only cattle bought in Burnet and Llano that I know of, were bought by John C. Tate for Mr. Blacker. Only 4,000 or 5,000 head were bought. Prices paid were $8 and $12, and cut very close at this price. The Grangers and many others are going to drive their own cattle by throwing together and letting some one of their number take them to market.

—J.M.H. (J.M. Hubbs), *San Marcos Free Press*, San Marcos, Texas, May 13, 1886

For two hours, Old Jack drove the wagon from Bluffton through forest and around hills. He was grateful to have the company of the schoolteacher and John B, even if it was only temporary.

"Thanks for rescuing us, Mr. Barringer," whimpered Fannie May.

"Call me Jack," grumbled the senior Barringer. "And I'll call you Fannie May."

After a pause, Fannie May spoke again. "Did you know we are planning to marry?"

"Nope," replied Old Jack, with no further words.

After several minutes of silence, Fannie May asked, "How did you happen to come for us today?"

"Heard tell that my son was in Llano jailhouse, and in serious trouble." After a moment he continued, "His ma sent me to find out what he done. Sheriff said he got off at trial but there could be more trouble."

"Seems like the sheriff has a nose for trouble," conceded Fannie May. "John B warned me. We need to hasten out of this county. We plan to go to Arizona, to see your brother Daniel."

"Daniel is a big wheel out there," agreed Old Jack. "Are you sure he will be favorable to your arrival?"

"Yes, we have something he is looking for."

"Precious rocks, I presume," said Old Jack.

Fannie May nodded.

"After what I saw today, seems like you might not survive a trip to Arizona. There's only three ways to get there and I don't think John B is up to any of them."

"Why do you underestimate your son?" asked Fannie May. "He has proven himself through this most vexatious summer."

"I reckon you have enough grit and gumption for two, ma'am. But my boy was seconds away from meeting his maker if you hadn't been there."

"I beg to differ with your notion. When John B recovers, we can talk about how he plans to get us to Arizona."

For three days, Fannie May tended to the injuries of her intended. After a while, John B was able to sit at the kitchen table and eat solid food. The wounds on his neck were healing. One evening, while Fannie May and Mrs. Barringer cleaned dishes, Old Jack brought up the pending trip to Arizona.

"There are only three ways you are going to get to Arizona, boy," claimed Old Jack. "Train, wagon, or cattle trail."

"Since there is no railway north of Llano, I was thinking horses and maybe a pack mule," responded John B.

"You could take the train back east from Austin to St. Louis. Then ride the Atchison, Topeka, and Santa Fe back to Winslow. Mighty costly. Probably take a month, depending on weather and outlaws along the way," suggested Old Jack.

"That would be most comfortable for Fannie May and me, but I wonder if Clyde would be troubled by the trip. Can't leave my pardner behind."

"Then that leaves wagon train or cattle drive. Either way, you are looking at six months. What with winter delays, my advice is, take the next cattle drive north along the Western Trail to Dodge City. Then spend the winter there and decide your mode of transportation to Winslow."

"Sounds reasonable, Pa."

"It's late in the season, so even if you hook up with a cattle drive, you may run into weather along the trail. Last winter came early to Kansas. Any drive leaving now is flirting with the winds of November."

"That was mighty unusual weather from what I heard, Pa. Even the Austin newspaper says it seems unlikely to get two such winters in a row."

"That may be. But there are those who are preparing for the worst. This summer they built a series of fences and gates along the Canadian River inside Indian Territory."

"How does that help ranchers?" John B asked earnestly.

"The early snow drove some of the cattle from Kansas and Nebraska clear past the rail-head. Most of them were rustled by hungry Indians or low-down Texans."

"Weren't they branded? The law should have been able to identify them."

"The law never stopped desperate types from re-branding or butchering beef on the hoof. Brands only keep an honest man honest."

"Sounds like a lot of cattle got lost or stolen."

"Some died from the cold. The few that were rounded up and driven back to the railways were run-down from starvation or Texas fever."

"What about Fannie May?" asked John B. "A school-teacher may not be welcome on a cattle drive." He coughed a plug of phlegm into his handkerchief.

"If I had a gal like that, I wouldn't worry too much," his father replied. "That one seems tough enough. Bet she would be welcome in any chuckwagon."

"Pa, what do you know about cattle drivin'?"

"You were a youngster when I was conscripted to fight in the war against the North. Your ma and you looked after the farm as best you could. When the war ended, we had no money and no crops, and soldiers had burned everything but the house. So, I signed on with a cattle company for a few years. You and your ma took care of things while I was away. By the time I returned, you were twelve or thirteen and had rebuilt most of the fences and buildings. You learned a lot about carpenterin' without me teachin' you anything about livestock or crops."

"I have a lot to learn if I want to work as a trail hand."

"Son, you already know how to ride a horse. I assume you can shoot a gun, even though I ain't never seen it. But I have seen you go for days without food or water. 'Bout the only thing I can teach ya' is how to throw a rope."

Fannie May gasped for air when she set the saddle on the ground and looked up—it was over eighteen hands to the Clydesdale's back.

Barringer leaned against the rail fence while he watched her struggle. "I wish I could help you." He groaned as he tried to stand without the support of the fence.

"What's the matter, John B? Did I squeeze your head too hard between my legs?" asked Fannie May with a smirk. "I bet that took your mind off the noose around your neck."

"Not sure what was on my mind at the time. But I won't soon forget that vision."

"You and your visions."

"Still. I reckon it would be more fun without the rope," drawled John B.

"Stop fantasizing and keep your mind on healing!" declared Fannie May. When she touched the scars on Barringer's neck, she was flooded by a rush of emotion. She turned away to blink back tears. Suddenly, she bent down and jerked the saddle to her shoulder, then rested it against the side of the horse as she regained her composure. "I can take care of saddling Clyde until you heal up."

Clyde threw his head high to convey his displeasure. Barringer pulled down on the bridle and rubbed the big horse's face. Fannie May got her shoulder under the saddle and then heaved with both hands until her arms were fully extended. Still the saddle was barely balancing on the back of the horse. Both ends of the cinch and billet straps were dangling beside her. She held her left arm rigid and only after several attempts was she able to lob the straps over the horse so that they hung on the opposite side. With incredible speed she grabbed an end of the rear billet strap and pulled it under the horse, gripping it with both hands and putting her full weight on the strap until the saddle moved up and across the horse. Still puffing from the effort, she attached the buckle of the rear billet. Now that the saddle was in place she was able to attach the front cinch and tighten all of the straps. Clyde inflated his body every time he felt her pull.

"OK, Clyde. This is not my first rodeo!" Fannie May exclaimed, as she poked a sharp elbow into the horse's side. At last she was able to tighten the straps properly. Turning to Barringer, she said, "I'll set things up with Sheriff Russell so that you can withdraw your five thousand dollars from the bank when you are healed."

"Thanks. But be careful. No tellin' what Chewy might try if he sees you. And Dora-lee is still blaming you for the loss of our good friend, Mr. Wills."

"I have a plan, John B," whispered Fannie May. "Those two won't bother us."

"Just don't be breakin' the law," mused John B. "I don't want to see that pretty neck on the end of another noose."

"A neck that's not so pretty now," said Fannie May, pulling down the kerchief hiding her rope burns.

"Pa will sell me a horse and I'll meet up with you in Llano next week. A pack horse. So down the road, we'll get you a proper trail horse."

Fannie May threw her arms around her man. "John B, I just want to wake up beside you every morning."

John B flinched when her arms pressed against his injured neck. "Well, my kin may not be regular churchgoers, but they are still afeared when it comes to unmarried acts of procreation."

"Acts of procreation can wait until you are healed. Still, I miss being at your side."

"I reckon I will get healed enough to share a bed in time," whispered John B.

They embraced silently for minutes, each thinking about the time they would be apart and the road that lay ahead.

22

Llano, Texas, 1886

School has opened, and the children are rushing down to Huntstable and Mooe's shoe store by the hundreds to buy their solar tip shoes that never rip and hardly ever wear out— prices for the best are $1.25 for 5s to 7s, $1.50 for 8s to 10 ½ and $2 for 11s to 12s.

—Dallas Daily Herald, **Dallas, Texas, October 12, 1886**

As she rode away, Fannie May wondered if John B noticed that Clyde was no longer sporting white feathers at the ankles. Most locals identified his big black horse by the three white ankles. Discreetly, Fannie May had blackened them to avoid being associated with the horse's owner.

On the trail to Llano, Fannie May couldn't help but wonder what was happening at the Bluffton schoolhouse. By now, her replacement would have cleaned up the mess from the lynch mob. Students should be back at their desks. She would miss the laughs and cries and squeals of the children. Wiping a tear from her eye, she refocused on the need to recover John B's money. They were still in danger from the lynch mob and the five-thousand-dollar cash withdrawal would be additional bait.

"Sheriff, what time does the bank open in the morning?"

The sheriff looked up from his desk to see a woman standing in the doorway of the jailhouse. She was dressed in canvas pants and a Coulter shirt. Her hair was covered by an over-sized Stetson. The scar on her neck was only slightly visible above the neckerchief she wore. She carried a leather saddlebag with both pouches bulging. "I'll be jiggered. Is that you under there, Miss Fannie?"

"Yes, but let's keep that under your hat."

"Bank opens tomorrow at 10:00 am. You making a deposit?"

"No, John B needs to make a large withdrawal, and I assume the bank will need to bring in cash on the stage."

"Oh, yeah. 'Spect everyone around here knows about that five thousand he got for selling his mine." The Sheriff lit his pipe while he pondered the transaction. "Well, if you like, it might be best if I go inquire on his behalf."

"Thanks. It might be safer if I stay here. Can you put me in a cell till you get back?"

"If you reckon that's necessary. You remember John B's favorite cell. Help yourself."

Sheriff Russell set the smoldering pipe in the dark glass ashtray on his desk before hoisting his bulk off the chair. He fumbled for the keys on his belt and then led Fannie May to a cell at the back corner of the jailhouse. After the sheriff unlocked the iron gate, Fannie May quickly entered the cell and closed the door.

"Do you want me to lock you in there?" asked the sheriff. "I will only be gone for a few minutes."

"Yes. I will feel safer if you do. But leave me the key, if you would."

Sheriff Russell shrugged his shoulders and disconnected the ring of keys from his belt. "I don't see no harm in that. Here you go," agreed the sheriff before leaving for the jail.

Fannie May sat on the hard bed frame, thinking about the times she had visited John B in this very cell. Those were tense times including the night they slept together. She wondered whether the times ahead would be better or worse. Just the same, Fannie May knew that she would face anything to be with John B.

Barringer was massaging the side of his neck with a balm his mother had made from pork fat and wild plants. After several applications, he was convinced that the rancid odor overpowered the soothing effect.

"I saw Fannie May riding out on Clyde this morning," stated Old Jack, standing at the window. "Where to?"

"She needs to get our affairs in order so we can hit the trail."

Old Jack nodded, then turned his gaze down to his son's neck. "It's gonna leave a mark."

"'Fraid so," agreed his mother. "Our boy is marked for life now."

When John B finished applying the ointment, he stood to face his parents.

"It's not the mark that makes the man!" declared John B. "It's up to the man to make his mark."

"How do you plan to do that?" inquired his father. "Looks to me like you are running from your troubles."

"I can't help how it looks any more than I can erase these scars. But with Fannie May, I can make a life somewhere else."

"Did ya do it?" His father was demanding an answer.

"Did I do what?"

"Did ya kill the rail boss?"

"No! I did not kill anyone!" shouted John B. "Why do you always think the worst of me?"

"But ya know who did," surmised Old Jack Barringer.

John B had no response to placate his father. The truth was too incredible. Two men had perished at the hands of persons close to him. John B knew who had shot the rail boss. He knew who had restrained the Westinghouse engineer and left him for dead. He knew the fate of another person who had gone missing. But John B would go to his grave before he revealed this to another living soul.

23

Llano, Texas, 1886

Recently the citizens of the town [Llano] have been disturbed at night by some person or persons going out of town, full of "red-eye" and giving the "war-whoop," and turning their "bull-dogs" loose and shooting into houses. A 44-caliber ball now rests in the end of the Methodist church. We are sorry that these "desperadoes" can't go to Mexico, or some other foreign land, to do their shooting and yelling.

—*Fort Worth Daily Gazette,* Fort Worth, Texas, January 13, 1886

When Sheriff Russell returned to the jailhouse, he tried to hide the grin under his mustache. He leaned on the cell bars as he said, "Good news from the bank manager. He says that he can use Western Union to send the money to Winslow by telegraph. I think his words were 'wire the money to Winslow.'"

"Do you really believe that?" asked Fannie May. "Sounds like snake oil to me."

"The man claims Western Union has been doing it for years, even though this here bank has never done one. So, I said why not give it a try."

"Sheriff. Get over there and stop that wire transfer."

"Don't you believe in this modern world?" asked Sheriff Russell.

"I can't believe that you do. Now please get a move on."

The sheriff burst out laughing. Then he doubled over and leaned on the bars of the cell.

"What's so funny?" asked Fannie May. "I'm going to go over to that bank myself."

"Ho ho ho. You should'a seen the look on your face, Miss Fannie. I was pullin' your leg. Oh God, I figgered I'd let you go over to the bank all riled up. But I can see now that might have been a bad idea."

"Sheriff Russell. You son of a biscuit-eater. What the heck did you expect? You may as well have told me that money grows on trees in Winslow."

The sheriff stood up, panting to catch his breath.

"I could not resist. Imagine sending paper money down a wire. Reckon they roll it up real thin and push it along the wire? Ha! Who suckers in for that?"

"So did you actually arrange anything with the bank?"

"Banker says he can have a shipment of money coming by stage with two days' notice. So let the bank know what denominations and when John B can sign for that five thousand dollars."

"Thanks. John B will be pleased when he gets to town."

"Let yourself out of the cell," mumbled the sheriff.

"No, I am staying here until John B comes for me."

"Well, why don't you stay at a proper hotel?" asked the sheriff, as he noticed the schoolteacher's tangled hair. "Get cleaned up and eat some proper food and drink."

"You are putting me on. Half of the people in the hotel were in the mob that tried to lynch us. I'd sooner be hungry and tired behind these bars."

"Land sakes, Miss Fannie. You are one stubborn woman. Now give me those keys."

"I'm keeping the one for my cell," declared Fannie May. She broke open the key ring and put one key in her pants and passed the others through the bars. "Sheriff, I need a good rest. I'll skip breakfast tomorrow. Can you check to see I am awake in the afternoon?"

"Suits me. I am in the courthouse tomorrow morning. I'll lock the front door so you won't be disturbed. Although, someone will bring you lunch around noon." The sheriff went back to his desk, shuffled some papers, then locked the front door of the jailhouse on his way out.

Fannie May lay on the hard cot, contemplating her plans for the bank. Sleep came in less than forty winks.

When the morning sunlight entered her cell, Fannie May sat up on the cot, splashed some water on her face and brushed her hair. She pulled the clothes that she had borrowed from Ma Barringer—undergarments, skirt, blouse, gloves and bonnet—out of her saddlebag and quickly changed her appearance. Fannie May adjusted her bonnet in a mirror to ensure the straps covered the remaining rope marks on her neck. Except for some wrinkles in the blouse, she looked like a lady of means.

Fannie May unlocked her cell and walked out to the sheriff's office, where she found a key to unlock the front door. When she stepped onto the street, she resembled the wife of a wealthy rancher. She walked to a church next door to the bank. Inside, she sat in pew near a window where she could view the entrance to the bank. She took a pair of hymnals and pretended to read from one in case anyone else came into the sanctuary. At 10:00 am, she saw the front door of the bank open and the bank manager step onto the wooden sidewalk. The man checked his pocket watch, tightened his suspenders, and then doubled back into the building.

Fannie May rose from her seat and went directly to the bank, where she was greeted by a teller.

"How can I help you, ma'am?" asked the tall clean-shaven man behind the wicket.

"I would like to see the manager about opening a new account," lied Fannie May. "My name is Frances Henderson."

The manager came to the front promptly after the teller announced the visitor's name.

"Hello, Miss Henderson. Is it Miss or Mrs.?"

"It's Miss. And to whom do I have the pleasure?" asked Fannie May, extending her gloved hand for the manager to kiss.

"I am Mr. Sutherland, the manager in charge of this financial institution. Welcome to my office."

The manager was charmed to meet such a beautiful and sophisticated woman. Such a woman was not common among his customers, and he wanted to make an impression. "Are you any relation to the Frances Henderson that was the wife of the first governor of Texas?"

"Why, yes. Such a remarkable woman," lied Fannie May. "And as my aunt she was an inspiration."

Now that Sutherland was suitably impressed, Fannie May described to him the service that she hoped his bank could provide. She explained that she had inherited some land which was about to be sold for one thousand dollars in one-dollar bills. She wanted to deposit the money on the Tuesday of the following week.

"Are you sure that your deposit does not include any silver dollars or gold coins?"

"Why, yes. I would not be able to lift a load of silver dollars. Paper notes are legal tender, are they not?"

"Oh, indeed. Paper money is the way of the future. It's just that many people in Texas have been slow to adopt paper money since 'The Crime of '73'. You are much too young to remember that time, but folks here in Texas tend towards coins of gold and silver since then. Hard currency, you see."

"Yes, I was only a girl in pigtails back then. But I did read something about that in the history books. I believe the sequence of events was over-expansion, major disasters like the Chicago fire, and then the government raised interest rates, causing railways to go bankrupt and workers to go on strike."

"Well, I am impressed, Miss Henderson. You appear to be familiar with the monetary situation."

"And yet I am still prepared to consider paper money as legal tender. I should give my head a shake," laughed Fannie May.

The manager chuckled politely and then asked her to fill in a signature card before he gave her a ledger book for her account.

As they stood to say goodbye, Fannie May asked, "How big will that deposit be? Will I need a footlocker to carry that much money?"

"Oh no, you would be surprised how compact paper money is when it is properly stacked," assured the manager. "I always like to say that five hundred bills will take up the same space as both testaments in the Bible beside your bed."

"I value your reverence," advised Fannie May. "So my deposit will be about the same size as two Bibles."

"Exactly, and just as easy to carry."

"Oh, but I should have a proper bag to carry the money. So it doesn't get spilled or caught in a breeze. What do you suggest?"

"We have canvas bags with drawstrings that we typically use to transport coins. I can give you one of those," volunteered the manager. He reached under a counter and pulled out a white canvas bag with "First National Bank" printed on it.

"I am much obliged, Mr. Sutherland. I will see you next week." Fannie May gave a subtle curtsy.

"Our pleasure. We look forward to your deposit on Tuesday, Miss Henderson."

Fannie May walked from the bank to the mercantile. She was careful to keep her face lowered behind the brim of her bonnet. She preferred to be incognito during this week in Llano. After the other customers had left the store, she paid the merchant for a pad of writing paper and three envelopes. When she noticed several cans of chewing tobacco on the glass counter, an idea came to Fannie May.

"Do you know a man called Chewy? Does he buy chewing tobacco here?"

"Shor do. Young whippersnapper. Always got a wad in his craw."

"Can you tell him that Professor Badu has a message for him?" She set some coins on the counter as she asked the question.

"If'n I see Chewy, I will tell him to look up the piano player."

"I am beholding to you," remarked Fannie May as she left the business.

Fannie May walked to the train station and entered the telegraph office. She hoped the telegraph operator did not recognize her from a previous visit. The operator was heads down, receiving a transmission and converting the Morse code to characters of the alphabet. Fannie May printed a message on one of the forms on the counter and placed it in a woven basket. After a few minutes, the tapping stopped. The operator tapped a few more words to acknowledge, then reached up for the basket.

He read the message aloud to confirm what Fannie May had written.

"To Pinkerton Detective Agency, stop." The operator raised one eyebrow. "Accomplice in the Llano rail-boss murder has admitted to pulling trigger. Stop. Goes by Chewy. Stop. At Dabb's Hotel Llano. Stop. Other residents in danger. Stop. Sincerely Miss Dora-lee. Stop."

The operator counted the words and looked up. "That will be two dollars on account of the urgency."

Fannie May passed two dollars and twenty-five cents across the counter, keeping her eyes lowered. Then she asked, "Can you type a copy for me?"

Fifteen minutes later, Fannie May was back in the jail-house, writing notes.

Dora-lee frequently delivered the lunch meal from the Dabb's to the jailhouse and just as frequently enjoyed conversation with a hungover trail hand or a rogue gambler who was temporarily in custody. But when Dora-lee walked into the jail with lunch for a female prisoner, both women were surprised.

"So maybe there is justice in the world," chuckled Dora-lee. "The schoolmarm is behind bars after cheating the lynch mob."

"If it's justice you seek, then turn yourself in for stealing my clothes. Starting with that dress you have on."

Dora-lee shrugged. "I took the whole trunk. Some of the other ladies in the crowd emptied your boxes and chest of drawers. No use letting them go to waste."

"Sorry, I don't have anything here for you to take."

"I'd be satisfied if you would admit you and your lover pinned a murder on Andrew Wills. He would still be alive and well."

"That old Scot may not have committed murder, but his fate was the result of too many empty bottles of bourbon," Fannie May responded. "I pity you for your lost lover. In fact, I forgive you for your role in the lynching attempt."

For a moment, Dora-lee looked surprised. Then she grinned and spat on the lunch. "Hope you're hungry." She slid the plate under the door of the cell.

"I wrote a letter to you this morning," stated Fannie May, as she pulled an envelope from her blouse. "Please take it."

The frustrated harlot took the envelope and strutted back to the Dabb's Hotel. There, she sat at her dressing table and opened the handwritten letter.

> *Dearest Dora-lee,*
>
> *I was your friend and peer in the past when we worked in Paris, Texas. And I know you loved Andrew Wills. He was a good friend to John Barringer, and I have made every effort to honor that friendship. The trial should not have found guilt with either man. In the meantime, John B has received a written confession from the actual killer. I value your friendship and have some money to prove it. If you come to the bank next Tuesday at 10:30 AM, I will give you $1000 and the letter of confession to clear Andrew's name. In any event, you will never see John Barringer or myself after Tuesday.*
>
> *Sincerest regards,*
>
> *Fannie May Henderson*

Sheriff Russell returned to the jailhouse shortly after lunch, as planned. His morning had been squandered waiting for a judge to sort out water rights between a grain farmer and a cattle rancher. Back in his office, the lawman pulled some biscuits and jerky out of his desk and called that lunch. As he gnawed on a slab of jerky, he walked back to the cell where Fannie May was lodged. There was a plate of stew and bread sitting on the floor of the cell.

"I see the caterer has brought you lunch. It's getting cold there, Miss Fannie," he observed.

"Yes, but the server was a surprise. Dora-lee brought that plate over from the Dabb's and I am not sure I am brave enough to cat it."

"Suit yer self. I don't blame you for being suspicious, but there ain't no other food comin' for ya."

"Well, why don't we trade?" suggested Fannie May, pointing at the sheriff's slab of jerky.

"That's a good idea," chuckled the sheriff as he handed the jerky through the bars. "In fact, I'll just have the Dabb's make lunch for both of us tomorrow, and then Dora-lee won't know which one to put the poison in. Never realized what a goddamn perdicament having a woman in jail might turn out to be," he murmured, as he swiped a finger through the beef stew and poked it in his mouth.

"Can I ask you to deliver a note to Professor Badu?" Fannie May pulled a sealed envelope out of her pocket. "Just thought I should let him know I'm in town."

The sheriff nodded and took the envelope, "Should see the professor later tonight. Reckon he owes me a drink."

That Friday evening, Dora-lee had regular patrons in her room, one after another. Her last patron of the night was Chewy. He was young and vigorous, but he was quick—usually in and out in less than fifteen minutes. But he always paid for a full hour.

Even before Chewy was off of her, Dora-lee was lost in thoughts about the offer from Fannie May. Despite this night of steady traffic, she would be scraping the bottom of the barrel to pay for her hotel room at the end of the week. And she had been scrounging leftovers from the kitchen when nobody was watching. With the end of summer, cattle drovers had moved on to places such as Wichita, Newton, and Dodge City. No more of their hard-earned money would be coming her way.

Chewy had left his boots on, this night, which apparently reduced the time required to get dressed. Dora-lee was still pulling her under-trousers over her aching thighs when Chewy flipped two silver dollars onto her dressing table. Then he dug around his vest pocket until he found a tin of tobacco and proceeded to stuff a wad into his cheek. Chewy waited and watched while Dora-lee wiped some of his greasy yellow drool from her neck and bosom.

"I'll be back next week. Are you gonna miss me?" grinned Chewy.

The offer from Fannie May flashed across her mind, and Dora-lee announced, "I am going to be out of town next week." She avoided looking at the loathsome man. "You best check with one of the other girls."

"Out of town? You are gonna miss me, ain't ya," declared Chewy, as he tightened his belt. "But make sure you come back quick so you can get some more of little Chewy."

Dora-lee was holding the soiled handkerchief between two fingers like she was holding a dead skunk by the tail. When she heard Chewy close the door, she carried the ruined article to a waste basket. "Fuck you, Chewy, and the horse you rode in on!" murmured Dora-lee to the empty room. "And Fannie May, too." Dora-lee decided it was unreasonable to seek revenge on someone who was prepared to buy forgiveness. Vengeance would not bring back that sweet old Scotsman who made her laugh. But with a thousand dollars, she might find the company of another man in another town.

At the bar in the Dabb's saloon, Professor Badu was enjoying a glass of beer with the sheriff. The lawman gave Fannie May's envelope to Badu, but the latter did not open it. The two men leaned on the bar, conversing about the lynching attempt that had been made at the Bluffton School.

"This is unbelievable," ventured Badu. "I understand the school board firing the schoolteacher when they discovered her shady past. But that's not a hanging offense."

"No argument here," agreed the sheriff. "Mighty extreme and just as illegal. There are no laws that say former harlots can't become schoolteachers."

"Do you think they were really after Barringer, and Miss Fannie was considered a conspirator?"

"There were some in the crowd that were under that impression," agreed the sheriff. "Here comes one now, fresh off a harlot."

"You mean Chewy?" asked Badu.

"Yeah, he fashioned the nooses, at the bidding of Dora-lee."

"Can you arrest him?"

"For what? Attempted lynching?" laughed the sheriff. "I am doubtful that it would get far in court. In the end, I'd just be poking a stick in his cage."

"Looks like he wants to poke your cage. He's coming over here."

Chewy's spurs jingled as he walked, bow-legged, towards the bar. He approached Badu and said, "Just the guy I'm looking for. Professor Badu."

"W-why?" stammered Badu, looking back and forth between Chewy and the sheriff.

"OK, Chewy. What d'ya you want with the Professor?" demanded the sheriff.

"He's got a message for me."

"W-what message?" questioned Badu.

"Some lady has been leaving word around town. Told me to pick up a message from Badu. Probably some gal too shy to come in here." Chewy spat a gob on the floor and ground it under his boot. "You gents know the ladies tend to fancy me. Reckon it's a love note," chuckled the scoundrel.

Badu grimaced as he pulled the envelope out of his pocket. Inside, there was a short note and a folded envelope labeled "Chewy." Badu read the note and kept it to himself.

Dear Professor,

*Please pass the enclosed envelope to Chewy
when he asks for it. Please do not mention
who sent it to you. I can explain if you visit
me while I am in custody.*

Regards, Fannie May Henderson

Badu handed the smaller envelope to Chewy and folded the note back into his pocket.

"Need someone to read that for you, Chewy?" asked the sheriff.

"Nah, I figger there ain't no big words in there. You know. Big words like trumped-up charges," laughed Chewy, as he walked out into the dark street. He was curious to read the anonymous note, so he wandered over to the railway camp where some of the immigrant workers were sitting around a campfire.

"'Scuse me, coolies. I just need to borrow some light."

The workers mumbled in their foreign language and disappeared into their tents. Chewy sat alone by the fire and removed the telegram from the envelope. After he read it several times, he realized that Dora-lee was pinning the murder of the rail boss on him.

"Tarnation! That low-down slut!" mumbled Chewy as he walked away from the fire. "So, she's going out of town. Bitch is skipping town and framing me." As he headed down the street, he wondered why Dora-lee would resort to this fabrication. Then it came to him: there must be a reward for this information. Dora-lee was falsely accusing him of murder to collect a reward. Well, he was not going to stand for that. Chewy knew that he was fortunate to be forewarned of Dora-lee's treachery. But he never questioned the source of the telegram or the motive behind it.

On the seventh day of her stay in Llano, Fannie May asked the sheriff if he had any glue. When he handed the jar to her, she asked him to leave her alone in the jailhouse while she got dressed and spiffed for a trip to the bank. He noticed a pair of black hymnals on Fannie May's bed. As far as the glue was concerned, he decided not to ask questions. The less he knew about the dressing habits of the female species, the better.

Fannie May proceeded to modify the two hymnals she had filched from the church only days before. She carefully removed the covers and spines from the bound pages. Then she glued some dollar bills on the front and back pages. The stack of pages now appeared, at first glance, to be a pile of dollar bills—a pile the same weight and size as one thousand paper dollars. She packed the phony money in the canvas deposit bag that had the name of the bank stenciled on it.

Utilizing the hymnal covers, Fannie May created two small boxes that looked like hymnals to the untrained eye. The top end of each was a paper flap, which could be opened to allow a pack of bills to slide inside.

Fannie May quickly pulled on the frock that she had worn on her previous recess from the hoosegow. "I'm ready, Sheriff Russell."

24

Llano, Texas, 1886

Llano, Tex., March 19.—E. L. Houghton, Esq., one of the leading attorneys of this county, was killed on the 16th inst., in San Saba county, about thirteen miles south of the town of San Saba, on the road leading from that place to Llano. Mr. Houghton left Llano on Tuesday, the 16th inst., for San Saba in company with William Van, for the purpose of defending a young man by the name of Bybee, who was charged with theft of a horse. Tuesday night they stopped at Van's house in Cherokee, and on Wednesday morning proceeded to San Saba and attended the preliminary examination of Bybee, who was acquitted. Some time after noon the three started for Llano, Houghton and Van in a buggy and Bybee on horseback. When within about two miles of Cherokee, Bybee, the only eye-witness of the tragedy, says Houghton and Van got into a dispute about who should drive the team. Bybee, who was riding a little distance in advance, returned to the buggy and tried to get the men to settle the difficulty, when Van became angry and threatened to shoot him for interfering, at the same time raising his Winchester and firing. Bybee rode away a short distance to a clump of trees and underbrush, and, on looking back, saw Van standing on the right hand side of the team, gun in hand, Houghton, sitting in the buggy, with one hand on his forehead, and at the instant he heard Houghton say, "Shoot, if you want to, you can't hit anything." Van now fired, the ball striking Houghton in the breast ranging downward a little and coming out near the lower point of the shoulder blade, and the body of E.L. Houghton, who had left his wife and three sprightly little children the day before in the vigor of his early manhood, fell to the ground a lifeless mass, the victim of a drunken, cowardly dastard. Van escaped to the brush and is still at large. The remains were brought here yesterday evening and interred at 6 pm., by the impressive services of the Episcopal church, Rev. Dr. Stanley officiating. This is another one added to the long list of those who have died at the hands of the cold-blooded murderer and assassin.

We have had a nice warm shower of rain to-day, and consequently people are in fine spirits, all anticipating a good crop year and prosperous times.

—*Fort Worth Daily Gazette*, Fort Worth, Texas, March 23, 1886

Barringer had received a letter from Fannie May with instructions to arrive at the Llano bank by 10:00 am on Tuesday. He trusted she had a plan that would allow them to withdraw the five thousand dollars from the bank and then take a powder. By now, he expected that the failed lynching attempt was a Llano County legend. There would be questions asked by anyone who knew him, whether they could see the scars or not. Barringer was counting on the colors of his red polka-dot neckerchief to camouflage his injuries. Were he to encounter suspicious strangers, his pat explanation would be that he had been attacked by highwaymen, who had hanged him from a tree, and that, fortunately, a battalion of soldiers had arrived minutes later to chase off the outlaws and cut down the lynch rope.

John B planned to reunite with his cherished horse, Clyde, at the Llano livery stable. In the meantime, Old Jack Barringer provided him a buckskin quarter-horse for the trip west. In return, John B turned over the reins to his wagon. The two-year-old buckskin was well-muscled, especially in the hind quarters, and would make an excellent pack horse. As he rode the path to Llano, with the sun on his back, John B was glad to be back in the saddle, despite some lower body injuries that needed time to heal. He checked his pocket watch and estimated that he would be at the bank a few minutes early.

At 9:55 am, Barringer stood beside the buckskin filly waiting for the bank to open. He watched his bride-to-be walk up to the front entrance with the sheriff on her arm. At the appointed time, the manager unlocked and opened the door to the bank allowing Fannie May and the sheriff to enter. Barringer promptly joined them inside the building.

The manager noticed that Fannie May was carrying a cash bag which had obvious heft. His expectation was a large deposit from the distinguished lady. She explained that she would not be depositing until later that day and that she was merely sharing the company of Sheriff Russell and Mr. Barringer during the latter's large withdrawal.

"Oh, I see," acknowledged the bank manager, although he had no idea what he saw. "Mr. Barringer, I am glad you brought the sheriff. It's not every day that a client withdraws five thousand dollars. We trust that your business here today is confidential."

"Yes. Now shall I sign for the withdrawal?" asked Barringer.

"Sign these two pages where it says 'account holder," said the banker, as he presented the papers.

After signing, Barringer said, "I would be obliged if you provide a cash bag like the one this lady is holding."

The banker brought the stacks of five-dollar bills to the wicket and let the teller count them as Barringer looked on. The sheriff was keeping a wary eye on the front door to prevent any unwanted disturbance during this drawn-out process.

Across the street from the bank, two men dismounted and tied their horses beside Barringer's buckskin. One man had a heavy black beard. The other had a scar from his nose up to his left ear. As they watched from across the street, they noticed a third man appear in the narrow gap between the bank and the saddlery store. That man was holding his right hand tucked in his vest.

The two strangers stepped back into the shadow of their horses. "What the hell is Chewy doing here?" asked Blackbeard.

"Probably same as us," growled Scar-face. "Ain't no secret that five thousand dollars is going to hit the street."

"I'm not splitting nothin' with Chewy."

"Let's wait for him to make his move. He might do the dirty work for us."

"Agreed. As long as that sum-bitch don't leave here with the money," said Blackbeard.

They looked towards the sound of a buggy coming up the street. It stopped directly in front of the bank, blocking their view of the door. They saw the bank door open and a man's boots appeared on the opposite side of the carriage. A woman's shoes and long dress descended next to the boots.

Blackbeard and Scar-face waited to hear any conversation between the hidden parties.

"Stay right there, Dora-lee," boomed the sheriff. "You can go into the bank as soon as Miss Fannie and Barringer complete their business." He looked up and down the street but took no notice of the strange horses tied on the opposite side.

Dora-lee stood silent and motionless.

"What's the harlot doing here?" asked Blackbeard overhearing the sheriff's instructions.

"Probably making a deposit from last night's earnings," whispered Scar-face.

"You watch Chewy," whispered Blackbeard. "I'll keep an eye on the harlot and the sheriff. See what happens when Barringer comes out of the bank."

"Keep yer eyes peeled for the schoolteacher," Scar-face cautioned. "Remember that Westinghouse man that paid me to steal some crystals from a feller in the Bluffton Hotel. He reckoned that Barringer couldn't teach a hen to cluck without that schoolmarm."

"Let's see which one come's out totin' the money and who's totin' the guns," answered Blackbeard.

When the bank door opened, Barringer was carrying a canvas cash bag. Fannie May had a hymnal in each hand. The sheriff stood between Dora-lee and the couple but kept his eyes on the harlot.

"I decided to take that money you offered, Miss Fannie," muttered Dora-lee.

Fannie May clasped both hymnals to her chest and screamed, "Don't shoot!" The shrill scream surprised everyone within earshot. The carriage horse bolted and the driver steered the carriage away from the bank.

Dora-lee did not flinch. She scowled at Fannie May.

Fannie May raised both hands above her head, still holding the hymnals, while a bewildered John B gawked at her. The sheriff kept his eyes on Dora-lee's hands but saw no weapon.

"Give her the reward money, John B!" yelled Fannie May with fear in her voice. "Give her all of it!"

Dora-lee shrugged at the clamor and shouted, "Don't know what yer game is. Just give me the money and that letter of confession. Like you promised!"

"Give her what she wants, John B!" screeched Fannie May. "You know she means it!"

Barringer obeyed and dropped the bag at Dora-lee's feet. Then he slowly raised his hands high.

Fannie May stepped in front of the sheriff before he could draw his sidearm. "No need for the gun, Sheriff," she said calmly.

Dora-lee picked up the bag. "Just getting what I bin promised." Then she hiked up her skirt, and chased after the carriage.

Fannie May lowered her arms and whispered, "Let her go, Sheriff. I did promise that bag to her."

"What the hell?" cried John B. "She's getting away with *my* money."

"Trust me, John B. She's not getting away with anything," Fannie May murmured as she tapped the hymnals against each other.

Dora-lee had almost reached the carriage when Chewy emerged from his hiding place, and standing directly in her path, shouted, "Stop right there, bitch." He pulled his pistol out from his vest and waved it at the cash bag while he extended his left palm. "Hand over that bag. You're not going to spend a dime of that reward."

"What are you talking about, you dumb bastard? What reward?"

"The reward money for sending me up the creek. For that rail boss that got shot."

"That's not what this money is for. Besides you didn't shoot that man. Fannie May gave me this money to leave her alone."

"Likely story. The same Fannie May that you and I were fixin' to string up?" asked Chewy. "I ain't that dumb."

"Well, I am not stupid enough to give you this bag," responded Dora-lee, holding it behind her back. She noticed Chewy's eyes were fixed on her chest. Apparently, he was distracted by the exposed skin where the dress buttons restrained her bosom. When Chewy tried to reach around her, Dora-lee wrapped her free arm around Chewy's right arm. She was no stranger to a fight, and had a few pounds on the scoundrel. Tugging on the canvas bag, moving in circles along the street, they looked more like partners in a promenade than hooligans fighting over loot.

Bang! The gun went off. Dora-lee released her grip and fell onto the gravel-covered street. As Chewy stood there with brown drool running down his cheek, Dora-lee kicked him in the ankle.

"You stupid ass," screamed Dora-lee. "Take the damn bag. And go get the doctor before I bleed to death." A red stain spread slowly through her dress just below her left thigh.

Chewy yanked the bag away from her and asked, "After what you done to me? Why should I care if you bleed to death?" Then he headed for his hiding place between the buildings with the cash bag in one hand and his gun in the other.

Blackbeard stepped out of the saddlery, his pistol leveled at Chewy. "I'll take that bag."

Startled, Chewy's first reaction was to swing his pistol towards the voice. Two shots rang out. Chewy, still gripping the money bag, stumbled backwards and fell on top of Dora-lee.

"Got what you deserved, asshole," she groaned, then yelled, "Someone get this son of a bitch off me. And get a doctor."

Fannie May gripped John B by the arm to hold him in the doorway of the bank. The sheriff went to assist Dora-lee, silently waving his sidearm at the bearded man who had shot Chewy.

Scar-face came into view from the opposite side of the street with a rifle leveled. "Stand your ground, lawman," he commanded. "I would not shoot the sheriff—unless I have to."

Blackbeard laughed. "And we know the undertaker don't have a box wide enough fer ya."

The sheriff dropped his pistol and stood beside Dora-lee with his hands at his side. Blackbeard yanked the money bag from Chewy's dead hand, walked across the street and tucked the sack into a saddlebag. Scar-face kept his rifle aimed at the sheriff until Blackbeard had saddled up and towed a horse over to him. Then the two robbers hightailed it west in a cloud of dust.

Lying in a puddle of blood, Dora-lee continued to make demands, but her voice was quieter now, and garbled. Sheriff Russell kneeled beside the wounded woman and rolled Chewy's dead body to the side. When he pulled a flask from his vest pocket and poured a swig into Dora-lee's quivering lips, she could barely swallow. The sheriff saw fear in her wide eyes that he had never seen—fear far greater than the woman had ever experienced.

Before long, the sheriff returned to the bank entrance where Barringer and Fannie May were sheltering. "You two get out of here before someone decides you were involved. I'll get the preacher for Dora-lee. Don't reckon the doc can put all that blood back in her."

Clutching two hymnals, Fannie May hugged the sheriff and asked, "Who were those wicked men?"

"The Van brothers. I recognize Willy as the one with the scar. I've got a poster wanting him for past misdeeds," growled Sheriff Russell.

"We are beholdin' to you, Sheriff," Fannie May pressed some paper bills into his hand. "I have to say good-bye to Dora-lee."

Barringer shook the lawman's hand and said, "Take care of yourself and the Professor."

Fannie May walked over to the wounded Dora-lee, and knelt close to her, careful to avoid the pool of blood. "Dora-lee. Where's the list?"

"Waah. Gwah." gurgled Dora-lee struggling to breathe.

Fannie May felt along the hem of the dress that Dora-lee was wearing—*a* dress that Dora-lee had stolen from the schoolhouse. Fannie May found a buttoned pocket on the inside of the hem exactly where she expected. She deftly opened the pocket and removed a folded piece of notepaper. Both women knew the significance of that folded paper.

Dora-lee took a feeble swing at Fannie May and then stopped moving. Fannie May stood and walked back to where Barringer and the sheriff were standing.

"What in tarnation did you say to Dora-lee?"

"I just told her that the dress looked better on me."

Before Tuesday noon, Sheriff Russell had witnessed a bank robbery, recorded the murder of a venerable prostitute, documented the shooting of a local ne'er-do-well, and released two bodies to the undertaker. He believed that he had earned his pay that Tuesday. He spent the rest of the day in the Dabb's saloon gilding the tale of the Llano bank robbery of '86.

25

Dallas, Texas, 1886

We say western cattle trade, because after all the impressive fact of the convention, though it included stockmen from all parts of the Union was this—that the vast area of trans-Mississippi territory from Texas to Montana has already become the great cattle raising ground of the world and yet, while this industry is assuming such gigantic proportions, in view of the largely undeveloped resources of the west, it may still be said to be in its infancy. As it has been well summarized, some idea of the magnitude of the interests represented can be gathered from that statement that west of the Mississippi there are not less than 23,000,000 head of cattle being fed and ranging on the grazing grounds of Texas, New Mexico, Colorado, and the other states and territories, and west of the Rocky mountains. The capital represented by these herds is simply stupendous.

—"The Cattle Convention," *The Emporia Weekly News*, Emporia, Kansas, November 27, 1884

Cotton MacLachlan sat at the bar, watching the bubbles float through amber liquid to form a white topping on his full glass of beer. He had given the bartender two bits and told him to keep the beer glass full while he waited for the evening crowd to straggle in.

At twenty-two years, Cotton was one of the youngest lead hands at a cattle ranch. But he had demonstrated his ability working at the Double Lightning Cattle Company for the last six years. During that time, the ranch had experienced range wars, Indian attacks, organized rustlers, Texas fever, and bad winters. None of the Texas ranchers had been spared from these disasters, yet they remained committed to raising beef cattle, driving them north to the rail-heads, and shipping the live animals to major cities in the east.

Cotton had been a dollar-a-day man on his first four cattle drives. After being promoted to trail boss the previous year, he had demonstrated his competence to the owners of the ranch. There were bigger men and meaner men, but Cotton had never lost a hand-to-hand fight. Even when angry drovers brought a knife or whip to a fight, Cotton had been able to bring the dispute to a satisfactory conclusion. Usually, the opponent backed down from the look in his eye, but there had been brief occasions when Cotton had to render his opponent unconscious with a swift kick to the jaw or a combination of blows.

Many drovers and ranch hands were not so devoted to the industry. There was a high turnover among the men who herded cattle out of Texas. The work was seasonal, so men had to have another source of income during the winter months. In many cases, this eventually drew them to a different vocation. The hazards of the job caused a high rate of attrition among even the most dedicated of cowboys. Pushing three thousand head of cattle for one hundred days over six hundred miles of hardship and danger could bring about a loss of enthusiasm, not to mention life and limb.

Cotton wondered whether he could convince any men to join his crew at this late date. Most of the dollar-a-day men were already on a drive. He hoped that some had returned from the spring drives, but any drover with experience knew that starting in September was flirting with bad weather in Kansas. So, he would need to offer those men more than the standard one hundred dollars at the completion of the drive. Either that or he would need to hire an inexperienced crew and train them along the trail. Cotton had been down that road in years past. And he knew greenhorns would slow down the drive and weaken morale.

Today, Cotton would rely on word of mouth among people in the saloons to give trail hands the lowdown. He had already recruited some elderly riders who had been on multiple drives. During his conversations he was surprised to hear the descriptions of two men who might be available. Apparently the men known as Bucktooth and Stubby had proven themselves on several cattle drives.

Cotton tipped back his glass of beer and ran his fingers through his tight blond curls to dry them. He placed his Stetson on his head, nodded to the bartender, and turned to view the men entering the saloon. He recognized two of them from a past altercation. Bucktooth seemed to have fewer teeth than Cotton recalled. Stubby had a new bandage covering his left ear.

"Looky here, Stubby," ribbed Bucktooth. "If'n it ain't the feller that showed you the sole of his boot, a ways back."

"I hear ya. Let's have a conflab with that boy," replied Stubby as they approached.

"You boys didn't come back for more, did ya?" asked Cotton.

"Maybe you ain't so tough when there's no womenfolk around," replied Bucktooth.

"I got a notion this youngster won't fight with his fists," said Stubby.

"Look, fellas. I would be glad to give you another lesson in street-fighting," stated Cotton. "But I would prefer to offer you a job."

"You pullin' my leg, mister?" asked Stubby.

Bucktooth got right to the point, "What kind of job?"

"Riding herd to Kansas," said Cotton. "Chisholm Trail."

"Reckon you're teasing the weather, ain't ya?" chuckled Bucktooth.

"Yah, how you going to pay us if snow flies early? Hell, last winter was early and some drives didn't make it past the ford on the Cimarron," added Stubby.

"Pay is one hundred dollars plus one dollar for every day that there is snow on the ground," answered Cotton.

"Whose payin'?"

"Double Lightning Ranch," Cotton said. "Hackett brothers' spread down on the Colorado. Day's ride east of Austin."

Stubby looked up at Bucktooth and shrugged. "Count us in. Do we need horses?"

"No need for horses. The Double Lightning will provide a remuda. If you got a horse here, sell it or board it." Cotton tipped back the rest of his beer and headed for the exit. He stopped with one hand on the swinging door and addressed the new recruits. "I'm taking drovers on my wagon down to the ranch in two days. Bring your pack. We leave at sundown."

Stubby, Bucktooth, and a few other cowboys nodded.

After Cotton was gone, Stubby asked, "Did any a'ya catch that feller's name?"

Another cowboy leaning on the bar spoke up. "MacLachlan. Cotton MacLachlan. Born in Dodge City but has been workin' on the Double Lightning since he could ride a horse. I've ridden flank for him a couple of drives. I figger you boys late to the game will probably ride drag."

Bucktooth stepped up to the bar, "You figger he means it about supplying the horseflesh? I'm partial to using my own ride when I can. That gelding is more like a brother to me."

"You fellas realize winter is likely comin' before you finish the drive," volunteered the bartender. "That's why they're providing the horses. If your ass gets too cold, you can't just ride away. Stealing a horse from the remuda might get you out of the cold and into a noose."

Stubby scratched his head, then said, "Well, if it's two bits a day to board a horse and I get paid a hundred dollars for a three-month drive, I reckon that's the same as workin' for only six bits a day."

"Seems we best be selling our horses in the next couple of days," muttered Bucktooth.

26

Waco, Texas, 1886

From Kansas City to this place there are at convenient distances most admirably conducted "Depot hotels," where the weary can rest as long as they like, sure of good meals and attendance at a fixed and reasonable charge, all under the management of the well known Fred Harvey, manager of hotels for the Atchison, Topeka & Sante Fe railroad.

—"A Boston Doctor in New Mexico," *Las Vegas Daily Gazette*, **Las Vegas, New Mexico, January 18, 1882**

Una sat on the chair beside a third-floor window of the private infirmary in Waco, her gaunt figure hidden within an over-sized hospital gown. She gazed out this window every day, hoping for some clue that would trigger her memory. Some clue that would give answers to the questions that tormented her. Was Una her real name? Where was her family? What had happened to her? Was she really eighteen years old? According to her nurses, Una had been in a coma until after her sixteenth birthday. They believed she came from someplace north of Waco.

The nurses described how the doctors had provided nutrition to her during the comatose period. Apparently, they had delivered remedies and fluids using tubes in

Una's rectum, nose and throat. Several doctors came to study her until, to their vapid satisfaction, Una regained consciousness. Then the doctors quit attending. Now that she was awake, Una was left in the care of two nurses. A local parish was funding her accommodation in the infirmary, but they were hopeful Una would regain her memory and return to her home.

Una lived within the cloth partitions around one of six beds on the third-floor. There was a sink and indoor privy. Una had never seen another patient since her awakening. For two years she had been struggling to regain her memory.

She was told her name was Una. Her nurses called her that. She had vague memories of a mother — she knew her only as "Mother". She remembered two young boys — maybe brothers — but no family names came to her. She had dreams of other people. Mostly her dreams were filled with older men. They called each other "Brother". None of these men had names but they conjured up feelings of guilt and vulnerability, feelings which lingered since regaining consciousness.

Through her window, Una would often see men, somber and stern men in dark suits, walking or riding along the streets of Waco. Like the men in her dreams, these men triggered only unhappy memories.

Una looked for clues among her meager possessions — a leather suitcase, clothes that no longer fit her growing body, an empty music box. When Una placed the music box on the windowsill, she noticed a scrap of newspaper tucked in the lining of the box. She retrieved it and read both sides: an article about storm damage in the Gulf of Mexico on one side and an advertisement for workers in a Dodge City restaurant on the other side. No date was visible on the clipping.

Una spent time reading books and periodicals supplied by the infirmary. When newspapers were available, Una read them front to back. Advertisements for workers in Harvey hotels and restaurants were prevalent in almost every issue. She wondered what was special about these restaurants that they needed so many workers. None of those ads mentioned Dodge City.

Una wondered why she had kept an advertisement for women to work in Dodge City. Why had she saved that particular clipping? There must have been something about the dining hall in Dodge City that had attracted her before her illness.

Una pinned the advertisement to the hem of her sleeve where she could retrieve it each morning. Silently, she would read the advertisement over and over again, hoping for a memory to emerge. *Are the clues to my past in Dodge City?*

"Where is Dodge City?" Una asked one of her nurses.

"It's north of here," said the nurse. "All the way up in Kansas. I have heard some drovers talk about going there."

"What do they do there?"

"Heavens, I guess they do whatever cowboys do after they have delivered a herd of cattle. It's a long trip for them. Heaven knows the kind of trouble a bunch of men can get into."

"Oh, what kind of trouble?" asked Una.

"I have no first-hand knowledge, as I have never been there," admitted the nurse. "But I do know one thing about men. Their manners do not improve when you get more than one in a room."

In the summer of 1886, Una was regaining strength. She believed that physically, she could survive outside the institution. As she watched the street, she recalled riding a horse but could not remember the color of the horse. The distant bawling of passing cattle drives reminded her of milking and feeding cows. She longed to leave the infirmary and contemplated joining a cattle drive going to Dodge City.

One fall evening she saw a wagon-load of cowboys stopped at the livery stable down the street. She watched as the men in the wagon untangled their limbs, climbed down, and straggled out of view. Then the driver of the wagon removed his hat to wipe the sweat from his brow.

Una gasped. Memories flooded her mind. The shocking white hair of this cowboy was intimately familiar to her. This man had saved her from two hooligans who had accosted her in the street. A street on the way to a barn or possibly a church. She had been on a wagon next to her mother. Her two brothers had been watching from the back of the wagon. There had been some confusion after church and that cowboy had given her a ride to her home.

And the name of that cowboy was clear in her memory: Cotton.

As Cotton was paying the livery man, he noticed a waif running across the street towards them. The woman was wearing an over-sized hospital gown. Her face was gaunt and partially obscured by her long red hair blowing in the breeze.

"Mr. Cotton. Wait. I need to talk to you, Mr. Cotton."

"Well, I reckon you could," Cotton mumbled, as he squinted towards the unfamiliar voice. "But I am baffled. Should I know you?"

"I know you!" replied Una, "I remember you! Please talk to me."

"Miss Una, is that you?"

"Yes. I am Una. And you are Mr. Cotton." Tears filled her eyes and she wrapped her arms around him and pushed her face against his shirt. "I think you know me. Please tell me how we know each other."

Cotton was confused by her words but nonetheless curious to know how the girl he met in Dallas had come to be in the Waco hospital. He held Una gently and whispered, "Let's get off the street. Can we talk inside the infirmary?"

Una stood back and motioned for him to follow her.

Across the street, Bucktooth elbowed Stubby and nodded towards the girl bundled around Cotton. "That piece of calico look familiar? Not dressed up this time."

"That was a while back. Looks like she's been rode hard," drawled Stubby.

On the walk to the infirmary, Cotton admitted to looking for Una several years ago. "I rode out to the Clark farm to ask about you. Your ma wouldn't tell me where you were but one of your brothers was out in the yard chasing chickens. He said you were gone because of a fever. But that's all he would say."

"The Clark farm! That's my name! Una Clark!" exclaimed the girl. "Tell me how we met. What else happened when we were together?"

As Cotton described their previous meeting, Una started to piece together the memory of her family. She remembered her mother and brothers. The events Cotton described were hazy but brought back feelings of guilt — feelings that were hard to comprehend when it was she who had been forsaken for the past four years. Regardless of the situation, Una was determined to start a new life. She was unsure where that life would be. She did not know how she would survive. Perhaps her future was in Dodge City. Perhaps she would become a Harvey Girl. But for now, Una knew in her heart that Cotton would keep her safe.

Una begged Cotton to take her on the cattle drive but sensed he was reluctant to have a frail young woman on the trail. She promised that she would not be a burden and that they could abandon her at any town along the way if she was not useful.

"I have no money, Mr. Cotton. But I promise to work for my keep."

"I reckon that might work. Can you cook and clean?"

"I don't remember. But I suspect I had to do those things at one time."

"Well, I reckon skill will come back to you," groaned Cotton. "Go pack your things and you can ride with us at daybreak."

27

A reliable rumor reached this place this evening that about 11 o'clock last night, by moonlight, two masked men entered the express office at Paige station, in Bastrop county, and leveled their pistols at Agent Nash and compelled him to open the safe. They got two or three dollars for their trouble. All of the contents were not disturbed. No clew or arrests as yet.

—*Fort Worth Daily Gazette*, Fort Worth, Texas, October 14, 1886

Barringer and Fannie May fled Llano along the stagecoach trail leading towards Fort Mason. The trail ran almost due west with minor diversions crossing creeks. At the end of August in 1886, the creeks were running low. Barringer kept a wary eye on the surrounding foliage whenever the couple was exposed in open stream crossings.

"Ya figger those bank robbers are out here?" asked Barringer, as he kept his head on a swivel. "If we come across them, we might have a chance to recover my money."

"That's highly probable," answered Fannie May. "They might even turn around when they open that money bag and discover they have only twenty dollars."

"What d'ya mean, twenty dollars?" challenged John B.

"The bag is weighed down with mostly paper," Fannie May explained. "When those bandits look inside, they will see what appears to be a stack of paper money. I glued some dollar bills onto the pages from two hymnals. You see, John B, I gave Dora-lee a few dollars and a pile of songs. That's what those robbers got away with."

"S'pose they try to divvy up the loot?"

"Then they will be pissed off at someone. I'm guessing they might come back looking for the rest of the money."

"So, is the money still in the bank?" asked Barringer.

Out of her saddlebag Fannie May pulled the two hymnals. She opened the loose flap on top of each to reveal the packs of bills inside.

John B laughed when he realized they had most of the money. Then he puckered his brow as he tried to retrace the sequence of events that morning. "When did you make the switch? The banker gave *me* a money bag to carry the five thousand."

"And then I asked if I could get a few dollars to buy a dress..."

"And that's when the sheriff went out to see Dora-lee arrive in the carriage. You had both money bags when everyone was distracted," conceded John B.

"That was good luck more than good planning. But it gave me time to take the money from your bag and slide it into these hymnals from the bag I was carrying. Then I stuffed my bag with the fake money packs into your empty money bag. If anyone looked inside they might assume that the extra money bag was there by mistake. It took me no time at all," gloated Fannie May.

"What if someone asked about the hymnals you were carrying?"

"I could say that I was on my way to return them to the church when we stopped at the bank. But it turned out that no one noticed nor cared about the hymnals."

"I suppose ya gave the sheriff a heads-up?" Barringer speculated.

"No, the sheriff and the banker still think the villains got away with our money. They are probably tacking up 'Wanted' posters as we speak."

The pair rode a few more miles before Barringer spoke again. "So, back at the bank, were those doings one of your three-cornered circles?"

"You mean Rock-Paper-Scissors tag. I would say that's true for the most part."

"Reckon you could explain your logic, now that it's bygone?"

"OK, the money was in the middle. Everyone in the circle was competing for the money. In my plan, Chewy was Rock. I gave him reason to suspect that Dora-lee had betrayed him. So, his greed brought him to the bank. He was on a full boil because he thought Dora-lee was accusing him of the murder that you were acquitted from."

"I assume you had a hand in that."

"Guilty as charged. Rock breaks Scissors. So, Dora-lee was Scissors. Dora-lee was motivated by fear. Any harlot over thirty knows her working days are numbered. She dreaded the prospect of growing old in a bordello. So,

Dora-lee was contemplating a way to retire. That could be by getting a bundle of money from Paper. Scissors cut Paper."

"But how did you know that Blackbeard and Scar-face would be there? Was they both Paper in your scheme?"

"No. They were a happy coincidence," reasoned Fannie May. "*I* was Paper until they showed up. I promised a thousand dollars to Dora-lee, which was really the fake money. For Paper to cover Rock, I planned that either the sheriff or I would shoot Chewy in self-defense or in revenge for Dora-lee. Turned out the Van brothers took over as Paper."

"Happy coincidence? In the great state of Texas?" queried John B.

"Paths cross, even in Texas, I suppose."

"But mighty dangerous to rely on that, Miss Fannie. Any one of those others might have shot you. Where was your gun?"

"Everyone suspected Dora-lee was fired up to finish what the lynch party started. But no one suspected that I had already neutralized her by offering a secret payment. Turned out a thousand dollars and her advancing years made her hatred go away."

"I am asking again. Where was your gun?"

"Well, I would have to borrow one from the sheriff, if he wasn't going to step in."

"Damn lucky those other scoundrels showed up to take your place. Sometimes you scare the shit out of me, Fannie May Henderson. Glad we are on the same team."

They both laughed. They had retained the money and avenged the attempted lynching. But a somber feeling came over John B as they rode. He wondered if he could protect his bride-to-be from peril on the trail. Despite her ingenuity, her fearlessness was a concern to him.

Fannie May had no concern about what lay ahead — assuming they acquired weapons and training. She doubted that John B and his old Navy five-shooter would be much help in a gunfight. Since her shotgun had been abandoned at the schoolhouse, the couple shared only Barringer's sidearm and the Winchester rifle.

"Have you ever traveled this way, John B?"

"Only as far as Fort Mason. Reckon we have no choice but to head north from there and leave hill country. That's where we're most likely to catch a late cattle drive. The cattle will slow down to graze once they get north of Peg-leg Crossing on the San Saba."

"I heard that most of the people in the town of Mason speak German," said Fannie May. "How do you propose we communicate?"

"Pa used to buy horses from the quartermaster at Fort Mason. The men there are U.S. Army. I assume they still speak our language. And as far as what I propose—I think that would be a dandy place to get hitched."

"Well, you are such a romantic. We can get married by an Army Captain and spend our honeymoon in the barracks," replied Fannie May sarcastically.

"I figgered that would make you happy."

"I am happy that I am pledged to you. And you are right. For the next one hundred days we are going to be more familiar with our horses than each other. I will marry you, John B. I will marry you in Fort Mason tomorrow."

"I have already bought you a wedding present."

"You found a diamond ring in Llano?"

"No. I wrote a letter to the quartermaster in Fort Mason and asked him to line up a good horse for a trip to Arizona. It should be waiting for you when we get there."

"Whose mare am I riding now? Does she have a name?"

"Tarry. I got her from Pa."

Fannie May flashed a wry smile. "Tarry as in 'dawdle,' I suppose, based on the pace we are setting today."

"Not even close. Tarry is short for Secretariat. Pa thought that was a good name, but I shortened it."

"And you'll be riding Clyde to Arizona. He's no spring chicken."

"We will see about that, won't we, Clyde?" roared Barringer, as he slapped his horse on the neck. The big horse snickered and trotted ahead. John B chuckled as he called back over his shoulder, "Don't Tarry there, Miss Fannie."

Barringer and Fannie May rode into Fort Mason after dusk. The front gates were still open, as civilian workers were leaving the fort.

A sentinel at the gate stopped the couple at the entrance: "Please state your name and business."

"John Barringer. I have business with the quartermaster about a horse."

"And you are traveling together?" asked the soldier, who was wearing corporal stripes.

"Good evening, Corporal. I am John Barringer's bride," answered Fannie May, skirting the truth in the name of propriety.

"Yes, ma'am. The quartermaster-sergeant is in the building next to the stable. There is a sign on the door."

"Much obliged," said Barringer, as he touched the brim of his hat in an imitation salute.

The corporal returned a formal salute as the couple rode through the gate.

The quartermaster's store was a long narrow building with two stories of items for sale. In many respects it reminded Barringer of a trading post, where trappers and hunters could trade furs for food and merchandise. Fannie May made her way through the narrow aisles while Barringer waited for the quartermaster-sergeant to look up from the counter.

"Can I help you, fella?"

"I hope so. Name's Barringer. John Barringer. I wrote about a horse."

"Oh, yes. You're the son of Old Jack Barringer out of Bluffton. Right? Well, come on out to the stable."

A woman with white hair and leathery skin stood up to tend the counter after the two men left through a side door. Fannie May came to her and asked, "Is there somewhere I can get some fine clothes in Mason?"

"Certainly not in here," laughed the woman. "But try Schmidt and Bauer in town. They have some fine ladies' clothes and accessories. Even speak English to the good customers."

"Thanks. I am attending a wedding tomorrow and have very little selection in my saddlebag," said Fannie

May, as she pointed out the window at the bag on the back of Tarry.

"We do have some larger saddlebags and packs if you might be in need of such."

"Yes, I will need some fittings. Do you have any handguns?"

After a double take, the white-haired woman said, "For sure. We have new guns and some that have seen action. Most of the new ones are imported from Germany or Austria. That's what these newcomers are looking for."

"What about American-made guns. Don't you sell them?"

"Indeed. But there arc so many that have been surrendered by the rebels or various army contingents that we don't need to be bringin' in new stock." The clerk escorted Fannie May into a back room, where guns were hanging on the walls, piled on shelves, and heaped in barrels.

"Yes, I see you have a selection of Colt pistols. I would like to get holsters and belts for two Colt 45s. I think that would be a good wedding present."

The woman showed her a selection of pistols and belts hanging on a wall. "These two were owned by confederate officers. Rumor has it that General Beauregard used these pistols in the Battle of Mexico City."

Fannie May held each gun to get the feel in her hand. Then she spun the cylinder, pulled back the hammer, and looked down the barrel. Both guns showed signs of wear, but if they were truly owned by General Beauregard, she expected they were cleaned more often than fired. She set them on the counter and asked for two hundred cartridges.

"Have you a good rifle?"

"As it happens, I prefer a shotgun, but let me look at a Winchester lever action as well."

While John B was out in the stable, Fannie May purchased guns, ammunition, holsters, scabbards, leather bags, packs, and bedrolls—for a grand total of one hundred and seventy-five dollars. The clerk helped her carry the merchandise to the horses tied in front. As she was fastening the second scabbard onto Tarry's harness, Fannie May saw two men walking across the courtyard: Scar-face and Blackbeard. The Van brothers.

The gun-belt, with both pistols, was coiled around Fannie May's neck and under one arm. She ducked behind Clyde and loaded six cartridges into one of the Colts. She crouched to look under Clyde's belly to see if the would-be robbers were coming her way. They had stopped in the yard and were talking with some soldiers. Fannie May dashed back into the quartermaster store and asked to see knives and hatchets. Quickly, she grabbed a pair of Bowie knives with ankle sheaths and threw five dollars at the clerk. She strapped on both knives—one per leg—before leaving through the side door.

"John B. Get out of sight," Fannie May whispered as she pulled him towards the wall of the building. "Scar-face and his pal are out there."

"Paths cross. Even in Texas." muttered John B before asking, "Did you get some weapons?"

"Yes, but let's not pick a fight in the middle of the Fort."

"I 'spect they are thinking the same thing."

"Do you think they will recognize the horses?" asked Fannie May.

"I hope not. Clyde is famous, but I don't think they would have seen him in Llano," said John B. "I'll ask the quartermaster-sergeant to keep an eye on our horses."

"Where we going to spend the night?" asked Fannie May.

"Well, Miss Fannie, that barn is probably the cheapest place for a night."

"OK. I'll get the rest of the guns."

28

There came men unto me, but I wist not whence they were: And it came to pass about the time of shutting of the gate, when it was dark, that the men went out: whither the men went I wot not: pursue after them quickly; for ye shall overtake them. But she had brought them up to the roof of the house, and hid them with the stalks of flax, which she had laid in order upon the roof. And the men pursued after them the way to Jordan unto the fords: and as soon as they which pursued after them were gone out, they shut the gate.

—Joshua 2:4-7 (King James Version)

The quartermaster-sergeant agreed to let the carpenter and schoolteacher stay in the loft of the barn for one night. When they opened the double doors, the lanterns carried by both men revealed a well-organized barn. There were stalls for eight horses on the ground floor but only one was occupied. Harnesses hung along the wall opposite the stalls. A ladder attached to the far wall led up to a large opening, where they could see stooks of oat straw piled in the loft.

Fannie May scrunched up her face at the irritating odor from years of horse sweat and manure.

Barringer noticed her reaction and said, "She was only the farmer's daughter, but all the horsemen knew 'er."

The three of them chuckled, even though they had all heard the joke before.

"Can you folks give me a hand bringing in the livestock for the night?" asked the quartermaster.

"Have you got room for our horses?" asked Barringer. "They might bring some undesired attention in the open."

"If you leave your pack horse out in the corral there is a stall for the Clydesdale next to your new gelding."

"What new gelding?" questioned Fannie May.

Barringer pointed to the stately red-brown gelding tethered in a stall. "He's for you." Then he handed his lamp to Fannie May.

The horse was a bay, with black mane and tail. At seventeen hands, he was not as large as Clyde but obviously bred from a draught horse based on his breadth and brawn. The large head was bisected by a narrow white stripe and a star blazed between dark, bright eyes. Pristine white socks adorned each powerful hind leg.

"That big fellow. Mostly Percheron, I figger," announced the quartermaster.

Fannie May was in the stall with the horse instantly. "Oh. John B. This is the horse I would have chosen from hundreds of others. What is his name?"

"Monte," stated the quartermaster. "He came from a ranch down by Packsaddle Mountain. Too good a horse to call him 'Packsaddle.' He is more of a mountain, so hence the 'Monte.'"

Barringer tied his own horse, Clyde, in the stall next to Monte while soldiers brought six other horses into the barn and removed any unnecessary harness before tying them in stalls.

Fannie May was still bonding with Monte when the quartermaster-sergeant checked his pocket watch.

"It's five minutes of ten," announced the officer. "I'll be leaving you on your own for the night." He closed the barn doors from the outside.

Barringer walked up behind Fannie May. "Reckon Monte wants to get some shut-eye before tomorrow's adventure with Fannie May Henderson."

"You mean Fannie May Barringer, after tomorrow," she whispered as they embraced.

"I reckon you never heard. The captain is off base for two weeks. We can't wait for him to perform any nuptials." John B ran his left hand along her buttocks.

"John B, you are pulling my leg. Tomorrow, someone in this fort is going to make an honest man of you—or else."

"Or else we just sleep together until we find a preacher on the trail." He was pulling the folds of her dress up her legs.

"So, you're feeling better, are you? Not now, John B. Not until we are married."

"What's that idea? Why wait? You already know me in the biblical sense."

"And that won't happen again until we are married."

"It's been so long. Don't reckon you can reclaim your chastity before we marry."

Fannie May pushed him away and glared at him. "If you really want to marry a whore, then go ahead. But it won't be me."

"Dang it, woman. You were once a whore."

Fannie May slapped him and ran to the base of the ladder. John B gave chase but stopped at the bottom rung when he realized his injuries had not healed enough to catch up to her. He held his lamp up to watch his bride-to-be stepping off the ladder onto the loft floor. From that angle he could see a knife in a scabbard on her left ankle.

Barringer paused. He turned back towards the barn door. When he stepped into the open air he felt his back pocket for his tobacco pouch. A minute later he lit a roll-your-own. Each pull of smoke into his lungs removed some burden from his troubled mind.

Barringer knew he would survive another night without the warmth of her body next to his. But he also knew that he needed her by his side — not for a night but for a lifetime. Baring his lust was easy. But the man struggled to bare his soul.

"Forgot to take your boots off at the door, young feller?" said a voice in the shadow of the store. Barringer hadn't noticed the quartermaster on the porch just over the corral fence.

"Ya might say that," replied Barringer. He drew in a long breath of smoke before throwing down the cigarette butt and crushing it with his boot. "Not sure where to put the hitch pin tonight."

"Come here!" ordered the quartermaster-sergeant. "You'll figger things out better after a good sleep. And this will help."

Barringer walked over to the corral fence where the quartermaster was holding out a bottle. They alternated swigs of the whiskey until the quartermaster pushed it away.

"You take that bottle and make sure it's empty by morning."

"Much obliged," said Barringer as they both turned back towards their respective lodgings.

Barringer went to the ladder and looked up into the moonlit loft. He took another long swallow from the bottle, extinguished the lantern and set both items on the floor at the foot of the ladder. Awkward and apprehensive, he climbed up to the loft. He saw Fannie May standing near a window across the room. Moonlight tinged her night clothes blue and silver. Her cheeks glistened with tears. Barringer kept his distance while he stared at her in awe.

A breeze came through the barn walls and aroused Barringer from his trance. Feeling the effects of the whiskey, he retreated to a corner where stooks of oat straw were piled. There he took off his gun-belt and chaps. Barringer removed his outer clothes and rolled them up into a makeshift pillow. He nestled into the stack enshrouded by sheaves of straw.

"Goodnight, Fannie May," Barringer stated cautiously. There was no response from the schoolteacher. One of the horses responded with a collection of snorts and groans.

When Barringer's snoring reached a steady tempo, Fannie May settled into the straw. She was agitated by John B's lack of sensitivity, but she knew her nerves were on edge. Logically, the challenges that lay ahead were more demanding than a marriage ceremony. Nonetheless, she had tired of sacrificing her happiness for the hardships of life in the west. Her security had been on the line more often than she could recall and the time had come to squeeze some happiness out of each day.

As she adjusted her clothes to keep warm, she felt the scabbards firmly attached to each ankle. "Oh, John B," she whispered. "You are lucky the knives did not come out." The slipshod straw bed kept her warm, and eventually sleep came to her.

The sound of hooves shuffling and halters clinking awoke Fannie May. She sat up slowly and saw lamplight flickering up through the ladder hole. She clambered through the straw towards Barringer, expecting an intruder to poke his head into view anytime. Hopefully, Barringer had brought his gun-belt to bed with him.

The lamplight cast a rectangle on the roof of the barn. A shadow appeared in the rectangle when the ladder treads groaned from the weight of an intruder. Fannie May crouched behind some sheaves near the top of the ladder. Nobody with good intentions would be climbing into a loft full of straw with a coal-oil lantern. The back of a man's head appeared above the loft floor. The intruder set the lamp on the floor and quietly climbed into the loft.

Fannie May heard a voice from below ask, "Are they up there?"

Then she watched the man in the loft pick up the lamp and turn towards her. When his face came into view, she gasped. She recognized Scar-face from the bank robbery. He was holding a pistol. She wanted to scream, but could not predict how this man would react. She assumed he and his partner had come for the money. Would he kill her—or John B?

"I'll give you the money." Fannie May spoke quietly.

"Damn right. Where is it?" asked Scar-face.

"Down below. Hidden in the stalls."

"Get your pretty ass down there!" ordered Scar-face. "And don't try anything or you both die."

"OK," agreed Fannie May. "Don't wake him or he might get foolhardy."

Fannie May wrapped her gown tight to her legs before descending into the darkness below. Near the bottom, Blackbeard wrapped his arms around her waist and pulled her off the ladder.

Fannie May was surprised by the mixture of emotions she felt in this man's firm embrace. In spite of the danger, she was attracted to the deep voice, compassionate eyes and muscular physique of this villain. Blackbeard's grip on her was more beguiling than threatening. In the huge man's arms she felt protected.

"Just give us the money and no one gets hurt," Blackbeard assured her.

"Where is it?" demanded Scar-face as he hung the lamp on a nail near the ladder.

"There is a saddlebag," she stammered. "It's hanging in the first stall. All the money is in that bag."

Blackbeard dealt Fannie May to Scar-face and grabbed the lamp. "Hold on to her while I check."

No sooner had Blackbeard turned away, than Scar-face pushed Fannie May onto the dirt floor. She expected only danger in the grip of the man with the eerie face. Fannie May had been attacked by men before but never before had she feared for her life. Steadfast and tenacious she refused to scream for help. She tried to reach the ankle scabbard on her right leg, but Scar-face pushed her arm back against the floor and gripped both her wrists tight with his left hand. She realized this was a life or death struggle.

In the darkness, Fannie May felt a calloused hand clawing and groping at her undergarments. She felt his breathing grow louder and faster. His breath was putrid from whiskey and rotten teeth. Once her clothing was torn away she was able to move her legs. As she writhed beneath her attacker, she tried to free her right leg. For a minute her right arm slipped free but she was unable to retrieve the knife from that ankle.

Fannie May felt fingers fumbling in her midsection. Scar-face was loosening his belt. He lifted her left leg high in the air. She stiffened her body to resist the impending violation. Bile rose in her throat. She tried to ignore the grunting. She tried to kick him with her free leg. Then she felt hands grip her left ankle. Her attacker had hands everywhere. Maybe Blackbeard was helping.

She thought she could feel the knife slip out of the left ankle scabbard. Did they plan to kill her first? Before Scar-face achieved gratification? Fannie May was not prepared to die. Not before her wedding.

"Help John B! Shoot! Follow my voice!" screamed Fannie May at the top of her lungs. "They are going to kill me! Get down here! Wake up John B!"

Wham! A fist came out of the dark, slammed into her chin and drove her head into the dirt. Stunned she lay motionless while Scar-face manipulated her limbs for his convenience. He pulled her left arm over her neck and gripped both wrists in his sweaty left hand. She felt his unshaven face next to hers. She felt spittle in her ear. His weight on her body made it hard for her to breathe. Fannie May bit her lip in an attempt to avoid passing out. The effort was futile.

When Fannie May regained consciousness, her attacker was gasping for air. For a moment, Fannie May felt the entire weight of his body pressing on her, crushing her right leg and mid-section. She struggled to breath. Now her arms were free. Quickly, she reached for her left ankle but felt only an empty scabbard. She noticed that Scar-face's snorting had turned to a gurgling sound. Then, a hot liquid sprayed onto her chest and ran around her neck. She covered her face to prevent droplets from filling her eyes and nose. When she gasped for air, the liquid tasted like a tin cup.

Then the attacker's head was lifted away and his body rolled to her right. Somewhere, lamplight flickered, silhouetting a man in a stetson standing over her, a knife in his hand. The muscular right arm of John Barringer was holding a knife — her knife.

Light suddenly filled the room. Fannie May saw Scar-face laying motionless beside her. Blackbeard was running towards them, holding the lamp in one hand and a saddlebag in the other. He struck Barringer on the shoulder with the lamp. Glass shattered and cut Barringer's left arm. Coal oil splashed on his clothes. For a moment, the barn went dark while Barringer swung the knife aimlessly.

Flames brought the room back into focus. The debris on the barn floor was burning. The barn door was open and there was no sign of Blackbeard. Barringer's scant outfit was now ablaze. His legs were blistered as he struggled out of his skivvies. The naked carpenter stood over Fannie May and extended his left hand to help her up. The pair hugged for an instant, amid the pandemonium of fire crackling, horses neighing, and hooves kicking the stalls.

"The horses!" screamed Fannie May. She ran to Monte's stall, untied her gelding, and led him to the door before slapping his rump. Then she ran back to rescue Clyde and the other horses from their stables.

Barringer stood over Scar-face, whose lifeless eyes stared up at the timbers above. Blood still squirted from where his throat had been sliced open. The liquid pooled around Barringer's toes, delaying the encroaching flames. Bare legs apart, Barringer stood over the body. As he pissed on Scar-face he yelled, "A clean shirt'll do ya!" Then Barringer stabbed the knife into the corpse over and over until the blade lodged in an eye socket.

Fannie May and the horses were free of the barn. Flames had ignited sheaves of dry straw and licked high along the wooden walls. Through the smoke, she could see an outline of a man in a stetson standing spread-eagle. Then the man bent over and jammed a knife, repeatedly, into the shadow on the floor of the barn.

Fannie May was vaguely aware of a bell tolling beyond the corral. She called out, "John B. Get out of there!"—then she ran to the far end of the corral, where she tied Clyde and Monte to a rail. The other horses ran back towards the barn. She saw John B in the doorway waving his arms to prevent the panicky animals from returning to the flames. She was relieved to see the arriving soldiers open the corral gates to let Tarry and the other horses free.

Barringer, naked from the neck down, walked out of the smoke-filled barn. He was attempting to cover himself with his charred stetson in one hand while holding a whiskey bottle in the other. Fannie May grabbed his arm and pulled him between their horses. The heat of the fire was still uncomfortable at this distance, but the stunned couple stared at the barn, which was now fully engulfed with flame.

The quartermaster-sergeant came running towards them with an angry expression. "Did my horses get out?"

"Yessir," declared Barringer. "Leastwise, Fannie May got everyone out except the man who started the fire."

"Who was that?"

"One of the men who was following us," replied Fannie May. "The other one got away with our saddlebag."

"You are both dripping blood. Are you wounded?"

"No. But you should see the other guy," Barringer replied.

The quartermaster-sergeant looked at Barringer's exposed legs and grinned. "Reckon you'll sleep with your boots on next time, Barringer. Go into the store. My wife can find you some clean clothes, if you're not too shy." Then he turned to join the bucket brigade.

Barringer handed the whiskey to Fannie May who took a snort. "Why were you wearing those knives?" he asked.

"There were two men on our trail and a fort full of men who have not been with a woman in months. Obviously, two knives were not enough protection. I am glad you were there, John B."

"I'm sorry about taking you for granted. You are not my harlot," said Barringer.

"What am I to you?"

"You are the woman I would defend with my dying breath. You are the woman I will follow to the ends of the earth. You are Fannie May, the woman I love more than anything else." said Barringer.

Fannie May looked into his eyes. "Thank you, John B. Just marry me and we can get on with our lives."

"Ya' reckon we should wait until the fire is out?" asked Barringer.

"I won't wait for another day, even if the fire goes on for a week," said Fannie May. "I must be a sorry sight standing here with nightclothes covered in blood and soot."

Barringer put his arm around her shoulders. "You look like just the gal for a man wearing nothing but a coat of blood."

Random gunfire started within the barn.

"Probably our burning ammo," shouted Fannie May.

"I reckon all the new guns and harness are in the fire," replied Barringer.

"We can buy new ones, John B. At least we are safe."

"Goddamn. What are we going to buy them with?" asked Barringer. "Blackbeard took the saddleba…."

Before he could finish his sentence, Fannie May turned around and pulled a blanket off of Clyde's back. Hidden under the blanket was the saddlebag in question.

Fannie May laughed. "Once again, the bad man took the wrong bag."

29

Fort Mason, Texas, 1886

"Mr. And Mrs. C.M. Wheat announce the marriage of their daughter, Minnie, to E.R. Holland, Wednesday, December 1, 7:30 o'clock, pm., Commerce Street Christian Church, Dallas Texas, 1886."

Miss Minnie Wheat is one of the most charming and lovely young ladies in all this city. The *Herald* returns thanks for the invitation to witness the marriage ceremony, and in advance trusts that much may be theirs all through their lives.

— *The Dallas Daily Herald*, Dallas, Texas, November 20, 1886

Fort Mason had four small cells in an isolated stockade shack. In one of these, Barringer stood looking through the barred window at the charred remains of the barn and stables. His memory of the previous night was fuzzy. Had he been arrested? Or was this the only vacant bed available? Did Fannie May acquire comfortable lodging? Was her sleep every bit as fitful as his own?

Barringer was startled by a loud clang against the cell door. After the click of a key, a private opened the door, snapped to attention, and loudly announced the presence of the captain of the fort. To Barringer it sounded like he said:

"Gall prizner shreddy foreign speck shun by thap ten uvvort Mason."

Barringer could not see other prisoners, but sounds from adjoining cells indicated that others were rising from their beds, spitting and coughing the remnants of a bad night.

The captain entered the hallway and stopped at each cell, while the private called out the name and charges pertaining to each prisoner. The charges were either drunkenness or absent without leave—until they came to Barringer's cell.

"Unknown civilian, charged with arson and murder."

"Who are you?" asked the soldier in a captain's uniform. "And why are you at Fort Mason?"

"John Barringer, sir. I am a carpenter traveling with my bride-to-be. We stopped here to buy a horse."

"So how did that end with burning a barn and killing a man?"

"Long story, sir. The lady and I, we witnessed a holdup at the bank in Llano. It seems the two scoundrels followed us here and when they discovered us sleeping in the barn, they attacked us with sidearms. I had to defend the lady, so I killed one man with a knife."

"Explain the reason for the fire," ordered the captain.

"The other man threw his lantern and fled," Barringer answered.

"The quartermaster-sergeant tells me that you and your lady rescued his horses from the fire."

"Two horses of our own and a half-dozen others. My betrothed rescued them all while I dealt with one of the men who attacked us. We were lucky to escape with our lives, so I don't understand the charges against me."

"You admit to killing a man," stated the captain. "While your lady rescued some valuable livestock."

"That seems to be the way of it."

"Well, carpenter, pending consideration, I may suspend any charges."

"What does the captain mean by consideration?"

"Considering you are a carpenter it seems fitting that you rebuild the quartermaster's barn."

"I appreciate that consideration, sir. Before I agree, can you please tell me where Miss Fannie is being held."

"Oh, she's not being held. I chatted with her earlier today, and she told me a different story. Seems she thinks it was her knife that cut the man's throat when he attacked her person."

"I have known Miss Fannie for over a year, and I doubt that she could kill a man."

"Indeed. I drew the same conclusion at first meeting her," agreed the captain. "Either way, that's self-defense in my books."

"D'ya know the dead man?" asked Barringer.

"The fire didn't improve his looks. But apparently the cadaver had several pre-existing scars from knife injuries—on his face, in particular."

"Scar-face," Barringer mumbled.

"I have see a reward offered for a scoundrel named William Van, that bears resemblance. In any case, you need to get cleaned up. Go with the private here and then come see me in my office," ordered the captain.

The private escorted Barringer to the officers' barracks. There he was provided with a hot bath, work clothes, gloves, and a tool belt. The captain waited in his office until Barringer—clean and dressed—joined him.

"Much improved, Mr. Barringer," commented the captain.

"Sir, may I assume that you are a captain of the United States Army and ranking officer of this fort?"

"Yes, that is the popular opinion. But the reality of the situation is that Fort Mason was abandoned by the United States Army back in '71. The soldiers you see here are a ragtag team who fought in the Civil War. The majority of them were Confederate Army and fought with General Lee during his command at this fort. After the war, this fort was used by the U.S. Army sporadically, depending on the situation with savages or rustlers in the area."

"So, were you a Confederate soldier?" asked Barringer.

"No. I still hold my rank in the Union Army, even though the Fort is not official."

"Where do you hail from?"

"I came here from Montana Territory with General John Porter Hatch, who was the last official commander of this fort. The state of Montana is like most of Texas— rugged and spread out. But the people there don't have as much interest in wars. You Texans always seem to be itchin' for the next battle." The captain paused, awaiting a response from Barringer. When none came, he asked, "But how about you, Barringer? Too young to have fought, but I suspect your family had sympathy for the Confederate cause."

"Can't rightly say. My pa never really declared who he fought for. He wasn't much for talking about it. I know he was keen on protecting his property, but I never saw any slaves on our farm."

"War left the country with a lot of hate. Hard to tell who is right and who is wrong."

"How's that?" asked Barringer.

"Well, losing the war didn't change much down here. Just made people bitter. They still treat blacks as slaves. White men still fight Indians. Men still rape and disrespect women. Ranchers still hate settlers."

"Tough to keep the peace. Especially wearing that blue uniform."

"You got that right. The blue uniform just means the government keeps us in ammo."

"Tell me, Captain—if this is not an official U.S. Army fort, how do you keep it going?"

"We have our quartermaster-sergeant, who retains his rank and influence. Q, as we tend to call him, runs the store like a trading post—as you know, your bride has taken advantage of the clothing and weapons for sale. And his rank oversees other forts which remain active. So, you can make your own assumptions how that might work in our favor."

Barringer scratched the side of his head and nodded. After a pause, he said, "Much obliged for the clothing. May I see Miss Fannie now?"

"Sorry, fella'. She has gone into town for some haggling. She seems determined that you are going to marry her before you leave Fort Mason."

"But there is still a murdering bank robber around here looking for her."

"You mean the other Van brother?" asked the captain, as he pulled two wanted posters from his desk, each with a black and white likeness of a man's face: Skip Van had a long, thick beard, and Willy Van had a distinct scar on the left side of his face. The heading on the posters read "Wanted Dead or Alive." Below the sketches, rewards of two hundred dollars were offered for each.

"I reckon those are the men. This one here died in the fire," said Barringer. "This other one could still be after Miss Fannie."

"And you as well."

"What d'ya mean?"

"Think about it, Barringer. One can assume that Skip Van doesn't know who killed his brother. And what were they really after last night? I would say your necks are stuck out equally. But you can relax for the moment. I asked for volunteers to escort Miss Fannie to various merchants in Mason. Damnedest thing. I got eight volunteers. Seems your intended, Miss Fannie, cleans up real nice. So, I let four officers offer me bribes so they can guard her today."

"I am grateful."

"As am I. Because tomorrow I will need four more bodyguards to accompany your Miss Fannie to town. And this will continue until you marry her."

"I'd be beholdin' to ya if you'd marry us tonight," said Barringer.

"You think this is your lucky day, Barringer?" The captain could not hide the grin on his face when he continued, "You won't get lucky until I see a barn out back. Even then, it will take a day or two to decorate the mess hall for a wedding. And that's assuming I am not tied up by any Army red tape."

"Sir, I don't figger you as a man who'd deprive me of my nuptials."

"Days are getting shorter. Nights are growing colder. If I was you, I'd get out there and organize that barn-raising. Q knows where the matcrials are stored, and there is no shortage of unskilled labor."

"Yessir," answered Barringer as he started to leave. At the door, he turned back towards the captain and added, "If I'm not mistaken that poster says 'Dead or Alive'. Reckon you can pay the reward to Miss Fannie." Now the grin was on Barringer's face.

The barn-raising went quickly with fifteen soldiers working twelve-hour days. Barringer was given authority to manage the project, including giving orders to officers. The quartermaster-sergeant had sufficient lumber and hardware on hand to build three such barns, so there was no waiting for material. At the conclusion, Fort Mason had a new barn, complete with stalls, straw, and harness. On the fourth night, eight horses were comfortably stabled in the barn.

Barringer and Fannie May went to find the captain in the Officer's Club. Several officers were smoking cigars and having a drink of brandy.

"Tell me you have good news, my new friend," said the captain.

"Both good and bad news," stated Barringer.

"So the barn is complete, with horses ensconced within?"

"It is," said Barringer.

"They are," added Fannie May.

"So what color is the barn?"

Fannie May looked at Barringer. He shrugged.

"Er, the color of new timber will fade over winter to a gray shade," said Fannie May.

"Has Q no paint? Shouldn't a barn be red?" asked the captain.

"I have the utmost confidence that your men can paint a barn without my supervision or assistance," declared Barringer.

"He is right, Captain," said Fannie May. "Now it is time to marry us!"

The officers laughed in unison. Then, just as the laughter subsided, one of them would blurt out some wedding-day humor and the others would whoop in response.

"It's time, Captain!" snorted an officer, pounding the arm of his chair.

"Two coats of paint, you say?" snorted the other.

All three officers were doubled over.

"What's so funny? We have spent more than enough time at your behest," said Fannie May.

"Stop, Miss Fannie. Please stop," said the captain, looking around at his giggling lieutenants. "My officers are spattering brandy all over the floor. We agree. We came to the same conclusion before you came in here."

"Yes. Admirable work, John Barringer," said another officer.

"We will have a wedding tomorrow," declared the captain. "The mess hall is being prepared as we speak."

The door to the Officer's Club swung open, and the quartermaster-sergeant burst into the room. "I hear the wedding is tomorrow. We have a good supply of whiskey and some wine if the captain so orders."

"That's an order, Q. Now go tell the drill sergeant to bury a pint of whiskey at the spot where the vows will be spoken."

"It's supposed to be buried a month before the wedding to keep the rain away," replied the quartermaster-sergeant.

"No time for that, but it can't hurt. Then Mr. and Mrs. Barringer can dig it up and start the celebration with a snort!"

The wedding day was an unforgettable celebration. Fannie May looked beautiful in the dress that she had purchased from a German seamstress in the town of Mason. Barringer was able to purchase a slightly tarnished gold ring from the quartermaster's store. Many townspeople attended the wedding and assisted with the catering of an outdoor barbecue. A wedding cake was provided, as well as a variety of dainties.

There was no shortage of whiskey, beer, and wine. An orchestra with a guitar, accordion, and drum played country dances and German polkas. The celebration went into the early hours of the morning.

The quartermaster-sergeant set up an actual bed in a stall of the new barn. His wife had provided fancy bed-clothes and curtains. The captain placed guards on the door. Again, he had no difficulty finding volunteers.

As the couple undressed, John B noticed Fannie May hesitate. Unsure of the problem, he said, "I am sorry for dragging my feet, Fannie May. There is nobody more keen for this night to arrive."

Fannie May peered through the curtains into the back of the barn. Where she expected to see a ladder leading to the loft, she saw stairs partially enclosed by a partition. She closed the curtain and continued to disrobe. "Thanks John B. I know you care."

At sunrise, Fannie May was saddling her trusted steed, Monte. The quartermaster's wife had offered to replace the guns and harness lost in the fire as a wedding present. Fannie May insisted on paying the same amount as she had paid originally.

Barringer was attaching packs of bedding and food supplies to the mare, Tarry.

Clyde snorted and whinnied in search of similar attention.

"Don't worry, big fella," laughed Barringer. "We are not going without you."

The quartermaster-sergeant and his wife hugged the couple before they mounted their horses.

"Take care on the trail," said the quartermaster's wife. "You know there is a wanted man out there watching for you."

"Much obliged for how you have treated us on our special day," said Fannie May.

"There's word of a drive and a wagon train crossing the San Saba in the next few days," said the quartermaster-sergeant. "You can catch them if you don't run into any more trouble."

"Thanks, Q," replied Barringer. "Trouble seems to have a way of finding us, but I figger we are due for some good luck."

"Luck was smiling on you when you found your missus," chuckled the quartermaster-sergeant as he watched them ride away.

Several townspeople were gathered at the gate to wish happy trails to the newlyweds. Some of them threw rice to congratulate the couple. Most of the rice landed short of the target and sprinkled the horses instead. Both Monte and Clyde threw their heads high and snickered through their lips, adding to the hullabaloo.

After man and wife and three horses had left the noisy crowd behind, Barringer looked over at his new bride. "You make me very happy, Fannie May Barringer."

"I'm glad we are married, John B. Do you think people will look upon us differently?"

Barringer thought for a minute. "I guess that's true. Family and friends will be more comfortable when we share a bed."

"That's why I agreed to marry you."

"What d'ya mean by that?"

"You know I only married you to share your bed," said Fannie May, trying to hide her smirk.

"I reckon that was your number one reason. But number two was that pair of hymnals."

"You guessed it, John B. I married you for your church singing."

John B grinned like a fool and broke into song. "Onward Christian soldiers, marching as to war..." Fannie May joined in, and they sang as many verses as they could recall.

BIBLICAL PROPORTIONS

30

Chisholm Trail, Texas, 1886

The last two winters has virtually settled the range cattle craze, at least for Kansas and the Indian Territory. Thousands of range herds will be destroyed and their owners bankrupted this winter. We dread to see the final returns.

—*Wichita Daily Eagle*, Wichita, Kansas, February 6, 1886

Cotton's cattle drive of 1886 set out from the Double Lightning Ranch with fifteen hundred head of beef cattle. The majority of the herd were Texas longhorns: bulls, cows, and steers. Fewer than one hundred head were Hereford steers. The rancher was keeping most of the Hereford bulls and cows on the ranch for breeding stock.

In addition to the cattle, other livestock accompanied the drive. The cook would keep some chickens and goats to butcher in the early days of the drive so that trail hands wouldn't get tired of eating only beef. The remuda for this drive included a pool of eighty horses and three mules. The crew included fifteen drovers and six support staff. There were five supply wagons, each pulled by a four-horse team.

This drive would follow the Chisholm Trail, north through the Texas towns of Waco, Fort Worth, and past Bowie, to the shores of the Red River. Beyond Red River Station, the trail crossed into the area known as Indian Territory. The herd of cattle would travel eight to twelve miles in a day, depending on the terrain and availability of grass and water. To serve the cattle drives and occasional wagon trains, small trading posts had been established along the trail. Each of these outposts had a stream or well to provide water for the herd to drink. At some stops, a water tank supplied only enough water for human consumption and the livestock would go thirsty until a future stop.

Rivers crossed the Chisholm Trail in many places. This afforded opportunity for cattle to drink, but the physical crossing of a river presented a strain on the animals and the trail hands. A swollen river might carry some animals downstream. Sometimes, the cattle would panic during the crossing and turn back against the herd. The banks of the river also presented a hazard. Frequently, banks could not support the pounding of hundreds of animals climbing the slope. Animals could break a leg on river rocks or rodent holes. On some banks, the soil dissolved into powder or mud, causing the herd to lose traction and remain trapped in the riverbed. On other riverbanks, quicksand and mud pits could swallow a horse and rider whole.

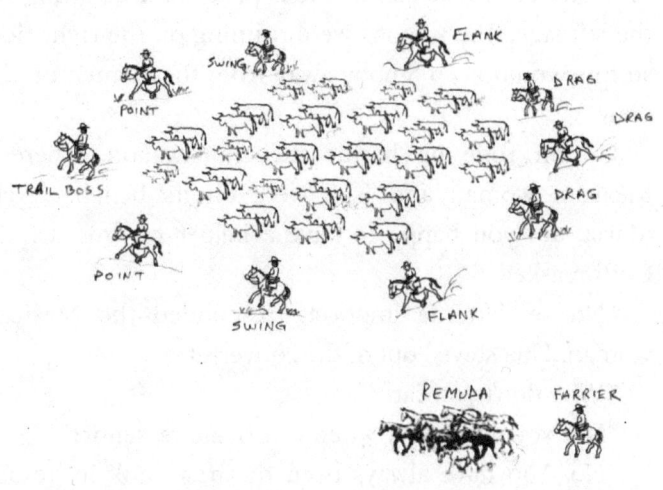

Every river crossing risked the lives of animals and herders. Trail bosses had experience crossing rivers and were familiar with the tried-and-true fords. As long as there were no major surprises in the weather conditions along or upstream of the trail, an experienced trail boss could avoid losing too many of his beeves. Cowboys new to the cattle drive learned to respect the trail boss. Those who did not follow instructions were frequently injured from falls, gored by a longhorn, drowned in a river, or trampled in a stampede. Drovers would either learn from the experience or die on the trail.

As the trail boss, Cotton usually rode near the front of the herd, in the *point* or *swing* position. But for the first day of the drive, he rode *drag*, so that he could keep an eye on the new members of the crew. He was pleasantly surprised with Stubby and Bucktooth. They had been on previous drives, so he let them pick flank or swing on the left side. The wagons were running on the right side, so this would keep Stubby away from the women on the crew.

Cotton rode up beside the chuckwagon, where a Mexican woman and Una were on its bench. "Well, Maria, are you happy to have a helper on this drive?" Cotton asked.

"No se. No me importa," responded the Mexican woman. Una stayed out of the conversation.

"Why don't you care?"

"Did you go hungry when I work alone, señor?"

"No. You have always been the best cook in Texas," Cotton laid it on.

"But now you give me this girl who has never been on the trail." Maria scowled in Una's direction.

"Una will learn. And Una can clean and sew. There is always that work."

"I see you," Maria scolded. "All men are drooling. Es el sueter de carne."

"Una, will you promise to earn your keep and do what Maria asks?" asked Cotton.

"Yes, Mr. Cotton," Una piped up. "I'll do whatever Maria asks, but I don't always understand. My Spanish is poor."

Cotton laughed. "That's probably a good thing."

"Vete pal' carajo," growled Maria.

"Si, señora. A good thing Una does not understand you. I am going to leave you alone now. We will stop in Round Rock tonight and Waco tomorrow. Make a list of any supplies that you need. We will stop at Morrison's Drug Store in Waco. Need to get a supply of Dr. Pepper. Miss Una, have you ever tasted Dr. Pepper?" Cotton inquired.

"No. Is it a tonic?"

"Well, some people think so. Sort of like sarsaparilla. Good for what ails ya."

"There's a stray, señor. Vamoose," Maria shouted.

"OK. Si." Cotton laughed as he moved on up the right side of the herd to ride in a wayward steer.

Maria turned to Una. "You watch out for that one. I can see he has eye on you."

Una blushed and picked up the apron she was mending.

On the far side of the herd, Stubby's horse stood still until Bucktooth caught up to his position. Stubby was straining to see the chuckwagon on the opposite side. Clouds of dust wafted above the cattle, blurring his view.

"I reckon that girl really has ya vexed," said Bucktooth.

"Can't get over it," admitted Stubby. "She smells so good up close. And that hair. Like a red mare."

"Best you forget her," said Bucktooth. "Cotton's got her hog-tied already."

"Nah. Cotton has his mind on the drive. He's just playin' fatherly."

"Dunno. More than that from where I'm sittin'."

"I got a plan. Aimin' to finish what I started back in Dallas."

"Stubby! Keep it in your pants till we get to Kansas. I don't feel like diggin' your grave anywhere along this trail."

"I know a guy," bragged Stubby. "Remember those Commancheros that hung out at Old Suggs Tank?"

"Ya mean that campground just past Reid Store?" Bucktooth asked.

"Yep. Skinny feller with one eye. Can't grow a proper beard," said Stubby.

"Oh, yeah, they call him Whisker, don't they? And his brother who always cheats at poker?" asked Bucktooth.

"Whisker and Shady. That's the pair," Stubby said, as he spit some tobacco juice on the ground. "Ya figger those two could be motivated to create an ambush around Silver City?"

"Them's probably yer guys."

"Hand to God," grunted Stubby. "Hand to God." When he noticed Cotton watching them from a knoll, he spurred his horse and rode up-herd into the left swing position.

The drive went slow for the first two weeks. On September 22, they stopped at Round Rock to pick up supplies. When they started out the next morning, a wheel came off the chuckwagon, causing the wagon to spill. Two horses had to be put down. Both women were scraped up, but no bones were broken. Most of the supplies were salvaged, but the wagon had to be unloaded until the wheel was repaired. This resulted in a two-night stay at Round Rock. After dark on the second night, Cotton lay awake in his tent, wondering how he could make up some time. Without warning, the door flap opened and Una crawled into the tent. She was shivering.

"What's the matter, Miss Una?"

"It's late September and I really should be back at school. You know I haven't finished my schooling, don't you?"

"OK. But I had to pull a lot of strings to get you on this cattle drive, and now you want to go back to Dallas?"

"No, I don't want to go back. But I do want to finish my studies. Do you think they have a good school in Dodge City?"

"We ain't going to Dodge City. We are going to Newton."

"I know. I'll catch a train or a stagecoach to Dodge City. But what do you think? Does it bother you that I don't have my diploma? And I don't even know how to be a chuck cook?"

"No. I reckon you are already pretty smart. And you will learn lots on this cattle drive. Tell me what you need to learn and I'll try to help."

"I need to learn about courting. And making woo."

Cotton chuckled nervously and started to respond. But when he looked in her eyes, two shining pools of green took the words right out of his mouth. He put his arm under hers and drew her close. Then he kissed her cheek lightly. "Are you sure you're ready to learn that stuff?"

"I'm all growed up, Cotton." Una ran her fingers through his curly hair. "Teach me." Una moved her lips to Cotton's cheek. After a pause, he turned and kissed her. Her mouth was warm to his tongue. Cotton had never felt such passion in a kiss.

Una pressed her body tight to his. After another lengthy kiss, she pressed her face to his ear. "Keep me warm tonight. I will learn to please you if you teach me."

"That's dangerous for us both."

"I'll be discreet," said Una.

"You can't never be seen leavin' my tent. The men will begrudge any favor I show you."

"You don't need to show me favor. Just hold me for awhile."

Cotton lay awake with Una's head resting on his chest and her hair tickling his nose. The clash between his libido and his responsibility occupied his waking thoughts. Eventually, he gently rolled Una to the side and was able to sleep, bundle-board style. When he awoke the next morning, Una was dressed and pouring coffee for some of the hands sitting around the campfire. She was silhouetted against the pink light of dawn. Cotton admired her from his tent before crawling into the open. He stood upright and pulled on his pants. Una pretended not to notice him as he wandered around behind a horse to urinate. With the pleasure of Una's company, the cowhands paid no mind to Cotton.

When Cotton approached the campfire, Una poured him a cup of coffee.

"Thanks, Miss Una," said Cotton before turning to face the crew. "We should push hard for the next few days to make up some time. Hopefully, we can get the herd to Waco by the end of the month and on to Alvarado."

"Ya' reckon we have time to stop in Fort Worth? I have a lady waitin' for me there," commented one of the drovers as he winked at the other men.

"Let's see when we get there. As you know, we are flirting with winter instead of women."

"Nah, last year was a rarity," responded the drover. "If I'm riding point, we'll get to Kansas before winter."

"We are all countin' on that," Cotton said and raised his cup towards the drovers.

Just then, Bucktooth and Stubby came over to the fire. Bucktooth held out a tin cup for Una to pour him coffee. Stubby sat down on a pail before holding out his cup. When Una bent over to pour the coffee, he was disappointed that she was wearing a high-collar blouse. But his gaze never met her eyes.

"Did we miss anything?" asked Stubby.

"Not really," answered Cotton. "Every mile counts from here on in."

"What about them fences? I hear that some settlers have started putting up barbwire around their fields," grumbled Stubby.

"I'll just cut 'em," answered the drover riding point.

"Alright by me," said Cotton. "Then the men riding drag can patch 'em up when we are through."

"I heard there's quarantine fences on the Kansas border," Bucktooth added.

"Nah, that's only on the Western Trail," replied the point drover.

"What's a quarantine fence?" asked Una.

"Some northern ranchers are afraid of Texas fever," said Cotton. "They believe that longhorns from the south carry a fever, and they don't want those herds coming into Kansas. So, they built some fences this side of the Kansas border along the North Canadian River. It doesn't stop a cattle drive, but it holds them up if the northern ranchers care to inspect the herd."

"I heard they just start shooting any longhorns," said Stubby.

"I heard they shoot the drovers, too," added Bucktooth.

"Settle down, fellers," ordered Cotton. "I am told that most of the quarantine fences are on the Western Trail. And we are running late in the season, so I don't expect to run into a Winchester quarantine at the Kansas border."

"What if yer wrong, boss?"

"If I'm wrong, we can deal with it then. Guns and ammunition will be provided to any man who needs them. Stay alert, but don't forget the purpose of this cattle drive. You should be more afraid of river crossings than a few strands of barbwire. Now let's move 'em out."

31

Western Trail, Texas, 1886

Reports from Texas indicate a disastrous drouth, and that the cattle are dying by thousands for want of water and grass. There is very little grass anywhere near water and that little is so dry and dead that it does not contain enough substance to do cattle any good. The cattle are very thin and getting thinner every day, and if no rain comes within thirty days the cattle business in west Texas will be ruined. People are very gloomy over the outlook.

— *Western Cyclone*, Nicodemus, Kansas, May 27, 1886

The Barringers crossed the San Saba River at Peg-leg Crossing on September 23, 1886. The stream was shallow due to dry conditions that summer. Monte, the gelding John B had purchased for Fannie May, was skittish during the crossing, but Fannie May stopped midstream to calm him.

"That's fine, Monte. Now you have it. Good horse."

Clyde, the big stallion, crossed the river with his usual quiet confidence. Barringer's stirrups stayed dry because his saddle was over eighteen hands above the riverbed.

"Where to now, John B?" asked Fannie May.

"According to the map that the quartermaster drew for me, there is a pass about eight miles north. Cow Gap is what he called it. The trail funnels through there, so we may catch a drive in the pass."

"Looks like some fresh tracks and cow pies up ahead. Are you sure they will be glad to see us?" Fannie May asked.

"Doubtful, but at this time of year beggars can't be choosers," professed John B.

"You mean that the real cowboys have already finished their cattle drives and only crazy people are pushing cattle this late in the year."

"That's how a schoolteacher might figger it. But a carpenter with a sense of adventure sees this as the perfect opportunity to learn a new skill."

"Well, I hope there is someone prepared to teach us roping and riding alongside a herd of dumb animals with pointed horns," Fannie May threw out.

"Hell, I'm not frettin' about those bovines. I'm worried about whether the weather will turn to winter."

"OK. I will add that to the list. Weather, wind, winter, water, hoofs, horns, horses."

"Don't forget food and fornicating."

"Right. Fornicating is my biggest worry," laughed Fannie May. "But you're getting better at it."

Barringer grinned and shook his head. "Happy to practice anytime."

After another hour, the Barringers could hear a dissonance that could only be a herd of cattle—bulls, cows, and calves all expressing hunger and thirst. The sound grew louder as the dust cloud came into view. Now human voices could be heard above the din. Some of the words were blasphemous. Some were expletives. But most of the shouting—"Hiya." "Hey, boss. Come, boss." "Yippee. Yahoo." "Get up. Get in. Giddy-up." "Yeah. Head 'em out."—could only be understood by bovines.

"What are they saying, John B?"

"Words of encouragement. Words of encouragement," John B pronounced.

The chuckwagon and supply wagons were stopped at the entrance to Cow Gap, waiting for the herd to exit on the north end before rolling into the pass. As the dust settled, Barringer rode over to talk to the man driving the chuckwagon.

"Good day, sir. Am I talking to the cook of this cattle drive?"

"Yessir. Name's Kenny. Who are ya'?"

"I'm John Barringer and this is my missus, Fannie May. We are hoping to tag along with a cattle drive to get up to the railroad in Kansas."

"Howdy, ma'am," said Kenny, as he tipped his hat and banged some dust off. "I can't rightly say if you are welcome to join us. That will be up to the trail boss, and as you can see he is mighty busy right now."

"We can both help," claimed Fannie May. "I can ride or cook."

"I can sure use some help getting the chuck ready. Just hang back behind the herd until we stop for the night. We won't get to the Colorado River till tomorrow, so hopefully there is a watering hole coming up soon. Then when the campfires are going, you can have a chinwag with boss Montana."

The Barringers followed the wagons at a safe distance until they stopped for the night.

The trail boss was a bow-legged man with a wiry frame. His face was tanned and wrinkled from long days in the sun. His hair was thin on top, yet he managed to keep a long ponytail. The mustache and beard were unkempt and covered most of his face. He talked very little, unless there was work to be done. The Barringers approached him together after he had eaten his supper.

"Are you the trail boss?" asked Barringer.

"Who's askin'?"

"My name is John Barringer. This is my wife, Fannie May. We are making our way to the railroads in Kansas."

The man nodded and looked them both over, head to toe, then offered an approving grin at Fannie May.

She responded, "We would be glad to pitch in if you can use any help. Our main desire is to have some company on our way."

Montana nodded and looked over at the crew. Some were grinning at the shapely figure in the firelight. Others were shaking their heads in disapproval.

"Ever rode a trail before?" asked Montana.

"No, sir. I am a carpenter. I have been riding that big horse for a few years, so I know what he can do."

"And I am a schoolteacher. But I can cook and clean."

"Well, carpenter, we have all the drovers we need. But we can use a wagon hand. Figger you could maintain the wagons?"

"Reckon so. If you have tools, I can fix a wagon wheel or repair any harness."

"How about farrier work?" asked the trail boss.

"I am a good shoer but never been much of a smithy."

"There will be some blacksmith shops turn up where you least expect it. And believe me, they will see us comin.'"

"Can I pitch in?" asked Fannie May.

"Ma'am, if y'all can see eye to eye with old Kenny on the chuckwagon yonder, well then, join in."

"I'd be honored," said Fannie May.

"Well, that fits right in," said Montana. "In yer spare time the two of ya can gather fuel for the fire and organize the tack?"

Both Barringers were nodding in agreement.

"Can't pay you much," continued Montana. "Maybe a hundred dollars to share when we reach Dodge City. You can use your own horses if they are up to it. The drovers will be requiring everything my remuda horses can give."

"We have three horses," said Fannie May. "Clyde and Monte will be up to the task but not sure about Tarry, the pack horse."

"If it'll help, go ahead and put some of your pack on a wagon," suggested Montana. "But before y'all get settled, I have one question."

"Ask away," said Fannie May.

"Can ya' sing?" asked the trail boss, looking at the comely woman.

"Huh? Sing what?"

"Sing songs. Anything. Calms the men and the cattle. I sing a bit, but the throat gets parched quick."

"I would be glad to sing along with some music if you have it."

"Yep. Guitar and a harmonica. You two go see Cook Kenny and get settled in. Breakfast is before the sun gets up."

"How shall we address you?" asked Fannie May.

"Huh, how what?" Montana asked.

"What do we call you?"

"Name is Tommy Montana. But on the drive, you just call me the 'big dog.' Don't ever argue with the big dog, because the big dog is always right."

Both the Western Trail and the Chisholm Trail gathered herds from southern Texas and ran north to rail-heads in Kansas. Cattle drives on either trail traveled more than ninety days, forty of which were spent crossing desolate Indian Territory. Both trails crossed the same major rivers at different points. At the Red River the crossings were only thirty miles apart. Both trails harbored the same challenges. But the late weeks of 1886 would present challenges never before experienced on any cattle drive.

Divvied up between both trails, Tommy Montana had experienced twenty-four cattle drives. He thought he had seen every type of danger known to man or nature. But number twenty-five presented a new obstacle. Montana was perplexed by the stories of barbwire fences constructed along the Canadian Rivers. Fences that would slow the drive. Fences that represented interference by men who opposed the Texas ranchers. And in his experience, there were two sides to a fence, and that meant there could be a fight. Even without any delays, Montana predicted these twenty-five hundred head of cattle would not reach Dodge before December 1, 1886. Unfortunately, the trail-boss had no inkling of the real calamity awaiting his crew.

The Barringers promptly fell into the daily routine. Fannie May's typical workday was: make breakfast, make coffee, clean, pack, prepare food, cook supper, serve supper, clean, pack, sing, set up tent and bedroll, sleep. By the second day, Fannie May was performing her role without instructions. Breakfast for the crew was served at first light. Packing up the chuckwagon after breakfast had to happen quickly so that the wagon did not get left behind.

On her first morning, Fannie May brought Montana a warm breakfast. He was ruminating over a map that had been hand-drawn on the back of an envelope.

"Can you show me where we are?" asked Fannie May.

Montana pointed to a dashed line running north from west Texas to Dodge City. "This here line is the Western Trail. We are a good bit north of the Colorado River and approaching the Wichita. Right there."

"Did you draw this map yourself?" asked Fannie May.

"Absolutely. Wouldn't trust any New York map maker to understand the cattle trails."

"Nor would I," agreed Fannie May. "They would be overly concerned with the correct spelling of the names of rivers."

Fannie May winked when Montana glared at her.

Montana's scowl turned into a big grin. "Just remember what I told you, schoolteacher. The big dog is always right," he growled as he watched her walk away.

There was less formality around the lunch meal. There was no need for the chuckwagon to stop when cowboys came sniffing around for some jerky or biscuits. The schedule for supper depended on arrival at a river or watering hole. Three wagons formed a barrier against the wind. Barringer and the drovers built a couple of campfires while the evening meal was being prepared. Hot food would be served in the first hour after sunset. Then drinking, card playing, and singing would commence among the entire crew.

Montana ordered a curfew for drovers at 10:00 pm so that all could get a peaceful night's sleep. The point and flank riders took shifts watching the herd. Barringer would keep an eye on the wagons and the horses while he worked on repairing harness. Horses spent the night on the string. They would be first to react to the presence of strangers or predators.

The lowing of the cattle was continuous through the night, but experienced drovers could recognize the sound of a cow or calf in distress. The entire crew would be awakened to protect the herd and campsite at the first sign of rustlers, coyotes, or lightning. The night shift was never boring but rarely was there any loss of life.

The daily routine for John B was: build the morning fire, eat, inspect wagons, ride to next stop, gather buffalo chips, build a fire, eat, repair harness, inspect horse hooves, sleep. He was busy each and every night repairing damaged harness or wagons under the light of a kerosene lamp. His eyes grew tired from the strain and long hours.

Fannie May worried about him and pined for him to join her in their tent.

"John B, can't that saddle wait until morning."

"Reckon the rider doesn't plan to ride bareback tomorrow. I will get some shut-eye as soon as this stirrup is repaired."

"Forget the shut-eye. I'd be happy with *you* riding bareback."

"Right after I finish stitching." Barringer was in the tent with Fannie May an hour later.

Tommy Montana's crew knew that river crossings were a mixed blessing. In dry seasons, the humans and animals welcomed the cool water. But real danger lay in the water and on both banks of the river. For this reason, the trail was mapped out to show fords in the rivers, which allowed a cattle drive to cross with the least jeopardy.

Doan's Crossing on the Red River was named for the trading post established by Jonathon and Corwin Doan. In the fall of 1886, there was a store, hotel, saloon and a school. The post at Doan's Crossing catered to cattle drives, wagon trains, buffalo hunters, and American Indians. After a successful crossing, the drovers were usually rewarded with some time to unwind in this semblance of civilization.

The Red River was the widest and least predictable of all the rivers on the Western Trail. There was a wide shallow basin with gentle slopes at entry and exit. Spring rains often caused the river to run fast and wide, but at this time of year the river meandered around shifting sand bars and pockets of quicksand. The drive entered the ford at Doan's Crossing on October 25, 1886. Tommy ran point to appraise the optimum route across the wet sand and shallow water. When he was satisfied that the riverbed would support two million pounds of beef on ten thousand hooves, Tommy waved his hat in a circle from the north side of the river.

The drovers mustered the front of the herd along the riverbank and then punched them into the river bottom. As soon as the lead cattle waded into the soft sand, the others fell into lines behind. By the time the lead animals were climbing out the far side, there were over five hundred head sloshing through the muddy river with another two thousand pushing down on them. In the first hour, over half of the animals had crossed the river.

The riverbed took a pounding from the herd, turning into an opaque brown soup. Larger animals stood motionless as the sticky mud gripped their legs. Some smaller animals disappeared into the quagmire and were never seen again. The drovers had seen this before. They knew that there would be some losses during this crossing. They continued to push the cattle down into the river and encourage them to climb out the other side. As the last of the herd entered the river, the riders in the drag position rode into the muck and lassoed animals that were struggling. The dead animals were also towed to the shore unless they had already floated out of sight.

Next, the wagons entered the river, one at a time. Barringer unhitched some of the wagon horses so that only two horses were tethered to each wagon. Ropes were strung from the sides of each wagon and pulled by outriders. The outriders could prevent a wagon from rolling over by turning it into the current. The crossing went smoothly for the first two wagons. They stayed upright from one side of the river to the far side.

The third wagon was heavier since it contained barrels of beer, bottles of whiskey, and canned goods. This wagon rode lower in the water and the wheels cut into the riverbed. The two horses were unable to pull the wagon out of its stuck position. Outriders tugged on the ropes, but the wagon would not move. Kenny, the cook, was driving this wagon. He jumped to the right, landing in shoulder-deep water on the downstream side of the wagon. When the horses felt the lines go slack, they bolted in the downstream direction. The sudden torque on the hitch pole flipped the wagon on top of Kenny.

"Give me a hand, fellows," yelled Barringer. "Kenny's under the wagon."

"Where is he?" replied a rider. "I can't see anything in this shit."

"He should be over here by the back wheel."

Both men jumped into the water, feeling below the surface frantically.

"I got an arm. Help me pull."

"He's stuck under the wheel! We need to lift the wagon."

"Pull, goddammit. Pull."

"Someone get a pole and pry up the wagon."

Two riders came splashing up to the wagon and pushed a dead tree under it as a pry bar. Three of them tried to raise the wagon, to no avail. Fannie May rode up to where the two horses were still splashing nervously. She grabbed their lines and pulled them upstream. Suddenly the wagon flipped back onto its wheels.

Kenny's body floated up from the bottom. The outriders tried to revive him by standing him upright and banging on his back. Kenny, the cook, was at the end of the trail.

After the cattle were settled on the north side of the Red River, Tommy announced that the next day would be a celebration of Kenny's life. A banquet and reception—prepared by Fannie May and the Doans—would follow a morning burial. The crew needed an opportunity to grieve and reclaim their morale.

32

We all get the same amount of ice.
The rich get it in the summer.
The poor get it in the winter.

—Bat Masterson

The loss of the chief cook was devastating for the entire crew. Most of the men understood the danger to themselves, but they never imagined that the cook would lose his life on any drive. Fannie May was able to keep food coming for the hungry men, with some assistance from John B and the drag riders.

North of the Red River, the river crossings went smoothly. In fact, the trail boss was surprised by the schedule they maintained crossing Indian Territory. But fences along the north banks of the North Canadian River posed an ominous threat. Montana stopped the herd while he scouted the fence for trouble. There were no gates. There were no guards. There were no signs. He ordered the wires cut and assigned Barringer to replace the wires after the herd was through.

At the supper campfire, Fannie May asked Montana, "What's the purpose of those fences?"

"They say fences make good neighbors," laughed Tommy. "Kansas ranchers want to keep longhorns with Texas fever from mingling with their herds. And Texas ranchers want to prevent Kansas herds from moving south to graze. So, ranchers from each state maintain fences across Indian Territory because they don't trust the other guys."

"What does the government say about this?" asked John B.

"Depends which way the wind is blowing. There are associations and conferences to settle the cattle trails. Some ranchers want open grazing all the way north to the territories in Canada. Meanwhile, homesteaders would like to protect their crops with more fences. Something is bound to change, and it won't be good for Texas," said Montana.

"That barbed wire seems like a simple solution," said Fannie May.

"Except that every time you turn around the wires get cut," said Montana. "Hopefully, responsible trail hands will hang the wire back up. Otherwise, you just have a bunch of bare posts in a long row."

"How many more rivers to cross?" asked Fannie May.

"Just the Cimarron," answered Montana. "In a few days, we will be in Kansas. From the Cimarron we have clear run up to Dodge. Should be counting our money in Dodge by *Mary Celeste* day."

"Not sure what you mean by that. Who is Mary Celeste?" asked Barringer.

"Not a who. A what. The sailing ship *Mary Celeste*," replied Montana.

"Did it sink in December?" asked Fannie May.

"No. Never sank. On December 4th, 1872, sailors on a ship from Canada found the *Mary Celeste* abandoned in the Atlantic. Sails were set. Cargo and provisions all intact. Just the crew and one lifeboat were missing. I like to celebrate the survival of that ship," declared Montana.

"Why?" asked Fannie May.

"What else can we celebrate in early December?"

"Were you a sailor, Mr. Montana?" Fannie May wondered.

"What d'ya mean? I still am. I'm the captain of a crew of sailors taking a cargo of beef across the prairie oceans with prairie schooners."

"Arr, that we be," said John B. "And we embark on this Indian Ocean ere long."

The three laughed at the notion of John B as a pirate, but agreed that the cattle drive was, indeed, akin to a seafaring voyage.

A sudden cold breeze drove them from the fire to their tents. The Barringers had purchased a buffalo hide in Mason and were grateful to share its warmth. By morning, the wind had grown fierce, causing the sides of the tent to flap.

Barringer looked at his pocket watch. "It is late, Fannie May. We must be burning daylight." He opened the tent flap and saw nothing but white. Snow was traveling sideways, and drifts covered the fire ring. "Snowstorm. Get dressed!" he shouted, pulling on his trousers.

"A snowstorm can't last, can it?" Fannie May said skeptically.

They both dressed quickly, and Barringer went out to check on the horses. The canvas had blown off one of the wagons and was flapping in the wind. Another wagon had blown over onto its side. The horses, Monte and Clyde, were pulling at their leads tied to the chuckwagon.

There was no sign of Montana—or anyone—in the blinding snow. Barringer was baffled by the situation. He had never experienced a blizzard, but he assumed that the cattle drive and all its crew were in danger. His shouts were answered by a distant bawling of cows on the wind.

Fannie May came out of the tent, fully dressed for the day. She went to the chuckwagon, where Barringer was throwing a saddle on Clyde.

"Is this a blizzard?" asked Fannie May.

"Your guess is as good as mine," replied John B.

"Should it blow over, like a dust storm?"

"In any event, I reckon it will leave behind some snow."

"What do we do?" Fannie May screamed over the howling wind.

"I think the drive is over."

"Do we need to find Tommy, or are we on our own?"

"Listen!" shouted Barringer. The thunder of hooves was discernible among the bawling sounds of the herd. "The cattle have turned with the wind. Get on your horse. We have to go now!"

"OK, I'll get our bedroll while you saddle up," suggested Fannie May.

"No time. Just get on Monte and ride east. Don't wait, I will try to keep up."

Fannie May untied her horse. "Which direction?"

"East," shouted Barringer, as he lifted her onto the gelding. "Just let him run with the wind. And hold on!" Then he slapped the horse on the rump.

Barringer pulled Clyde behind the chuckwagon and noticed Fannie May's saddlebag and rifle in the wagon. He threw them over his shoulder and climbed onto Clyde. Some longhorn bulls ran past. They were heading south.

"Giddy up, Clyde," yelled Barringer and steered Clyde to the east with his legs. The Clydesdale bolted forward and collided with a cow running across their path. Both animals ignored the collision.

The snow on the ground and in the air created a complete whiteout. When Barringer looked where he thought the sun should be, he could only see a blur of cattle stampeding across their path. Clyde demonstrated an uncanny ability to maneuver through the herd. Horse and rider galloped with the wind.

Barringer looked in every direction and could not see the sun nor a shadow cast by his horse. There was no distinguishable horizon. All he could see was white. But his steed continued to follow the wind and, with any luck, Fannie May's trail. Barringer hoped for the best as he tucked low on the horse's back. In this position he was able to share some of Clyde's body heat as he rode.

By noon, Barringer estimated that he had traveled twenty miles without seeing any sign of Fannie May. It seemed now that Clyde was walking downhill. The wind died down in the lee of a ravine, and Barringer could see they were among some trees along a creek bed that emptied into a river ahead.

"Good job, Clyde. Let's follow the river." The horse came to a sudden halt before Barringer had finished the sentence. At that point, Barringer noticed fence posts and four strands of barbwire blocking their path.

"Shit," Barringer muttered as he rubbed Clyde's neck. He pulled the rifle over his head and checked to see if it was loaded. Then he held the gun where the horse could see it.

"Easy boy. I'm going to open that fence the hard way. That wire is as tight as a violin string." Barringer fired a shot at the point where the wire was attached to a post. It snapped, and the end whipped back towards Clyde. Barbs sliced along the horse's chest. Clyde reared, and Barringer fell into the snow below. Blood was dripping from the horse.

"Sorry, big fella. Reckon I didn't see that coming." Barringer moved the horse back a safe distance and tied him to a shrub. Then he went directly in front of the fence post and shot the remaining three wires. They whipped in both directions harmlessly.

Fannie May thought she was literally frozen to the back of her horse. She gripped Monte's neck tightly, grateful for his body heat. Snow had accumulated on her back and was soaking through her clothes. Fannie May had never imagined this degree of cold. She wondered how long a human could survive these conditions. How would she find some shelter? She guided the horse along the fence line, looking for a way to get down to the river valley.

"Whoa, Monte. Did you hear a shot?" she asked the horse, as she waited to hear the noise again above the howling wind. She waited for over a minute and was sure she heard additional shots carried on the wind. Then she dug her heels into the horse's ribs. "Let's turn around, boy. There's someone back there with a rifle."

Fannie May steered her horse back the way they had come. Now they were riding into the wind with the fence on the left. For the moment, she could see four or five fence posts ahead. They plodded into the wind for a half hour before she saw the outline of a horse and rider coming from the opposite direction. And riding on the opposite side of the fence. The rider wasn't looking in her direction. He was looking down the slope of the river valley.

"That looks like it could be John B. At least the horse is big enough," Fannie May whispered to no-one. Then she screamed at the top of her lungs, "Eeeaak."

The rider did not look her way. She wished she had a gun, but she had no weapons and no tools to cut the fence.

Fannie May guided her horse close to the fence. Then she tore a blue ruffle off her dress and wrapped it around the top strand.

"See this wire, Monte. You're going to jump this wire, Monte."

Fannie May had watched her father jump a horse in equestrian events but had never done it herself. She reined Monte away from the fence and dug her heels into his sides until he reached a cantor. Then she steered him in an arc, back towards the fence. By the time the blue cloth came into view, the horse had only seconds to react. Fannie May closed her eyes and held tight to the horse's mane. She felt the horse leap up. To Fannie May, they seemed to float farther and higher than required to hurdle the fence. When the front legs of her horse touched down, Fannie May fell forward and lost her grip on the mane. She landed, unharmed, in a drift of snow-covered sagebrush. The horse continued down the slope towards the other rider.

Cold, sore, and exhausted, Fannie May struggled to get her feet under her. She screamed at the horse and rider. She tried to catch up with Monte, but the snow was too deep and she fell awkwardly.

Barringer was shocked when Monte trotted up beside him. Clyde snickered when the gelding touched him nose to nose.

"Sakes alive," Barringer shouted. "Where is Fannie May? Whoa, Clyde. Stop!"

He looked up the slope but saw only white, with small patches of vegetation poking through. He reached down and grabbed the reins from Monte. Then he turned both horses on a path backtracking hoof prints up the slope. Moments later, they climbed a small ridge and Barringer saw movement in the snow. It was Fannie May, crawling through snow too deep to walk through. Her shivering face managed a grin at John B as he approached.

Barringer climbed down and scooped Fannie May out of the snow in his arms. Her clothes were wet, and she was shivering. He held her close to his body to shield her from the wind.

"Can you ride, Fannie May?"

"Yes. But I am freezing. Which way do we ride?"

"With the wind. We can follow the river valley east. Hopefully, there will be some trees along the bank, where we can take cover."

John B helped her onto her horse. He noticed that ice had formed on the hem of her dress and around her shoulders. She lay forward, trying to extract warmth from Monte.

"We will stop soon, I promise," said John B. As they rode, he wondered how long his bride could survive the frigid temperature. If they did not find shelter soon, she would succumb to the cold and he would not be far behind. His legs were tingling from the effects of frostbite, so he could only imagine the condition of Fannie May's legs under that long, frozen dress.

As they neared the river, he saw tracks in the snow and steaming cow manure. Maybe some animals had found a break in the fence. Once again, he pulled the Winchester off his back as the horses continued to plod through the snow.

"Mwaa." Barringer turned to see a calf running towards him. Several adult longhorns were following fifty yards behind. He readied the rifle and chose the largest of the animals as his target. The cattle plowed through the snow, throwing their heads and horns from side to side as if looking for an exit to this white prison. Frozen mucous covered their steaming nostrils. There were icicles hanging from their underbellies.

The horses deftly sidestepped the charging animals. Barringer fired once and the bullet ricocheted off the forehead of an approaching bull. It stopped and shook its head but did not drop. Barringer fired again, this time hitting the bull in the shoulder. Blood ran down the front leg and the bull dropped to its front knees. Barringer leapt to the ground, slipping on the snow into a sitting position directly in front of the agitated bull. The bull roared and pushed forward with its back legs. As its head rammed Barringer, Fannie May screamed. Then Barringer pushed the barrel of the gun against the bull's eye and pulled the trigger.

Blood sprayed from the animal, covering Barringer's face and hands. The bull fell on its side, motionless. Barringer struggled to his feet and opened the saddlebag. He retrieved one of the knives Fannie May had purchased at the Fort.

"What are you doing?" asked Fannie May.

"I am gutting this bull. Get down, and you can help while he is still warm."

Barringer rolled the bull fully on its side so that two feet were pointing up to waist height. Then he slit the bull's throat. Warm blood drained out of the neck.

"Put your hands in his throat. That will warm them up."

Reluctantly, Fannie May wiggled her fingers through the slot in the animal's neck. The temperature inside was painful to her frozen fingers, but her upper body was warmed by blood running along her arms. Barringer continued to cut a line from the neck, down the brisket, and through the center-line of the animal's underbelly. He struggled feverishly to slice the hairy cowhide and pull it away from the fat-covered hulk.

After he exposed the rib cage, he opened the hide along the animal's underbelly where he could access the internal organs. He pulled out entrails ranging from the apple-sized gall bladder to the pillow-sized rumen. Red, yellow and green liquids stained the snow. Barringer's shirt and arms were dripping blood.

"What's that awful smell," asked Fannie May.

"I must have punctured one of the stomachs. In a rush."

"What do you mean, *one* of the stomachs?"

"Bovines have four stomachs. That big one there is the rumen."

"Why are you doing this?" asked Fannie May.

"Shelter from the storm. Bully boy will keep you warm for the night."

Fannie May looked at the colorful fluids melting the snow around Barringer. She removed her hands from the warmth of the bull's arteries and turned away. Then she doubled over and vomited in the snow.

"Are you OK?" asked Barringer.

"Do you have to ask? Is it my fate to die in the bowels of a bull or to die of frostbite? Or maybe both! Where are you going while I am inside the carcass?"

"I'll be there with you, real cozy-like," replied John B. He couldn't tell if she was shaking her head in disapproval or because of the cold. To lighten the mood, he pointed at her mouth. "You have a little chunk of something on your lip there."

Barringer pulled out the lungs and heart and some miscellaneous organs. Then he helped Fannie May into the dark, murky cavern. She lay with her legs extending into the bull's rib cage and her body resting in a pool of bloody fluids.

"I won't forgive you for this, John B. Aside from the smell and the color, though, I have to admit this is like a warm bath. But I will never forgive you."

Barringer scooped snow on top of the carcass, burying the front quarters. He took off his chaps and lay them across the opening in the bull's hide.

"Look out. I'm coming in." John B slithered his wiry legs into the wet rib cage, next to Fannie May. They lay face to face. Fannie May maneuvered her head onto the shoulder of his muscled right arm.

"What about the horses?" she asked.

"I untied them so they could seek shelter."

"If we die here, nobody will find us."

"Is there anyone looking for us besides that bank robber? I'm just happy to be here with you," whispered John B.

"I love you, Mr. Barringer. But next time we do this, we take off our boots."

Sometime during the first night, Fannie May shook Barringer awake. "I have to pee, John B. Can you let me out of here?"

"No. Just piss in your bloomers," groaned John B.

"What if I need to do more than piss?"

"Same thing. I already did. Reckon our clothes are already dirty. Besides, it saves some heat."

"I'm pissing on you right now. No offense intended," growled Fannie May.

"None taken," chuckled John B.

There was no light entering their refuge. The howling of the wind drowned out any other sounds. For now, Fannie May shivered while soaking in a warm stew of the fluids from two species.

"I am afraid John B. What if this storm lasts for days?"

"Reckon the sun will come out tomorrow and we can mosey on."

"It's so dark in here. If you weren't here, I think I would cry."

"Me too," mumbled John B and almost immediately began to snore.

Fannie May pondered their situation. Was it good fortune to be sheltered in this cavern of flesh and bones? Was she suffering the slings and arrows of outrageous fortune that she had read about in *Hamlet*. The entire soliloquy wormed its way through her mind until her tears mixed with the bloody ooze below. She whispered, "For in that sleep of death what dreams may come."

A dream did come. Fannie May lay on a bed of sand and gravel. Even in the perfect darkness, she sensed she was inside a wooden crate. A man hammered on the lid. He spoke in words that were muffled but she recognized the voice. She raised her hands to push on the top of the crate. She tried to scream but no sound came from her throat. The hammering grew louder. A sliver of light appeared at the lid of the crate. The hammering went faster. Then suddenly a bright shaft pained her eyes. Quickly she attempted to sit up but her forehead struck the lid of the crate. The dream ended.

Fannie May gasped when she awoke. Her vision was restored in the light. She could see her crate was actually red meat. Eight inches above her, she saw the depression her forehead had left in the fatty flesh. She turned towards the light and saw John B using a knife to chip ice away from the opening in the hide.

John B asked, "Are you awake? Did you get a good rest?" He continued to hack the frozen shroud.

"Yes. No."

"Sorry to wake you. I thought I should look out and check the weather. There is still snow blowing down."

"I had a nightmare. The Westinghouse engineer trapped me in a crate."

"'Twas a sudden turn of events."

"Bad karma. I am not sure which is more frightening — the crate or the carcass."

"I reckon the crate. We are temporarily taking shelter in a carcass but being trapped in a crate probably does not bode well at anytime."

"You're right, assuming this is temporary," Fannie May admitted. "We are here by choice. No one chooses to be locked in a crate."

"And in this first-class carcass you get breakfast in bed," John B proclaimed as he presented a chunk of snow to Fannie May.

Conversation was limited while the storm continued throughout another day. The newlyweds slept in fits and spurts. Fannie May had never felt so discouraged as she did when the storm continued into the second night. Even as John B sang a raunchy version of Darling Clementine, she remained woebegone.

By the following morning, Fannie May's low spirits were infecting John B's mood.

"I'm starting to sour on this storm," declared John B. "It has to end soon."

"If you say so," mumbled Fannie May as she squirmed to find a comfortable position.

"I say so. Tomorrow I am going out to build a fire, rain or shine."

In silence, Fannie May stared blankly at the ceiling of raw meat inches from her face.

The storm continued into the third night. The disheartened couple was hungry and cramped, yet the temperature in their den stayed pleasant. John B talked about their past adventures and their future plans. But the present dilemma was never far from his thoughts. The few responses from Fannie May were testy.

Sometime in the night the wind subsided. Fannie May listened for the wind to return but only heard the heavy breathing of her husband. Suddenly she felt at home. Her body relaxed and she went back to sleep.

In the morning, light coming through the snow was blinding to both of the stowaways. John B rubbed his eyes and looked at Fannie May's face. To his surprise she was smiling.

"John B. I am glad we are here together. I would not have survived the first night alone. Imagine the trail hands separated from the others by this storm."

"They would have the company of their horse."

"And imagine being thrown from a horse or a wagon in the middle of the open range covered in snow. The loneliness would be terrifying."

"You are talking like a city person. There are hundreds of men and women who arrive in the West alone, they travel alone, they eat alone, they sleep alone. Miners or hunters or spinsters. Probably prefer to be alone."

"I can only say that I was terrified of losing you. Terrified that you would try to brave the storm looking for help. And more terrified that you would not find help."

"I won't leave you alone. And I hope you don't leave me alone." That day, John B realized how much Fannie May needed him. Almost as much as he needed her.

33

Chisholm Trail, Indian Territory, 1886

The government had paid the Indians the full price of the lands, and while the original understanding was that Oklahoma should be used as a colony for Indians and freedmen, that idea had long ago been abandoned, and the only use made of Oklahoma, Clark said, was that of a pasture of the herds belonging to the cattle barons. He said that a cattle company formed at Lawrence, Kans., had leased the lands from the Indians for $100,000, and had sub-let it at a considerable advance to other cattlemen. He wanted the territory opened to settlers.

—*Emporia Weekly News*, **Emporia, Kansas, February 4, 1886**

In 1886, most cattle drives had moved west, leaving behind the trading posts and watering holes that catered to the needs of the Chisholm Trail crossing the middle of Indian Territory. But late in that year, Cotton was determined to deliver the herd before the onset of winter by taking the shortest route possible. He decided that the Double Lightning crew would enter Indian Territory at the ford named Red River Station. The Red River crossing was the most unpredictable on the Chisholm Trail.

Fortunately, when they arrived, they found that the river had enough water to provide some buoyancy to the cattle but not so much that they had to swim for their lives. The experienced drovers and wagon drivers got the herd across in just half a day, and that night, they set up camp in a post called Blue Grove. Celebrations were in order, and Cotton made sure the deserving men got all the whiskey they could drink. As the crew retired to the warmth of their bedrolls, Cotton watched the fire recede to embers. He took off his boots in the dark, took one last swig of whiskey, and then crawled into his tent. In his stupor, he did not notice the rise under his blanket until he lifted a corner.

"I've been waiting," whispered Una.

"What in tarnation?" exclaimed Cotton.

"Shh, you don't want the crew to hear."

"Shh. Don't want crew," slurred Cotton in a voice that the cattle probably heard.

"Make love to me," whispered Una.

"Nah. Oh well. Stayin'… nnn … awake to make love …." Cotton's voice trailed off.

Una felt Cotton roll on top of her in the dark tent. He mumbled incoherently as the two of them unfastened and tussled for five minutes. Una was uncomfortable but determined. When Cotton's grunting turned to snoring, she struggled to roll his heavy body off of hers. The experience was neither as grim nor as gratifying as she had anticipated. Still and all, she was pleased: she was a woman now. She was a woman, and he was her man.

The following day, the cattle drive moved north into Indian Territory. They reached a post named Reid Store. Most of the crew were tired and hungover from the previous night. They talked around the campfire for an hour after eating supper. Cotton did not hear any comments about his intercourse with Una, and he wondered if it had been a dream—until Una joined him again in his tent that night. She was able to wake him long enough for a union more satisfying than the night before. And Cotton would remember this time.

While the crew was sleeping, Stubby borrowed a horse from the remuda. He knew the consequences if he was caught in the act, but he was dead set on meeting with a previous acquaintance living in the area. He was gone for only a couple of hours and returned the horse undetected.

Stubby crawled into his tent and shook his bunk mate.

"What? Mornin' already?" asked Bucktooth.

"You know that item I been cogitatin' on," said Stubby. "Figger it's high time I took a wife."

The Double Lightning cattle drive continued north without any major problems. The campfire discussions centered around the burgeoning relationship between Una and Cotton. Cotton stayed aloof to the comments and innuendo. Unless Una was mentioned. Then he was quick to rebuke any cowboys that besmirched her character. But after Cotton left the campfire, the banter degenerated quickly.

"Can't really hear any squealin' and moanin' over all the racket from the cattle," said one of the drovers.

"Maybe Cotton can't get his pants off."

"If it was me in the tent with that filly, buttons would be flying every direction."

"I bet Cotton knows his way around buttons and belts. This isn't his first rodeo."

"Bet he don't bother to take his boots off."

The men around the fire broke into spontaneous laughter. Then the conversation became even more graphic as the drovers talked about women they had been with in saloons and brothels along the trail.

On the morning of November 13, the cattle drive crossed the Canadian River at Silver City. At the end of the day, when the cattle were settled, most of the men rode back to Silver City for an evening of gambling, drinking, and womanizing. Nobody noticed the drop in the overnight temperature until they gathered for breakfast the next morning. They built a huge campfire and sat around it, groaning and shivering. There were no thermometers to indicate the morning temperature of forty degrees Fahrenheit.

As the sun came up, the crew pointed at the silhouettes of four riders on a ridge less than a mile to the northeast. One of riders appeared to be wearing a feathered headdress.

Stubby pulled a spyglass from his pack. "Looks like Comanches to me. Wonder if we are grazing on their land?"

Cotton replied, "The government pays fees to the Comanche, Apache and Kiowa tribes to allow us to graze here. That was all setup by Quanah Parker and Sam Burnett back in '84."

"What d'ya think they want?" asked Stubby, as he passed the scope.

"They might have a fence ahead of us. Even if we can legally cross their land, they still have the right to fence it."

"Reckon they just wonder what a cattle drive is doing so late in the season," Stubby suggested.

"Stubby, you keep an eye on them with that spyglass, will ya?" asked Cotton. "If they get any closer, I'll go have a conflab."

Stubby nodded to Cotton and turned away to wink at Bucktooth.

The unknown riders followed the cattle drive from a distance. Cotton and Stubby shared the spyglass throughout the day. The next morning the point rider stopped the herd at the base of a small rise. He sent word back to Cotton that there was a barbwire fence across the trail ahead. Cotton rode up to have a look.

"Is there a gate in the fence?" Cotton asked the point rider.

"Not that I can see. It's probably easiest to take down the wire for a couple of furlongs."

"OK. Cut the wires by that tree on the ridge and lay it on the ground in both directions. Then I'll supervise a crew to tack it back up. That's probably why we have spectators following us. Just want to make sure we put the fence back the way we found it."

On the morning of November 15, the sky was clear and a cold wind blew from the northwest. Dust was in the air, and a gray wall appeared on the western horizon. By afternoon, the dust clouds had rolled across the cold, dry plain and enveloped the Chisholm Trail. Cotton wondered if he should stop the herd near the Yukon settlement and delay crossing the North Canadian River. He was shading his eyes in an effort to see through the dust when suddenly one of the drag drovers appeared.

"We finished hanging two strands of barbwire back where we cut through the fence," said the rider.

"What about the other two strands?" asked Cotton.

"Can't see well enough to find the wire."

"Any sign of those strangers on the flank?"

"Can't see them, either. No one came to us."

"Just wait here." Cotton rode downwind until he couldn't see the other rider. Then he turned his horse back into the wind and returned to the drover. "Visibility is about thirty yards. We can't cross the North Canadian in this," Cotton shouted over the roar of the wind. "We'll stop the herd at the edge of the river. Spread the word up the right side. I'll go up the left."

Cotton rode around the left flank and told Bucktooth to spread the word up that side. Bucktooth disappeared into the dust as he rode north along the left side of the herd.

When he came to Stubby's position, he lowered his bandanna and yelled, "Cotton says to stop the herd before the river. I'll go tell the others up the line."

"Can't see anything in this wind. I doubt that I can join up with my wedding party in this weather."

"You mean kidnappers," said Bucktooth. "What do you need them for? Just take your prize and ride into the wind. Nobody can track in this."

"Shit. This weather feels wrong," mumbled Stubby.

"We need to take cover. Can't even light a cooking fire in this."

"Go. I'll see you back at camp." As Stubby rode to the back of the herd, he worried that his plan was falling apart. He had arranged for a crew to follow the drive and kidnap Una after they crossed the North Canadian. Stubby planned to stay on the drive for another couple of days so that he was not suspected. Then he would ride out, on the pretense that he knew where they took her. But with no visibility, the plan fell apart. He was running out of time to act. He would have to improvise.

When Stubby got to the wagons, he found Una standing by a horse in the lee of the chuckwagon. He galloped over and shouted above the wind, "Cotton told me to come and get you. Let's get to safety. He's setting up camp in the river valley."

Una had never experienced a dust storm on the open prairie. She was afraid to stay and afraid to go with Stubby. She assumed that she could ride back to the safety of the wagon if Stubby had deceived her. Una climbed onto the horse and protested when Stubby grabbed the reins from her. Then he led them directly into the wind.

Una could hardly see Stubby's back, and the roar of the wind drowned out the sounds of the cattle. She put her head down and pulled a scarf around her mouth and nose. The ride seemed to go on forever.

"Where are you taking me?" Una yelled. But Stubby did not answer. He just pulled harder on the reins.

The dust started to bite her face. There were tiny bits of ice in the dust. Una covered her eyes with one arm and held on to the saddle horn with the other. Suddenly the air ahead turned white. Snow was blowing directly in her face. The ground ahead was already white with snow.

On the north side of Yukon, the herd huddled in a grassy field. Blowing snow pelted the cattle and the crew. Drifts were forming between the few buildings of the town. Cotton ordered the crew to group their wagons and teams beside the livery stable at the edge of town. The cowhands tied their horses along the board fences and signposts. Cotton assumed Una was safely sheltered in the chuckwagon. He focused on seeking lodging somewhere in town. Through the whiteout, Cotton saw no signs of life when he rode into the middle of town. Snowdrifts were covering the sidewalks. Signs were hanging askew, that is, if they weren't blown completely off the buildings. Someone had abandoned a wagon in the middle of the street. There was no trace of any team that had been hitched to it. There were no horses to be seen anywhere down the street.

Cotton spotted an orange glow in the window of one building which, even without a sign, appeared to be a place of lodging. He rode his horse up the step and could see people huddled around a fireplace. He tied his horse and went inside.

"Howdy, folks," said Cotton, as he banged the snow off his hat.

"Where'd you come from, stranger?"

"I'm herding for the Double Lightning Ranch. Name's Cotton."

"Where's yer herd, mister?"

"Right outside town. We got stopped by this storm."

"Where are yer men?"

"They're just out there also. I wonder if there is a place we can hole up for the night. We'll head for the river in the morning."

"Son, that's assuming this storm lets up. Folks here remember last winter. It came about this time."

"Yeah. That storm lasted a week, and the rest of the month was just plain old winter."

"We can put you up for the night right here if you have your own bedrolls," interjected an elderly woman. "I'm afraid we don't have food enough to feed a whole crew."

"We got our own food. And a couple of good cooks. Just need to thaw them out," replied Cotton, as he started for the door. There were some posters on the wall beside the door. Most were tattered "Wanted" posters, for outlaws that were probably dead and gone. A poster on white paper appeared to be newer than the others. The Van Brothers were wanted for a bank holdup in Llano.

Cotton was scanning the wall for any reference to men on his crew who might be wanted elsewhere, when he heard a loud crash in the street. When he opened the door, longhorn cattle were thundering past — bawling and hooves pounding louder than the wind. The stampede was moving downwind, and nothing could stand in its way. Cotton's horse broke its tether and was swept into the furor.

Cotton stepped to the walkway and yelled down the street, "Una, look out," but his words were drowned by the stampede. He watched in horror as the herd demolished everything in its path. From his vantage point, he saw the trading post and livery trampled to the ground by thousands of hooves. He knew his crew were tied up directly in the path of the stampede. When he stepped onto the porch, a horn from a passing animal caught him on the hip, tearing his chaps and skin. Cotton fell. He rolled with the herd until he was under the porch deck and the hooves were no longer pounding his legs.

In pain, Cotton waited. He was afraid of what he would find when the stampede was over. How could anyone survive the maelstrom? Would they have had any warning? By the time they saw the animals coming, they would be crushed. Was the chuckwagon enough to protect Una?

As the last few cows ran past, Cotton crawled into the street. With difficulty, he stood and limped to where the chuckwagon had been parked. The wagon was on its side. The canvas was flapping in the wind. Two panicked horses, still harnessed to the wagon, were dragging it in circles. Cotton grabbed both horse collars and calmed the steeds. When he staggered over to the upset wagon, there was no sign of Una. As Cotton looked around, he saw nobody from his crew. They had disappeared along with the herd. He knew he had to find Una but did not know where to start.

Una felt like she was in a different world. A world where everything was white. A cold world where her hands and feet went numb. Una touched her forehead, but it felt like a stone. Tears had frozen around her eyes, and she wiped them with her hand, hoping to see something. She could see the head of her horse but, besides that, she could only see her reins tensing towards an invisible rider on an invisible horse. She knew Stubby was still there. In her mind, she could feel his groping fingers. She could smell his putrid breath. She could hear his lewd grunts. In her mind.

Una had no sense of time. Had they been riding into the wind for minutes—or hours? Somehow, she was able to focus in this moment. She was no longer with the cattle drive. She was getting further from Cotton every minute. She had been captured by Stubby, and now survival was her only priority.

Una was afraid of what Stubby was planning after dark. Or would he wait until the storm receded? No, he would take her body. He would take her warmth. To Stubby, she was an object for his pleasure. Una knew she must escape in the storm. Better to die cold and alone than to be violated by the sinner who was leading her into the tempest.

Una leaned forward, but she could not reach the reins. She talked to the horse. She pulled the sides of its halter.

"Stop, horse. Whoa, boy. Whoa."

The horse was close to panic. It knew that this strange world meant danger. It only continued because it chose to follow the lead horse.

Una struggled to climb onto the horse's neck in an effort to lean over its face and grab the reins. But her movements scared the animal. It reared to the side, sending

Una tumbling into the snow. For a moment, she saw one of the reins dangling, then the horse disappeared into the opaque atmosphere. Una lay flat on the ground, trapped in a cold white room—a room smaller than a wagon yet larger than the county. Una could see the hoof prints from the two horses. She started to crawl in the direction from which they came. Her hands and knees were wet and cold from contact with the snow. The wind blew cold on her back and legs. There was no escaping the cold, whether she lay still or crawled. So she continued to crawl.

The storm was unending. Snow filled the hoof prints. Soon Una realized that she had likely angled off the trail. The wind was coming from her left side now. She felt she could go no further. Her thoughts were scattered, and she seemed to be dreaming. Dreams about Cotton. Dreams about her family. Dreams that her father was coming to find her. Dreams that she was traveling down a steep slope. Una dreamt that her hands were warm. It felt good even if it was in her imagination. She had heard of mirages in the desert. This warmth must be the snow storm equivalent of a mirage.

Suddenly her arms descended into a soft and warm ooze. Below the snow, the surface was wet and tepid. As she moved forward, her arms sank further into the warmth.

The sensation was startling — and confusing. Una wondered if she was waking from a dream. Maybe she was still in the granary of wheat back home. But this felt wet and warm. She could sink in it when she moved, and the warmth felt good. Then, suddenly, the bottom fell away, and Una plunged headfirst into the mire. She held her breath and twisted so that her body floated above her feet. Frantically, she reached over her head and felt around until her hand gripped a solid object. Una pulled herself to the surface and gasped for air. The air smelled like rotten eggs and left a bitter taste on her lips. She held tight to the rocky ledge with her frozen fingers. Fumes and steam were rising from the surface around her.

Una did not know where she was. But she had heard about quicksand. Was it quicksand that was sheltering her from the relentless cold? As the storm continued into the night, Una felt safe for the time being, stranded in a warm, wet, dark pit.

34

North Canadian River, Indian Territory, 1886

The Treasury Department has received a large quantity of paper money which had been burned in a railroad smashup and conflagration. Although to the inexpert the money could scarcely be recognized as fragments of money the treasury experts expect to make out the denominations and estimate the value.

—Indian Chieftain, **Vinita, Indian Territory, December 8, 1887**

Almost two feet of snow fell during the three-day storm that swept through Indian Territory. The wind never stopped, but it did change directions from night to day. Any obstructions in the path of the storm created snow-drifts up to six feet deep. Tall weeds, sagebrush, and oak trees appeared randomly above the surface. Otherwise, the lands along the border with southern Kansas were completely white.

Una slept in fits and starts, floating near the top layer of the warm quicksand. She had discovered a ledge under the surface, where she could sit with her head protruding into the open air. Steam rising off the hot spring water smelled of minerals but created a layer of warm air so that Una's exposed face did not freeze despite the discomfort. Tiny icicles formed in her dark red hair, creating a crown-of-thorns appearance.

Una's religious upbringing helped her fight the loneliness. She thanked God for providing this sanctuary during the storm. She recited passages from the Bible that she had committed to memory. She waited patiently for the storm to end.

Una dared not drink the smelly brew surrounding her, but she was able to lick snow that accumulated above the spa. She ignored her hunger. There would be no food until the storm subsided.

On the fourth day, the sun came up in a clear blue sky. The temperature climbed above freezing, and snow melted at the edges of the hot spring. Carefully, she felt her way along the ledge to a point where she felt solid ground under the snow. Climbing into the cold air was both a relief and a shock. Her clothes and hair were steaming. But her wet skin was cooling quickly. Una thought about building a fire, but she couldn't see any dry fuel. Nor would she be able to start the fire without matches. She heard some birds singing. Then a horse whinnied in the distance. She scanned the horizon and saw a large black horse pushing snow off the ground to find some grass below. There was no rider on the horse and the reins dragged in the snow. But it had a saddle and bag.

When Una began to walk, she realized that she had lost her boots in the quicksand. Socks were all that covered her feet as she ran towards the horse. When she got close, she slowed and spoke softly.

"Good horse. What a good boy." Carefully she grabbed the reins, and the stallion threw his head high and whinnied loud. Una rubbed his nose with her warm hand. She hoped she had gained the horse's trust and moved to mount the saddle. The horse was so tall that she had to jump to grab the saddle horn and lift herself to get a foothold in the stirrup. After a couple of attempts, she successfully mounted the big black horse with three white legs.

Una shook the reins and clicked her tongue. Clyde turned and started walking west along the valley of the North Canadian River.

Barringer was awakened by cold water dripping on his lower back. When he moved, he disturbed Fannie May.

"What's happening now?" asked Fannie May.

"I think the storm is done. Some of the snow is melting," replied Barringer, as he probed his breathing hole with the knife. "I can see blue sky."

"Let's get out of here!" rasped Fannie May.

"I'll see if the horses are still here. I haven't heard them for a couple of days."

They struggled to shift stiffened limbs, then lurched through the snowdrift that covered the dead bull. Once out of the cavern, they stood staring at each other. Barringer had dark red stains on the right side of his clothes and body. Blood dripped from his shirt and pants, staining the sparkling surface surrounding his boots.

Fannie May looked at him in shock before gazing down. Her blood-soaked dress clung to her body from the neck down. Her exposed skin had transformed from milky soft to crusty sorrel. Her hair was matted with a cinnamon-like powder. "I would sooner freeze than get back in that coffin of meat and bones," said Fannie May.

Barringer grimaced, hearing the exasperation in her voice. When he looked at her sunken cheeks and the dark bags below her eyes, he said, "Let's try to build a fire." Barringer kicked some snow aside and pulled his chaps out of the drift. Then he looked around in a complete arc. "We need to find Clyde. The saddlebag was on him."

"And the matches are in the saddlebag!" wailed Fannie May. "John B. The bloody matches are in the bloody saddlebag with all the bloody money!"

Barringer put his chaps on without saying a word. He put the knife in his belt and the rifle over his shoulder. Then he scooped up a handful of snow to quench his thirst. Barringer wondered if they could survive long enough to find either horse. Never had he been so dependent on a horse as at this moment. And there were no tracks. No neighing or pounding of hooves. Not even any horse shit.

The Clydesdale plodded upstream along the bank of the North Canadian River with an ice-coated rider. Una clung to the horse for dear life, grateful for the companion. She hoped the horse was in search of shelter and food. Or was its owner nearby? After an hour, Una and Clyde entered a grove of live oak trees. Some saplings and ferns protruded through the snow. The horse started to graze on these, waiting for further instructions.

The air felt warmer in the sheltered area. Una saw some dead-fall among the trees and opened the saddlebag to see if there were any matches. Her spirits were lifted by the sight of the hymnals in the bag. Hymnals would make good kindling, and there were wooden matches. Una threw the saddlebag to the snow below and dismounted. Quickly, she gathered some dead weeds, tree branches, and leaves. She arranged them in a tiny steeple on an exposed stump. Then she tried to open the hymnals. Una discovered that the covers were glued shut but a flap on top opened to reveal hundreds of notes where she expected song pages. Una had never seen paper money before but assumed the bills would burn as well as any other paper. She stuffed some into her tinder and lit them with one match. As the paper and kindling worked their magic, Una warmed her hands over the tiny fire. Then she set about gathering more wood.

John B and Fannie May heard a horse whinny downstream. They tromped through snow and mud for two miles before they rounded a bend in the river. There they could see a grove of trees. Gray smoke wafted above the leaves. As they got closer they could smell wood-smoke. Once inside the grove, they saw a tiny person resting against a tree and a giant horse beside a fire.

Clyde whinnied loudly as he saw the Barringers approach. John B held his rifle at his waist while Fannie May approached the foundling. The person stood up to hide behind a tree.

"Don't be afraid," said Fannie May softly. "We saw your fire and heard the horse."

The coating of frozen mud and mineral scale concealed the gender of the small stranger. Strands of red hair protruded from the gray ooze covering their head. Hazel eyes were dull behind the earthen mask that covered other facial features. Streaks appeared below their eyes, where tears had dissolved the scale. Fannie May waited for a reply before deciding whether the stranger was male or female. At first glance, she thought the stranger was a girl, but Fannie May recalled another tiny stranger who had deceived her by pretending to be a man.

"That is *my* fire," stammered Una. She paused to muster more confidence and shouted, "I made that fire."

"We don't mean to scare you, miss," declared John B, drawing his own conclusions. "My name is John Barringer and this is my bride, Fannie May."

Fannie May took Una's arm and guided her back to sit at the fire. She spoke softly, trying to comfort a fellow survivor. John B proceeded to gather more wood, and when the fire was roaring, he went to check on Clyde. The horse would have struggled to get enough feed during the blizzard, so Barringer gathered leafy branches and tall grass. He noticed that the saddlebag was missing from the back of the horse.

When John B went back to the fire, Fannie May was wiping the mud from the face of a weeping girl. He gathered from the conversation that this girl, Una, had been kidnapped from the company of a trail boss on the Chisholm Trail. Her captor had taken her into the blizzard, where she escaped on foot and, by the grace of God, came across a sand-filled hot spring. After the blizzard, she was looking for help and came across his horse.

"God answered my prayers and delivered your horse and saddlebag to me," alleged Una. "I built this fire with matches and papers found in the saddlebag."

"I bet those papers were fivers," said Barringer. "How many did you need to start the fire?"

"I used at least ten. What is a fiver?"

"Five dollars. That's OK. You only burnt fifty dollars to start the fire," Fannie May said.

"Fifty dollars? How can I ever repay you?"

"You have repaid us," assured Fannie May. "You saved our horse and the saddlebag. You built a fire for us to get warm. That is more than enough."

"It's easy for you to say," said John B. "It's my money yer burnin'."

Una's eyes darted from one to the other. After a pause, Fannie May burst out laughing and John B grinned. Una relaxed when she realized they were taking the situation in stride.

"John B, you should take Clyde for a ride. See if you can find my horse. While you are gone, Una and I will be getting some of the filth off our clothes and bodies."

"How do you plan to do that?" wondered John B.

"Never you mind. Just don't be in a rush to come back here," Fannie May ordered.

The women watched Barringer climb into the saddle, tip his hat, and then ride downstream. Then Fannie May started to undress.

"What are you doing?" asked Una.

"Getting these bloody clothes off!" exclaimed Fannie May. "We can scrub our clothes and skin with snow, then dry them by the fire."

Una followed the older woman's lead. The two of them stood naked by the fire while they rubbed themselves with melting snow. Their skin came reasonably clean. Hair and clothes were a bigger challenge. Fannie May filled her bloomers with snow and held them close enough to the fire that the snow melted and dissolved some of the blood from them. After a couple of rinses, she realized that they would never be white again. She fashioned a tripod of branches near the fire and draped the clothes over it. Then she helped Una do the same.

Una knelt by the fire rubbing snow into her long auburn hair and along her limbs. Her limbs were long and thin, like those of a child growing faster than normal. The cold water cleansed the mud and revealed ribs distending the pale skin of her torso. Each handful of snow revealed more of Una's delicate frame.

Una noticed Fannie May staring at her figure and attempted to cover herself with arms and hands.

"I am sorry, Una. You seem so young compared to me. Can I ask how old you are?"

"I am eighteen."

"How did such a young girl get into such trouble?"

"I had trouble at home when I was fourteen. Then I became ill with the fever. I was in a hospital until a few weeks ago. I fell in love with a cowboy and was accompanying him on a cattle drive when this storm separated us."

"What's his name?" asked Fannie May.

"Cotton," swooned Una. "He is the handsomest man I ever saw. He saved me once from a man named Stubby, who attacked me. And that same man kidnapped me in the storm. He will be in big trouble when Cotton finds him."

"Did Cotton convince you to join the cattle drive?" inquired Fannie May.

"No. I did the convincing because I wanted to get to Kansas. Dodge City, Kansas."

"Why Dodge?" asked Fannie May. "It's reputed to be a wild place."

"I don't remember," Una admitted. "Maybe I want to be a Harvey Girl." Una picked up her dress and removed a safety pin holding a soggy piece of newspaper. She unfolded the paper to show Fannie May. "They are looking for Harvey Girls in Dodge City."

"I have heard about Fred Harvey and his restaurants. That sounds like a good job."

"Where are you and John B going?" asked Una. "If you don't mind me asking?"

"We were going to Dodge to catch the train. Then west to Arizona. We joined up with a cattle drive for safety. There is an outlaw tracking us for that money you saw in the hymnals."

Both women continued to soak their clothes and wring the dirty water out of them. The sun was setting and the light of the fire cast shadows of their naked forms against the trees. One shadow was slim and twig-like. The other athletic and curvy.

Fannie May took the opportunity to explore her concerns. "Look at those shadows. I look like a porker compared to you."

"I see nothing wrong with your body Fannie May." answered Una shyly.

"Beyond some blood stains and saggy skin," laughed Fannie May. "But I think we both could use a hearty meal. How was the food where you came from?"

"The drovers did not leave much food untouched on the trail. Most of my meals were cold scraps."

"And before the cattle drive?"

"I think the Waco nurses tried to feed me well. But there was not a lot of food, and I had no money to contribute. I prayed that God would provide for me."

"I think we all need a good meal when we get to town. Perhaps God has delivered you to our care for that reason." Secretly, Fannie May started to wonder where their next meal would come from.

Barringer rode east along the river valley, looking for the other horse. Clyde stopped to give a loud snicker at regular intervals. They had no luck before dusk, so they turned back towards the fire flickering among the live oaks.

"Whoa, boy. I think we came back too soon," whispered Barringer as he noticed firelight reflecting off shiny white skin.

"I have an idea, Clyde. Let's go upstream and find that bull carcass."

In the light of a full moon, Barringer was able to find the footprints that led back to the bull carcass. He took the knife from his belt and started hacking chunks of meat out of the hind quarters. He noticed the liver where he had left it, half-buried in the snow. He bundled the cuts of meat in a piece of hide and hung them on the horn before settling into the saddle.

Just as Barringer reined Clyde towards the campsite, the horse reacted to a sudden movement on its right. A dark horse was approaching from the east, at a gallop, the snow exploding in front of his legs. Monte had returned.

Barringer and horses rode to the edge of the grove of trees, where Clyde announced their presence. The women hustled to cover themselves with clammy clothes. Fannie May whistled when it was safe for John B to enter the bluff. He cooked the meat from the bull, and the trio ate until they could eat no more. There was liver left for another meal. They reveled in their survival by singing from the few pages left in the hymnals, followed by compositions that would never be heard in a church. Sleeping in dry clothes, on a bed of branches, near a warm fire was a comfort that they would never again take for granted.

The next day, they set off—Barringer on Clyde and Fannie May and Una on Monte—trudging through the drifts of snow in the river valley. The horses were hungry, and the footing was difficult. The party covered only twenty miles before the horses needed rest. Barringer found a patch of willows sheltered from the wind at the edge of the river. There were blades of grass showing, and the riders were able to scrape away enough snow to let the horses graze. That evening, Fannie May and Una built a fire, again using five-dollar notes as kindling. They cooked the remaining liver.

The following day gave new life to the horses. Travel was less difficult, since the horses now had experience with snow on the ground. The riders were comfortable as the sun warmed their backs. Early in the day, Barringer pointed to a heavy black wall atop the crest of a hill ahead of them.

"What is it, John B?" asked Fannie May.

"I don't know. It seems to be along the fence line."

"Why are those vultures circling? There must be two dozen."

"Let's have a look," Barringer suggested, as he rode up the rise.

As they ascended the north bank of the river, the abomination became apparent. There were dead and injured cattle piled against the barbwire fence—thousands of cattle piled on top of one another. There was no movement. They made no sounds, although warm breath could be seen rising in places. Even the ones standing on all fours were cold and lifeless —propped up by the remains of other dead beasts.

"What happened?" asked Una. "Whose cows are these?"

"Reckon they are all that's left of a cattle drive," said Barringer. "The cattle turned south in the snowstorm. They would not be able to see the barbwire, so I figger the first ones ran into it, then the ones who were following just piled into the back of them. They froze to death or died from injuries."

"I see breath coming from a few," said Fannie May. "Maybe we can save them."

"Unlikely," replied Barringer, as he climbed down from his horse. He went over to a calf that seemed to be breathing and tried to drag it out of the pile. Its legs were tangled among larger animals. When he pulled the small animal free from the drift, its legs hung loose—broken.

Barringer waved the women to look away before taking his knife and cutting the animal's throat.

"We should check the brands so we can report this at Dodge," suggested Fannie May. She and Una dismounted and walked behind the carcasses, trying to distinguish any visible brands. Fannie May was surprised when Una stopped dead in her tracks. She stared at Una bending over and vomiting in the snow. When the girl stood, she had a frightened expression.

"Have you been sick a lot," asked Fannie May.

Before Una could answer, a rush of nausea required Fannie May to double over. She grabbed for Una's outstretched arm to maintain her balance as she retched vigorously.

Barringer walked across the backs of the dead animals. Looking to the west, he could not see the end of the carcasses. Thousands lined the fence. Black, gray, and brown hair. Longhorns, Herefords, and Brahmas. There were some horse carcasses in the jumble, too. Barringer saw a cowboy hat stuck on the horns of one animal. He took notice of the brands from the herd on the trail. And he counted another dozen brands that he did not recognize.

Preoccupied by the carnage, Barringer stepped on a black creature. The vulture expelled a guttural hiss at him before taking flight. Then he noticed several other vultures taking flight from the carcasses in his path. Their rasping squawk could only be described as petrifying. Barringer lost his balance and fell onto a head where the bird had removed a bull's eye, leaving bloody and stringy remains. He struggled not to vomit when he heard the accompanying retching from the womenfolk.

"Are we finished airin' the paunches, gals?" John B asked as he returned to them.

Fannie May wiped the drool on her sleeve and asked "How many different brands?"

"At least fifteen. I recognized three brands from Tommy Montana's drive."

"How many head do you estimate?"

"Thousands, but I couldn't see to the end," bemoaned John B.

Una quietly asked, "What happened?"

"These cattle died a horrible death. They were starved and half-licked from the long trail, but they ran their hearts out to escape the storm. Then they piled onto each other and broke bones and crushed heads. Any that survived the affray will either die from the cold or starve before they can get free of this pile."

"We should put some out of their misery," said Fannie May.

"Not on your life. You get hanged for rustling, so you get hanged for killing someone's animals. 'Sides, there ain't enough bullets in the Union Army to do the job," lamented Barringer. "Saddle up, ladies. We keep heading west."

They had ridden only a few yards when Fannie May screamed. She was pointing to the carcasses about fifty feet ahead. A horse head protruded from the pile. Its front legs were on top of a steer as if it had tried to climb over the carcass. Its ears were twisting in the wind. Its eyes were wide open. The back of the horse was pinned under more bovine carcasses. A saddlebag was pushed up beside the horse's neck.

"That's Tarry," yelled Fannie May. "She's still alive."

"No. She can't be. Her ears are just flapping in the breeze."

"John B. You need to check."

Barringer dismounted onto the back of a frozen bull and clamored over another dozen carcasses. When he got to Tarry, he felt her mouth and neck. Everything was ice-cold. He patted the top of the horse's head. The horse did not move. Barringer struggled to pull the saddlebag out of the pile. When he looked inside, he saw some jerky and a canteen that had burst from freezing.

After he climbed off the pile of dead animals, Barringer threw the canteen into the snow and passed the jerky to Fannie May and Una. Then he hung the saddlebag on Clyde. The group was silent as the horses trudged on through the knee-deep snow.

35

The agricultural editor of the Garden City Sentinel sensibly says:

The heavy snowstorms of the past week, though personally unpleasant, are highly valuable to the country. They supply the needed moisture for the wheat and fill the soil with water preparatory to next spring's crops. There is little doubt that with a continuation of the snowstorms, next year will bring us a harvest which will be unparalleled in the west. Every wonderful harvest will double the population of this country, and we ought to be able to bear the personal inconvenience of snowstorms without grumbling. A snowy winter invariably precedes a fine crop season, while a dry, open winter, while it is an excellent thing for cattle on the range, means a dry spring, no wheat, late corn, hot winds, hard times and general desolation. Give us the snow, even though it comes in blizzards, rather than the mild, open winter which precedes drouth.

—*Dodge City Times*, Dodge City, Kansas, November 25, 1886

Cotton survived the three-day blizzard by taking cover in the Yukon jailhouse. The only brick building in the village, it withstood the horrendous wind. Some of his crew members were able to find shelter in the local buildings. For three days, they waited for the snow and wind to abate. When the weather settled, people appeared on the wooden sidewalks to take stock of who had survived and who was lost.

Most buildings were able to maintain some heat with wood or coal stoves, but a number of chairs and tables had to be used as fuel. Some residents had frozen fingers and toes from venturing out in the storm. Dogs and cats were discovered trapped under the porches and steps of buildings. A goat was leaping from snowdrift to snowdrift until a local resident shot it.

Everyone agreed that no living person had ever witnessed a winter storm so brutal in this western territory. Remarkably, the Yukon outpost had survived it.

On the fifth morning, the town deputy had a list of twenty-three people who were missing and another four who were found deceased from exposure. The doctor insisted the bodies had to be thawed out before he declared them deceased. Then bodies were wrapped in blankets and placed in outdoor sheds until an undertaker could come through town.

Cotton's entire remuda had broken free and only a few of the horses stayed in the shelter of the town. And many of those animals were suffering from exposure and thirst. The livery man had taken shelter in his stable and kept a dozen horses fed and watered. After the storm, hay and supplies were delivered around the village by a team of two horses using a stone boat as a sled.

Cotton rode out of town looking for Una. He found most of the cattle and horses piled up along the fences at the South Canadian River. He also found the bodies of some members of his crew, including the cook, Maria. There was no sign of Una or Stubby or their two horses.

When he returned to the saloon in Yukon, Cotton sat down with the remaining trail hands. "The drive is finished, men," Cotton announced. "The herd is gone, mostly dead. Same for most of the horses."

"What happened to those two womenfolk?" asked one of the cowboys.

"I found Maria's body. No sign of Una."

"What about Stubby?" asked Bucktooth. "He's missing too."

"Yeah, that's right," replied Cotton. "Anyone know anything about that?"

The drovers all shrugged. All but Bucktooth. He turned to avoid Cotton's gaze.

"We gonna get any pay?" asked a drover.

"Yeah, how we s'posed to get out of this place?" mumbled another.

"I'm gonna pay you each fifty dollars plus one horse. And I'll see what the ranch wants to do for you in the spring when the next drive comes around."

"What if there ain't nuff horses."

"Reckon some of you will need to partner up until you find a horse for sale. I'll buy you a horse where I can." Cotton started passing out money. He bought another round for everyone before they went their separate directions. Except for Bucktooth. "As for you, you need to come clean about your pal Stubby."

Bucktooth looked sheepish as he spun an empty whiskey glass.

"OK, spill the beans. What do you know about Stubby and Miss Clark?" asked Cotton.

"Ain't fair that I'm payin' the price for Stubby's bent action," moaned Bucktooth.

"Tell me what he did, or I'll kick the livin' shit outta ya."

"Those Commancheros were his idea. They were s'posed to come in before the storm and take Miss Una. Before she went into your tent."

"So when the storm came up, what did Stubby do?"

"Far as I know, he wasn't waitin' for the Commancheros. Don't know fer shor but s'pect he went for the girl on his own."

"Where would he take her?" Cotton prodded.

"Reckon he would ride with the wind."

"I doubt that. I bet Stubby rode upwind. To the west along the river. The storm would cover his tracks quicker."

"Must'a been like pissin' into the wind. Stubby probably froze out there."

"Not to mention Miss Una!" shouted Cotton. "She would be no better off than your bastard friend. I'm going to ride upstream to look for them."

"Want me to come along?" asked Bucktooth.

"No. And forget your pal. He is a dead man riding."

LONG AND SHORT OF IT

36

Dodge City, Kansas, December 1886

The editors and managers of the Vox Populi have been, are now, and always will be opposed to anything that the editors, or managers of the Dodge City Times advocate. They intend to wage a persistent and relentless warfare upon any and all things emanating from this source. Their opposition to this scapegoat faction is just and right; no decent newspaper or set of men with the least claim to respectability could do otherwise. The editor of the *Times* is, and always has been a scurrilous and unscrupulous vagabond; his treacherous and fiendish acts drove him from Missouri; the same purile mendacity that characterized him in Missouri, and stamped him as a villain of the deepest dye, has manifested itself in Kansas. The goddess Nemesis, who so effectually squelched him in Missouri will crush him here. His days are short. The time has about arrived when he will fold his government blanket and seek the shelter and assistance of a friend, as he did when he left Missouri for Dodge City. His cry that the gang must go will soon recoil upon his own vile and putrid carcass with such force that he will be left the shattered and pestilent remnant of an obliterated faction. "The gang," as this vile wretch sees fit to call the element that opposes him in Dodge, will sweep him and his little coterie of venomous reptiles that answer to his beck and call, and grin and acquiesce in all he says and writes into the eternal depths of perdition.

—W.B. Masterson, *The Vox Populi*, Dodge City, Kansas, November 1, 1884

Over the years, there were several newspapers in Dodge City. The *Dodge City Times* was first published in 1876 and was recognized as the primary source of news in the area. The gang was largely opposed to the anti-gang slant of the *Times* and labeled it as a branch of the Democratic party.

Ransome Cooper, a reporter from Chicago, had set up a commercial print shop in Dodge. Operating a print shop business fell short of his lifelong dream to become editor of a prominent newspaper. His occasional forays into publishing were limited to single-page issues when time and money allowed. Bat Masterson met Ransome during the Dodge City War. After the town returned to peace, Bat had obtained a picture of eight gang members, which he labeled the Dodge City Peace Commission. Bat enlisted Ransome to print copies of the picture for the Gang members. This was the editor's first official business with the Gang, but it would not be his last.

Bat sought the printer's assistance to issue a four-page newspaper entitled *The Vox Populi* in November, 1884. The issue was intended to influence Dodge City voters to support Masterson's preferred candidates in the upcoming civic elections. The November 1 edition was written almost exclusively by Bat, but he did not have the initiative to continue. The *Vox Populi* had only one issue.

The interest generated by the vicious content in the *Vox Populi* encouraged Ransome. He now realized that he could publish whatever he could imagine. The *Vox Populi* had included fraudulent and spurious claims. The response from the *Dodge City Times* was less vile but equally fraudulent. The fact that Bat's accusations were in black and white was never questioned. Readers who supported Bat and the Gang would believe those claims. And readers who opposed the Gang and its cabal of candidates would ignore them. In fact, there was no need for readers to go beyond the front page of the *Vox Populi* to understand the opinions of the editor.

Ransome concluded that print news was no more reliable than the spoken word. The stories in a newspaper might be truth or might be fiction. Either way, the message conveyed was open to interpretation by the reader. These weekly or daily publications reminded Ransome of Aesop's fables. Readers knew the stories were contrived, yet they accepted the message in principle. Even children knew that a tortoise could not actually challenge a hare, yet the message of the story rang true. Aesop, if he truly existed, may well have been a newspaper editor in another life. Newspapers were merely conveying a story. It was up to the reader to consider, "What if it is true?"—and then decide.

As a result of this experience, Ransome created the *Dodge City Fable*, a single-page newspaper which he issued as frequently as advertisers demanded. The *Fable* was able to solicit advertising from traveling peddlers and mail-order vendors who made no effort to offer truth in advertising.

The *Fable* garnered popularity among the residents of Dodge. It was easy to read. It cost only two cents. Some places of business provided free copies to their customers. One reader's letter to the editor complained, tongue in cheek, that there wasn't enough paper in the *Fable* to bother taking it to the outhouse. In the next issue, Ransome expressed regret that readers preferred the *Dodge City Times* for cleaning their backsides.

By 1886, the advertising in the *Dodge City Fable* had grown to the point that Ransome considered hiring assistants in the print shop. He grabbed a copy of the *New York Times* to see the content and format used in "Help Wanted" advertising. Buried in the back sections were two advertisements that inspired him to expand his business further:

> Harvey Restaurants and Hotels request applications from women to perform service duties in elegant hotels being built on the AT&SF line through Missouri and Kansas. Excellent salary and accommodations. Apply to Fred Harvey at Box 44, Leavenworth, Kansas.

> Mail-order Bride service. Young ladies seeking matrimony with suitable Kansas men. Guaranteed compatibility and security for qualified maidens. All expenses paid. Apply to Box 16, New York Times, NY, NY.

Ransome wondered if a woman could provide the assistance he required. He decided that even the most robust woman would not be physically capable, but that two women should be able to lift and tote paper rolls and bundles. At the time, the Treadwell Press was promoted as a machine that even women could operate. And if he were able to recruit a bevy of capable women, he could broker them as domestics, mail-order brides, or even as serving staff in one of Fred Harvey's rail-side dining establishments.

Ransome set up his press to print another issue of the *Dodge City Fable*, advertising positions for women. After proofreading the first page, he wondered whether it might be a good idea to advertise outside of Dodge City. So, he came up with a scheme to print fake versions of popular newspapers from major cities. Although it would take days to do the setup, he had the equipment to print the *Fort Worth Daily Gazette* or the *New York Times*. And then he could sell those counterfeit issues. Ransome was captivated by the idea. He could run off a few copies of the *New York Times* which would include some of his own advertisements and original content.

Over several weeks Ransome printed thirty counterfeit papers and sold them in Dodge City for ten cents each. The money barely covered the cost of materials, yet Ransome wallowed in the knowledge that his articles and advertisements were being read by very important people.

Ransome enlisted the help of his brother, who was living in New Orleans, Louisiana. This brother operated an emporium that catered to riverboat travelers. He would mail Ransome outdated copies of the *New Orleans Times-Democrat*. Ransome would set his type with a new date and change some of the advertising. Then he would send a bundle of twenty back to his brother, who would sell them to the tourists. Of course, they had no idea that the news they were reading might be six weeks old.

After a few months, Ransome began receiving responses to the advertisements in these counterfeit publications. Mail poured in from women seeking positions and fulfillment in the Kansas frontier. The number of appealing candidates overwhelmed Ransome. He planned to invite one woman per week for an internship at his office. Anticipating more women applicants than he could employ, he advertised "Ladies Seeking Positions" in his newspaper.

Ransome got down to business preparing the next issue of the *Dodge City Fable*. He needed to fill one column of the page to capture the attention of readers so they would continue to read the advertising—including his advertisement for female assistants. He had heard people talking about a couple from Texas who had survived the big storm on the cattle trails. As far as he knew, the *Times* had not conducted an interview.

Ransome went to the Long Branch to ask about the couple from Texas. The hotel clerk checked the register and said, "Seems Mister Barringer has two rooms. Number 3 and 4."

"Why's that?" asked Ransome.

"No idea. Those rooms are identical."

"Is the lady staying in a separate room? I thought they were Mister and Missus."

"Oh, they are. But there is a girl. Maybe she has her own room."

"A girl, you say? Like a daughter?"

"Can't rightly say, Mister. They were all mighty grubby. Looked like they mopped up the bloody floor of a butcher shop. Smelled bad, too."

"Sounds like they will fit right in at the Long Branch. I'll go see what I can ascertain."

Ransome knocked on the door of Room 3. A man's voice asked, "Who is it?" After Ransome identified himself, the door opened. John Barringer stood in the doorway.

"You must be John Barringer from Texas. Pleased to meet ya," said Ransome, as he extended his hand.

Barringer shook hands with him and looked him over. Ransome had a slight build and stood about five foot seven. He had black hair which curled up at his shoulder. A thin mustache and goatee made him look about thirty years old.

"To what do I owe the pleasure, stranger?" said Barringer.

"Welcome to Dodge City. I am owner of the *Dodge City Fable*, which is a small newspaper in town. Hearsay has it that you survived the blizzard down in Indian Territory. My readers will be excited to hear your tale."

"It was nothing like I could describe. Even the snow you got around here is nothin' compared to the coverin' down south. Colder than a witch's tit."

"And how many were in your party, Mr. Barringer?"

"Call me John B."

"Fine. And you can call me Ransome. I heard your wife was with you."

"That's right. And we ran into young Miss Clark. She's sleeping in the next room, so we won't disturb her. And my wife—Fannie May is her name—she is having a bath. You can judge by my appearance that I'm needin' some soap and water myself," said Barringer, as he ran his blood-stained fingers through his matted hair.

"You must have faced ruination. Like a near-death experience?"

"Shor nuff. When the storm hit the cattle drive, we headed east. Couldn't see nothing but white on white, so we got separated. Eventually the wind died down, and she heard me fire my gun."

"Where did you take shelter?"

"Couldn't see no trees or buildings and then a bull came running past. So I shot him. And gutted him. Then we crawled inside to stay warm."

"Inside the bull?" exclaimed Ransome. "Land sakes, Barringer! How did you think of that?"

"Well, my pa and I butchered a few cattle in our time. I knew how to hollow out a carcass, lock, stock and barrel. There was still lots of warm blood and other liquids in there. Fannie May wasn't real fond of the smell."

"So you got inside the bull's carcass and were warmed by the blood," Ransome recited, as he scribbled notes on a paper pad. "And then what did you do during the rest of the blizzard?"

"Abide. Nothing more. Just abide. I reckon we were in there for three days—maybe four. Nothing we could do but abide."

"That's incredible, Mr. Barringer. Most people would have frozen in that time. What happened after you escaped the carcass?"

"The storm died down, and the sun came out for a spell. The horses were gone, so we started walking towards the sun. Eventually we came upon my horse, Clyde, and Miss Una."

"You mean the girl in the next room. Is that Miss Una?"

"Young Miss Clark. Well, her name is Una Clark."

Ransome scribbled some more notes, then asked, "Tell me about Miss Clark?"

"Skinny redhead gal. We all had red hair from the time we got out of that bloody bull's gut. Miss Una cleans up real good but reckon she could use a few more square meals."

"Well, that gives me a bit to write about, Mr. Barringer. I look forward to meeting with you and your bride so you can tell me more."

"Like I said. Call me John B. And there is lots more to the story whenever it suits ya."

"Will you be staying here for awhile, John B?"

"'Spect so. We need some rest." Then Barringer chuckled, "Will abide, once more."

37

Atchison, Topeka, and Santa Fe Railroad, December 1886

PARIS, TEX., May 24. The examining trial of Miss Lizzie Clements was begun this afternoon at 2 o'clock before Justice Ryan. Miss Lizzie is a young girl of perhaps seventeen or eighteen years of age. She is just up from a long spell of typhoid fever. She is medium size, light complexion, light auburn hair, dark eyes and has a piercing look. Her face is rather oval shape and has a very pleasant look. She is charged with the burning of J.W. Rodgers' mattress and hen-house on Friday, May 14, also with firing his barn two days afterwards, on Sunday, May 16 last.

—*Fort Worth Daily Gazette*, Fort Worth, Texas, May 25, 1886

The Pinkerton Agent was traveling on the AT&SF railway at the request of Pinkerton headquarters. He had been instructed to travel to Chicago, where he would receive further details. This mission was of utmost importance, and personal attendance was required. The week-long trip from Texas to Chicago epitomized a phrase from the company motto — *Because at Pinkerton, we never sleep.*

Agent H.A. Clark had met with Allan Pinkerton on previous visits to the headquarters, but since the founder's demise, the director of the organization was his son, Robert Pinkerton. Clark assumed that his assignment would be to investigate organized labor activity on the railroads. When he arrived in Chicago, however, he learned that his mission was not only classified—it was off the record.

"No note-taking here," ordered Pinkerton, as Clark entered his office. "We never had this conversation, if anyone asks. You were never in Chicago this year. In fact, you took an indefinite leave of absence from the company."

"I see. What did I do to deserve this treatment?" Clark asked.

"You don't know. Since we never had this meeting."

"OK. What do you have for me?"

"Sorry Clark," said the director. "Excuse my boorishness. I never offered you a drink."

"I don't drink, sir. But you could offer me a chair."

"Sit down, agent," ordered the director as he stared at Clark for a moment. "Didn't you wear an eye-patch last time we met?"

"Correct. Does my blurry eye bother you?"

"I've seen worse. Is it healing?"

"No sir. I am still blind in my trigger eye. But the patch is uncomfortable to wear. And the exposed eye bothers in cold weather or in a breeze. So depending on the occasion I chose whether to wear the patch."

"That would drive me to drink," stated the director. "But I will send for some tea for you."

"Are there more details for this clandestine mission?" Clark asked, hoping to conclude his business with the director.

"Obviously. Are you aware of President Cleveland's pending act to establish an Interstate Commerce Commission?"

"No. Should I be?" replied Clark.

"This president and his Secretary of the Interior are going after the railroads. This commission will legislate the return of millions of acres of land that is currently owned by railroad companies as potential right-of-way."

"And railroad companies are a large portion of our business."

"The railroad companies are *all* of our business!" exclaimed Pinkerton. "As long as labor unions continue to disrupt progress, the Pinkertons will be engaged to quell them."

"So, our railroad friends want our help to prevent the government from reclaiming those lands?"

"Exactly. And we are pursuing all of the legal avenues available to the railroads. But *you* are going to gather some dirt on the people involved. And that dirt will give us the leverage the railroads need to stop this action."

"What kind of dirt?" Clark requested.

"We already know that President Cleveland has a thing for young women. That Halpin woman for one. We have her picture." The director handed a black and white photograph to Clark. "Some White House aids found a letter in which the young Cleveland declared his attraction to her rounded chin, curved mouth, and pale complexion contrasted by dark hair and dark eyes. Personally, I think he was more likely thinking about her curved buttocks and rounded bosoms. But alas, I don't have a picture of them."

"So you suggest I sniff around the women of New York who may have been with him?" inquired Clark.

"Better than that. I have names and places. And some of them are familiar to you."

"Like?"

"Mollie Brennan, formerly of Ellsworth and Cantonment Sweetwater."

"I've heard the name but as you can appreciate, I have not made her acquaintance."

"Brennan died in 1876. Find some witnesses who knew her and show them this likeness of Maria Halpin. I suspect there is a resemblance. Cleveland bragged to his cronies that Halpin did reflect the type of woman that could stir him up. I'll bet he is on the *list*."

"What list?" queried Clark.

"There is a tale about Mollie Brennan and Bat Masterson in a shoot-out in Sweetwater. Rumor has it, Mollie kept a punter's list — the list of her customers over the years. I guess that any smart harlot would do that."

"*Cave meretricem qui legit et scribit*," Clark declared.

"Sorry Clark. I am not up on my French," Pinkerton grumbled.

"Latin in this case. *Beware the harlot that reads and writes*."

Pinkerton laughed as he wrote the words on his writing pad. "Is that a quote from Hippocrates?"

"No, just my advice to leaders," replied Clark. "And I suggest someone carve those words into the headboards at the White House."

"Aah. But we digress. It's rumored that Mollie's list ended up in the hands of the Jolly twins, girls who worked in the dance hall where the shooting occurred. Find that list. I bet that Cleveland is on it. Or someone who has the goods on Cleveland."

"Where do I start?" asked Clark.

"Dodge City. The Jolly twins recently worked at a newspaper there. And they associated with Bat Masterson and the Dodge City gang."

"I will catch a train tonight," yawned Clark. "When I get the list, do you want me to telegraph the whole list or just verify that Cleveland is on it."

"The whole list of course," confirmed Pinkerton without looking up.

Clark rose to leave.

"Wait a minute Clark. There is another name we suspect is on that list."

"Who's that?"

"Oh, it's a name you know. He's a big supporter of Grover Cleveland, even in the face of this scandal. Henry Ward Beecher."

"The preacher and reformer, Henry Ward Beecher?"

"The same," acknowledged Pinkerton. "That's why we picked you, Clark. You're a believer. You're one of his followers. And a God-fearing man like you can be trusted not to ignore any inconvenient facts."

On November 15, 1886, Agent H.A. Clark was asleep in his cabin when the train conductor knocked on the door.

"Train is stopping here. Everyone has to disembark."

"How long are we stopping," yawned Clark as he sat up.

"Don't know. Blizzard has blocked the rails."

The blizzard pinned Clark down for five days in Newton, Kansas. The Newton stockyards closed for the winter and rail service was interrupted in both directions. Passengers scrambled to get accommodations, but Clark was anxious to continue his mission, so he slept on a bench in the station, hoping to catch the first available transport. He found a bundle of old newspapers and repurposed them as bedclothes to sleep under. Passersby assumed the man on the bench was just another vagabond riding the rails.

During the days, Clark entertained himself by reading his quilt of many stories. A story about an eighteen-year-old girl who was arrested for several arsons caught his attention. The girl had survived typhoid fever but suffered setbacks to her mental and emotional maturity. The description of the girl reminded him of his daughter, Una. He recalled the day that a messenger had presented him with the certificate stating that his only daughter had succumbed to typhoid fever on the way to Waco hospital. Assuming her death was the Lord's will, Agent Clark bemoaned the fact that his daughter had refused to seek penitence, not unlike the Fort Worth girl who survived typhoid only to commit further serious crimes.

"Be strong, and let us show ourselves courageous for the sake of our people and for the cities of our God and may the Lord do what is good in His sight," prayed Agent Clark under his shroud of weeklies.

Passenger service to Dodge City on the AT&SF was not restored until November 21. An unbathed, disheveled man presented his first-class ticket when he heard the announcement. Clark intended to continue to Dodge in hopes that the Jolly twins were there. In any case, there were other persons of interest for him to see as part of his investigation.

Although the snow had ceased, the temperature remained twenty degrees below normal. Train passengers huddled around a pot-bellied stove in the station until the conductor called "All aboard." Clark noticed two women who looked very much alike in the group of passengers. Had they been wearing the same frock, he could not have picked one from the other. Clark watched the pair board the train in Newton, pondering the coincidence that he was seeking twins matching their gender and approximate age. Unfortunately, he had no further description to go on. His follow-up with members of the Dodge City gang might confirm his suspicion. Unfortunately, the overtired Clark fell asleep in his first-class cabin and did not see the ladies disembark.

Upon arrival in Dodge, Clark plastered the town with posters offering reward for information about Mollie Brennan. He chose not to include any reference to the Jolly twins in hopes that they might come forward. Clark decided to wait in Dodge until the new year, in the event that any outstanding cattle drives or travelers from Texas arrived with useful information.

On the morning of December 8, Agent Clark looked out of the second-floor window of Klara's Boarding

House. Since he had arrived in Kansas, the weather had gone from autumn to winter in less than two weeks. More trains were canceled on the AT&SF due to snow. Fatalities aboard stagecoaches caused operators to cancel all passenger service through Dodge City for the entire month of December.

Frustrated with his lack of progress, Clark folded up a map and picked up the Bible on his bed. He sat reading some passages in a whisper. He felt confined to his quarters. Then his mind wandered to the women he was seeking. If they were in Dodge, where would he find them? Had they continued a career in entertainment or prostitution? If not, were they God-fearing women? Were they married or working?

Clark's wait for more cattle drives proved fruitless for the rest of that winter. It was rumored that fewer than a dozen souls entered Dodge during December of 1886. And unknown to the Pinkerton agent, those arrivals included John Barringer, Fannie May Barringer, and Una Clark.

38

Dodge City, Kansas, December 1886

Dodge City welcomed some newcomers last week. Mr. and Mrs. John Barringer, from Bluffton, Texas, both of whom were caught in this year's early winter storm, arrived in our beauteous city after being separated from a cattle drive bearing the same destination. By the grace of God and Barringer's ingenuity, the couple rode two large horses through the blizzard to survive the Great Die-Up. Understandably, they declined to report their harrowing story before getting accommodations at the famous Long Branch Hotel and Saloon, where they will be treated to relaxation, libations, and jocularity.

—*Dodge City Fable*, Dodge City, Kansas, December 8, 1886

Cotton rode through deep snow and icy waters along the North Canadian River. Over five days he saw thousands of dead longhorns tangled and stacked along the quarantine fences. Carcasses of cattle and horses were also scattered along the river bottom. One bull carcass in the valley had been mutilated. But there was no sign of Una or Stubby. On the sixth day he rode into Dodge City. Cotton doubted that Una could have escaped from Stubby and survived. His soul was filled with anguish and guilt when he thought about the last days of the girl's life.

There were lots of cowboys and railway workers gathered at the Lady Gay Saloon. Cotton went straight to the bar and ordered a whiskey.

"Here's yer bourbon, mister. That should warm yer innards," said the barkeeper.

"Much obliged," said Cotton. He emptied the drink in one gulp and tapped his finger on the empty glass.

"Did you survive that storm on the Western Trail?" asked the cowboy standing next to him.

"Nope. But same storm hit the Chisholm Trail. Killed all the beeves."

"What are ya doin' in Dodge, then?" asked the cowboy. "Wudda been closer to Caldwell, wouldn't ya?"

"Lost some of my crew," replied Cotton, as he watched the barkeeper refill his glass. "Reckon some maybe came up the North Canadian or the Cimarron."

"Right into the teeth of the wind. Seems a little farfetched, mister!"

"I hope not. There's a red-headed girl special to me. And a drover named Stubby."

"What's the red-head answer to?" asked the bartender.

"Una. Tell me you've seen her!"

"Can't say I did," replied the bartender. "If I had, I'd reckon there'd be some reward, wouldn't I?"

"She's valuable to me," warned Cotton. "Keep that in mind if you get wind of her. I figger on stayin' upstairs for about a week."

Cotton dropped a quarter on the bar and walked away from the second glass of whiskey. He stood looking out the front window of the saloon at the snowflakes blowing past.

"Hey, mister. Ya didn't finish yer whiskey," called the bartender. Another cowpoke was quick to chase down the orphaned drink.

The Barringers and their foundling had washed their clothes and bodies vigorously in the powder room shared among Long Branch guests. Bloodstains remained on Fannie May's clothes and undergarments. Dried blood was under her fingernails and in her hair and her ears. She dared not imagine what liquids had entered other body cavities.

"John B, we won't get clean for weeks!" announced Fannie May. "How can we go out in public?"

"Let's just stay in bed," said John B.

"And pretend we are inside a bull carcass," grumbled Fannie May.

"Kinda ruins the mood when ya put it that way."

"Who can we get to bring us some new clothes?"

"I should'a asked that newspaper man. Ransome something."

"Who's Ransome something?" demanded Fannie May.

"He was here to get our story. While you were bathin'."

"So, what did you tell him? Did you mention Una?"

"Well, he seemed to know about Una."

"Get dressed, John B."

"I thought you said we need new clothes. What's so pressing?"

"We have to stop your newspaper man before he exposes Una.

"What d'ya mean exposes Una? Is she on the run?"

"We don't know if the man who kidnapped her is still around. We weren't the only people to survive the storm."

"I gather you think she's at risk even in our company."

"Especially in our company, based on recent history. Now, get your clothes on. We have to find this guy, Ransome."

Ransome Cooper was setting the type in his Treadwell Power Press by the light of several candles. His fingers were cold, causing him to fumble with the movable lead letters. He had just bent over to pick up a letter that dropped on the floor when he was startled by pounding on his door. As he stood, his head hit the bar on the press and he fell to the floor, dazed. When he looked up at the front entrance, he saw a striking brunette cupping her face against the glass to see inside. Ransome got to his feet and opened the door to admit the fair stranger.

"Come in out of the storm," said Ransome.

"Thank you," said Fannie May as she entered.

Barringer stepped out of the shadows. "Much obliged," he said, before Ransome could close the door in his face.

"Sorry, Barringer," said Ransome. "Didn't see you there. So, this must be your bride, Fannie May."

"Pleased to meet you, Mr. Ransome. And please excuse my clothes. I am obviously in need of a tour of the Dodge shops, but we felt this discussion could not wait."

"I am in the midst of setting the type for tomorrow's *Fable*. Could we not postpone a day?"

"It is urgent that we agree on the content of your newspaper before it is issued," said Fannie May.

"Now, that is highly irregular. I don't usually make changes so late."

"Mr. Ransome. You undoubtedly have deduced that there is a young woman in our party.

"Yes, Miss Una Clark, I believe."

"Miss Clark has suffered a great deal of trauma on the journey to Dodge. Prior to that she was victim to a lengthy period of convalescence."

"Perhaps the church-goers here in Dodge could be of some assistance. And the publicity of my reporting will sit well with them."

"At some point in the future, perhaps, but in the meantime there may be a villainous man in pursuit of Miss Clark. Not to mention the highway robber following John B and I."

"Would you accept a short report that the two of you have come through great peril to arrive in Dodge at this unfortunate time?"

Fannie May looked at John B before answering. "That should be fine. We will trust you to be discreet."

"And the sooner we mention the villains, the sooner they will turn up. Assuming they are here in Dodge. I suggest we expose the details of your story on a gradual basis. That helps me gain readers from week to week.

"Well the villain tailing us is Skip Van," offered Barringer. "There is probably a wanted poster in the county office."

"That's the spirit," replied Ransome as he picked up his note book. "I can use that in next week's issue."

"How about the following week you cast a net for a man that goes by Stubby?" suggested Fannie May. "That will tell us whether it is safe to reveal Una's location."

"Sure, now you are thinking like a newspaper editor. Then there is no Fable over Christmas so we can introduce the rest of your adventure in the new year, if agreed."

"Sounds fair," answered Fannie May.

"Including Miss Clark. And these stories will be exclusive to this publication. I expect you to refuse interviews with the *Dodge City Times*."

"I have another favor to ask of you, Ransome. Do you have contacts with the Gang?" inquired Fannie May.

"The Gang?" demanded John B.

"I mean Bat Masterson and his hooligans," explained Fannie May.

"Well, the gang does a lot for this town, including this newspaper," Ransome replied. "I resent the hooligan inference."

"My apologies," responded Fannie May. "I guess I have been reading too much into the articles in the *Times*."

"The *Times* is certainly not a fan of Bat Masterson," agreed Ransome. "However, I will be glad to provide introductions when Bat is in our town."

When Ransome saw Fannie May unfold some five dollar bills, he added, "Of course, whatever I can do to help."

"Then we have a deal?" asked Fannie May as she handed fifty dollars to the newsman.

Ransome considered the money in his hand. "Perhaps there is a better way. I have need of two female assistants. Would you and the nameless girl assist me in my press room?"

"That is not why we have come to you. We are not seeking employment."

"Nevertheless, I would be beholding to you. You see, I am unable to recruit qualified ladies until transportation is restored to our city. By working on the press you will also be able to censor my publication," Ransome suggested.

Fannie May looked at John B, shrugged, and then lifted her hand gracefully to allow Ransome to kiss it. "I accept your terms on the condition that the girl's identity remains secret for now. She will remain incognito until the new year. Hopefully her pursuer is located by then. And you will pay us both fair wages in January."

"Agreed. And here are your wages for the first week of January," Ransome grinned, as he handed the money back to Fannie May.

"Now, will you please entrust me with the story of Mr. and Mrs. Barringer surviving the Great Die-Up of 1886."

"What do you mean by the Great Die-Up?"

"That's what I am calling those dead cows. That's my headline."

The Barringers looked at each other. Then Fannie May grinned. "Certainly. But that story will have more details than you have time to gather tonight. You might be able to fill several pages before we discuss the fate of a red-headed girl who was lost in the storm."

Ransome started jotting in his notebook. "Please sit down. We can craft the story now." Then he threw some ground coffee into a pot on his stove.

39

Dodge City, Kansas, December 1886

The cattle stampeded in the blizzard for three days and three nights. Even while the Barringer couple were safe inside the carcass of a dead bull, they could hear the distant caterwauling of injured cattle. When the storm let up enough for them to move out, they retrieved their mounts and rode beside the North Canadian River, where cattle had lodged in the barbwire fence. The animals were piled four or five deep against the fence. And if they looked closely, they could see a horse trapped among the beeves at every one hundred yards or so about. Sometimes they saw signs that the horses had riders. There were hats, boots, saddle bags, and frozen human limbs exposed in the snow and hides. As they watched for movement among the carnage, they found a man trapped between his horse and several steers. Buzzards were picking at his eyes, and he was screaming at them, but his arms were pinned or broken. They tried to free him from the amassment but could not. He was very weak but was able to speak. He said he did not know his Christian name, but everyone knew him as Stubby. He claimed that he was escorting a young woman to the safety of the trading post in Woodward. He said that a stampede overcame them and pushed them into the conglomeration. He nodded to the east, where he had last seen the girl. Mrs. Barringer sat with Stubby and gave him water from her canteen. John Barringer walked across the rows of dead and dying animals. He came across a blood-stained bonnet protruding from the snow. A locket was tied to the strap. But after Barringer removed all the snow from the area he was only able to find a dead horse. There was no sign of an eighteen-year-old girl nor any other persons. Mrs. Barringer comforted Stubby until he stopped breathing. To this day, Mrs. Barringer finds the events more horrific than words can describe. The Fable hopes that she can get over her shock by sharing the remaining details of the Great Die-Up with our readership.

The Fable is predicting that the weather is bound to improve after Christmas, when the days start getting longer.

—*Dodge City Fable*, Dodge City, Kansas, December 15, 1886

Bill Tilghman was the deputy sheriff for Ford County. He had a small ranch west of Dodge City at the time of the blizzard. Sometime during the first night of the storm his herd disappeared from his corral. He assumed they had traveled downwind, and when weather permitted, he rode south to retrieve the animals.

Tilghman found only a few calves, dead in the snow. After he scared off buzzards with his sidearm, he determined they had been trampled. He had no inkling of the disaster he would find when he reached the fences at the North Canadian River.

"Get lost, you dirty scavengers. Poor little fellas never even grew old enough to get branded."

Most of the hoof prints were covered by snow, but Tilghman was able to track what looked like a stampede. When he arrived at the drift fence, vultures and coyotes were gnawing on the heads and shoulders of dead cattle. Tilghman dismounted and fired a couple of shots to ward off the predators. He walked on top of the frozen carcasses, taking note of brands. He identified at least twenty head from his herd among the hundreds in the vicinity. Despite the cold weather, the remains were starting to rot. Tears came to the big man's eyes.

Tilghman felt obligated to report this carnage to Pat Sughrue, Ford County Sheriff. There was a visitor in the sheriff's office when he arrived. A tall slender man, dressed entirely in black. The man had a black cloth patch over one eye. Without introduction, Tilghman assumed the man was from the Pinkertons. Sughrue took down the information regarding the dead cattle and shared the reports that had been filed by other witnesses.

"Bill, you look like you could use a drink," observed Sughrue. "Will you gents join me in a glass of rum?"

"That's a fine offer," answered Tilghman.

"Not for me," asserted Clark. "I am a total abstainer. And I predict your ungodliness will come to an end soon."

"No offense intended, Agent Clark," said the sheriff, as he put the rum bottle back in his desk.

"I did not come to Dodge to preach prohibition, although I find a calling in this town. I come here seeking information about Mollie Brennan and the Jolly twins." The Pinkerton man continued on for some time with an inspired rant about sin and redemption, occasionally deploring the influence of the Gang.

Tilghman had worked up a thirst by the time he left the sheriff's office. He headed to the Long Branch Saloon, where he expected to find members of the Dodge City Gang. Bat Masterson saw Tilghman enter and waved him over to a table where he was sitting with Charlie Bassett.

"Come sit with us, Bill. But why the long face?" asked Bat.

"My herd is gone. And I found them trampled and frozen among hundreds."

The others sat quietly as they watched the grief welling up on Tilghman's face. Bat slid his glass of whiskey over to Tilghman and waved at a woman serving drinks to bring more.

"We've heard the tale from others, but never imagined your herd was in there," said Bat.

"That's tough, Bill. Are they all dead?" asked Bassett.

"Dead and gone," replied Tilghman. "That's the end of my ranching. I came to town to report to Sheriff Sughrue."

Ignoring the somber mood, Bassett said, "There was a couple came to town and reported dead animals on the drift fence. Ransome at the *Fable* says they survived the storm inside a bull's carcass. He's calling the whole thing the 'Great Die-Up.'"

"Whatever it's called, it's the end of my time with cattle. I'll appreciate any work the Gang has for me," admitted Tilghman.

"The gambling and alcohol business has been impacted by these Reformers and Bible-thumpers," Bat said. "Down to two saloons in Dodge—and this is the only one contributing to the Gang. Look around at the empty chairs."

"So, you sayin' you can't use me?" asked Tilghman.

"I am saying that you should maintain your credentials with the various law-enforcement agencies. I recently received communications from our esteemed politicians in Topeka. They struggle with the distribution of county seats in the western regions of our state—in particular, Garfield County and Gray County. The governor and attorney general have asked me to assist in the process of selecting county seats."

"You mean so they don't end up with egg on their face like a few years ago? Wasn't that Comanche County?"

"Exactly," answered Bat. "Money was spent on a county seat despite the fact there were no residents in the county nor in the fictional town. Just a paper town."

"How are you involved?" Tilghman asked Bat.

"The government believes they need to deputize a team to oversee the nomination and selection of county seats. I am appointed Chief of Special Deputies, based on my experience surveying new communities. Not to mention my experience as a lawman and newspaper publisher."

"Slick. What's in it for the Gang?" asked Tilghman.

"I am authorized to select deputies," said Bat. "Paid positions. Other members of our Gang can stir up sponsorship from competing communities. And when we know which way the wind is blowing, we buy up all the properties ahead of the election. There is money from government, money from the campaigns, and eventually money from the real estate."

"Count me in. When does all this start?" asked Tilghman.

"The spring of 1887 will be the Gang's finest hour."

"Thanks for the pep talk—and the whiskey. I needed that after the cattle and the run-in with the Pinkerton man."

"What Pinkerton man?" asked Bat.

"I'm surprised you have not crossed paths with Agent Clark. You see the posters looking for information on Mollie Brennan?"

"Yes, I am aware of the posters but did not realize a Pinkerton Agent was here. I would have expected he would be looking in Sweetwater."

"He's here in Dodge, and on top of it, he's a Bible-thumper. Probably getting some of those Reformers fired up while he's in town," said Tilghman.

"I'll keep my ear to the ground. Reformers are enough trouble. We don't need them joining forces with Pinkertons." Bat paused in thought. "I am going to chat with the couple who survived inside that bull carcass. What did you say the name was?"

"Barrington. Or Barringer, maybe. Bet they are staying right here in the Long Branch as we speak," replied Bassett.

"I intend to find out more about their trip," Bat announced. "Maybe we can use their story to drum up some government support for cattlemen."

40

Dodge City, Kansas, January 1887

The churches are taking no uncertain positions against anarchy and saloonocracy. The Christian Evangelist at St. Louis, says the temperance movement is a conflict between devilization and civilization, between sin and righteousness, between heaven and hell. It does not see how christian people can train with foreign anarchists, gamblers, brothel-keepers and cut throats. The christian must take one side or the other. "Every christian not only has the right, but it is his duty to demand that the party which asks his vote shall be unequivocal in its enmity to this devilish traffic. Whenever the twelve millions of Protestant church members in the United States determine that there shall be no more curse they will be reinforced by a large enough following from the world to sweep down the saloon under an avalanche and bury it forever."

—*Dodge City Times*, Dodge City, Kansas, October 28, 1886

On a cold Sunday, Agent Clark attended a morning service at the newly founded First Christian Church of Dodge. This was the first service in the year of our Lord, 1887. The congregation listened intently to the Pastor's sermon condemning the sins occurring in Dodge City. Clark felt solace and comfort in this gathering of God-fearing

Christians. After the service, he talked with many members who were actively reforming life in Dodge City. The Pastor was grateful to meet Agent Clark and invited him to the rectory for dinner that night.

"Our congregation is aware of your pursuit of sinners. And our prayers are with you. Have you found any information since your arrival in Dodge?"

"Not anything definitive, but I have suspicions," replied Clark.

"I share your suspicions. This town is full of fallen women and those who take advantage."

"Anyone in particular that I should interrogate?" Clark asked.

"Probably any member of the Dodge City Gang. They tend to meet at the Long Branch Saloon but can be found anywhere."

"Does Masterson run the Gang?" asked Clark.

"Bat Masterson seems to be at the center. And he has several lieutenants. Charlie Bassett and Bill Tilghman reside in Ford County almost year-round. Wyatt Earp and Doc Holliday when they are in town."

"What about newspapermen? They often have a handle on who's who."

"The editor of the *Dodge City Times* will probably help you," said the Pastor.

"How about the *Dodge City Fable*?"

"Ransome Cooper. He has talent as a writer, but he's not afraid to protect the Gang members. Or should I say, he is afraid *not to protect* Gang members. There is a rumor he was part of the Gang at one time."

"What makes you say that?" urged Clark.

"In '85 there was a fire that burned almost all of the business district in Dodge City. The *Times* building was next door to the Lady Gay Saloon. Witnesses say both buildings went on fire at the same time rather than spreading from one to the other. The owners of the Lady Gay have been long-time competitors of the Gang. Publicly, the Lady Gay management supports reform but that puts them in conflict with their financial interest. And since the fire, the *Times* openly opposes Bat Masterson and other members of the Gang."

"So, was it ever proven that the Gang was responsible for the fire?"

"Not proven, but by coincidence the *Fable* and another saloon— the Long Branch — were untouched by the fire—on a street where many other buildings burned."

"Very suspicious, proof or not," agreed Clark.

"Perhaps the Pinkertons can help the God-fearing residents of Dodge eradicate Masterson and the Gang," replied the Pastor.

"In the meantime, I hope the reform-minded people of Dodge can assist in finding the Jolly twins."

The winter weather left Cotton stranded in the Lady Gay for over a month. He spent his waking hours in the saloon talking with cowboys who might have seen Una. More than one of the patrons had heard that the Pinkertons were offering a reward for information about harlots from Texas, including twins who had resided in Dodge City at one time. A bartender sent a telegram to the Pinkerton office in Dallas describing the white-haired trail boss who was taking a special interest in the whereabouts of young women.

"Hey, young fella. Do you go by the name of Cotton?" asked a weasel-faced gambler.

"Who's asking?"

"Some of us thought there might be a *ree-ward* for information about you and yer little woman."

"I am that Cotton. And for the right information, you'd be rewarded."

"Well, it might be fittin' for some recompense in advance," said Weasel-face.

"If you think you deserve an advance, I recommend you check with the Pinkertons first."

"Check what?" asked Agent Clark, who had just entered the Lady Gay Saloon.

"Well, speak of the devil and a one-eyed Pinkerton appears," said Weasel-face. "Reckon you gents might find these women quicker if you ante up some reward money."

"Who's this guy looking for?" asked Agent Clark. "The Jolly Twins?"

"Who are the Jolly Twins?" asked Cotton. "And who are you, Mister? Besides being a Pinkerton man."

"Agent H.A. Clark. I am with the Pinkertons but, more importantly, I seek information on a harlot named Mollie Brennan and a pair of twins from her establishment."

"You just keep lookin'. Cuz I have no idea who that is, er, who they is."

"I am going to ask again," Clark growled as he gaped his coat and laid his hand on a sidearm. "Who is it you have been asking about?"

Cotton raised his hands above his shoulders. Then he said, "I have no issue with the Pinkertons. These men were just spreading gossip on whiskey row."

"Let's talk, outside," said Clark, nodding towards the exit.

"Hey, what about a round for us citizens who rounded him up?" asked Weasel-face.

When the two men were outside of the saloon, Cotton lowered his hands and spoke up, "They call me Cotton, if yer interested. And I will look ya up if I see any trace of a Mollie Brennan."

"So for the third time, what woman are you looking for in Dodge?"

"Miss Clark. You probably ain't seen Miss Una Clark," Cotton barked.

"Don't play games!" ordered the Agent. "Una Clark died four years ago."

"The Una Clark I am talking about is probably dead. But only for four weeks if she is gone. Red haired woman."

"Una Clark died. Not sure why you intend to antagonize me. My daughter died according to the death certificate I received four years ago!"

Cotton was dumbfounded. He did recall Una mentioning her father worked for the Pinkertons but questioned the coincidence. "I don't know. But the gal I am looking for was alive until the blizzard hit our cattle drive in the town of Yukon. I have been tracking her since," explained Cotton.

"What is this girl, this impostor, to you?" asked Clark.

"Er, well, I am not talkin' about a girl. This woman was helping out with the chuckwagon on the trail when we got hit by weather in Yukon. That spooked the cattle, and they stampeded back on top of us."

"And yet you seem no worse for wear?" asked Clark.

"I was checkin' for lodging in the Yukon hotel. When I got back to the wagons, Miss Una was gone, along with most of the crew and all of the cattle."

"Were you betrothed to this woman?"

"No. Just cared for each other."

"Did you have physical relations with this woman?" inquired Agent Clark.

"She's been on the chuckwagon since Waco. About three month's back."

"Not what I asked," said Clark, squinting his exposed eye.

Cotton was offended by the man's questions even if this man was in fact Una's father. Both men jumped when the sound of gunfire erupted a short distance down the street.

"Something's happening at the Long Branch," Cotton said, seizing an opportunity to escape the conversation. "I'm gonna go see."

"You won't escape. God will punish fornicators!" yelled Clark at the fleeing cowhand.

After six rounds, the gunfire stopped. Men gathered around a cowboy who was slurring his words and waving his pistol.

"Goddamn weather. Goddamn hoss," said Barringer. "She up and died. Can you believe it? My favrit hoss. I'm gonna miss that hoss."

"Settle down thar, feller. Gunfire won't bring yer horse home," said the piano player.

"Nuttin' gonna bring her home. Goddamn dead horse. Dead, I tell you!" Barringer mumbled. He watched a white-haired man running towards him, followed by a man wearing a patch over one eye. Behind them, he saw Fannie May spirit Una out the alley behind the Long Branch. Then he continued his rant, "Stone-cold dead. Colder than a witch's tit."

"Can I help you, friend?" said Cotton, as he ran to Barringer's side. "Had a few whiskeys today?"

"Tarry. That's what we called her. Best mare a man could have, that Tarry."

"Is this feller stayin' here?" asked Cotton.

The bartender was watching from the doorway. "Yeah. Was behaving up till today. He's been tipping a few in the saloon."

"A few indeed," said Cotton. "What's yer name, feller?"

"Barringer. John Barringer. And my horse Tarry. I'm gonna miss that gal."

"I'll take him up to his room," said Cotton, as he looked over his shoulder to see the Pinkerton man standing in the street at a safe distance. Cotton took the gun from the drunken actor and guided him up to his hotel room. On the way he asked, "Barringer, are you here alone?"

"Nah, got the old lady. Fannie May," Barringer slurred. "You should see her. She's a real piece of calico."

"Did I read about a Fannie May and John Barringer in the paper? Was that you?"

"Shor nuff. But that paper didn't say nothin' about my hoss, Tarry. She was some mare."

"Here you are," said Cotton at the top of the stair. "Hope Fannie May doesn't mind you coming home drunk."

"Much obliged. I owe ya. Reckon ya deserve a drink, stranger."

"Name's Cotton. But another time. I reckon we will meet again."

Fannie May and Una were shivering in the cold air when Ransome opened the back door of the *Fable* office.

"Come in, ladies," said Ransome, a huge grin on his face. "Set by the stove in this room."

"Thanks, Ransome," said Fannie May. "Una, this is Mr. Cooper. I made some arrangements for his assistance. He runs *The Fable* and this print shop."

"Please call me Ransome. And may I call you Una," he asked, lifting the girl's bony fingers to kiss them.

"Certainly," replied Una. "I am so excited about becoming a Harvey Girl."

Ransome looked at both women in disbelief. He stammered, "Harvey Girl? Where?"

"Harvey Girl?" asked Fannie May.

Una reached inside her dress and fumbled with the safety pin holding a piece of newspaper. "Because the advertisement says to write to this office."

Una handed over the scrap from the *New Orleans Times-Democrat*.

> **Wanted: Young women 14 to 20 years of age, of good moral character, attractive**

*and intelligent, to waitress in Harvey
Eating Houses on the Atchison, Topeka
and Santa Fe Railway in the West.
Wages, $17.50 per month with room
and board. Liberal tips customary.
Experience not necessary. Write in care
of The Fable, Dodge City, Kansas.*

"Well, I guess that is a testament to advertising. And you certainly look like a girl who could qualify. But that advertisement was valid some time ago. I don't know when the next time Mr. Harvey will be requiring new staff around here."

"When will you meet with him?" asked Una. She could hardly contain her excitement.

"I am at a loss," said Ransome. "Mrs. Barringer, were you aware of Miss Una's desire in this regard?"

"Not particularly. We have not discussed it since the storm."

"Then you and I are of similar mind. The arrangement remains that Miss Una will work and live here at the *Fable* for the near future. In the past, I have protected young women and arranged employment with great discretion. But I have no need of a Harvey Girl."

"Una, Mr. Ransome will keep you safe until it is safe for you to find another position, although it may not be as a Harvey Girl."

"I thought I could stay with you and John B. The three of us," said Una.

"We felt it best that you stay out of sight for a bit," replied Fannie May. "While John B tries to find your friend Cotton, you and I will be working here during the day."

"Do I have any say in the matter?" asked Una, on the verge of tears.

"This is temporary," assured Fannie May. "We want to keep you out of harm's way. Mr. Ransome, will you be able to keep Una hidden if she stays here?"

"As long as she can work the printing machine with me, Una can stay here."

"What if Cotton comes for me?" asked Una. "He will."

"And while you wait," said Ransome, "you'll have a comfortable home with warm food."

"Why, I don't really know," Una whispered to Fannie May.

"What are the lodging arrangements, Mr. Ransome?" asked Fannie May.

"There is a loft over the printing press," said Ransome. "I'll show you the room where Una will have her own bed and lavatory. There is even a bathtub."

A torn piece of a poster caught Fannie May's eye. Before they left Ransome's office, she picked up the scraps as if she was cleaning up behind Una. The characters on one scrap read: *gram to Pinkerton Dall.*

Ransome led the ladies up a steep set of stairs to a musty-smelling room with two beds and a chest of drawers. At the far end of the room was a door to a closet. Ransome opened the closet, revealing a bucket toilet, a tin washtub, a basin on a shelf, and a large enamel pitcher.

"You can bring up water from the kitchen in that pot," Ransome said, pointing to the blue speckled pitcher. "I have another pail in the kitchen you may use to fill the tub for bathing."

"Why are there two beds in here?" quizzed Fannie May.

"As you are aware, I will need two workers in the press room. At one time, I had two sisters who Bat Masterson recommended but they now have homes of their own," replied Ransome.

"And you share the kitchen?" asked Fannie May.

"Yes, I'll show you," said Ransome, as he started down the stairs. "If Miss Una cares to cook for both of us, I can deduct the cost of food from her board."

Fannie May inspected all of the rooms and was satisfied. Una agreed to stay with Ransome on the basis that Fannie May was there during the day.

"Remember to stay out of sight, cautioned Fannie May. "If there is something you need outside of this shop, you must ask Ransome or I to fetch it for you."

"I will remember," said Una. "And I am grateful to you and Mr. Barringer for your assistance."

"We are your friends. No thanks are necessary."

Barringer sat beside a fireplace in the largest and most luxurious room in the Long Branch. He had a blanket over him and half a cup of coffee on the table at his side. "Goddamn, this town is cold," he complained. "And it is still snowing."

Fannie May brought a pot of coffee and filled his cup. Then she put another log on the fire and sat across from Barringer. A shawl covered her shoulders, and she was wearing white cotton gloves.

"You'll get warm in bed. Patience is a virtue," laughed Fannie May.

"Well, I guess I have time for a cigarette," Barringer said, as he folded some tobacco into a paper and rolled it on his leg. "Did I tell you that I met the man, Cotton?"

"No, you didn't say. Whereabouts?"

"Right here in the Long Branch. He showed up while I was putting on that distraction out front."

"Maybe paths don't cross so much in Dodge. Una goes out the back door and Cotton comes in the front," Fannie May said. "Did he seem like a fine fellow?"

"I gathered as much. However, he was being polite, 'cause a one-eyed man was on his tail."

"A one-eyed man? Probably a member of the Gang," Fannie May speculated. "What else can you tell me about the trail boss?"

"Well, he's a strapping lad. Curly white hair, as expected. I reckon some womenfolk might call him handsome. And strong as an ox when it came to helping this drunkard up the stairs."

"I don't think it's safe to bring him to Una until we know more about him. Do you think Cotton will stick around?" asked Fannie May.

"Until the snow melts, I reckon. Now that he rescued me, it might be appropriate to deliver him a box of cigars and a note of from Una."

"I think I need to build a Rock-Paper-Scissors circle," said Fannie May.

John B frowned and shook his head. "There are far too many people involved. Most of them outside the law. Who would you pit against Cotton and the trail hands?"

"I have chatted with some of the Reformers in Dodge. They're a formidable group. And they say they have a Pinkerton man coming to services now."

"Shit!" declared John B. "Not another agent devoted to prohibition."

"From what Una remembers about her father, he was extremely pious. And a Pinkerton man." replied Fannie May.

"Hold on there. Una said her last name is Clark. And she grew up in Dallas. You don't think her father is the Agent Clark that arrested me in Bluffton last summer?" asked John B. "He was from Dallas."

"Maybe paths do cross. But we don't know that this Pinkerton man is Agent Clark. Even in that rare circumstance, I doubt that Una wants to meet him. From what she has said, she has no desire to return to her family or childhood home."

"What's an agent doing here in Dodge?" John B wondered.

"Apparently the Dallas office is responsible for those Mollie Brennan posters around town. Could be related to those."

"Or maybe something related to the Llano bank robbery." John B speculated.

"We can only hope that he's on the trail of Skip Van," admitted Fannie May.

"Like you say. Paths cross, even in Dodge. But getting back to your circle of three foes. You only have the

Cowboys versus Reformers so far. What group of godless men will be the third party?"

"Bat Masterson runs everything here with his Gang of peacekeepers," said Fannie May. "And Ransome, the editor of *The Fable*, is tied to the Gang."

"Have you seen much of them around town? I mean, the Gang?" asked Barringer.

"I have overheard a few conversations in the tearoom. According to the pastor's wife, Bill Tilghman is definitely keeping an eye on you and I. She says that Bat Masterson, Wyatt Earp, and Charlie Bassett are gone to Garfield County. They are supervising the election of a county seat. The town of Ravanna versus the town of Eminence. And most of the gang members are supposed to go stuff the ballot boxes in Ravanna," said Fannie May.

"That kinda leaves Dodge in the hands of the Reformers," said John B. "Cotton's cowboys don't have a chance of claiming Una against Pinkerton guns and the Reformers."

"No one can run away from this situation. We did not survive a blizzard only to ride off into snowdrifts. If Cotton shares Una's affection it will be hard to predict what the youngsters will do when they come face to face."

"Probably rub up against each other." chuckled John B.

Cotton awoke to a knock on his door. He wondered which of his fellow drovers was looking for him this early. There was only a blush of light in the east.

"Who is there?"

"John Barringer. I would speak with you, privately."

"Barringer. You mean the drunk man with a loaded gun?"

"Not today. I am, however, beholdin' to ya."

Cotton pulled off the feather tick and pulled on a pair of ice-cold pants. Then he opened the door to see Barringer holding a small package.

"Sorry to intrude. I brought some cigars. Gran Corona from Alberto Turrent in Mexico."

"Why?"

"The Mexicans say that the smoke fills your lungs, but the aroma brings lost lovers to your eyes." Barringer handed the box to Cotton and whispered, "For your eyes only." Then he turned and headed down the hall.

Confused, Cotton sat on the bed and opened the box. There was a folded note inside.

> *Dear Cotton,*
>
> *My love, if this letter finds you, then I am jubilant that you survived the storm. Survival in the storm was less tortuous than my escape from Stubby but some new friends are working for my benefit. Trust Fannie May and John Barringer when they come to you with this letter.*
>
> *I don't know when we can be together but I ask you to be patient. Please wait for me in Dodge until I am able to join you.*
>
> *All my love,*
>
> *Una Clark*

Paper

Cotton stuffed the letter in his pocket and finished dressing for the day. Then he headed out into another day of wind and snow.

41

Dodge City, Kansas, January 1887

There was a party of newspaper men who went out to Nevada once to write things about "Bat" but he was no "poser," and would not open up for them. They told him of the money they would make out of it, all of it lost if he refused. "Bat" dove into his pockets, drew out $4—all he had— and said: "You fellers can have $3 of this if you like—I need the other dollar myself."

That was "Bat"—square as a die and businesslike!

— *The Washington Times*, Washington, D.C., February 19, 1905

A gust of cold wind alerted the man behind the counter of the Modern Cafe that a patron had entered. The patron wore a patch over one eye and was dressed entirely in black.

"Welcome, Agent Clark," said the man in the apron. "Would you like the special?"

"I would, assuming it is the same Wednesday special that you have served me twice before?" specified Clark. He sat on a stool at the counter.

"Guilty as charged," laughed the proprietor. "Denver sandwich served Colorado-style."

Clark looked around the diner to see if business was booming today. There was a woman sitting alone, four tables back. She appeared to be in her early twenties, dressed in a navy Edwardian dress and ruffled white blouse with a cameo brooch at the collar. Her long brown hair was arranged in a single French braid under a gray sinamay hat. Her eyes had a dusky tone, and she forced a smile when she noticed his gaze. She was cutting the pickle of her own Wednesday special.

Clark tipped his hat, then turned back to the man in the apron to converse about the weather and the continuing search for survivors from the storm.

When the woman finished her meal, she came up to the counter to pay the restaurant owner. She was close enough that Clark could smell her perfume. The bouquet reminded him of the ladies he had seen on the train from Newton.

"Excuse me, ma'am. Did I see you on the train before Christmas?" Clark inquired.

"Yes, I have been in Dodge for over a fortnight."

"And you were sitting with another fine young woman, who I would venture was your twin."

"Well, I am flattered that you remember my younger cousin and I. But she continued on to Colorado. Assuming the tracks were clear."

"The resemblance is remarkable. Manners would dictate that I introduce myself. I am Agent H.A. Clark from Dallas."

"Yes, I recognized you from church last Sunday. I am Agnes Robinson, from Kansas City," replied the woman.

Agnes extended her hand for Clark to kiss her fingers. "I gather you are looking for friends of Mollie Brennan in Dodge City."

As she listened to Clark's response, Agnes was reminded of her own arrival in Dodge at a young age. Her mind wandered to the life forced upon Anna and herself. From the age of eighteen the twins had been passed from man to man, including two Masterson brothers, Ransome Cooper and, until recently, two brothers in Missouri named Robinson.

Clark was still talking to her. "There is a trail boss in Dodge by the name of Cotton. I don't trust him, but he also seems to be looking for a young woman traveling under a false name."

"What name is that?"

"Una Clark. That was my late daughter's name. She passed some four years ago."

"I might be able to help you. Meet me here, tomorrow, at breakfast," Agnes said abruptly. As she went out the door she looked back and added, "I should have some information about this impostor."

Clark watched her leave then turned to the man at the counter with a skeptical gaze. Both men shrugged their shoulders before Clark returned his attention to lunch.

On their first day, the new *Fable* employees learned how to operate the Treadwell printing press, feed sheets of paper into it, and remove the product. Fannie May was impressed with how quickly Una picked up the routine. Business was booming for Ransome, as the *Fable*'s reports on the Big Die-Up continued to attract readers and advertisers. After working twelve hours for five days in a row, Ransome suggested that they should celebrate by having a special meal.

"May we invite John B to join us?" asked Una. "He and Fannie May have been my guardian angels."

"That's a good idea, Una. And I have invited a special guest that I want you to meet.

The next day, Ransome closed the print shop early for the celebratory supper.

"I hope you like barbecue pork ribs," announced Ransome. "Una, can you clean up the press and then join me outside to help prepare the meal."

"Certainly. I have never had barbecue," Una cheered.

"I'll help too," declared Fannie May.

"No, let Una help. You have a guest in my office and I would regret keeping him waiting."

"Who? I don't expect anyone."

Ransome pointed to his office. "It's important. He's waiting."

Fannie May went to the kitchen and washed away as much ink as she could in a few minutes. Then she removed her apron and tidied her dress before going to the office.

When she entered the room, all she could see were the hands of someone sitting behind the desk reading a newspaper.

"Hello," said Fannie May.

The hands folded the newspaper shut revealing a man with dark features. His hair was neatly cut and combed.

He had a thick black mustache over thin lips. He had a penetrating yet friendly gaze. His attire could match any bank manager in New York City. He got up from his chair with the assistance of an ornate walking stick. Even without the conspicuous hat, the man was unmistakably, Bat Masterson.

Seeing the surprise on Fannie May's face, Bat spoke first. "Mrs. Barringer. Allow me to introduce myself. My name is Bartholemew Masterson." He spoke with a trace of an Irish accent.

"I am pleased. Uh, beyond pleased to meet you, Mr. Masterson." stammered Fannie May.

"Please call me Bat, if I may call you Fannie May."

"Yes, thank you...Bat," Fannie May said cautiously. She was afraid of this man, yet curious to hear what he had to say.

"Please sit down," suggested Bat, in an effort to ease the tension. "Can I get you anything?"

"No, I am fine. I expect to eat with the others soon."

"Indeed. Ransome's famous barbecue ribs. Not my choice, but most people enjoy them. Do you mind if I sit down?" Bat asked, as he lowered himself back into the chair.

"I am surprised you wanted to see me, Mr. Masterson, er Bat. I thought you were out of town."

"I was. But in my line of work, there is much travel. No rest for the wicked, as they say."

Fannie May offered a polite smile.

Bat continued, "I have heard tales of your bravery and cunning. You and your John B have had some adventures.

But I come here today to ask for your assistance on a matter of great importance. You may be aware that I have not yet married, nor have I fathered any children. This creates a great vacuum in my life and obscures much of my legacy."

"I was not aware. But you are aware that I am married?" asked Fannie May.

"Oh, how awkward I have been," chuckled Bat. "I am not looking to you for that kind of assistance, although I could do much worse than to share your companionship. No, I am looking for something much more visceral. More faithful. More confidential. I am looking for someone to write a letter for me and to keep the contents secure."

"I see. Are you thinking of a lawyer or a justice?" inquired Fannie May.

"Never trust a man who is paid to keep your secrets and judge them at the same time. That is my motto. I only trust people who can look me in the eye and tell me the truth, regardless of the consequences."

"I am not sure why you are telling me this."

"Fannie May. I have met a lot of people in my life. Many of them sat across a card table from me. Many of them spoke through the bars of a jail cell. A few shared my bed. And in every case, these people have two eyes. I believe that a person has one eye which sees other people in the world. Their other eye looks out for them self. And, face to face, I can tell which eye is dominant."

"That's an interesting point of view," Fannie May observed.

"I see what you did there," laughed Bat. "Each time I talk with you, I can tell that you see other people with your dominant eye."

"But we have only just met," Fannie May noted. "How can you come to that conclusion?"

"We have met more than once. And I am better for those meetings."

"I don't know what you mean."

"As I mentioned, I travel far and wide. Including Paris, Texas."

Fannie May gasped. Memories of her younger life in a Paris bordello flooded her memory. Now, she remembered this man's voice. His hat. His dark eyes. But he had not carried a cane in those days.

"Is that what you came for, Bat Masterson?" shouted Fannie May as she stood to leave.

"No. If anything, I have come to apologize for the sins of *my* youth, not yours. Please sit and hear me out."

"I have gone to great lengths to leave that life behind."

"And I applaud you, Fannie May Barringer. That is exactly why I trust you to help me. I propose, in fact, that we can help each other. I want to protect my reputation as much as you do yours. But we both have skeletons in our closet. And those skeletons have value."

"Such as?" asked Fannie May.

"That bordello in Paris had a fashionable reputation in your time. Top men came from far and wide. Money was no object to those men of good repute. Like me, those men relied and continue to rely, on your discretion."

"And their names have never crossed my lips."

"But a written list of those names could prove invaluable. Priceless, in a time of need."

"What makes you think I have such a list?"

"I hope you do. Because I want to make a trade. Your list for mine."

"And is your list as valuable?"

"To me. A confession of my dishonesty."

"Your reputation is well traveled. That cat is already out of the bag. I can't imagine any villainy that would harm that reputation."

"That reputation serves me well. In Kansas," Bat emphasized. "My malicious and unscrupulous behavior provides prestige in Dodge City. It's Bat Masterson, the legend. Yet not all the legends and articles written about my exploits are based on facts. People like Ransome Cooper and others have taken my every experience and blown it out of proportion. They entertain their readers with the incredible and fantastic adventures of a man with a gun, a cane, and a funny hat."

"I never questioned your villainy," admitted Fannie May. "Should I have?"

"In this age of newspapers and paperbacks, every writer or editor tries to outdo the competition. I myself made the same effort in 1884 with the *Vox Populi*. That single edition was not a business success, but politically I was able to affect the outcome of the county elections."

"I am listening, but what has this to do with me?"

"Let me give you an example. I was involved in the Battle at Adobe Walls in 1874. Thirty men and one stubborn woman defended that fort from an Indian attack. I was one of the motley crew of buffalo hunters in that post. At the end of the battle, twenty-eight of the enemy were killed. Did I kill any of them? I don't know. There is a vast difference between shooting a buffalo in a herd and shooting a man on horseback who knows when to retreat. Chances are that I shot more trees or horses than men. Yet, after two days, the number of dead warriors exceeded the number of surviving defenders. Law of averages would suggest I must have killed one man. And an army report said I did. Then a captain decided that some buffalo hunters were better shots than others, so they probably did the bulk of the killing. His report credited me with shooting five of the enemy and nominated me for a commendation. Buffalo hunters as a rule, are inclined to "pretty up" the success of their peers. They, in turn, embellished the commendation to suggest that I had killed ten men. Subsequent and exaggerated reports from Texas preceded my travels. By the time I reached Dodge City, the public were reading how Bat Masterson single-handedly killed all twenty-eight raiders in defense of the Adobe Walls saloon."

"And so a legend begins," acknowledged Fannie May.

"And grows from there. But a legend in the west will be considered a criminal in polite society. I have friends in the eastern cities who keep my company in Dodge City but would deny our acquaintance in New York City."

Fannie May thought for a moment then added, "It's impossible to maintain the lore that surrounds you in both situations."

"You are correct. But when the die is cast, history will choose versions of truth from words written on paper. My documented history, largely fictional, disrespects the families of my alleged victims. They deserve to know the truth."

"And when do you think they can handle the truth?" inquired Fannie May.

"I hope I will know. Probably not as long as I live and breathe in the west. But my pursuits in the east may require dilution of my reputation. That is why I am asking you to pen a sworn statement from me. And I will ask you to guard that document until I request it or until you feel justified in exposing my truth."

Fannie May retrieved a stack of blank pages and took down the information as dictated by Masterson. The dictation filled four pages. Fannie May read the notes back to Bat for his approval.

"Truer words were never spoken," affirmed Bat. "I entrust them to your discretion."

"In exchange for my list of *top men*?" confirmed Fannie May. Then she squatted behind the desk to retrieve a note from the pocket on the hem of her skirt. She flattened the stained and wrinkled paper on the desktop. Despite exposure to rain, snow, fire and blood, the lion's share of the printed names were clear and legible. Fannie May printed several additional names and signed "Dora-lee Devito" on the bottom.

"I have a clear memory of the men who paid for my company," Fannie May stated. "I have added them to Dora-lee's list but I will not put my name to any of them. The late Dora-lee worked brothels from Paris to Dallas to Austin to Llano. She can take credit for the entire list."

Bat looked at the names. "Remarkable," he said with a grin. "This Masterson fellow might be the least impressive on the list."

Fannie May placed the list in a thick envelope and the legend in another. She applied a wax seal to each envelope.

"We shall guard each other's reputations until the die is cast," Bat declared.

"Until the die is cast," repeated Fannie May.

42

Dodge City, Kansas, 1887

After satisfying myself of the quality of the work, and that an important saving in price would be made over hand printing, but not finding the printers prepared to adopt it, I determined to begin the business of printing, and continue it until the printers should be satisfied that it would be for their advantage to adopt my press and purchase the right to use it. I built a second machine in 1822, to be operated by the same horse that carried the first. In this the bed and platen were of cast-iron, I having succeeded in adapting an old lathe to turn their faces. In connection with two gentlemen, General W.H. Sumner and Mr. Redford Webster, I purchased type, procured workmen, and made contracts with some booksellers to print several books for them, and otherwise obtained work where I could get it. With these two presses I continued operations in Batterymarch Street, in a building owned by Benjamin Bussey, for a year or two, the work being equal to any hand-press printing, and, being performed by females at the rate of nine or ten impressions a minute, the saving of expense was important. In 1822, one of the principal booksellers of Boston purchased my establishment with the patent right for Massachusetts. It was removed to another place, and two more presses added. The establishment was burned in 1826.

— Morrill Wyman, *Memoir of Daniel Treadwell* (John Wilson and Son, 1888)

The heat of mesquite coals cooked the pork ribs quickly. Ransome tended the meat while Una stood next to him, heating the corn and hash potatoes. Like any good journalist, Ransome was inquiring about Una's family and life in Dallas. Thinking she was talking with a friend, who would be discreet, Una related the events leading up to her being shut out and contracting a fever. When she noticed Ransome writing some notes behind her back, Una suspected she had shared too much. She made an effort to bring the others into the conversation.

"I don't recall cooking outdoors in Dallas," Una said. "I suspect that was to discourage any outsiders."

"What do you mean by outsiders?" asked John B.

"People who were not from our church. Especially boys who were not Brethren."

"Do you still feel that way?" asked Fannie May.

"No, of course not. I left that life." Una paused for a moment and nervously flattened her apron against her abdomen. She looked at the floor sheepishly and said, "Now that I have been with a man, I am considered an outsider."

"Will you ever return to the church?" asked John B.

"No, never," Una said loudly. "I am waiting for Cotton. I am sure he will come for me soon."

"No matter, girl," whispered Ransome, as he brushed her hair away from her face. Then in his normal voice he added, "When we have our meal, and some wine, you can tell us more about your miserable one-eyed father, the Pinkerton man."

"One-eyed man?" asked Fannie May. "Who are you talking about?"

"Jesus H. Christ!" shouted John B. "That's who I saw!"

"Cotton?" asked Fannie May.

"No. Clark. Agent Clark has an eye patch," John B repeated. "That's why I didn't recognize him. But he looked familiar. What happened to his eye?"

Everyone looked at Una who was hanging her head.

"When I was fourteen, before I got the fever, I sprayed perfume in his eye. I guess that may have caused permanent damage."

"When he arrested me last summer, I noticed his right eye was cloudy," John B recalled. "I just assumed he had an injury from a pistol misfire."

"I assumed that also," explained Ransome. "When he came into town, I hoped it might make a good story. But he explained that the eye was aggravated by wind and cold, so he frequently needed the patch."

A somber mood descended on the group as they digested the news about Agent Clark. Fannie May scarcely touched her meal and avoided the meat entirely. Eventually John B declared that the barbecue meat was the best he had tasted since leaving Llano.

In response, Ransome opened a bottle of wine and poured it into generous goblets. Fannie May declined and remained aloof. The drink lightened the spirits of the others, especially Una.

"Oh, I wonder if this is what dancing feels like," Una said in a squeaky voice.

"Why do you ask that?" asked John B.

"I have never danced, but the room seems to be spinning slowly."

"I will dance with you, Una," Ransome said, as he lifted her from her chair.

With wobbly feet, Una awkwardly waltzed around the kitchen following Ransome's lead. Fannie May and John B joined in for a few spins before Una collapsed into Ransome's arms.

"Oh, I just want to close my eyes," said Una.

John B laughed, "Seems this is the first time Miss Una has been under the influence."

"I'm not sure Una should be drinking wine," Fannie May observed. "Come Una, I'll help you up the stairs so you can get to bed."

Once in the loft, Fannie May lay Una on her bed. "Get some sleep, Una. You will feel better in the morning."

"Ooh. I don't think so. Lately, the mornings have been the worst part of my day."

"Hopefully, it's just the water," grumbled Fannie May.

"I have sinned so much tonight. But that was so fun!" exclaimed Una.

"That's enough fun for today," said Fannie May as she left the girl's room.

Una started to undress but did not get far before her head fell on the pillow. She just needed some rest, and then she would change into her night shift. She closed her eyes and succumbed to the dullness.

Sometime later, Una noticed a shadowy figure extinguish the candles in her room. In her catatonic state, Una felt a hand moving under her dress. "No, no, no," she croaked.

"Give yourself to me," Ransome whispered. "I am better than that cowboy."

Una screamed, "No. No. He will kill you!"

Ransome removed his hand and quietly left the room.

Una kept mumbling, "No, No," until consciousness escaped her.

The next time Una awoke, she heard the sound of someone at the door of her room. It sounded like a key turning in the lock. The room was still dark. "Who's there?" she called.

There was no answer, but she heard footsteps and creaking as the person descended the stairs. She felt the top of her dresser for a match, but none were there. She crawled to the door and tried to open it. The door was locked. With tears in her eyes, she crawled back towards her bed, still dizzy from the alcohol. She puked into the dark closet and passed out on the floor.

When Una next awoke, light was filtering through the window blinds. Her head felt thick. She dragged herself into bed and covered her head to block out the dim light. Then she heard loud voices from the print room below.

"Give yourself to me," said a woman's voice. "You always said that, didn't you?"

"Stop, Anna," said Ransome. "You are going to hurt me."

"You will suffer this night. But only one night. We suffered dozens of nights."

"You bitch, untie me!" shouted Ransome.

"Suffer, you sick bastard."

"Aah," screamed Ransome. "Stop, Anna."

"Prepare to meet your maker," said the woman's voice.

"Nooo, no…no…." The words trailed off.

Confused and frightened, Una lay perfectly still. Seconds turned to minutes in the silence of the shop. Then she heard a loud clang followed by sounds of metal scraping against metal. Moments later, she heard the stairs creak as someone climbed towards her room. Una pulled the blankets tight around her neck and held her breath. A key turned, and the door swung open. A shadow knelt and slid something metal under the unoccupied bed. Una saw the figure of a woman with long hair wearing a dark blue dress stand and face her. A sliver of daylight reflected off something white pinned to the intruder's collar. The woman backed out of the room, closed the door and locked it again. Una heard her rapid descent on the stairs.

Una waited. Her mind was still in a stupor. Fractured events swirled in her thoughts. The building was quiet. Nervously, she crawled to the door and tried the knob. It was locked, as she had expected. Una looked under the bed where the woman had discarded something. In the shadow she saw a speckled trail of blood and two objects. She reached under the bed and pulled out the closest object. It was a kitchen knife, with blood on the handle and blade. In shock, Una threw it back under the bed. She pulled out the other object. It was a wire key ring with several skeleton keys on it. Blood was dripping from the keys.

Una held the key ring and crawled to her door. The second key she tried unbolted the door. On hands and knees, she crawled out of her room and peered between the rails of the stairwell. There were no signs of life in the shop below, except the flickering shadows of candlelight. But there were signs of misadventure: red smears across stacks of paper; bloody footprints on the floor leading up and down the stairs; and —Una gasped— a human torso protruding from under the platen of the printing press.

Una held back a scream in fear she would be heard, but bile rose to her lips. Then she vomited over the edge of the stairs into the mechanism of the press below. She wiped her arm across her mouth and realized she was still dressed from the previous evening. She stood to descend the stairs. A loud knock on the front door startled her and she had to fight to maintain her balance. Had someone come to rescue her? Both relieved and surprised she ventured down to the print room.

43

Dodge City, Kansas, January 1887

The punishment for rape under the United States is death, and yet the party injured may be in perfect health while the condemned dangles by the neck on the gallows.

—J.R. Hallowell (attorney), letter to the Topeka *Capital*, reprinted in the *Iola Register*, Iola, Kansas, October 14, 1887

The editor of the *Dodge City Times* was enjoying a breakfast biscuit and cup of coffee when a woman came storming into his office. She was dressed informally, in a gray cotton Mother Hubbard dress with buttoned front. Her hair was entirely hidden in a black bonnet, and she was wearing spectacles.

"Can I help you, ma'am?"

"Yes, I was passing the other newspaper office and heard a woman screaming. I thought you might know how to help."

The editor jumped from behind the desk and grabbed his coat. Then he yelled into a back office. "Samuel, bring your camera. Somebody, bring a lawman to the *Fable*." When the editor turned around, the woman in the gray dress was gone. He watched her run down the street, away from the commotion she had only just reported.

By the time Deputy Tilghman arrived at the *Fable*, the front door had been opened by force. Glass shards littered the floor. Several people were inside the print shop, including some passers-by. Among them, Tilghman recognized Doctor Swift. The doctor was busy consoling an overwrought redhead. The young woman's hands and clothes had blood on them.

Tilghman approached the doctor. "What happened to this girl?"

The doctor nodded towards the men gathered at the far end of the printing press. The deputy recognized the *Times* editor and a photographer.

"Hang on to the girl, Doc. I better see what's going on over there."

"Hold on to your breakfast, deputy," replied the doctor.

Tilghman was blinded momentarily when the photographer exploded his flash powder to take a picture of the carnage. When the deputy regained his vision, he was taken aback by the scene before him: a blood-soaked torso and legs were dangling from bloody tissue clamped in the printing press.

"Stop that before you blind us all!" yelled Tilghman. "Who is in there?"

"Should be Ransome," said the man from the *Times*. "Can't be sure until we open up the press."

"Reckon he is pretty mangled. Do you fellers know how to operate this contraption?" asked the deputy.

The newspaperman went to the front of the press, opened some latches, and cranked a steel wheel until the platen lifted slightly. Blood poured onto the floor, and the dead man's body slithered out of the press. Chunks of flesh and hair, snagged in the mechanism, tore away in stringy red flaps.

"God rest his soul. Reckon the Shawnee would have done a cleaner job of scalping him," said the deputy as he bent over the corpse.

The man from the *Times* turned to his photographer. "Don't bother takin' pictures. Can't figure out what we are looking at."

"Do ya figger it was an accident?" the deputy asked the man from the *Times*.

"No, the press won't come down until someone yanks that lever over there. Appears Ransome would have been reaching inside when someone else pulled the lever."

"So, is it your opinion we have a murder on our hands?"

"I am afraid so," replied the editor from the *Times*. "It would be extremely negligent to pull that lever when Ransome was clearly in harm's way. And then you see the blood on his trousers."

"Yeah. Right at the crotch. I'll get Doc to check if this gentleman is missing any parts," Tilghman grumbled. "OK. You people start clearing out of here. Doc, you and the girl can stay."

"You gonna lock her up?" asked the editor.

"Yep. I have some questions to ask when she sobers up. Smells like a wine bottle."

Agnes Robinson wore a navy-blue Edwardian dress and a blouse with pink flowers printed on it. She was sitting at the same table in the back of the Modern Cafe. When she saw Agent Clark come into the diner, she smiled and waved. Clark removed his stetson and sat down across from her.

"Agent Clark, I know where your daughter is staying."

"My daughter died. I saw the death certificate. That is an impostor."

Agnes smiled politely and continued, "Yesterday, I saw that redhead in the print shop. I could not be sure, but I got the impression the editor was berating her about something."

"What makes you say that?" asked Clark.

"He was upset about a note she was holding. Yelling something about keep quiet about Mollie."

"And you think this interests me since my dead daughter had red hair?"

"Red-headed teenager? Skinny but attractive?"

"There are more than one of such women. But if she has information about Mollie Brennan, I will want to talk with her."

"Why? What's your interest in this Mollie Brennan?"

"Are you familiar with the lady?"

"No. Who was she?"

"She was a harlot and keeper of a bawdy house in the Texas town about three days south of here. Back then it was known as Cantonment Sweetwater. Now it's called Mobeetie."

"Sounds like an awful woman," declared Agnes. "What does she do now?"

"The woman is dead. Shot by a sinner while in the company of another."

"I am intrigued by your interest in that story," Anna said softly and tucked some stray hair behind her right ear.

Agent Clark was happy to reveal the details of the "Sweetwater Shootout" to this woman who appeared both interesting and interested. He named all of the parties involved including the Jolly twins. The more he talked, the more questions Agnes Robinson asked. Eventually, Agnes looked up at the clock above the cash register.

"I don't believe the time on that clock. Do you have a watch?" she asked Clark.

Clark pulled out his pocket watch and said, "I have five minutes of nine o'clock."

"I have an appointment with the friseaur," Agnes said touching the hair dangling, once again, in front of her ear.

"If it is not out of your way, can you take me to the girl that you think has information about Mollie," requested the man in black.

Deputy Tilghman was gathering some details from Una when Agent Clark and Agnes Robinson entered the print room.

"So your name is Una Clark and you are employed by Ransome Cooper?" asked Tilghman.

Suddenly, Una's eyes went wide. "And that's the murderer," she screamed, pointing at Agnes Robinson. "She was here. She killed Ransome and put that knife in my room."

Agent Clark was dumbfounded. Gasping for air he asked, "Una? I had a daughter named Una. She looked much like you."

"I know who you are!" shouted Una. "Do you know who you are with? That woman murdered my friend. She murdered Mr. Cooper. I saw her."

"You are wrong, whoever you are. I was with this lady most of the morning. You must be confused," stated Clark.

"You ladies, stay here!" commanded Tilghman. "Agent, come over here by the body where we can talk."

Fannie May and John Barringer arrived to join the crowd gathered outside the *Fable* print room. Agent Clark spotted Fannie May over Tilghman's shoulder. He stared at her with his uncovered eye.

Now Fannie May understood what Bat meant by "one eye looks out for them self."

44

Dodge City, Kansas, 1887

Quite a sensation was created in Marquette last Saturday, when the rumor was spread on the streets that Mr. Sam Ruby, the proprietor of the Merchants' Hotel, had attempted to outrage the person of his hired girl, Miss Signora Riley. On the girl's complaint, Mr. Ruby was arrested for an assault with attempt to rape, and his case came up before Judge Ericson on Monday this week. Mr. Grattan, our county attorney, appeared for the state, and some lawyers from Salina were present as counsel for the defendant. The judge bound the defendant over to the district court and fixed his bonds at $300. The crime was committed on the night between Friday and Saturday of last week. The girl, who was sleeping in the kitchen when attacked, defended herself bravely and the man soon found out that he had tackled the wrong person.

—*Saline County Journal*, **Salina, Kansas, August 4, 1887**

A despondent Una Clark sat motionless on her jailhouse bunk while her father stood looking down at her. She watched him fidget with his hat in his hands, trying to find words. She did not understand the type of relationship they might have going forward. Una did not know what her father expected of her but she found it difficult to understand why he had given her up for dead without a second thought.

"Speak your mind, father," commanded Una.

"Daughter, you have disgraced your family and your church. In fact, you have disgraced everyone who has crossed paths with you since the day you met that cowboy."

"You have no right to judge me!" shouted Una. "I know I have sinned and I have suffered for it. But I have found love and friendship. More love than I was ever offered by my family."

"Consuming alcohol is a sin. Intercourse outside of marriage is unforgivable. And now murder. I can not abide your existence. God can never forgive you. Una, you have entered the abyss."

"God knows the truth. But truth means nothing to you. You assume my guilt and ask me to beg for mercy."

"God knows none of this would have happened if you had waited for your healing to be complete. If you had returned to your family and brethren instead of running off with some cowboys."

"So I should have returned like some prodigal son. But no. Your kind would never believe the words of a disgraced girl. You and your brethren were relieved that this unrighteous female had taken ill and died. No need for the celebrated Agent Clark to investigate that death. Game over. Brethren One. Girl zero. Did anybody even ask the hospital how I died? Hell, nobody bothered to claim my body. Why not?" wailed Una, trying to hold back tears.

"Even if we had claimed your body you would never have been allowed a Christian burial."

"So just wipe me from memory. Very bloody convenient? But not very damn convenient for me. I spent four years wondering who I was and why I was there. But worse than that was the sadness in the eyes of the nurses when I asked them the same questions. Everyday for four years I asked them. And everyday I brought them to tears."

"We didn't know you were alive."

"And now you do. I can't imagine how bitter today has been for you to discover your eldest child still lives. And lives in sin every chance she gets. But don't worry. I may never see the light of day again."

"Why did you take up with the first cowboy that came along. Why do you keep company with a harlot and an accused murderer — Fannie May and John Barringer?"

"Because they care. Those three people love me regardless of my past. They love me based on the future they want for me. They can't quote the Bible but they are better damn Christians than you will ever be."

"Cussing me does not change anything. You insist on another sin today by blaming an innocent woman for a crime she could not have committed. Lies do not prove you innocent."

"Father!" shouted Una. "Please hold your tongue and listen to me. I know what I saw. The only difference between the killer and the woman you call Agnes Robinson is the blood on their clothes. And the name, of course."

"What do you mean, *name*?"

"I told the deputy. I heard Ransome screaming at the woman who attacked him. He called her Anna."

"I can vouch for the innocence of the woman, Agnes. But Ransome was attacked by another?" asked Clark.

"It looked like the same woman," replied Una. "I am still so tired. Nothing makes sense." Una lay back on the cot. Her tears wet the cloth pillow.

Agent Clark paused to consider this information. "I did see another woman who looked like Agnes on the train. But, to my knowledge, she didn't get off in Dodge."

"But why kill Ransome?" asked Una. "Did he owe her something?"

"Dignity. From what you heard it sounds like Ransome took advantage of Anna. And she killed him to recover a piece of her dignity," answered Clark.

Una gathered her thoughts. "There were two beds in that loft. He said there were two other women there before me. Ransome talked about some jolly girls who worked with him a few years ago. Those women could have been the Robinson twins —Anna and Agnes —seeking revenge for Ransome's assaults. I might have sought revenge, but they got there first."

"Not the Robinson twins. They were both married to men named Robinson. They are the Jolly twins. Of course, and now I've let them escape!" exclaimed the Pinkerton man.

"That's their name? Jolly? I thought Ransome was talking about their mood, as in happy-go-lucky." Una looked up at her father, "But I don't care about them. I want to know what's going to happen to me?"

"If you think Ransome raped you, then you had motive to kill him. Or, maybe it's Cotton who had motive for murder."

"Well, I don't believe Ransome did rape me. Either way, that don't mean I killed him."

"You will have to show the law that someone else had motive."

"Will you help me father? I'm innocent."

"I have orders to catch the Jolly twins. As an agent of the law that is my duty. They may or may not provide information that helps your case. But as your father, I can't help you. You will always be a sinner in my eyes and the eyes of God." Clark took a gulp of air. Una couldn't tell if it was a sigh of relief or a sigh of despair. Then he said, "God will give me a sign if you are innocent. Until then, I have to leave you here."

"It wouldn't be the first time you abandoned your only daughter."

"Your undoing is the result of disobedience. You ignored our teachings and instead put trust in an advertisement in a newspaper. That was foolhardy. Brazen. Blasphemous. You were brought up not to trust any readings outside of the Bible."

"Yes, you raised me to ignore the outside world. But that is no way to live. Inside a cage. There were more bars around me then than in this jail cell. Can't you see that?"

"That's not how God sees it, Una. God will not forgive you without penitence."

"God has nothing to forgive. I did not commit a sin."

"Fornication is a sin. But the court will decide if you committed a crime. I can only help the court find facts. And the fact that you were not Ransome's first victim is important. Ransome always planned to bring in women that he could take advantage of. I suspect there were others stripped of their dignity. At your trial, the judge will take this evidence into account. I will gather what I can on Anna and Agnes, the Robinson sisters or Jolly twins as they may be. It will take me away from Dodge City."

"You go ahead and gather evidence. But trial or no trial, I intend to reclaim *my* dignity."

The citizens of Dodge City were in an uproar as the news of the murder spread. Several versions of events circulated with diverging opinions about the guilt or innocence of the parties involved. Some Reformers thought the murder was probably justified. After all, Ransome's support of the Gang's activities left little doubt that he had been doing the devil's work. But the woman had sinned by taking a man's life not to mention her many other sins.

The drovers and trail bosses were sympathetic to Una and Cotton. They were all impressed that Una had survived on the trail, lived through a blizzard, and escaped numerous rape attempts by whatever means at her disposal. Even Bucktooth remarked, "That fiery redhead is much more than just a piece of calico. Reckon she left Stubby's body to the buzzards. That newspaperman would have been smart to keep his distance."

Bat Masterson received a telegram from Ford County partially explaining the events at the *Dodge City Fable*.

Since he and his Gang were fifty miles away, rigging the county seat election in Garfield county, and since snow continued to restrict travel, Bat responded that the Gang would not return to Dodge unless either the weather improved or the murder trial was scheduled.

Deputy marshal Bill Tilghman was uncomfortable holding Una for trial without the support of the Gang. He expected the other factions to cause more trouble than he could handle. The life of the lawman was difficult at the best of times. And this might be the worst of times in Dodge City.

Cotton's gut reaction was that Una had protected herself and should not be prosecuted for it. Cotton looked for advice from the other cowboys. Rumors spread that the cowboys were going to break Una out of jail. He contacted Barringer and Fannie May to see how they could assist.

"That girl doesn't have a mean bone in her body," said Cotton. "I can't stand by to watch her go on trial, let alone hang for this."

"Do you have a plan?" asked Fannie May.

Cotton shrugged and said, "Not a real good one. S'pect the deputy will get shot if we raid the calaboose. Even if we free Una, our lives won't be worth a plug nickel."

"And if the deputy backs away, either the Gang or the Army will step in," Barringer added. "That could put Una on the run for years. And you with her."

"Her pa, the Pinkerton man, came to me." said Cotton.

"What's his plan?" asked Barringer.

"He says she is guilty of many sins, but Ransome deserved to die. Plans to track down some witnesses to prove it. But, he told me to stay out of it and stay away from Una for the rest of my life."

"He's determined to make her life miserable," said Fannie May. "How do you feel about spending some time in the hoosegow, temporarily of course?"

"Ain't on my bucket list, but anything if it helps Una," replied Cotton.

"OK." Fannie May mapped out her plan. "Find a cowpoke you can trust. Someone a couple inches over five feet. Skinny. Should have red hair. We need a group of cowboys. Make sure they all like whiskey."

45

Dodge City, Kansas, January 1887

... the Chief of Police in Kansas City has pronounced upon the proper dress for a lady to wear upon the street. In restricting the movements and dress of women, these officers interfere with the rights of a vote-less class. We hope a test case will soon decide justly upon the merits of this matter. What right this officer has to interfere with the comfortable and healthful "Mother Hubbard" is a profound mystery to most people. Physicians and sensible people pronounce the "Mother Hubbard" a boon to the race, and an altogether decent and becoming garment. If the war had been made on "tie-backs" people possessed of "gumption" would be able to see some justice in it.

Not long since a young lady of our acquaintance, stood chatting with a friend upon the sidewalk in front of her residence. Although the day was sultry, and the lady eminently respectable, and her conduct irreproachable, Chief Spears pounced upon and arrested her. It now costs the price of a handsome dress to be seen in a "Mother Hubbard" in the city in which Chief Spear's dictum is law.

—*Saline County Journal*, Salina, Kansas, June 24, 1886

The schedule for the AT&SF railway was limited until the end of January of 1887. After waiting several days, two women boarded a first-class cabin on a westbound train at Dodge City. They were not much for looks in their gray Mother Hubbards and the black puritan bonnets tied tight around their faces. As the train pulled away from the station, one of the women pulled out a flask. She opened it and said, "And here's to you, Mrs. Robinson," then raised it above her head. "Jesus loves you more than you will know." She tipped back the flask and swallowed twice before the other woman said, "Whoa, whoa, whoa."

When the flask was promptly passed across the cabin the second woman said, "God bless you, please, Mrs. Robinson. Heaven holds a place for those who pray."

The conductor opened the door to their compartment. "Are you ladies comfy? I'll come by for tickets shortly."

"Yes, thanks, conductor. We are going all the way to Winslow."

The conductor nodded and then proceeded to the next cabin. He opened the door to see a man with an eye-patch. The conductor winked, and the man in black handed him a sawbuck. No words were spoken between them. Outside, snow was spraying up beside the windows, as the car jostled from the forward motion.

The volume of freight handled by rail increased threefold that winter, since teamsters were unable to navigate through the snow and mud. George Hoover, founder and mayor of Dodge City, continued to operate the most profitable wholesale alcohol business in the state. He brought in barrels of spirits and beer from St. Louis and Kansas City by train. Then he bottled, blended, and sold them to saloons and hotels. In the severe weather of 1886-87, he continued to receive stock by train but was not able to ship much product beyond the confines of Dodge City. So, when Fannie May offered to subsidize the sales of whiskey in Dodge, Hoover was more than helpful.

"Mr. Hoover, please set the price of whiskey at a quarter of normal. I will pay you for the three quarters' difference."

"You realize saloons will be selling whiskey for pennies a glass," chuckled Hoover.

"Of course. That will mean that whiskey is cheaper than water. Saloon patrons will be crocked early in the day."

On January 24, the Long Branch Saloon planned a birthday celebration for Fannie May Barringer. That morning, a glass of whiskey was priced at two cents. The cattle crew from Double Lightning was lined up, waiting for the Long Branch Saloon to open its doors. Cotton was buying. Drovers from other establishments got wind of the clearance and arrived soon afterwards. In the late afternoon, cowboys were celebrating in the streets with enthusiasm. Some had their shirts off. Some were trying to write their names in the snow. Some were being towed by rope, skiing behind horses. Shots were fired into the air.

Deputy Tilghman was warned by several members of the public that there might be bloodshed or a fire. Fannie May found Tilghman watching from a merchant's window.

"Deputy, how do you plan to stop these drunken hooligans?"

"I don't reckon I can. The sheriff and other deputies are working up in Ravanna."

"Well, you need to get creative. May I make a suggestion?" asked Fannie May.

"You would not be the first to offer advice. Go on," replied Tilghman.

"I have been watching these cowboys for several weeks. That white-haired fellow they call Cotton is one of the instigators. And he's got a short, red-haired man and a bucktoothed man who do his bidding. I suggest you arrest those three and some others. If you throw the trouble-makers in a cell overnight, the rest will settle down."

The deputy nodded. "Uh-huh."

"Some of the churchgoers will surely act as your posse. My husband John Barringer will join in."

"Uh-huh," said Tilghman.

"Sounds logical, Deputy," said the storekeeper, who had been listening to Fannie May's advice. "If you wait much longer there will be broken glass and who knows what."

Deputy Tilghman gathered some Reformers in a posse to approach the mob. Barringer stood with the posse. The cowboys were boisterous, but they kept their guns at their sides.

"Sorry, fellas. I have to go with the deputy," shouted Cotton. "He's got a shine on me."

"Hey, wait up. We can just move the party," yelled Bucktooth.

"I'm bringing my whiskey!" declared a red-haired cowpoke.

"Hey, Deputy. How many beds you got over there?"

"Off we go. Cotton will need our support."

"I bet Cotton wants to share a bed with you-know-who if she's still in that jail."

"Reckon we all want to share that bunk!"

"Mmm-doggie."

"Yahoo. To the calaboose."

In their drunken state, the drovers were more than cooperative. They surrendered their firearms at the jailhouse entrance and marched into the cells. There was some struggling with the keys when some drovers fought over who would share a cell with Una.

"There is only one man there I care to share my cell with," shouted Una over the din. Her eyes met Cotton's.

"Look, there ain't nobody sharing cells with this gal. It's a jailhouse, not a bordello," said Tilghman, as he crammed six drovers in one cell and locked the door. "The rest of you, come with me across the street to the county jail."

"That's not fair, Deputy," whined the short, red-haired man with Cotton.

"I'd be in favor of being in the same building as the rest, even if it is a little tight," said Cotton.

Tilghman unholstered his pistol. "I said, let's move it. There's empty cells across the street, and you can worry about your love life when you sober up. The rest of you, sleep it off, and we will see what tomorrow brings."

"Have you got any food, Deputy?"

"How we gonna piss with this here gal around?"

"Boys. Boys. Let's get a guitar so we can do some jailhouse singing."

As the deputy was showing Cotton and the remaining cowboys to their county cells across the street, singing erupted back in the city jail. One cowboy played "Oh! Susanna" on a mouth organ, and the cowboys on both sides of the street joined in.

Men and women of the Reform movement were gathered in the street between the jailhouses. The preacher passed out hymnals so the gathering could sing louder than the cowboys. The awful sound echoed down the main street, with overlapping lyrics that sounded like:

Nearer my God to thee

With a banjo on my knee

"Go on home now," shouted the deputy. "They'll settle down when we get some food in them. I reckon some of you ladies could bring some biscuits and other fixin's."

Tilghman's prediction was correct. The singing and shouting stopped as soon as food was provided. Some of the cowboys had already fallen asleep on the cell floor.

Cotton was sitting on the wooden bed next to the short man with red hair. Both men looked dejected. They had expected to be locked up across the street in the same jail as Una.

"So much for the lady's plan," said the redhead cowpoke.

The *Fable* building cast a long shadow across the street. Barringer walked back to the Long Branch to meet Fannie May before dark. He wondered how she would fix this mess. Did she have a Plan B, or were all these cowboys serving time for naught?

He noticed the silhouette of a man at the back door of the *Fable*. A man with a walking stick and a bowler-style hat. Barringer walked towards the building and saw Bat Masterson gesturing for him to come over.

"I thought you were in Garfield County," said Barringer.

"That's what you and everyone else are supposed to think. Come into the office so we can talk privately."

Inside, Masterson explained that he was concerned about Tilghman's state of mind after the loss of his herd. He wondered if Deputy Tilghman would be able to maintain law and order without the support of the sheriff or the other gang members. He offered Barringer a plan to finish what Fannie May had put in motion.

"That gal of yours is canny and wily. I will be sorry to see her leave Dodge."

"Yer right, Mr. Masterson. There is no man that will tame Miss Fannie."

"Including you," agreed Bat, grinning. "Now take my keys and I will see you in the Livery tomorrow."

Barringer took two key rings from Masterson and waited in the alley at the back of the Ford County jailhouse. After sunset, the singing stopped and the Reformers dispersed. Then he piled up snow under the jail window and stood as high as he could before speaking. "Psst! Cotton, you in there?"

"Yeah, who's asking?"

"It's John B. I have the keys to get you out of there."

"Where'd you get those?"

"Never mind. I'll throw them up. When you hear me whistle 'My Darling Clementine' you sneak Red across the street. You know the song?"

"Yep. I'll wait for your signal. *And her shoes were number nine.*"

On the second throw, the keys disappeared into the dark window.

"Got them," whispered Cotton.

"OK. See you over at the city jail. If you have any trouble start whistling 'Oh! Susanna.'"

Barringer casually walked into the street. Seeing no others, he unlocked the front door of the city jailhouse and left it ajar. He looked out through the curtains and watched as Cotton and the redhead dashed across. The redhead tripped on the step and fell into the door of the jailhouse. Cotton picked him up but the commotion disturbed the inmates.

"Zat you, Deputy?"

"What's the commotion? We are trying to sleep back here."

Barringer wondered if he could keep these inebriated cowboys quiet and in their cells. The three of them went back to the cells to settle things down.

"Hey, where's my mouth organ. I know some more songs, fellas."

"How come Cotton is out of jail?"

"Shut up, fellas!" said the redhead.

"You shut up. Who let you out?"

While Cotton tried to calm the drunk tank, Barringer opened Una's cell. She jumped up and hugged him, then went to Cotton. They embraced for a few seconds, then Cotton took her and the redhead cowboy to the front office to explain the escape plan.

One particularly stalwart prisoner was hungry, tired, and agitated. He saw Barringer carrying keys, so he reached through the bars and grabbed Barringer by the throat. He pulled him against the cell and yelled, "Give me those keys!" Barringer could hardly breathe, but he fought to stay conscious. He threw the keys down the hallway with a clang. He saw Cotton pick them up just before the world went black.

Tilghman came back to the jail around ten o'clock the next morning. The night had been cold, and some of the men were huddled together on the cots. The cells reeked of whiskey and urine. Men that were alert rousted the others. Una appeared to still be asleep, tucked under a blanket in her cell.

"OK, fellas. You had yer fun. I don't want to be dragging you back here tonight," shouted Tilghman, as he opened the cell full of stinkers. "You just stay right there, Miss Una, and I'll get these inebriates out of your way before your breakfast."

"Who's he calling inebriates?"

"Dunno. I thought we were just drunks."

"Let's see if we can get that whiskey river flowing today."

Some of the cowboys tipped their hats to the deputy. Some of them cussed him under their breath. They all grabbed their sidearms on the way out. As they left the jailhouse, there was no audience of Reformers. Two of the offenders took the opportunity to take a piss off the deck.

"Don't eat that yellow snow, Deputy."

Tilghman went across the street to the Ford County jail. Three men in the cell were standing at the bars waiting for him. The redhead stood behind them, his hat pulled low on his face.

"Same as I told the others, I don't want to be dragging you back here tonight. Go home or go find a warm piece of calico, but don't be disturbin' the peace." Tilghman opened the cell door, and the four stumbled out into the street.

Two of them followed the other prisoners shuffling towards the Long Branch. Cotton and the redheaded fellow marched directly to the livery stable. Tilghman assumed they had horses that needed tending. He followed them partway and then noticed parallel troughs carved in the snow, as if someone had been dragged along the street. He decided to check on that after he had enjoyed a warm breakfast at the Modern Cafe.

When his belly was full, the deputy asked for an order of hotcakes to take back to his jailhouse for Miss Una. Tilghman was a married man, but he couldn't help admiring Miss Una regardless of her alleged crime.

"Here you go, Miss Una. Bacon and hotcakes, nice and hot off the grill," said Tilghman when he returned to the city jail.

Tilghman waited as Miss Una got off the bed, stood in the light of the hallway, and lifted her bonnet. As long spirals of red hair fell to the ground, he heard a man's voice. "You can call me Miss if you like, as long as you don't call me late for breakfast." Then the redheaded prisoner raised one hand, and Tilghman saw that he was holding up a pair of scissors. He clicked the blades twice.

Fannie May was in a panic when Barringer did not return. She had expected him back at the Long Branch before morning, after the cowboys were safely locked away. She could only presume that he had been confused with the cowboys and locked up with them.

According to her plan, the redheaded cowboy was to change places with Una in the city jail. She and John B were to be at the livery at sunrise with four horses saddled and packs on two other horses. When John B didn't return, she knew she had to proceed on her own. Alone in the barn, she had managed to saddle two horses and was struggling to put a saddle on Clyde.

"Come on, big fella," she said softly. "We are going for a ride in the snow today."

"I could sure use a morning in a hayloft."

Fannie May jumped at the sound of her husband's voice and turned to see John B struggling to get free from soiled straw piled in the corner.

Fannie May couldn't help smiling at the sight. "If that's true, you should have cleaned up first. Where were you last night?"

"I got caught up in a jailhouse fight. You should see the other guy. Hair on my neck probably scratched his arm just before I passed out."

"That poor neck. But how about Una and Cotton?"

"Don't know. The plan changed when Cotton and the redheaded stranger got put in the county lock-up instead of the city jail."

"So, what were you doing?"

Before John B could answer, another voice joined the conversation. "I can explain the intricacies of the evening." Fannie May and John B turned to see Bat limping through the barn door.

"Mr. Masterson. What are you doing here?" asked Fannie May.

"I am only an observer and will be on my way out of Dodge momentarily. Your plan was as resplendent as this vision before me. As adroit as a lesson from the Bluffton school. Except the number of boisterous prisoners exceeded the capacity of the city calaboose. And the chivalry of Deputy Tilghman required segregation of prisoners based on their gender."

"You mean Cotton and the redhead were not in the same cell as Una?"

"They were not even in the same building. But your lionhearted husband was able to correct the situation with the provision of latchkeys."

"I did free Cotton, Una, and the redhead, but that was as far as I got before another cowboy jumped me. I figger Cotton took care of the rest. Somebody must have dragged me here."

Just then, the barn door flew open and two figures entered. Cotton's large frame and shock of white curls were instantly recognizable. The diminutive figure beside him was a mystery for only a few moments. The person lifted their hat, and Una's smiling face appeared. Even after most of her hair had been chopped away, she was uniquely beautiful. Quickly, Fannie May gave Una and Cotton each a buffalo-hide coat. They proceeded to saddle up, and Bat stood by the barn door.

"Did my father help you rescue me?" Una pleaded. "Did you get the keys from him?"

"I can't say," said Barringer, glancing at Bat.

"I can assure you that your father is chasing new evidence," responded Bat. "Agent Clark was seen boarding the last train heading west."

The group rode single file through the barn door as Bat held it open. Barringer stopped to tip his hat. "I don't reckon we will meet again, Mr. Masterson. Much obliged for all you have done."

Bat tapped his cane against the side of his derby and replied, "Follow the rails where you can. There will be shallow snow."

Barringer spurred the big Clydesdale. Cotton and Una high-tailed after Barringer.

Fannie May held her horse back at the exit to address Bat. "I appreciate your assistance and your discretion, Mr. Masterson. Is that true? Is Clark looking for evidence to support Una's claim that one of the Robinson women killed Ransome."

"You mean the Jolly twins."

"The Robinson women are the Jolly twins?"

"As I confessed in the written affidavit you hold, the Jolly twins shot Sergeant King and Mollie Brennan over a decade ago in Sweetwater. No one could blame them for shooting King in self-defense. His attack on them was in progress when Mollie and I entered the room. One of the girls had King's pistol in her hand. I believe that she was about to shoot King when we entered the room. In the commotion she opened fire, hitting Mollie and I. When King grabbed her she threw the gun to the other twin. That one shot King with his own gun."

"So why did the gang cover up the truth? And you took the blame for shooting King."

"Not blame. Credit. Nobody considered King's death as a tragedy. And he had initiated the situation. As far as I was concerned, the twins had just reacted in fear for their lives. Besides, nobody could tell which twin shot King and which one shot Mollie."

"And the law would probably just ignore the death of a harlot. So the gang took two murderers into protection, here in Dodge," observed Fannie May.

"That's where their lives went from bad to worse. Gang members who could reveal the truth forced the twins into servitude. Marshal Ed was involved with them until he got shot. Then Ransome took them in. He eventually sold them off to the Robinson brothers."

"Sold them? That's slavery! Not to mention pandering."

"How do you think Ransome bought all that fancy printing machinery?"

"So your brother Ed was already dead. And now the twins took revenge on Ransome. Does Agent Clark know any of this?"

"According to my railway sources, Clark is after the names on Mollie's list. A list of names as distinguished as those you entrusted to me. Agent Clark thinks the Jolly twins have it. It is entirely possible they did have it at one time, but I doubt they appreciated its value. It may well be ashes in the wind but who knows the lengths the Pinkertons will go to in the search. By now, Clark probably suspects that the Robinson women are the Jolly twins. "

"More importantly," observed Fannie May, "Una's innocence could be proved if her father captures the Robinson's."

"I wish him luck. But Clark might sell those wildcats short. He could be their next victim."

"Aren't you afraid they will come after you, Bat?"

"That die has been cast. I carry this cane as a reminder that one of those girls put a bullet in me and may want to finish the job. But they are not the only people who scare the dickens out of me." Bat tipped his hat to Fannie May. "It's time for you to go west Miss Fannie."

"As you say, the die has been cast," laughed Fannie May as she spurred Monte to a gallop.

Several minutes west of Dodge, Fannie May caught up to John B. He had stopped while Cotton and Una were in a passionate embrace.

The die had been cast that day. Before her nineteenth birthday, Una Clark was a fugitive from the law.

46

New York, New York, 1911

**William Barclay Masterson, more or less widely known as
Bat Masterson, brought suit yesterday against Frank B. Ufer
to recover $10,000 damages for slander. He alleges that on
September 14 last Ufer said:**

**"Bat Masterson is an alleged bad man and gun fighter who
made his reputation by shooting drunken Mexicans and
Indians in the back."**

**The complaint says that this meant that "plaintiff was guilty
of discharging a firearm toward a human being." The statement is false, the plaintiff says.**

—*The Sun*, New York, New York, October 14, 1911

Bat discovered sports betting late in life. Live boxing
matches were popular sporting events for the partici-
pants, the audience, and the gambling community. Bat
was known to work boxing matches as a timekeeper. In
this role, he was ringside for the heavyweight champion-
ship bout between Jake Kilrain and John L. Sullivan in
July 1889. Masterson was working in the Kilrain corner
and had positioned Luke Short and several other gangsters in the crowd. The result was controversial when
Kilrain's manager threw in the towel after seventy-five

rounds, against the boxer's will. There was no evidence of wrongdoing by Bat, but the Gang's presence suggested they had bet against Kilrain. This fight was the last world heavyweight title to be fought under the London Prize Ring Rules of one-minute rounds until either boxer threw in the towel.

In 1892, Bat became manager and owner of the Palace Variety Theater in Denver, where he began a relationship with Emma Moulton, his future wife. He moved on to other gambling establishments in Colorado and continued his interest in prizefighting. At one point, Bat opened a boxing club in Denver, promoted the sport and began writing weekly sports articles in a Denver newspaper.

Bat obtained a temporary bodyguard position for a prominent New Yorker, who introduced him to the rich and famous residents of New York. Even though Bat returned to Colorado, he was attracted by the social life in the big city. In 1902, Emma and Bat moved to New York. Bat was arrested immediately upon arrival and charged with conducting illegal gambling and carrying a concealed weapon. The bunco charge was dropped, and he paid the ten-dollar fine for his revolver. Shortly after arriving, the *Morning Telegraph* hired Masterson as a sports reporter.

Stories of Bat's checkered past, both fact and fiction, followed him to New York. Lurid accounts of dozens of killings attributed to Bat Masterson had appeared in newspapers from New York to Denver. Numerous publications reported that Bat had killed twenty-eight men over his career. Bat was able to ignore the falsehoods until 1911, when Frank B. Ufer, a reporter from a competing paper, wrote that Bat had made his reputation by shooting drunken Mexicans and Indians in the back. This was the last straw. Bat launched a libel suit against the Commercial Advertiser Association, the publisher of the article. He retained Benjamin Patterson to seek ten thousand dollars in damages. The publishers engaged a prominent New York law firm, Simpson and Cardozo, to defend them.

Patterson insisted on reviewing Bat's testimony before each session of the trial. They met in the Masterson residence on May 18, 1913, two days before the trial was scheduled.

"Bat, can you tell me how much of Ufer's article is true?" asked Patterson.

"I object," said Emma to the surprise of both men.

"What do you mean by that?" asked Patterson.

"If they ask that question, you should object on the grounds that any answer would suggest there is some truth in any article Ufer may have written about Bat."

"She's right, Bat," agreed Patterson. "If Cardozo asks that question, don't answer. The judge will make him be more specific. Such as: Mr Masterson, do you have a reputation in this town?"

"Yes, I am well known," Bat answered pulling his suspenders forward. "I was well known prior to coming to New York, and now I am known by my articles in a popular newspaper. Have you read any of my articles in the *Morning Telegraph*?"

Patterson chuckled. "I am not sure that it helps to make fun of the defense lawyer. But if you do, watch for the judge's reaction. Let's try another question."

"OK, but the courtroom is still laughing," stated Bat. Emma was giggling behind her hands.

"Mr. Masterson, have you shot a great many men in your life?"

"No. But I may have future opportunities," replied Bat.

"How many have you shot before this morning?" retorted Patterson. "We won't worry about the rest of the day."

"I have shot many bullets with the intent of killing men," Bat admitted. "But on most occasions, I failed."

Emma tittered.

"So tell us about the times you did not fail," continued Patterson.

"I shot a man named Walker or Wagner. Which one escapes my memory. They were traveling together. One of them killed the marshal of Dodge City, who happened to be my brother. I shot at both as they ran away, but I only killed the one who killed Marshal Ed Masterson."

"So you shot him in the back?" asked Patterson.

"He chose which side I would have to shoot him. Had he run towards me, I would have shot him in the chest."

Emma continued to laugh at her husband's humor.

"What about all the Indians you shot at the battle of Adobe Walls?" asked Patterson in an antagonistic tone.

"I was sleeping off libations in the saloon at the Adobe Walls with eight other men, mostly buffalo hunters. Then seven hundred warriors attacked the building at sunrise.

We had no choice but to fight with guns, fists, and clubs. Some of the attackers were killed by our efforts. I can't take credit for any one of the dead attackers. Others might take credit for killing twenty or more."

"How many attackers were killed?"

"There were fifteen bodies on the ground after the first day, but a number had been carried away."

"And you were only nine? Your survival seems unbelievable."

"Only nine of us woke up in the saloon. There were another eighteen white men in the camp."

"Do you think these men were heroic?" prodded Patterson.

"I don't feel that I was a hero. But I am damn glad that the group of us did not give up. And I am damn glad the attack ended after a couple of weeks."

By the end of the day, Patterson was comfortable that Bat Masterson would make a formidable adversary for any defense lawyer.

During the trial, Cardozo referred to more than one newspaper report that Bat had killed twenty-eight men. Bat confessed to killing only three men, including the man who killed Mollie Brennan, the man who killed his brother Ed, and a wanted murderer from Texas. None of these victims were Mexican. He also admitted to shooting at attackers during battle but that it was not his fault if he did not hit them. Witness after witness downplayed the violence that Cardozo attempted to imply. Even those witnesses called by Cardozo could not provide any proof of wrongdoing by Bat.

In closing arguments, Patterson stated, "In *The Winning of the West*, Colonel Roosevelt spoke in the highest terms of Mr. Masterson." The judge ordered the jury to find in favor of Masterson and award him any amount over six cents. The jury awarded Masterson three thousand five hundred dollars plus court costs.

Cardozo filed for appeal within a few days. The Appellate Division of New York determined that if both parties agreed to lower the amount of the award to one thousand dollars, then another trial could be avoided.

Patterson arranged a meeting with Bat at the sports desk to present the offer. "Do you want to accept the new award? Even if you do, I don't think Cardozo will accept it. We are probably going back to court in any event."

"I suspect their game was to continue to shoot down my reputation. The money is not the issue. I have better things to do in life."

"All we can do is accept the thousand and see what they do," Patterson conceded.

Bat frowned. "I am a portly, graying old man of sixty-one, with more hair in my ears than on my head. As much as I like a mental joust with Cardozo, I much prefer to be writing about actual bouts of pugilism. How about we play dirty with Ufer and Cardozo?"

"What do you mean?"

Bat picked up a racing form that was on his desk and folded it six ways. Now the form was a tiny note with a list of racehorses on the front. "There are lists like this in every brothel around the world. But very few people ever see one of these lists."

"A list of horses?" asked Patterson.

"Not this list specifically. But a punter's list. A list of whore-mongers. Johns and Janes," declared Bat. "And I bet Cardozo and Ufer have their names written on more than one of those lists."

There were no further reports of this case in either the *Morning Telegraph* or the *Globe and Commercial Advertiser*. The case of Masterson v. Commercial Advertiser Association was not listed in the Court of Appeals records. Whether Bat received the thousand dollars is immaterial. The trial he initiated was now over and out of the public spotlight.

Bat continued reporting sports and followed heavy-weight boxing. In 1921, he witnessed Jack Dempsey defend his world boxing title. In October of that year, Bat Masterson died at his writing desk. The undertaker was surprised to find a decade-old racing form folded and tucked into the inside breast pocket of Bat's suit jacket. There was a circle around the name of one of the race-horses—*Fannie's Honor*.

Bat's adult life held two phases: thirty years of adventure in the West and twenty years of writing about that adventure while living in New York City. It might be observed that the second phase of Bat's life coincided with the years when he was happily married.

In his personal life Bat Masterson was a son, brother, husband, and loyal friend to many. In his professional life,

Bat Masterson can easily be described as a Renaissance man of the Old West, earning a living as a farmer, rail worker, army scout, buffalo hunter, teamster, surveyor, developer, gambler, gangster, lawman, politician, fight promoter, and journalist.

47

Western USA, 1870 - 1920

In the West, the turbulent days when Bat and his gun were in demand to keep the peace are gone. As a rule things are as quiet West of the Mississippi as a Sunday afternoon in a New England village. In recent years Bat has amused himself with a little business, some gambling ventures, and a good deal of sport. At last the East has become too bad to do without him. Bat has been summoned to deal gently but firmly with the unruly foreign element, the mafia, and the lawless millionaires of New York.

—*The Washington Times*, **Washington, D.C., February 19, 1905**

Bat Masterson's immediate family lived and died in Kansas. His parents and siblings are buried in Wichita, Kansas with the exception of Edward who was buried in both Fort Dodge and Dodge City. Bat died in New York in 1921; his wife, Emma Matilda Walker Masterson, died in 1932. Both are buried in Bronx, New York. The legendary life of Bat Masterson is reflected in over one hundred and fifty works of fiction, including books, movies, television episodes, and comic books.

Wyatt Earp's early occupations included teamster, pimp, gunslinger, and lawman. He moved to Dodge in 1875 and worked as assistant marshal on and off until 1879, when he left to join his brothers Virgil, James, and Morgan in the silver boom around Tombstone, Arizona. There, he worked alongside his brothers and close friend Doc Holliday maintaining law and order. Their reputations as gunfighters attracted disputes with a local gang known as the Cochise County Cowboys. The shootout at the OK Corral in 1881 resulted in one dead and one wounded. Seeking revenge, the Cowboys tracked the Earps and Holliday to the train station in Tucson. Sometime in the night, another Cowboy was killed, and Tucson authorities issued an arrest warrant for Doc Holliday.

To avoid a trial in Arizona, Wyatt Earp and Doc Holliday fled to New Mexico, and Colorado. Holliday was arrested in Denver and was about to be extradited to Arizona to face the Tucson warrants. Earp arranged the meeting with Bat Masterson in Trinidad, Colorado in 1882, where they concocted the plan to prevent Holliday's extradition.

Earp moved on to work in mining and gambling in Colorado, Idaho, California, Alaska, and Yukon Territory. Most of Earp's mining interests were gold mines in California and the Klondike. He also filed claims for copper and potash in California. He achieved some notoriety as a boxing referee, including the infamous Fitzsimmons-Sharkey fight of 1896. His life in Los Angeles included working as a consultant to Hollywood movie personalities.

In 1929, Wyatt Earp died in Los Angeles of chronic diseases and was buried next to his wife, Josephine, in Colma, California. Over his eighty-year life, Earp's travels took him far and wide. His careers were varied, and he outlived all of his gun-slinging friends and foes.

Like his friends Wyatt and Bat, Doc Holliday understood that reputation was key to his success and survival. In a newspaper interview, Holliday was asked if his conscience troubled him. He responded, "I coughed that up with my lungs, years ago." Despite Holliday's terminal illness, he maintained a reputation as a mean and deadly gunslinger until his death in 1887 at age thirty-six.

Charlie Bassett was a buffalo hunter who joined the Mastersons in law enforcement in and around Dodge. He was a founder of the Long Branch Saloon and had a similar venture in Kansas City, Missouri. When Luke Short was kicked out of Dodge, Bassett was the first to offer assistance by assembling the other gang members to form the Dodge City Peace Commission. Bassett suffered from rheumatism and died in 1896 at the age of forty-eight.

Bill Tilghman claimed the record of killing three thousand three hundred buffalo in less than a year. He opened the Crystal Palace Saloon in Dodge in 1877 and sold it a year later. He served as deputy for the county under Bat Masterson and Pat Sughrue, during which time he also owned another saloon and was accused of a variety of property crimes. After Sughrue, Tilghman was appointed city marshal. He resigned in 1886 to tend to his cattle ranch, which was later wiped out in the Great Die-up. For the next few years, he stayed close to the gang's activities and participated in the county seat war between Ingalls and Cimarron. Undaunted by his ranching experience, Tilghman participated in the Oklahoma land rush of 1889 and started another ranch, which included raising thoroughbred horses.

In 1892, Tilghman was appointed a Deputy U.S. Marshal in Oklahoma in an effort to combat the outlaw Doolin-Dalton Gang, also referred to as the Wild Bunch. In 1896, Tilghman single-handedly captured the leader, Bill Doolin, in a bathhouse in Arkansas, only to witness Doolin's escape six months later. All the same, the demise of the Wild Bunch followed within the year.

When Tilghman visited New York, Bat introduced him to Theodore Roosevelt. The two men had opposing political affiliations, yet Roosevelt respected the Oklahoma rancher and invited him to attend the 1909 inauguration ceremony of President Taft. These connections helped Tilghman become the senator for Oklahoma in 1910.

Realizing the power of media, Tilghman partnered in a movie production called *The Passing of the Oklahoma Outlaws*. He starred as himself and used the film to promote a largely fictional account of the taming of Oklahoma.

In 1924, at the age of seventy, Tilghman confronted a corrupt prohibition agent in Cromwell, Oklahoma. The agent was drunk and armed, and Tilghman was shot while attempting to apprehend the man. He died from his wounds. His funeral included an honor guard ordered by Oklahoma Governor Martin Trapp.

Mollie Brennan worked as a harlot in Ellsworth, Kansas until she got involved with gunman Billy Thompson. Thompson went on the run after shooting a sheriff. Mollie followed Billy to Cantonment Sweetwater near present-day Mobeetie, Texas. Legend suggests that she intervened when Melvin King tried to shoot Bat Masterson. The shot from King's gun is reported to have killed Mollie and wounded Bat such that he required a cane from that day forward.

Some stories include other Kansas prostitutes joining Mollie in Sweetwater. As many as seven sisters with the surname Jolly were mentioned. There may have been twins and there may have been minors in the family. There are no historical records to indicate that identical twins Anna and Agnes Jolly were ever in Norton's Dance Hall in Sweetwater. Marriage licenses proving they married the Robinson brothers do not exist. The Jolly twins were never apprehended by Kansas lawmen.

Dodge City founder and entrepreneur George Hoover traveled an undocumented route from Canada to Kansas. Like other Canadians, he may have been enticed by the riches and rewards described in the *Handbook to Kansas Territory*. Almost half the distance to Kansas may have been accomplished by ship, if Hoover boarded in Port Colborne on Lake Erie and sailed to Chicago. In the 1870s most freight was carried on schooners along the lakes and inland waterways. One such schooner was built by Edmond Fitzgerald and bore the name of its builder. That ship would meet its fate in November of 1883 when the captain tried to deliver one last shipment of wheat before the onset of winter. A snowstorm came up, and heavy seas ran the *Edmond Fitzgerald* aground before breaking it apart. The crew of seven men died when their lifeboats foundered within earshot of land.

In 1958, the longest freighter on the Great Lakes was launched. Its dimensions were the maximum allowed in the St. Lawrence Seaway, and it could carry twenty-nine tons of iron ore. This ship was named the *Edmund Fitzgerald* after its owner, the grandnephew of Edmond Fitzgerald. In November of 1975, the fully loaded *Edmund Fitzgerald* encountered gale-force winds and thirty-five-foot waves on Lake Superior. The ship and crew of twenty-nine men last reported they were "holding their own" at 7:10 pm. on November 10. The late singer-songwriter Gordon Lightfoot paid tribute to the crew of the *Edmund Fitzgerald* in his hit song, "The Wreck of the *Edmund Fitzgerald*."

Hoover's first stop in Kansas was Ellsworth, where he settled for a short time before looking for a more profit-able environment to do business. If Hoover met Mollie Brennan while in Ellsworth, the meeting was discreet and not historically momentous.

During the Civil War, Fred Harvey worked on the Burlington Railroad. He saw an opportunity to offer a fine dining experience to travelers and in 1876 opened a dining room in Topeka, Kansas, serving meals to travelers on the Atchison, Topeka and Sante Fe Railway. His second dining room was in Florence, Kansas, where the dining experience was formalized with silver utensils, linens, and fine china. In 1883, the restaurants switched to all-female wait staff, hiring women with looks, manners, and skill. The Harvey Girls, as they became known, were immortalized in the 1946 MGM musical of the same name. Besides fine dining, many of the Harvey Houses provided luxury accommodations.

At its peak, there were eighty-four Harvey Houses operating in twelve states. Most of these were located in towns on the AT&SF rail line and were eventually serviced by Route 66. When the Harvey Company was sold in 1968, it was the sixth-largest retail food chain in the United States. The restaurants are gone, but several of the sites in Arizona operate as tourist attractions in the twenty-first century.

I do not believe there ever was any life more attractive to a vigorous young fellow than life on a cattle ranch in those days. It was a fine, healthy life, too; it taught a man self-reliance, hardihood, and the value of instant decision... I enjoyed the life to the full.
—Theodore Roosevelt

By 1883, buffalo hunting had moved north to the Dakota Territory. Outdoorsman Theodore Roosevelt first tried to shoot buffalo in the badlands of present-day North Dakota. He was so impressed by the lifestyle in the West that he invested in two cattle ranches near the community of Medora. When his wife and mother both died on the same day in 1884, he retreated from political life as a New York assemblyman to raise beef cattle in a serious way.

Roosevelt was an organizer of the Little Missouri Stockmen's Association, which was created to address the problems of overgrazing and disease control. In 1886, he served as sheriff in Billings County and was able to hunt down several thieves. While the blizzard was raging across the western states that December, Roosevelt remarried in London, England. Edith Kermit Carow was his second wife until his death in 1919.

Texas longhorns were brought in along the cattle trails, and by 1886 Roosevelt had a herd of thirty-five hundred cattle plus a thousand calves. Before the ranch reached its potential, however, it was devastated by the winter of 1886-87. Although his cattle were not captured by the fences of the Big Die-Up, Roosevelt lost two-thirds of his herd to the cold winter. The loss was crippling, and Roosevelt returned to public life in New York.

Roosevelt was deeply influenced by the environment and lifestyle in the Dakota Territory. Back in New York he wrote a historical novel, *The Winning of the West*, which earned favorable reviews.

In 1901, he became the youngest person to be elected President of the United States, and during his eight years in office he was committed to preserving natural habitat and creating public lands through a system of national parks. The career of Theodore Roosevelt was as diverse and adventurous as any hero of the West. This affinity was not lost on Bat Masterson, when, in 1905, he received a request from Roosevelt to accept an appointment as U.S. Marshal for the Southern District of New York. The two became lifelong friends, sharing legendary histories whenever they met in Washington and New York.

The Plymouth Brethren ministry was based on the teachings of a nineteenth-century Irish biblical scholar, John Nelson Darby, and his interpretations of the King James Version of the Bible. Brethren Assemblies have existed in North America since the middle of the nineteenth century. The Dallas Paramount Brethren Assembly is a fictional church based on the beliefs of some assemblies during Victorian times. There is no historical basis for a Pinkerton Agent (H.A.) Clark or his daughter Una in a Brethren Assembly. However, Henry Ward Beecher has been referred to as the most famous preacher in the nation. He became the first pastor of the Plymouth Church in Brooklyn, New York in 1847 and went on to acquire fame through his support of the abolition of slavery, women's suffrage, and prohibition. Beecher employed humor, dialect, and slang in his ministry and supported Darwin's Theory as compatible with Christian beliefs.

Beecher was connected to Kansas in the build-up to the Civil War when he raised money for rifles—nicknamed "Beecher's Bibles"—to arm abolitionist forces in the Kansas Territory. In addition to other clergy, Beecher's personal network included presidents, senators, industrialists, bankers, and publishers.

Beecher was implicated in a number of sex scandals over the years, and eventually a civil action was launched in response to free-love practices with the wife of a former associate. The jury was split, and the church exonerated their leader.

Typhoid fever was only one of the many communicable diseases that victimized the American population in the 1800s. Treatments and medications were largely ineffective since few practitioners were able to distinguish between the source or symptoms among diseases — including smallpox, cholera, typhus, dysentery, yellow fever, scarlet fever, syphilis, rabies, measles, malaria, diphtheria, tuberculosis, and influenza.

Cowpox vaccine was introduced during the Civil War to mitigate the impact of smallpox. Pasteur developed a rabies vaccine in 1885. Typhoid fever vaccine was available in 1896. Vaccines for most of these diseases were not available until after 1920.

Antitoxin for diphtheria was discovered in 1894. Chlorination of drinking water became commonplace in municipal systems after 1900. Antibiotics for treatment of other infections were not available commercially until after 1943.

If Doc Holliday had been born in 1920, he probably would not have contracted tuberculosis and would have died with his boots on instead of on a bed in an infirmary.

John Barringer and Fannie May Barringer have no documented history outside of Llano County, Texas.

Nevertheless, after rescuing Una Clark from those who sought to harm her, they continue a fabled journey to Winslow, Arizona, in search of the Barringer meteor crater.

Una Clark is an entirely fictional character. Females in the late nineteenth century often faced misogyny, religious persecution, violence, disease, and pregnancy years before reaching adulthood. By consuming ice that her father brought from New Orleans, Una became infected with typhoid fever and endured a catatonic state, quarantine, medical experimentation, and amnesia. Even so, her adolescent years were presumably less dreadful than they would have been had she remained in her Dallas home. Una's escape from Dodge City in *Paper* sets in motion her disturbing future in *Scissors*.

THE END

ABOUT THE BOOK

Paper is NOT your average novel about the Wild West. Although it is not without a few gun battles, it focuses on the lives of powerful people willing to present their own "truth" as reality to get what they want. The story begins with the early lives of several Canadians who eventually achieve prominence in Dodge City at the intersection of fiction and history. One such person is Bat Masterson, who is not afraid to use a sheriff's badge to get what he wants in Dodge City. While supposedly working to keep law and order, he secretly leads the Dodge City Gang and gets rich on the proceeds of crime. Another is newspaperman Ransome Cooper, who has no trouble fabricating news stories to fill in the space around the advertising he sells for the *Dodge City Fable*. But advertising also has its own "truth", as Una, a young woman from Texas will discover. After seeing a job ad, Una decides to flee the stifling religious household in which she has grown up and start afresh in Dodge City.

To get there, Una must face the dangers of a late-season cattle drive in 1886. Along the way, she meets carpenter

John Barringer and his new wife, Fannie May, who are running from their own troubles. As a trio, they must depend on each other and their wits to survive—along with a strategy developed by Fannie May, which she has based on the Rock, Paper, Scissors game.

***Paper* is the second book in the exciting historical fiction series *Rock Paper Scissors* by Montgomery Colt, but it can also be enjoyed as a standalone novel. As in his first book, Colt adeptly weaves real historical players (such as Bat Masterson, George Hoover, Doc Holliday, Wyatt Earp, and Buffalo Bill Cody) and events with a fictional tale that makes the Wild West come alive, while telling a story that is particularly relevant in modern times.**

ABOUT THE AUTHOR

Montgomery Colt is the author's pen name. He grew up on a cattle ranch in Saskatchewan, Canada and was an active member in Valleyview 4H Beef Club. His early years included raising and showing beef cattle while attending a rural school. Later, he received a degree in Agricultural Engineering and worked on projects involving food processing, information technology, geology, and water management. He also taught as a university professor and has traveled extensively across North America. His frequent travels to Texas and Arizona allowed him to visit both ends of the adventure — Barringer Hill and Barringer Meteor Crater.

Today, Colt and his wife live on the shores of Last Mountain Lake in Canada. An avid reader of historical fiction and mystery novels, Colt wrote his debut novel, *Rock*, during the pandemic and continues the series with *Paper*. In his words, "I fell in love with the Barringer story on the day I discovered matching grave stones for John and Fannie in the cemetery at Bluffton, Texas. They struck me as a couple who would persevere in the face of danger.

And with the initials JB, John Barringer needed to embark on a fictional adventure in the spirit of James Bond and Jason Bourne.

 Printed in Canada